GULF
BOULEVARD

DENNIS HART

GULF BOULEVARD

THE PERMANENT PRESS
Sag Harbor, NY 11963

For information, address:
The Permanent Press
4170 Noyac Road
Sag Harbor, NY 11963
www.thepermanentpress.com

Library of Congress Cataloging-in-Publication Data

Hart, Dennis—
    Gulf Boulevard / Dennis Hart.
        pages cm
    ISBN 978-1-57962-353-1
        1. Lottery winners—Fiction. 2. Divorced women—Fiction.
    3. Swindlers and swindling—Fiction. 4. Florida—Fiction.
    I. Title.

PS3608.A7845G85 2014
813'.6—dc23   2013040024

Printed in the United States of America

For my daughters

Cheri, Angela, Jessica, and *Jenna*

ACKNOWLEDGEMENTS

I wish to express my most sincere gratitude to:

Amy Metz, Jeni Decker, and Ann Everett for their time spent reviewing my early drafts by chapter on our writers' forum. Thanks for the edits, suggestions, and encouragement.

I want to thank Sue Franco for suggesting that I put a sock in my mouth and let Jason tell his own story. You were instrumental with edits and comments as the book progressed.

Bill Greenleaf at *Greenleaf Literary* brought the elements of *Gulf Boulevard* together with his detailed analysis and guidance toward finding representation.

My agent, Joyce Holland, at *D4EO Literary Agency*, asked to represent the book immediately saving me the arduous task of writing additional query letters.

Thanks to Judith and Martin Shepard at *The Permanent Press* for putting their faith in a comedic mystery and for adding *Gulf Boulevard* to their prestigious list of titles.

And finally to Barbara Anderson who proofread my final draft and added her finishing touches to make it a better read.

Two Scales

"Only two things are infinite, the universe and human stupidity, and I am not sure about the former."

—ALBERT EINSTEIN

Salvatore Scalise drove his car down Atwells Avenue in the heart of Federal Hill, the "Little Italy" section of Providence, Rhode Island. Passing the small, quaint restaurant of his interest, he found a parking space on a side street. He maneuvered his large, bulky weight out of the driver's seat, stretched, and took in the superfluity of Italian aromas diffusing throughout the neighborhood of eateries. His stomach growled.

The sign on the awning read—Caesar's Ristorante. He stepped over to the front window and perused the menu displayed on an easel inside the restaurant. Fingering the choices from his side of the glass, he was certain he could order and then finish each item listed. But, he wasn't there to dine. Tonight was business. He had been asked there by Joey "The Nose" Di Matteo, a local capo, to accept a last-minute contract—an above-average contract. Something heavy was going down.

He opened the door and stepped inside. On his left, a dozen tables set with white linen, stemware, and centerpiece arrangements of fresh flowers. Several were occupied. On his right, a refrigerated pastry display, followed by a bar that ran the length of the establishment. Pictures of celebrities adorned the walls. Sinatra and Martin stood out. In another frame he saw the portrait of Don Vito Corleone surrounded by his sons, Santino, Michael, and Fredo, as they stared down menacingly at the patrons.

He closed his eyes and inhaled deeply. The aroma of basil and garlic permeated the room. On one table, he stared shamelessly at a dish of lobster fra diavolo until a waiter stepped in front of him with a plate of veal saltimbocca alla romano. After only several steps inside the restaurant, he had added several pounds to his bulk.

An attractive hostess, dressed in a low-cut, tight-fitting black dress approached, holding several leather-bound menus. "May I help you, sir?" she asked, smiling.

Before he could answer, a voice bellowed from the rear of the room.

"Hey, Sal, get your *culo grasso* over here!"

A wave of subdued laughter erupted from some of the diners and employees.

He looked beyond the hostess and found Joey at a table in the rear of the dining room, waving his arm as if hailing a cab. The hostess seemed stuck between a smile and a laugh. When Sal dismissed her with a nod, she slipped away, pressed the menus to her face, and let a fit of giggles escape.

Sal focused on the table in the corner. On one side sat Joey, his friend of many years, with a nose that started in one zip code and ended in another. Across from Joey sat a guy Sal thought he may have seen before, but wasn't sure. From where Sal stood, the man had chiseled features, broad shoulders, and a receding dark hairline. A napkin sprouted out from the man's neck protecting his white shirt, tie, and suspenders. Sal started walking, trying to place the face.

The floor creaked as he made his way past the tables. Several people gawked at him for a moment, but then lowered their gazes in capitulation. When he reached the table, Joey stood and embraced him, followed by heavy clapping on each other's back as if they were cowboys dusting one another off after a long ride.

"Sally, where you been, huh?"

"Laying low and on the go," he replied.

He tapped Sally on the cheek several times. "I want you to meet somebody," Joey said, sitting back down. "Boss, this is

Salvatore Scalise, a friend of mine I told you about. Sally, this here is the boss, Raymond 'Junior' Gulioti."

The Boss! Sal leaned over and extended his hand. The highest rank he'd ever met in any family was a capo, so sitting at a table with the underboss of Providence excited him. This *was* big, just as Joey had promised.

Gulioti ignored him, engrossed by the current twist of linguini on his fork.

"Sit," Joey mumbled, chewing on a meatball the size of a baseball.

Sal slowly drew his hand back, as he lowered himself in the seat. The chair moaned under the sudden avalanche of weight. Silence ruled the table as both men continued to eat. Sal stared at a plate of gabagool, and then at a serving of gnocchi in marinara sauce—both nestled between other plates of Italian cuisine dividing the capo and the underboss. Beads of sweat surfaced on his forehead. His mouth salivated. His tongue swept his lips. He wanted a bite of something.

"Bless me where I fuckin' sit if it ain't Salvatore 'Two Scales' Scalise," the underboss said, reaching for his glass of wine.

Joey laughed. "Two Scales. I haven't heard that in a while."

"*Madonn'*, have you ever once in your fuckin' life considered eatin' a salad?" Gulioti asked, raising the linen napkin to the corners of his mouth.

Salvatore "'Two Scales'" Scalise sat dumbfounded. All three hundred eighty-plus pounds on his five-foot, ten-inch frame, stilled at the ridicule tossed at him by the underboss. He didn't know how to react.

"Boss," Joey interjected on Sal's behalf. "He comes with a solid book. Short notice and all, huh?" Joey said, talking more with his hands.

Gulioti tore at a piece of bread. "I'm listening."

Joey leaned in. "Couple of years ago, that chili-shitter who raped the union boss's niece? I put Sally here on it. Turns out it's her neighbor. Sally finds the guy, sticks a blade in, but not enough to kill him. He calls me, I call the union boss. The union boss gets his justice by beating the living fuck out of the guy, but he don't have the balls to finish him being a civilian and all. So, Sally takes over. End of story." Joey rubbed his hands together to imply a done deal. "They ever find the body?" Joey asked, turning to Sal.

"A few pieces," Sal said.

"There you go, short notice and all, Boss. Sally's the man for the contract. He'll do it good," Joey said.

Gulioti turned back to Sal. "Do you really use two scales to weigh yourself? Like, add the fuckin' numbers together, or what?"

Sal lowered his gaze to the table. Ridicule and hunger were not mixing well.

Exasperated, Joey said, "Boss, we ain't asking him to run a marathon, huh?"

Gulioti leaned back in his chair as though deciding whether or not to offer the contract. Sal watched as Gulioti's eyes swept the restaurant in an apparent search to see if anyone was paying attention to their table. The closest ears belonged to two men sitting at the bar. Sal suspected them to be *soldati*—there to protect the underboss.

Gulioti gazed down at the table as he started to fold his napkin in a perfect square. "I got a finook in my crew. Name is Frankie Moretti, married with a kid. Can ya believe that shit? A good earner though, but I can't reconcile the two. If it ever gets out we're running a business with a queer in charge . . . for fucksakes, what a *tempesta di merda!* Even worse, he's the boy of one of my capos."

"It's a sad predicament," Joey inserted.

Gulioti turned to Sal. "Here's the paper. The guy's wife and kid are going to New York Friday afternoon for the weekend. We've made arrangements for Moretti to be picked up at midnight for a job down at the docks. So you need to be there and complete the paper beforehand. This is our window, short notice and all. I need it to look like a couple of *moulinyans* broke in for money and drugs. Fuck the place up. Take out Moretti, but nothing to the head. I want an open casket, understand?"

Sal nodded.

"*Bene.* Take the money, jewelry, and in your case the food . . . make it stink like one of them smash and grabs. Call Joey when you're done. Can you handle the job or what? We only got one shot at this, *capisce?*"

"No worries, Mr. Gulioti. I'll do you and Joey good."

"Sally here wants to make an impression, boss. Maybe when we can't get the Philly boys, on short notice and all, we call him. Ain't that right, big guy," Joey said, landing a playful fist on Sal's arm.

Sal remained stoic, the professional hit man's look. He had learned that from watching *The Godfather* movies.

Gulioti stared at Sal for a moment, shook his head as if questioning his decision, and then snapped his fingers, causing one of the men from the bar to step over to the table. The man reached under his jacket and removed a banded envelope. He handed it to the underboss and reclaimed his seat at the bar.

Gulioti pushed the envelope slowly in Sal's direction. "Twenty-five large now. Another seventy-five when it's done."

"Thank you, Mr. Gulioti," Sal said, reaching for the package.

Gulioti's hand reached out and grasped Sal's wrist. For a moment nothing was said. Then Gulioti leaned over and whispered, "Don't fuck this up."

❧

SAL TRUDGED up several staircases carrying a Francesco's Pizza box within an insulated delivery bag, which he balanced carefully in his gloved hands so as not to let the cheese slide. Inside was his favorite, a large extra cheese smothered with mushrooms and prosciutto. He rested at each landing and was tempted to sit on the top step and grab a slice while it was still warm. But he plodded on.

On the third floor of the apartment building, he rested again, caught his breath, and searched the corridor for apartment number 36. He balanced the pizza box on the handrail and removed the handgun from his shoulder holster. From his pocket he secured the silencer and screwed it on. Sal continued down the hallway, walking past a door with the number 32 tacked above a brass knocker.

A few muffled televisions could be heard, but other than that, the hallway was quiet. He paused for a moment to listen for traffic on the stairs or voices near doors. Satisfied, he stepped in front of apartment number 36. Balancing the pizza in one hand with his gun underneath, he lifted the knocker and let it fall two times. He stepped back in clear view of the peephole, so his target could clearly see his Francesco's Pizza delivery cap and delivery bag. He glanced down the corridor again to see if the noise of his arrival had attracted any meddlesome neighbors.

After a couple of seconds, the door opened until a chain pulled taut. A face appeared in the small opening.

"What?"

"Pizza delivery for . . . Moretti," Sal said, pretending to read the name taped to the side of the box facing him.

"Nobody ordered any pizza, Einstein," the man said, yet he sounded as if he wasn't sure.

"Hey, they told me Moretti in apartment 36. This is 36, right?" Sal asked, with the number inches away from him.

The man leaned out of sight. Sal thought about kicking in the door with the useless chain, but then it closed, followed by the sound of metal sliding. The man opened the door wide, stepped back, and waved for the pizza deliveryman to enter.

Sal stood staring for a second. The man in front of him was wrapped in only a towel. He was young, thin, and athletic looking. Mid-twenties, Sal guessed as he eased his wide frame through the doorway and slid the pizza box on the closest table.

"Is there any pizza left in it?" the man quipped.

Sal spun around to face the smiling man. He dropped the carrying bag and squeezed the trigger, shooting the man dead in the heart. As the body slumped against a wall and snaked to the floor, he reached over and closed the door gently.

Sal rested in a chair next to the pizza box. He placed the gun on the table and removed a small bag of cocaine from his pocket. He then spread the contents indiscriminately on the table to make it look like a drug deal had gone bad. In the background he heard the shower running. He'd shut it off in a minute, but first he wanted a slice. He walked over to the refrigerator and found a beer. Back at the table, he lifted the box cover, and massaged a heavy, grease-dripping slice, into a "V" shape.

"No, you finook, I'm not gonna leave any pizza," Sal scolded the dead body.

He took a large bite, cutting the slice in half. He moaned with pleasure as he chewed. His favorite pizza and a successful hundred-grand contract in one night. *Life is good. Well, for some,* he thought with a chuckle.

Another bite. He washed it down with a swig of beer, wiping his mouth on his sleeve. He started to reach for his cell to call Joey, when the sound of falling water stilled.

Sal reached for his gun and jumped to his feet as fast as his corpulent frame would allow. "Fuck," he muttered. They had assured him the wife would be out of town. He gripped the gun and headed toward the bathroom. His thoughts raced. He had a rule about women and children, but getting caught trumped all rules. He needed to act fast. Maybe catch her off guard and knock her out. Sal lumbered over to the bathroom door and listened. Someone was inside and moving around.

He surveyed the area. *Hide in the bedroom? Hide in the kitchen?* He had to get to her before she saw the body. A scream would . . .

"Hey, Vinny?"

The deep male voice from inside the bathroom stunned Sal.

"Yo, Vinny? I'm out."

"*Vinny?*" Sal mumbled. He looked at the sprawled body on the floor and realized he had killed the wrong guy. *No big deal. Shit happens,* he thought. Sal placed his hand on the doorknob and opened the door. A cloud of steam billowed out. He let the door swing in.

"Hurry the fuck up, handsome," the naked man said. "We ain't got all night."

Sal slid into the haze, lifted the gun and fired. The force of the shot pushed Frankie Moretti against the tiled wall. His body twisted, bounced off the sink, and slumped to the floor. Sal checked the pulse to make sure he was dead.

He emerged from the bathroom and searched the rest of the apartment to make sure he hadn't barged into Finooks "R" Us. After securing the other rooms, he settled in the bedroom. Male pornography and condoms littered the unmade bed. Sal shook his head in disgust. On a chair were draped two pairs of pants with shirts. He lifted the wallets, watches, and rings from the nightstand, bundled the clothes in a ball, and then returned to the pizza.

Chewing on his second slice, he opened one wallet, removed the cash without counting it and checked the license. Francis Arturo Moretti. He tossed the wallet over his head. The second wallet had a thicker wad of cash. He piled the bills on the table. The license in that wallet read, Vincent Nicolo Gulioti. He tossed that wallet over his head, too.

After he had consumed six of the eight slices, Sal moved around the apartment to make it look like a heist, as well as a bad drug deal. He grabbed a pillowcase and filled it with the jewelry, the clothes, a laptop, and an iPod. He opened drawers and emptied the contents on the floor. He turned over furniture. When the apartment was as disheveled as he suspected a *moolie* might leave it, he returned to the table to finish the pizza.

After a grunt for a job well done and a belch for devouring the whole pizza, Sal put the pile of money in his pocket, stuffed the pillowcase of goods inside the pizza bag, and reached for his cell to call Joey. The call was answered on the second ring.

"Hey, Sally, how's everything at the office?"

Sal nodded as he reviewed his efforts. "We're good, Joey. It was a two-for-one special tonight, but no problem. I won't charge ya."

"What? You walked in on him doing it . . . with a guy?"

"Close, but the boss was right. Now he ain't got no problem in the ranks no more."

Joey laughed. "Un-fuckin'-believable."

"Yeah, and the other finook got a name like the boss." Sal stood up, walked over to the wallets and found the one he was looking for. "Joey, the other guy's name is Gulioti." Sal paused as he read the name a second time. Something didn't feel right.

"Sally, don't fuck with me," Joey said with a nervous laugh. "Spell the name."

He spelled the name. Silence. It was becoming obvious to both men. Sal spoke next. "Joey, this can't be, right?"

Sounding suddenly distressed, Joey replied, "Sally, what's the first name?"

"Vincent."

"Oh, my fuckin' word, that's the boss's kid," Joey mumbled. "You know what the fuck you did?"

Sal knew now. But how was he to know the capo's son was finooking with the boss's son? "You saying the boss's kid is a homo, too?" Sal asked.

Silence.

"Joey?"

Sal could hear the muffled sounds at the other end. He wanted to ask if he was still getting paid the back end, all seventy-five large. His heart was beating fast. His agita was ready to blow, big time. A heavy weight fell upon him. He had whacked the boss's son. He gripped his chest as a flamethrower erupted inside.

"Sally, get your ass out of town tonight. You hearing me? Get the fuck out *tonight!* Far away, until I see how this plays out."

The call was abruptly terminated.

~ PART ONE ~

CHAPTER ONE

Is it Cold Enough for Ya?

"Oh, you hate your job? Why didn't you say so? There's a support group for that. It's called *everybody*, and they meet at the bar."

—DREW CAREY

My name is Jason Najarian. I live on a barrier island off the west coast of Florida, under lazy palm trees and salt-laden air. Warm breezes sway my hammock. Dolphins play in turquoise water just beyond my reach. Sandpipers dance along the shoreline. There's not a person in sight. I live here until I wake up each morning just north of Boston. This is why Ambien is my best friend as well as my travel agent.

Reality kicks in.

I slosh my way to the front entrance through a mixture of snow, slush, and crunchy rock salt; the result of a heavy winter snowstorm that turned to sleet before changing back to snow. When the skies cleared, the temperature promptly plummeted, freezing everything in place, as if my surroundings became a postcard.

Ah, New England weather.

It is the time of year when most people verbalize their contempt for the elements.

"It's too friggin' cold."

"What happened to global warming?"

Or my favorite: *"Is it cold enough for ya?"* Who answers *no* to that inquiry?

Six months from now, when winter is a distant memory, those same amateur meteorologists will ask: *"Is it hot enough for ya?"*

Who answers *no* to that inquiry? Me.

I'd rather be toasting my buns on a tropical sugar-white sand beach, under the fronds of a palm tree, surrounded by the scent of multihued flora seducing my senses, than trudging through knee-deep powder with air so cold it shrink-wraps my testicles.

I despise winter so much that my final wish clearly states the following: Cremate me; urn me; carry me to a warm, deserted shoreline; buy a beach chair and position it facing the setting sun; gently pour me out on the seat and leave me alone.

Go away.

Screw off.

I will disperse of myself when the first sea breeze embraces me.

I open the door, step inside, and shake myself like a dog out of water. I stomp my feet to remove the snow banks accumulated on my Merrell boots. The secretary, who usually greets me each morning with a grunt sound like "Mor-in," is busy preparing the conference room for another monthly staff meeting, which typically makes my ears bleed. I loathe sitting in one place for three hours while talking heads expound on how great their departments are performing. I don't drink coffee or energy drinks, or indulge in any substance worthy of giving me the jolt necessary to survive these marathon sessions of unadulterated boredom. Each time, I'm forced to stifle yawns and fight back heavy eyelids. I am living proof these monthly meetings-of-the-minds work better than any dose of the strongest sleep aid. I've often thought about secretly recording these conferences and selling them on eBay to the sleep deprived. It is on mornings like this that I reflect on the five years I've labored for Winchester Rope Company and realize how much I hate my job.

I start toward my office when suddenly I stop on a dime, literally. I lean over to claim my find when the tail side comes into focus. I ease back up, leaving the riches of bad luck to the unsuspecting.

"Mor-in, Jason," Barbara calls out from the conference room, as I try to scoot by undetected.

"Hey, Barbs." I stop and lean in. "Fine job as usual," I say, surveying the monthly reports neatly arranged in front of the tucked-in chairs. In the center of the table sits a pitcher of water with seven glasses. Barbara has been the company secretary/receptionist since before I was hired. She is friendly, outgoing, and attractive, but she will tell you she is currently overweight and attending hot yoga classes in an effort to slim down by summer. To my eyes, she looks fine.

Barbara is furiously erasing notations from a previous meeting on a wall-mounted dry-erase board. In the corner stands an easel with a thick pad of paper the boss defers to when the whiteboard is reduced to a confusing road map of numbers and arrows. I suspect he likes the paper display better as evidenced by the way he gently lifts each page, folds it over the top, and then irons it out with a gentleness better reserved for one of Barbara's copious breasts, before defiling the paper with a black Magic Marker.

"Mr. Steinberg wants to start promptly at nine this morning," she says, pointing the dry eraser at me. "Don't dilly-dally."

"Barbs, you know this is the highlight of my month. I'm already feeling bloated and crampy. But fear not, I'll be here at 8:59 sharp."

Barbara knows better. She dismisses me with a wave of the eraser.

I continue through the lobby, nodding silent mor-ins to a few early arrivals. I'm almost in my office when Jimmy DiLorenzo, our purchasing manager, pops out of his. He stands around five-foot seven, short dark hair, a round face, and an infectious smile. He apparently has a cigar stitched into every shirt pocket because I've never seen him smoke one.

"Hey, Jason, I put some receiving reports on your desk." He says this as he walks by me. He then turns and while walking backward says, "Is it cold enough for ya?"

My office sits at the end of the lobby, a room of four walls, no windows, and a threadbare commercial carpet. A wood-framed guest chair with torn upholstery sits in front of an old battleship-gray metal desk dented on three sides with drawers that stick shut every other day of the week. The walls are adorned with three oil paintings, of what I haven't figured out yet. If forced to describe them, I would say they are a cluster-fuck of colors painted, I assume, by a gorilla with a paintbrush between his toes. I can't emphasize enough how eager I am each morning to arrive in my opulent surroundings.

I toss my coat onto the chair in a heap. I find if I hang it neatly around the back of the chair, my coworkers will find this open seat an invitation to lower their butts and talk. They are less likely to do so if my coat is thrown on the seat in a ball. It leaves them compelled to stand, not knowing what to do with my garment. This has taken me years to refine. People who have to stand to wait for information tend to exit quickly. The exceptions are Jimmy and the warehouse manager, Carlos Alvarez, who both carelessly lift my coat off the chair and drop it to the floor before taking a seat. But it works with most coworkers, especially the boss. During the warmer months, however, I'm screwed.

I slip into my squeaky, high-backed chair and lower my briefcase to the floor. On my desk is a pile of papers thrown haphazardly at least two feet from my in-box. I'm a fastidious accountant, so finding my desk out of order can set me off. It's a quirk of mine that may need to be addressed on a couch someday. I shuffle the papers into a neat stack, paperclip them, and place the collection off to one side.

With a tap of a button, my virus-infected computer comes to life. As it boots up, it sounds like someone banging trash cans together in an alley. First things first, as I check for replies to my *Craigslist* advertisement under men seeking women. Why begin work when a rich widow or divorcee could be answering my listing for a passionate woman who seeks long walks on the beach and candlelit dinners? I'll even throw in a puppy. I'm prompted by two messages.

The first reply is from a woman who says she is a BBW with a great personality. BBW is an acronym for big, beautiful, woman, which is further translated by some to chubby chick. She writes that she loves to cook, and favors the Patriots over the Red Sox.

She is comfortable in her skin, and if I don't like BBW, I can move on.

The second reply is from a woman named Mistress Pandora, who is willing to teach me to crawl to her, lick her leather boots, and obey her every whim. She goes on to write that if I perform my duties to her satisfaction, she will reward me by strapping on her portable manhood and riding me like a bronco. I shiver at the uncomfortable image. All I have to do to experience this nirvana is reply to a website, make an appointment, and secure it with a credit card.

It appears my early morning choices are limited to a dominatrix-driven colonoscopy or possible suffocation should the chubby chick prefer to be topside.

I deliberate.

Jimmy glides into my office. He lifts my coat, drops it on the floor, and sits down. I quickly hit the minimize button, returning to my tropical island screen saver.

"Looking at porn?" Jimmy asks.

I toss him a look of disgust. "No, I was checking the stock market."

"The stock market ain't open yet."

"So? Hey, you think you can place the receiving reports in the tray labeled in-box?"

"Ready for the meeting?" he asks, ignoring my request.

"Yeah, I've been up all night in anticipation."

"Good. Let's kick some ass." As quickly as Jimmy entered, he bolts out of the chair and leaves my office. My coat remains on the floor.

I look at my watch: 8:55 A.M. *Plenty of time.*

I reach down to the lower drawer of my desk and wrestle with it. Inside, the desk elf is apparently awake and pulling back. It likes to play tug-of-war with me. At night and on weekends, I'm fairly convinced the elf comes out and hides my favorite pen and moves stuff around on my desk, just to screw with me.

I jiggle the drawer from side to side until the elf surrenders. With a metal squeal the drawer finally pulls out. This is the home of my sweet stash. I open the 56-ounce XXL bag and grab a handful of multicolored M&M candies. Spilling them onto my desk, I maneuver the mouse to the Club Casino icon for a few hands of "just for play" blackjack. As the program starts up, I sort my chocolate infatuations by color before devouring them like Pac-Man in a maze.

By 9:15 A.M., I'm up a few hundred bucks. Duty calls. I clear the screen, lift my coat back onto the chair and leave for the conference room. Barbara sees me coming, checks her watch and frowns at me.

"Don't hold my calls," I say, eliciting a smile from her.

I saunter into the meeting and slither into the remaining empty chair, which happens to be next to Jimmy. The whiteboard is filling up with information as Sam Steinberg, the boss, who is thin and stands over six feet with a perpetually dour expression peering out from behind thick black-framed glasses, is reading from my monthly report and highlighting the pertinent areas for the group to review. He turns when he hears me enter.

"Jason . . . we start at nine."

"Sorry, Sam, but the auditors called. They needed more info."

He adjusts his glasses and twirls the Magic Marker between his fingers. "Is something wrong?"

I have sensed for a long time that Steinberg fears the auditors. He is hiding something and I enjoy giving him his squirm du jour from time to time. "Nothing major," I say.

He stares at me for a moment longer, and then turns back to the board. Seconds later, a paper clip bounces off my chest. I look at Carlos, our resident shaved-head and tattooed Hispanic, sitting across the table, smiling. This is how Carlos playfully says good morning—he throws things at me. His inventory is endless; paper clips, crumpled donut bags, pens, rubber bands, or anything small he can grab usually bounce off my shirt. A few years back I started collecting his greetings and tossing them under the front seat of his 1982 Toyota Corolla. He hasn't noticed yet.

The meeting drags along like the flat line on a heart-monitoring machine. Steinberg continues to reiterate what is in my report, prompting a tidal surge of yawns from me. The first wave is small and I am able to either swallow them or cover my mouth. The next wave is substantial and infectious. Within minutes, my massive yawns cause the other managers to yawn uncontrollably while Steinberg talks to the whiteboard.

Soon after, as with every monthly meeting, the sandman floats into the room and puffs sleepy dust into my face, causing my eyelids to become heavy. As each department manager takes his or her turn dragging the meeting along with tedious bits of earth-shattering information, my eyelids start to flutter. Moments later, the weight is too much for me to bear and I unconsciously slip into la-la land until Jimmy saves me with a flick to my ear, startling me back to the meeting. I fear someday I will drift into a comatose state and expel one of those snort-snores that sound like you're gasping for your last breath, as the boss colors with his Magic Marker.

With our three-hour assembly concluded for yet another month, the bloating and cramps subside and I head back to my office. I click the favorites tab for *Craigslist* and find another reply waiting to convince me she is the woman of my dreams. She calls herself Jennifer and she works as a nurse at Massachusetts General Hospital. She considers herself gregarious, loves practical jokes, and italicizes the words *low maintenance*. I'm so taken with her reply I find myself sucking in my gut as I read it.

Steinberg saunters in. *Can't a guy have some privacy?* He looks at my coat bundled in a pile and decides to lean on the doorjamb. "Are you sure we're good with the auditors?"

"Yes, Sam," I say. "They were fishing for information I'd already sent them." I hate lying because it never fails to take on a life of its own, but it is good theater watching Steinberg age in front of me. Winchester Rope is a family-run business, so there is plenty he is probably manipulating when no one is looking.

He nods to my answer. Wavering in the doorway, he says, "Is it cold enough for ya?"

Christ. I smile. "Need to get these receiving reports posted before lunch," I say, placing my fingers on the keyboard. Steinberg checks his watch, issues me a salute, and leaves.

I check my watch: 12:15 P.M. My stomach grumbles for sustenance. But first, back to the letter from the nurse. I reach down to my bag of M&M's, snag a few and spill them blindly on my desk, totally captivated by my computer screen as I continue reading her reply.

"*. . . and I love the outdoors. Please be tall and considered handsome because I am over six feet tall. Sorry short guys . . . I don't want to look like a circus act.*"

My balloon pops. My tire deflates. I let out my gut and tap the delete key.

Disappointed, I look over at my M&M's and . . . I can't believe what I'm looking at! I stand up, push back my chair, and stare at my desk in amazement.

"*Holy shit!*"

Chapter Two

All Green Ones

"Marriage is a wonderful institution, but who wants to live in an institution?"
—Groucho Marx

"Jimmy!" I call out.

I can hear the clamor he makes while leaving his desk. I wait, still standing, until he appears in my office.

"Yo, what's up?"

"Look," I say, pointing to the M&M's on my desk.

Jimmy glances down. "Don't mind if I do," he says, reaching for the candy.

"No!" I say, gripping his outstretched arm. "These are special ones because they're all friggin' green. A minute ago, I reached into my M&M bag (I pull it out of the drawer and show him) without looking and . . . like magic or an omen, I end up with a handful of one color—all green ones. Come on, what are the odds of doing that?"

Jimmy looks at me perplexed. "I don't get it. You called me over here to show me a bunch of green M&M's? That's weird, man, even for you." He turns and leaves the office.

I remain spellbound. What *were* the odds of lifting eight M&M's of the same color in one handful from a multicolored bag? And all the color green to boot. It had to be a sign of good luck. I scoop my treasure and slip the candy into a ziplock bag for safe keeping. It is time for lunch.

Angelo's Sandwich Shop is located across the street from Winchester Rope. On a normal day, it's about a five-minute walk. I bundle up and venture out into the arctic freeze to face four-foot-high mounds of plowed snow on both sides of the street. The snow drift resembles those Jersey concrete barriers and are completely impeding my access to the other side where Angelo's is rustling up submarine sandwiches for the noontime famished. I think about stepping through the moguls in the hopes the frozen snow has crusted hard enough to support my weight. My only alternative is to drive, but allow me to explain the quandary.

Winchester Rope employs a crew of hard-working Vietnamese women who speak fragmented English and have little regard for reserved parking spaces. For as far back as I can remember, every time I left my parking space (clearly marked with a "Reserved for Jason Najarian" sign) one of the diminutive women would come dashing out of the factory, running in a way that resembled a shackled convict escaping from a chain gang, until she reached her car at the far end of the parking lot. She would then drive up front and occupy my coveted space.

This injustice takes place every time I venture out around the noon hour. It has become a game whereby the older women hide in the shadows waiting to ambush my spot. At times, they are so proficient in reaching their vehicles without being noticed, I swear these parking-spot terrorists have a network of tunnels dug from the ladies' room to the parking lot. Not wanting to lose my parking spot in this frigid cold, my only option is to scale the snow summit before me.

I dig the tips of my boots into the piled snow, making footholds from where I take three unbalanced steps to the top. Standing almost ten feet above street level on the crest of the mogul, I wish for two things: a net and a basketball to make my first and last slam dunk. I can hear the crowd going wild.

I contemplate jumping down from this elevation, but I subscribe to Murphy's Law, which guarantees I will slip on the icy landing and break something, if not end up on my ass. So instead, I begin my descent ever so slowly until Murphy sees what I'm attempting. Like a trap door below me, the mound of snow succumbs to my weight and swallows me up to waist level.

And there I stand buried in snow. Cars drive by slowly looking at the man with the missing legs. It has to be around eighty-five degrees in Florida.

I dig my way through the wall of powder and emerge onto the street. With Angelo's just a snowball's throw on the other side, I skate across and find firm footing in his plowed parking lot.

"Mr. Najarian," Angelo says, announcing my arrival in unison with the bells on his front door. "Is it cold enough for ya?"

I shuffle up to the deli counter and peruse the wall-mounted menu. I'm a regular customer here, so the ten to fifteen pounds . . . all right, twenty pounds I'm overweight, based on someone else's guidelines, can be attributed to Angelo's scrumptious sandwiches.

"How's it going, Angelo. It could be a little colder, though. I can't quite get my spit to freeze before it hits the ground."

He laughs. "What can I get you today?"

"How about the usual: small roast beef with lettuce, tomatoes, and mayo."

Angelo repeats my order to his sandwich preparers.

"Angelo, I'm feeling lucky today."

"How's that?"

"Well, what would you do if you grabbed a handful of M&M's from a multi-colored bag and they all came up green?"

"I'd eat 'em."

"You're missing the point," I say. "They were all *green*! What are the odds?"

Angelo shrugs his shoulders. "Candy doesn't make for a lucky day."

"Yeah? Watch me . . . let me have one of those twenty-dollar scratch tickets." I open my wallet and find forty-eight dollars. I slip a twenty-dollar bill over the counter as Angelo hands me the ticket.

I scratch the numbers for a few seconds while Angelo peers over the counter to watch me uncover my prize. When the last number is exposed without a match, he says, "See! Eat the candy, don't bet on it."

Undeterred, I ask for another ticket. My wallet is lighter by twenty dollars as Angelo shakes his head and says, "Remind me to never hire you as my financial planner."

Scratch . . . scratch . . . scratch.

Another loser. I can't believe it. Disappointed, I look up at Angelo who is holding my wrapped sandwich. "Don't bet on this sandwich if you happen to find *green* lettuce inside, all right? That wisdom will cost you $3.50."

I hand him a five-dollar bill and wait for change. As I do, I notice that the Powerball Lottery prize amount posted next to the register has ballooned to over $63 million. I reach for my three remaining dollars and say, "Let me have three quick picks for tonight's Powerball."

Angelo hands me my change, steps in front of the lottery machine and punches in my request. One ticket prints out. He takes my money and hands me the ticket.

"That was one expensive bag of M&M's," he jokes.

I look at the numbers:

11-30-46-57-59 +11
4-16-17-47-49 +18
3- 6-26-28-42 +11

"These numbers are terrible," I complain halfheartedly. "Look, you gave me two Powerball numbers the same. I want a do-over. What kind of operation are you running here?"

"Hey, Jason," Angelo says smiling, as he wipes his hands on his apron. "It's your lucky day, remember?"

When I arrive back at my desk, I find a telephone message from my ex-wife. Each time this woman calls is equivalent to receiving an audit notice from the Internal Revenue Service. It's never good news and whatever she wants is never of any benefit to me. I toss the sandwich on the desk and decide to tackle this annoyance before eating.

I met Megan in my final year of college. I'm not much of a ladies' man, having never mastered the verbal repartee required to garner a woman's attention, so it came as a complete surprise to me when this nice looking coed decided she had surpassed the alcohol requirement for placing her perfectly sculptured bottom into my lap during a loud and boisterous frat party. At first, I thought this petite, glassy-eyed brunette had missed her boyfriend's lap by maybe several frat houses, but after a few minutes of swaying to the tunes of *Nickelback,* she remained entrenched while her coconut-scented hair titillated my senses. Then I thought this had to be a mere tune-up for her late-night gig at the local strip club known as *The Golden Banana*. But after ten minutes, this fair-skinned woman remained in my lap, turning every so often with a smile that suggested she had nowhere else to be.

We dated exclusively throughout our remaining college days and got married a year after I was employed as the controller for Winchester Rope. She found work as a paralegal for an ambulance chaser. I had fallen in love with a woman who literally fell into my lap.

It didn't take long for Megan to grasp her mistake, or to finally become sober. When she realized life married to an accountant was not going to provide her with the glamour and financial security she anticipated after stuttering, "I . . . I . . . I . . . do," Megan started searching for another lap to beguile. After two years of marriage, unbeknownst to me, I took on the unenviable designation of cuckold. I found out about my wife's infidelity when a friend of a friend of a friend mentioned to a friend of mine that my wife had become very cozy with her physical trainer at New Body Fitness Center.

I suspected as much. It's easy to tell when your wife is cheating by the sudden increase in fake orgasms. What used to take an hour or more was reduced to maybe ten minutes, and included a spurious moan and an apathetic shout before the actress forged her climactic shudder. Still, I wasn't totally sure. I took my friend's advice and followed Megan to the fitness center one evening. Sure enough, I found the two of them surreptitiously pumping more than iron. When I confronted Megan, she immediately went on the offense by screaming, "Who the hell are you to be following me?"

Your husband?

Her muscle-head boyfriend flexed a few times then stepped in front of her to face me. The man was handsome, I'll give him that, with a physique to match: tall, shaved head, square jaw, and bulging biceps. I was no match. Megan stood behind him as if Muscle-head had to protect her from me. I felt inadequate. I felt like a loser. But I also wondered what the hell she saw in him beyond his physique?

Six months later our divorce was final. No kids, no assets to split. She went her way, I went mine. Soon after, Megan and Muscle-head got married. A couple of years later, Muscle-head met a woman from Down Under and left Megan, one cold and dreary New England day, for the sunny shores of Queensland. Life's a bitch, mate.

Ever since that impromptu parting, which was more impromptu for Megan than for Muscle-head, she has blamed me for everything in her life, from an early childhood bloody nose to yesterday's pimple on her ass. As I hold her phone message in my hand, I'm looking at a roast beef sandwich with a side order of ex-wife indigestion. I tap in her number.

"Hi, Jason. Thanks for getting back to me."

"What's up?"

"I have a business proposition for you."

"Not interested."

"I want to invest in a line of Happy Life Vitamins."

"Good for you and best of luck. Bye."

"Wait! I need some seed money."

"No."

"Jason, for chrissakes, I'll pay you back with interest as soon as I can."

"I can't hear you. My fingers are in my ears."

"Then who's holding the goddamn phone?"

I rake my face. "Riddle me this. Why should I invest in anything to do with Megan O'Mally?"

"Because, I'm still your ex-wife."

Huh? I scratch my head as I ponder the curse. "What about your fitness guru? Call him."

"He's dead to me."

"Can't I be?"

"Come on, Jason. Your money is sitting in some lame mutual fund losing value every day. This is a business opportunity for you."

"I like losing money in my mutual fund. Look, I just bought some Powerball tickets. If I win, I'll loan you what you need, all right? Are we good? See ya." I end the call hearing only the screech of "cheap bast . . ." as I remove the phone from my ear.

Later that night, with a plate of Rao's marinara over thick spaghetti with cut lobster meat, tail only, and a salad churning in my belly, I sit surfing the channels for a movie that will keep me awake. How is it with eighteen cable channels in high definition, I can't find a movie I haven't already seen? I settle on the *Discovery* channel and watch repeat episodes of *The Deadliest Catch*, *Dirty Jobs*, and *Storm Chasers*, which, for some reason, all remind me of my marriage to Megan.

At some point, I nod off until the wee hours of the morning when my internal mechanism decides to nudge me awake in order to shut off the television. I clean up my supper dishes, climb into my New England Patriots sweat pants and crawl into bed for sleep session number two. I have no inkling of what I have missed.

Live from the most exciting vacation destination:
Universal Orlando Resort. It's Powerball; America's number
one jackpot game. Good Wednesday night everyone, Scott
Adams here with you. Tonight's estimated jackpot is sixty-
three million dollars!

Powerball 10x continues until the number is drawn. You
can multiply all non-jackpot prizes up to ten times! Tonight,
your multiplier is four.

So let's get to it! First white ball tonight: 17
It's followed by: 4

Your next number is: 49

Here's a picture of Betty from Lansing, Michigan. She pulled down $100,000!

Next is: 16

And your final white ball tonight: 47

Time now for your Powerball and that number is: 18

Your winning numbers are: 17-4-49-16-47 with a Powerball 18.

Sixty-three million dollars! Good luck!

CHAPTER THREE

Ticket to Ride

"If you really want something in life, you have to work for it. Now quiet, they're about to announce the lottery numbers."

—HOMER SIMPSON

The sporadic buzz is annoying me.

I glance to my left, in the direction of the irritant, to find a monkey clinging to a bungee cord with one hand, while displaying what looks like an alarm clock in the other. The chimp has reached the lowest point, and is quickly springing back up into a thicket of fronds at the top of the coconut palm tree that supports my hammock, taking the buzz with it.

To my right, a naked woman sits reading a book on a large sleeping sea tortoise. She wears only black-rimmed glasses, and is holding a paperback titled *Murder and Mayhem in Goose Pimple Junction*. Her light golden-red hair rests casually upon her shoulders complementing her freckled, milky complexion. Her legs straddle the tortoise, and I can see the advertisement, *Sprint 4-G speed*, painted on its shell.

The buzz returns as the monkey on the bungee cord reappears. I reach to hit the snooze button, but in an instant the bungee whips back up into the palm tree.

At the other end of my hammock, a red macaw wearing a tiny captain's hat stretches its wings and starts singing a limerick.

"There once was a girl from Nantucket . . ."

Beyond the macaw, four gray dolphins play volleyball on the beach. I find that weird. I always figured dolphins for football.

"Who crossed the sea in a bucket . . ."

The chimp screeches his arrival and the buzz intensifies. This time my aim is good as I push the snooze button.

"I think you should answer that," the naked lady says.

"And when she got there . . ."

One of the dolphins leaps into the air and spikes the ball with its nose. *Point!* The two dolphins belly bump and exchange a high one with their flippers.

"They asked for a fare . . ."

"Pick up the phone, Jason," the naked lady urges me.

I reach over blindly for the cell phone vibrating on the night-stand.

"So she pulled up her dress and said . . ."

"Hello?"

"Good morning, sweetie."

I open one eye and look at the clock. The red digital numbers display 5:23 A.M.; a full hour before the alarm was programmed to drag me from paradise.

"Megan?"

"Do you miss waking up with me?"

Jesus Christ! "First . . . are you all right?" My words are slowed by the early hour fog on the highway from my mind to my mouth.

"Oh, now that's sweet. You still care."

"No, I don't care." I scratch my head, then reach down and take inventory of the jewels. "What's so important . . . *yawn* . . . that you need to wake me this early?"

"Well . . . you know I'm an early riser. The early bird catches the snail and all."

"Worm, Megan."

"Be nice to me, Jason."

"Catches the worm. The early bird catches the *worm.*" I actually pinch myself to escape this nightmare, but it doesn't work. I'm awake now at . . . 5:26 A.M., courtesy of my ex-wife. Why can't I have a real ex-wife who speaks negatively of me, and wouldn't want to be caught dead in the same country?

"Whatever," she says. "So I'm getting dressed while watching the early news when suddenly they report on something that's never happened before."

I'm lying back down, head on the pillow, my finger hovering over the end button on my cell.

"Can you guess what that is, Poopsie, or are you gonna play dumb with me?"

"Enlighten me, Megan. Then, hang up and go far away."

"For the first time ever, someone in Massachusetts has won the Powerball lottery."

"Whoopee-do."

"And the winning ticket was sold in Winchester!"

"Megan, I hear the rates at the Somalia Hilton this time of year can't be beat. There's warm water, sandy beaches, and wealthy pirates. What more could you ask for?"

"At a store called Angelo's Sandwich Shop."

I bolt up into a sitting position.

"Now, Poopsie, if I remember correctly, isn't that the sandwich shop across the street from your office?"

My early morning grogginess quickly dissipates. I try to focus on where I last saw the ticket I bought. I put the phone on speaker, throw it on the bed, jump out from under the covers, and retrieve yesterday's pants.

"And didn't you tell me you bought some Powerball tickets yesterday?"

After rooting through the pockets with no success, I search my jacket and then rifle through my briefcase for the lottery ticket. I come up empty.

"Talk to me, Jason. Are we megamillionaires or what?"

"*We?*" I reach for the phone. "How do you get *we* out of this? There is no *we*. A surgical laser beam split *we* into two distinct and separate parts: Me and you. Me bought the ticket. You didn't." I carry the phone into the kitchen, still searching.

"Jason, Jason, Jason. We made marriage vows until death parts between us. I don't take those vows lightly."

"*Death do we* . . . never mind. Seems you took those vows lightly at the gym when you and Muscle-head were working out the kinks. Then you go and marry the steroid." Frustrated, the only place left to look is at my office. Could a winning ticket worth $63 million be sitting on my desk for anyone to take?

"Temporary insanity. I told you that, Poopsie. My periods were wicked bad back then."

Temporary? "I have to get to work. Don't forget to check out priceline.com for those Somali rates." I end the call. A rush of adrenaline surges through me as I hurry into the shower. Could I really have the winning numbers waiting for me at the office? Or was I setting myself up for a major disappointment? And then I recall the green M&M's.

In record time I am out of the bathroom, dressed, and in my car headed for work at the ungodly hour of 6:05 A.M.

⸙

I PULL into the empty parking lot of Winchester Rope. Megan has already left three messages on my cell. It is still dark and cold as I step from the car. Icicles have formed on everything from overhead telephone lines to tree branches. It is so cold a seagull is perched on a street lamp near Angelo's dumpster with what looks like a frozen number-two hanging from its butt.

The snowplow guy has already sanded the parking lot and walkway, so I have to endure the fingernails-on-a-chalkboard crunch of sand while I walk to the front door. As I stand shivering in search of the office key, I glance over at Angelo's Sandwich Shop again. The lights are all on, and in the parking lot is a Fox news truck shining a klieg light on the front entrance.

I enter the lobby, flip on the lights, and run to my office. I wrestle out of my jacket, drop my briefcase and stare at my desk. No ticket. I'm not sure whether to panic or not. I suffer from PMS. Not the PMS you're thinking of, but Pessimistic Magnet Syndrome, whereby I attract all thoughts negative, and it is currently suggesting the winner is already being interviewed over at Angelo's. If that is the case, it will leave me sleep deprived and the owner of a brown nose for coming to work so early. I open the middle drawer of the desk. In my pencil tray is a ziplock bag of green M&M's and a lottery ticket.

What are the odds? I push the on button and listen as my computer clanks to life. When the *Yahoo!* screen appears, I type in a search for the Massachusetts Lottery, and wait.

The florescent lights above me hum.

The drawer elf within my desk snores.

I drum my fingers in anticipation.

What are the odds?

A list of threads are displayed on the screen and I select the first. In a few seconds the official site for the Massachusetts Lottery appears.

I look at the official Powerball results. Then I look at my ticket.

Then I nearly shit myself.

∽∾∽

I TRY to be professional. I really do. But the initial impact of the windfall turns me into a giggling imbecile. My heart pounds, my feet dance. I rush to the copier and make fifty copies of my winning ticket-to-ride. While I wait, I grab all the toilet paper from the bathrooms and toss ribbons of Charmin throughout the office. I am a one-man celebration. I leave notes on random desks announcing my retirement due to an M&M overdose. I bequeath my open bag of M&M's to Jimmy, with a note to play the lottery if he ever grabs a handful of green ones.

My PMS gives me pause for a moment. A sickening feeling overwhelms me. What if I read it wrong? I rush back to my computer and check the numbers again. I'm still a winner. I read it again. I'm still a winner. I read each individual number out loud. I'm still a winner.

I gather up my personal belongings, which amount to a ziplock bag of green M&M's, my briefcase, and my jacket, and exit Winchester Rope as an employee for the last time. Bye-bye monthly meetings. Bye-bye career. When I reach my car, a few warehouse workers are pulling into the parking lot. I give them all my biggest smile and longest wave. They look at me as if I'd just won the lottery.

I roll out of the parking lot and drive across the street to Angelo's. Channel 4 news has joined Fox in front of the store. Inside the sandwich shop, I can see a group of people surrounding Angelo with microphones and cameras. He is in for a pretty good windfall himself for selling the ticket.

The door jingles as I enter. Angelo notices me at the entrance and excuses himself from the media scrum. He nods and directs me to join him behind the refrigerated display case that holds all the ingredients to make his famous sandwiches.

"Well?" Angelo asks wide-eyed, his arms stretched out as if ready to catch me.

"Well what? I came over here to buy the paper."

Angelo deflates instantly. "Damn! I sold a bunch of tickets yesterday, but I was hoping it was you, Jason."

"Yeah, me too. Problem is you chastised me about betting on green M&M's. Negative karma," I say, pointing at him. My phone buzzes. It's Megan again. Talk about negative karma.

Angelo lowers his head. "I know, I know, but when I came into work this morning, I had a feeling you were the winner. So look." He points over to a table where he has taken all the large bags of M&M's off the sales shelf and lined them up in a row. "I was gonna start doing what you said. Put my hand in each one and try to grab all the green ones without looking."

I'm laughing inside. "Look, if you really want to be good at this, good enough to play the lottery and win," I say, reaching for my ticket-to-ride and waving it in front of him, "you have to have patience." I wave the ticket again. "You have to play to win." I hold the ticket with one hand and point to it. He isn't getting it. "And when people tell you to eat the candy, don't bet on it, you have to turn a deaf ear." I raise the ticket to my forehead and hold it there.

It takes a few seconds, but then Angelo lets out a howl, followed by a belly laugh. He screams my name at the top of his lungs, startling the gathered media, and proceeds to lift me high enough that my head almost brushes the ceiling.

"Here's your winner!" Angelo proclaims.

The media rushes over, shining their lights, yelling questions, and shoving microphones in my direction. I remain in Angelo's grasp, pumping my fist in the air. It is like hitting the winning grand slam in the last inning of the final game of the World Series, or catching the winning touchdown pass in the final seconds of the Super Bowl, or sinking a three-pointer with no time left on the clock to win the NBA finals. I am yelling. Angelo is yelling. What a picture.

"How does it feel?"

"What are you going to do with the money?"

"How did you pick the numbers?"

It is one long blur as my life begins to take on a profound new character. And then my PMS kicks in—*be careful what you wish for.*

CHAPTER FOUR

Palms Up!

"Revenge is sweet and not fattening."
—ALFRED HITCHCOCK

And then it starts. Family, friends, acquaintances, people I hardly remembered from college, guys I played softball with, women who rejected my overtures, men I stood next to in public bathrooms, females writing letters from prison, you name it, they all want to suddenly be my friend. The newspapers and nightly newscasts turn me into a celebrity. Charities for every illness, injustice, and calamity, locally and around the world, want a piece of my windfall. Political action committees call looking for me to support their agenda. *Am I a Republican or Democrat?* Youth sports organizations, police departments, fire departments, and my alma mater start lining up at my door, palms up. Even the Girl Scouts show up asking me to place a large preorder for their cookies. The phone calls are incessant, the mail endless. What a mistake I made going public.

"Hey Jason, it's your cousin Vinny from California. On your mother's side."

"*Who?*"

"Hi Jason, this is Beth Connors. You remember me from high school, right?"

"*Who?*"

"Jason, Ben Grainger here. We played a round of golf a few years back."

"*Who?*"

"Hello Jason, Cindy Hellman from college. You wanted to date me before you got involved with that whore, Megan O'Mally. Do you remember me?"

I did remember her. "Hey, Cindy, I do remember you. If I recall correctly, you turned me down when I asked you out, and then went out of your way to make a scene with the campus administrator. Something about sexual harassment if my memory serves me right."

She giggles. "I was young and probably having a bad period that day. I sure would like to make it up to you."

Why do I get all the bad periods? "I'm sure you would. Have a nice day."

I put my cell on vibrate and toss it on the sofa. Let the monkey deal with it.

The first week of being a megamillionaire is stressful. Everyone's needs, their financial problems, their overall suffering seem to be my responsibility. I'm torn with guilt that I can't help everyone, but also angry that I am a target for handouts. I need to escape the barrage of attention. I have to get out of Dodge.

Across the room, I stare at the giant check leaning against the wall endorsed to me in the amount of $19,672,531 and change. I mean literally a *giant* check: six-feet long by three-feet wide. The lottery had me hold it while snapshots were taken. The published picture on the lottery website shows me with a scowl on my face instead of a happy millionaire's smile. I think it was due to my confusion as to how $63 million was reduced to $19 million within minutes.

"Shouldn't I be holding a larger check?" I asked the lottery official.

He laughed. "This is as big as they come. Any bigger and it wouldn't fit in the picture."

"No, I mean the amount." *Dumbass.* "Is there a second check I should be holding?"

"This is it, Mr. Najarian. After you accepted the cash-out option and satisfied the taxes, this is your net."

"Sixty-three to nineteen," I muttered, as the cameras clicked away.

∽∾

My first order of business is to get my normal-sized lottery check deposited. I head down to the local branch of Bank of America where I have, for some time, suffered the indignities of having a checking account and a credit card with said bank.

When the great recession of 2007 hit, greed in the form of risky investments caught up to the banks, and they ended up taking it out on their customers. My credit line was lowered, which I discovered to my embarrassment while on a date, and my checking account fees skyrocketed. I challenged the bank when three of my checks bounced while attempting to clear on the same day as my paycheck deposit. The result: three overdraft charges of $39. One of the checks was only for $10.50. Livid, I met with the branch manager in an attempt to get these fees overturned.

"There's nothing I can do," the glorified teller said in broken English.

"You charged me $39 for a $10.50 overdraft!"

"Bank policy," she replied. I left muttering obscenities to myself.

I stand once again in the lobby and ask for the manager, carrying less anger than three years earlier. The same woman I met with before greets me with a smile and extends her hand. Her name is Maria Ramos.

"How can I help you?" she says. Her job secured with T.A.R.P. money.

"Remember me?"

She tilts her head to one side—confused doggy style. "Are you a customer of the branch?"

"Yes. We met a while back over some bank fees you refused to overturn." I knew she wouldn't remember, but it was fun to reminisce.

"I'm sorry, I don't recall. Is there something I can help you with today?"

I remove the lottery check from my pocket and display it for her.

"I wanted to deposit this with the bank," I start. Her eyes widen as she focuses on the amount.

"Oh, that's wonderful. I'll be happy to assist you."

"Maybe so, but I'm not happy to assist you."

Her head tilts again. *Rut roh.* "You see, Maria, the fact your bank was so arrogant with regard to lowering my credit card line and charging excessive fees tells me you don't care about your customers." I love watching arrogance squirm.

"I assure you, sir, we do care about our customers. Can I look back and see what happened to your account?"

"No. I just wanted to drop by and show you what $117 in fees ended up costing your bank. I'll be closing my checking account and won't need your credit card anymore." I drop the cut pieces of the card in her palm. "Well, you have a nice day." Revenge is sweet.

∽

I END up depositing the check into my brokerage account. At the same time, I meet with a financial planner and give him $10 million to invest. I want to earn at least 5 percent yearly on the principal, reinvest half, and live on the balance.

I warn the guy, "If you do a Madoff with my money, I will hunt you and your family down and butcher the lot." I end my threat with a *capisce,* to give the impression I am mob connected.

He smiles at me, but I remain serious. It's not like I can go out and win the lottery again.

My next order of business is to contact an agent to find what has been so prominent in my dreams: a secluded gulf-front property on a barrier island on the west coast of Florida with a bungee-jumping monkey, limerick-singing macaw, a naked woman riding on a sea tortoise, and dolphins playing volleyball. Should be easy. The agent's name is Maggie and she specializes in island property sales along Florida's southern Gulf Coast.

"I'll get right on it, Jason," she says while giggling.

Charity begins at home. My parents, Gloria and Sam Najarian, were married for twenty-two years until they amicably called it quits. I guess the warranty ran out. I am their only child, so they insist we remain close. Each year we spend the holidays together. My father brings his girlfriend and my mother her boyfriend. It was uncomfortable for me, the first few years, watching the wrong people kissing, but I got over it. In fact, their separation never really bothered me until now, when I realize I have to buy *two* houses for them instead of one.

Both of my parents love the water: my mother the ocean, my dad the lakes. In my case, the apple didn't fall far from either tree. I buy my mother a $1 million home in Wellfleet, on the Outer Cape, overlooking Cape Cod Bay. She enjoys dabbling in oils, so I figure she can spend the rest of her life on a porch painting seascapes nobody will recognize. Her boyfriend, Bradley, is in the academic field. Whenever he starts talking, I am prone to breaking out in hives. At Christmas, he wears a cashmere sweater tied in a knot around his neck. Really, who does that anymore? And he never wears socks. Each year, as the holiday festivities drag on, the professor slips one foot out of his loafers so he can pick his toes. What's up with that? When it's time to leave, I always make sure my hands are holding something to avoid his handshake. But Bradley makes my mother happy, so I take my constant urge to purge while in his company to another room.

My dad loves to fly fish. I buy him a $1 million log home near Danforth, Maine, where he can enjoy his passion on East Grand Lake. It took my father longer to hook up with someone after the divorce, and for a while I thought he had sworn off the opposite sex. But one Thanksgiving he showed up with a much younger woman on his arm, and my first thought was—"*You go, Dad!*"

My second thought was, "*You have to be shitting me!*"

As she strolled farther into the house I could tell she had circa 1960 hippie written all over her. It looked as if my father had taken Mr. Peabody's way-back machine back to a Vietnam-era, "Hell no, we won't go" rally, and enticed this young waif to follow him into the future. Her name is Tranquility. She has long hair and wears no makeup. Colorful beads dangle around her neck. Rings adorn each finger. She dresses in tie-dyed Bohemian garb—short enough to expose the fuzz on her legs, and she walks in sandals—even in the winter. She is friendly, with a wonderful smile, but my sense is she drifts through life in some utopian state well beyond the grasp of mankind. Plus, I fear she has braids in her armpits.

Over the course of several holiday gatherings, I've noticed Tranny has a tendency to pick her nose. Not a deep, full-finger exploration, but a more feminine pick around the inside edges. Luckily, I've never witnessed the removal of debris. Still, it is unsettling to watch her eyes cross as she guides her finger uphill. But Tranquility makes my father happy, so I force myself to turn away from her nostril infatuations and hope my dad has drawn the line on bushy armpits.

When I originally met with my lawyer, my intent was to gift the homes to my parents. But then I remembered last Christmas when I caught the toe-picker and the nose-picker exchanging flirtatious glances. It gave me pause. If these scalawags end up marrying my parents, they would gain access to my gifts. So I keep both houses in my name and force my parents to fork over a dollar each year for rent.

⚭

It takes less time than I anticipated for Maggie, the Florida property finder, to call me back. I suspect it is probably due to the current housing crisis in Florida. Property values have plummeted creating a surplus of homes.

"From my multiple listings, I found a property located on a barrier island just south of Sarasota. It's listed by Gulf Breeze Realty and the realtor's name is Phyllis Hammerstein," Maggie informs me. "I'm e-mailing you some pictures."

"That sounds great," I say, excited.

"If you like the property, let me know. I'll make an appointment with Gulf Breeze when you are ready to come down and see it in person."

The pictures are as if they were scanned from my dreams. I immediately call Maggie back and express my interest.

∽

As THE weeks turn into days before my escape to Florida, I still have affairs to settle. I contribute $1 million to *The Jimmy Fund*, a charity that helps in the fight against cancer in children. It leaves me with just over $6 million in the slush account. I planned for that donation to be my last, until I received a letter from Sarah Holland who represents a group supporting the families of fallen soldiers. She isn't begging me for money, unlike every other charity. She simply wants me to attend a meeting. I e-mail her back and agree.

I sit and listen to families commiserate about their dads, husbands, and sons who won't be returning from Iraq and Afghanistan. It is even more moving to hear that some moms and daughters aren't coming home either. I am humbled. I feel guilty that a schmuck like me won the lottery instead of one of these brave families. After the meeting, I hand Sarah a check for $500,000 to be used to assist the families of these heroes. One story in particular moves me: A twenty-one-year-old widow with a son her husband never held. She looks so young, frightened, and lost. Sarah tells me her name is Theresa and shares with me what I need to know about her. Sarah understands, for she lost her husband years earlier during the assault on Fallujah.

The next day, I inform my investment advisor I have adopted a family anonymously. I instruct him to take a percentage of my monthly return on investment and send a check to Theresa and her son every month.

∽

I AM days away from my appointment in Florida and I need to address one more issue: how to escape from my ex-wife. I have agreed to meet with Megan on a Saturday morning for breakfast—her idea, her treat—in an effort to put her in my rearview mirror.

I am sitting at a table sipping orange juice when in sashays Megan with an air of confidence that leaves a trail of dollar signs in her wake. She stops and scans the restaurant until she finds me. Megan breaks into a huge smile, waves her hand, and begins to skip in my direction.

"Hi, Poops," she says, slipping out of her coat. She arrives in trifecta form: good looking, smelling great, and dressed in an outfit so tight clueless men are forced to adulate her figure. If only there were a pill available to numb her mind, because I'd take her body back in a heartbeat.

"I have news to share with you," I begin.

She claps her hands and smiles. "When am I moving in?"

The hair on my neck stands out. "First, I need to ask you a question."

During the days following my windfall, Megan reached out to her attorney to determine what percentage of my gain she was entitled to. When the harsh reality of zero startled her like finding out broccoli crowns had lingered between her teeth all day, it was time for her to roll out Plan B. Over a four-week period, Plan B entailed carpet bombing me daily with love letters, sexy phone calls, casseroles, and e-mail greeting cards, just to name a few. She showed up one night at my doorstep naked, wearing only a winter coat. When I answered the door, she flashed her assets with a message that read, *We Love You,* written in red lipstick across her freckled breasts. Megan had her eyes on the prize and nothing was going to get in her way. Fearing she had nineteen million reasons to continue her bombing raid, I considered my options. Either get a restraining order, which any victim will attest doesn't work, or succumb to her assault. In the end, I succumbed by meeting her for breakfast.

"You're proposing to me here, Poopsie?" She looks mischievously at the tables that abut ours. My guess is she has been dusting off the old name, Megan Najarian, and meshing it with the new title of millionaire.

"Why did you meet with your lawyer after I won the lottery?"

Her smile quickly evaporates. The question catches her off guard, so she pauses for a moment before replying—like a black widow might pause before administering its poisonous venom.

"I wanted to see if I was entitled to something because of all the years . . . you know . . . that I serviced you."

"Serviced me? What are you? A gas station?"

"You know . . . the sex," she whispers, leaning closer to me.

"Yes, I know, but it was mostly self-serve, not full service. And all the *years* amounted to just three. Wouldn't getting paid for the sex make you a prostitute?" I whisper back.

She leans away and straightens her back. "Sticks and stones may break my bones, but names are a horse of a different color."

I massage my temples. "Wasn't the ten grand I offered for the vitamins enough?"

"Jason, forget the vitamins, I want you. *I love you.* I always have," she says, eyes watering on cue.

I look in her misty eyes. "If we get back together, how will I know there won't be another Muscle-head down the road?"

She takes my hands in hers. "I'd never make that mistake again."

"You'll be honest with me? No lies?" I ask.

"Yes, Poopsie." Excitement is building.

"You'll leave all your friends, your job, and follow me?"

"Yes . . . yes!"

"You'll sign a pre-nup?"

Her mouth freezes open. I can almost smell the rubber burning from the brakes being applied.

"If . . . if I have to," she stutters.

"Good. Next week I'm flying out of town to look at a piece of property. If it's as beautiful in person as it is in the pictures, I'm buying it."

Her eyes widen. "Where, Jason? Tell me! Tell me! Tell me!"

"It's gonna take a couple of weeks to get papers drawn up and checks cleared. When everything is settled, I'll call for you to fly out."

"Oh my God! Where, Jason?"

I remove a check from my pocket. "Here's the $10,000 I promised for your vitamin scam. Use it for airfare and whatever else you need."

"Jason! Cut the suspense! Where are we moving to?"

"California."

Megan jumps out of her chair and dances a jig until she has the attention of the packed restaurant. She slithers back into her chair and asks, "LA? Hollywood? San Fran? San Andreas?"

"San Andreas is a fault line, Megan."

"*Whatever.* Are you, like, buying a movie star's house? Tell me, Jason, please, you're making me have to pee I'm so excited!"

"I'm looking at a house on a bluff overlooking Paradise Cove beach in Malibu."

Megan starts fanning herself. "Oh my God! *Paradise Cove beach?* Is that, like, on the water?"

CHAPTER FIVE

Gulf Boulevard

"Money is better than poverty, if only for financial
reasons."

—WOODY ALLEN

In a midmorning phone conversation from my hotel with Phyllis
Hammerstein of Gulf Breeze Realty, she suggests I meet her at Two
Palms Marina in one hour. She gives me directions and then hangs
up abruptly before I am able to ask how I will know who she is.
My first impression of The Hammer leads me to believe she isn't
too excited about showing me the property. In fact, it sounded like
she had better things to do.

I leave my room at the Windjammer Inn in Englewood, jump
into my rented Ford Mustang convertible and head south on highway 775. On the way, I pass a Bealls department store, a few pizza
joints, a Steak 'n Shake, several bait shops, and numerous banks.
As I drive farther, I notice a modern looking single-story building
with a sign that reads, First Federal Bank of Florida. I decide I
will do business with this bank because I like their hunter-green
tin roof.

I come upon a boat dealership with a yard full of shiny new
vessels, inboards and outboards, cruisers and performance. I steer
onto the shoulder to grab a closer look. Like a kid outside a candy
store, I peek through the fence at Sea Rays, Bayliners, and Pro-
lines. A few high-performance Donzi boats catch my eye. I want
one of each. For me, the excitement of owning a boat is right up
there with owning a house on the beach. I can picture myself
cruising the warm gulf waters with a parrot on my shoulder, both

of us wearing pirate hats and singing, *Yo ho, yo ho, a pirate's life for me*. Does it get any better?

Back on the highway, I travel another several miles until I come upon the sign for Two Palms Marina. I turn right onto a crushed-shell road, and follow it for another quarter of a mile to the marina. Several boats are in the main yard being serviced. A forklift, used for lifting them out of the water, stands idle. Ahead of me a quay stretches out into the waterway. Located on the concrete wharf is a combination fishing gear and bait shop with two Texaco gas pumps at the far end. Along the length of the wharf are a dozen or so boat slips located between barnacle-covered pillars. I park the Mustang under two palm trees.

Behind me I hear the sound of tires skidding on crushed shells. In one quick motion the car comes to a stop and a woman, all five feet of her by the looks of it, comes swaggering into the marina. She is wearing a sundress and sneakers with oversized sunglasses nestled on top of her head. I'm guessing midforties. She carries a leather briefcase in one hand and a clipboard in the other. Her step is brisk as if she is trying to make up for lost time. The woman comes to a stop at the entrance to the quay. One look along the empty wharf convinces her I must be her appointment.

Turning to the boatyard she calls out, "Mr. Najarian?"

"Yes, that's me."

"Well, get over here snowbird. I ain't got all day."

I hurry over and introduce myself. "Jason Najarian," I say, extending my hand.

She lifts her briefcase and clipboard to show me. "If I had a third hand, Mr. Najarian, I'd welcome you. For now, take it for granted. Now follow me."

I think, *Hammer time.*

I follow Phyllis Hammerstein down the steps from the boatyard to the wharf until we reach the fifth berth where a center-console Carolina Skiff is tied off. She tosses the clipboard in the boat and fishes a set of keys from her briefcase.

"How was your trip, Mr. Najarian? You're in from Boston, right?" She steps down into the boat.

"Yes, Boston. The flight was smooth. In fact, everything was going great until I started driving over the Sunshine Skyway Bridge out of Tampa. That's one high bridge."

"Afraid of heights, are you?"

"No, not really. But it's a bit unnerving when I can look out my car window and see the astronauts playing poker inside the space station."

The Hammer grunts. "What really is unnerving, Mr. Najarian, is crossing the bridge with the knowledge that it fell into Tampa Bay back in 1980," she quips.

My jaw drops. "*What?*"

The Hammer is fidgeting with the boat keys at the console. "During a storm, a freighter slammed into a supporting pier, sending the bridge crashing into the water. It was a terrible scene." She looks up at me and winks. "FYI as you drive back to Tampa International."

Phyllis Hammerstein scares me. I start to think about changing realtors.

"Mornin' Ms. Phyllis."

The voice behind me belongs to an old, scraggly guy leaning on the outside of the bait shop. He wears torn jeans and a stained white T-shirt with rolled-up sleeves. He is bald on top and his side hair is combed back into a ponytail. His beard hangs unkempt. Thick-framed glasses lean against his nose, and around his neck is a lanyard that falls to his chest with what looks like a headlight hanging from the end. Clipped to his waist is a six-volt rechargeable lead-acid battery. I do a double take thinking Jed Clampett.

"Good morning, Memphis," Phyllis replies.

"I got 'er all gassed up for yous," he says, rubbing the scruff on his face. "Are yous takin' in the properties on the islands or just takin' in dis beautiful day?"

"I'm running over to Sand Key to show this snowbird the Double-D house," she says thumbing me. "Not that he's a buyer, mind you."

Memphis forces a laugh, and then chokes on his phlegm. He turns to one side and spits the interruption into the canal. "Just anudder nosey northerner, huh? Can't say I'd have da patience yous have with all dese snowbirds, Ms. Phyllis." I hear the skiff's motor turn over.

The snowbird reference is getting a little old with me. Plus, I feel anxiety building within me about driving back over the bridge, so confrontation comes easily.

"Say old man, what's that thing hanging around your neck, a headlight? Are you a motorcycle?"

"Mr. Najarian, please undo the dock lines," Phyllis says.

"*Na-jar-in?* Is dat one of dem terrorist type names?" Memphis blurts.

This guy looks like he just crawled out of a cave, and he's calling me a terrorist. "Do I look like a terrorist? Maybe if you turn on your high beam there," I say, pointing at his stomach, "you might see me better."

"Mr. Najarian, time's a wasting. I'll be late for my afternoon tee time," Phyllis warns me.

Memphis runs his hand over to the battery pack. He touches the switch and his stomach light shines brightly.

"You sneerin' at me, boy?"

Forget Jed Clampett. I start hearing the dueling banjos from *Deliverance*.

Memphis takes a few steps toward me and raises the light. "I'm the marina masta, *Na-Jar-Bin-Laden*. I guide da boats into da marina at night."

"So you're not a motorcycle? You're more like a lighthouse?"

"Mr. Najarian, please untie the lines while we're still young."

I keep one eye on Memphis as I attend to the cleats. I toss both lines into the boat and climb aboard. The Hammer pushes us away from the wharf until we drift into the waterway and then she shifts into forward. We cruise parallel to the quay leaving a minimal wake as Memphis keeps pace on foot. When we are beyond the wharf, she taps the throttle forward, forcing the bow to lift gently out of the water as we pick up speed. I look back at Memphis standing between the two gas pumps, his gut light swaying left to right. A crooked smile crosses his face.

∽

WE SET course through the open waters of the Intracoastal Waterway heading west toward a strand of barrier islands. The Hammer calls out the names of each one as we pass. After a few minutes we steer south within the channel markers until we approach an inlet. On our starboard side is Sand Key, a long, thin island covered with a thicket of mangrove trees. On a map it's shaped like a smoker's pipe: a bowl at the south end and a mouthpiece pointing north. The property I am interested in sits right on the edge of the mouthpiece.

As we get closer, it seems the island is uninhabited due to the thick overgrowth. Nothing manmade is visible, but as we enter the horseshoe-shaped lagoon, I notice six docks on the port side, and up ahead an area cleared for barge landings. As we approach the docks, our tsunami-like wake chases the crabs from the spiked mangrove roots—hundreds, if not thousands, of little crabs run for their lives. Once the disturbance floats by, the crabs race to regain their positions.

I spot an egret standing sentinel within the shrubs. In my excitement I yell, "Hey, Ms. Hammerstein, look at the bird." I forget this is as normal a sighting for her as a pigeon would be for me in Massachusetts. She doesn't look, but I think I hear her mumble, "Tourist."

The skiff settles in along the first pier. I drop the bumpers and toss the bow and stern lines onto the dock. I jump out and secure them to cleats. I offer The Hammer a helping hand from the boat, but she refuses by saying, "Mr. Najarian, I've been doing this since you were pooping in your diapers." Effortlessly, she places one foot on the gunwale and another foot on the dock while carrying her briefcase and clipboard. "Follow me," she says.

We walk the length of the dock that merges onto an old road made up of tar, shells, and sand. In the distance I can hear the surf coming ashore. A few song birds add to the calming effect. I've never heard anything so tranquil.

"This is Gulf Boulevard," she offers. Pointing south she says, "A hundred yards or so down the road is a bird sanctuary and beyond that are about two dozen homes. Some are year round, but most are rentals." Turning, she continues, "The road ends over at the barge landing. The development company purchased the end of the island with the intent to build six waterfront homes located just beyond this cluster of trees and shrubs. I'll go into that further in a minute. Follow me down this path and we'll take a look at the house."

The sun is warm with a slight sea breeze. I inhale the scent of salt blended with the island flora. It is so serene that each step we take sounds like crashing cymbals beneath our feet.

A gecko crosses my path.

"Hey, Ms. Hammerstein, I just saw a Geico."

"It's *gecko*, Mr. Najarian. When we get back to my office, I'll give you a coloring book so you can learn the names and color all the wildlife you've seen," she says over her shoulder while leading me down the path.

Funny Hammer. I think she could do stand-up comedy if she were tall enough to stand.

The foliage and trees thin out and a beautiful house emerges, surrounded by rolling sand dunes covered with sea oats. The house offers a 180-degree panorama of the Gulf of Mexico. Turquoise waters, gentle waves, sandpipers dancing, sailboats touching the horizon. It is absolutely breathtaking. I am mesmerized. I think about sunsets over the gulf.

"Follow me," The Hammer says, slicing through the stillness. The house is built on pilings, so the thump of The Hammer climbing wooden steps breaks me from my trance. As I climb each step, the view gets better. From the first deck, I can see a wider body of water. The vastness of the gulf is impressive. From the second deck off the master bedroom, the vista seems to explode. The breeze is stronger and I can see the strand of barrier islands from north to south. I am sold.

"Let's begin the tour here," The Hammer suggests.

I follow her as she points out the kitchen filled with stainless-steel appliances. The living room is larger, with wicker furniture, a sixty-inch, wall-mounted plasma television and a music system with speakers wired throughout the house. The floors are plank oak. The walls are painted in pastel colors. A study, laundry room, and full bath complete the first level. A wide oak staircase in the center of the house leads to the second floor. The master bedroom runs the width of the house with floor-to-ceiling glass walls facing the gulf, wall-to-wall carpeting, and sliding glass doors that open to the upper deck. A large master bath and a walk-in closet act as bookends to the master bedroom. Two smaller bedrooms sharing a full bath make up the second level. It is a big house for a single guy. Phyllis runs a finger down her checklist.

"The master bathroom is done in teak. The handrails are polished oak. The carpets are the finest quality. The roof construction is such that it is tied into the frame of the house to sustain heavy winds. You also have hurricane shutters on the gulf-side windows," she points out without pausing to breathe. Phyllis is rattling off so many details I can't keep up. "Any questions?" she goads.

I shake my head no in fear.

"Oh . . . and the home comes furnished. What you see is what you get."

I'm not getting a warm and fuzzy feeling over some of the furnishings, but I can live with it for a while. Next, she starts in on the history.

"Decker Development made its name after hurricane Andrew wiped out most of Homestead. They were one of the first builders on the scene to repair and construct new homes. Their logo was, *'Everyone wants to get their hands on a Double D.'* Back in 2002, Cyrus Decker and his wife, Jenna, wanted to expand to the west coast of Florida, so they started down in Naples building luxury homes and worked their way north.

"Sometime around 2005, Cyrus contributed campaign donations to the coffers of a politician, and like magic, a variance was granted to develop the land adjacent to the bird sanctuary, which I pointed out to you at the docks. Before anyone knew what was going on, Decker Development had permits to build on ten acres at the tip of the island. They started with a small desalination plant and then got this house up as a model before the great recession hit. I remember speaking with Jenna back in 2008. They had just lost their investment in Sand Key to the bank. Decker Development was filing Chapter 11.

"Anyway, the bank owns all the property now. Decker Development originally had it on the market for $1.9 million, but the bank reduced it to $1.5. Still, no buyers in this depressed market. And it won't get better anytime soon, now that BP is spilling its crude into the gulf. Unfortunately, this house will remain a fantasy for many. And I assume, Mr. Najarian, you'll be another on a long list of dreamers."

"Call me Jason."

"I can do that."

"Good, because I'd like us to be friends."

"Oh really? Look mister, if you're looking for a cougar, you've come to the wrong place." She says this smiling as she gently pushes a wisp of hair from her face.

"With all due respect, Ms. Hammerstein, I'd like to make an offer on the house."

The Hammer grunts. "The bank won't just give it away, Jason. Please understand I've had plenty of lowballers turn out to be a total waste of my golf time."

"I understand." I walk over to the glass wall and stare out into the gulf. "Baron de Rothschild once said, 'When there's blood in the streets, buy property.' The same can be said for oil in the water." I turned to look at her. "Inform the bank you have a serious buyer offering $1.2 million in cash, payable immediately.

Where our friendship comes into play, Ms. Hammerstein, is you convincing the bank that if the oil spill reaches the Florida coast, this property will be worth shit. Ask them if they want to take that risk."

"Fair enough. But why are you risking it?" she counters.

"Because the oil spill will never make it here." I know this from my dreams.

CHAPTER SIX

Moving In

"Some cause happiness wherever they go; others whenever they go."

—OSCAR WILDE

Years before my sudden windfall, I considered myself a supersti-
tious character with a fair share of idiosyncrasies. Since winning
my ticket-to-ride, I've edged into a mild state of paranoia aided
by my inherent PMS. I've spent a few sleepless nights worrying
the Massachusetts Lottery is going to call me to say, "Mr. Najarian . . . we've made a mistake. Kindly return the money." I've
learned this is not an uncommon delusion for instant millionaires,
but when coupled with my other quirks, it makes for a heated
debate between the fearmongers squatting in my head. The end
result usually leaves me with a pounding migraine, and at times
the urge to expel flatus in the closest Bank of America lobby. I
often wonder if Doctor Oz would consider my condition normal.

I part ways with The Hammer at the marina. She promises to
call the bank holding the mortgage as soon as she gets back to
her office. There seems to be a new commission bounce in her
step. Apparently I am no longer an annoying snowbird. In fact,
I swear as she was climbing into her car, she looked back at me
and blew a kiss. Don't hold me to that, the sun was in my eyes.
But I'm fairly certain there was some kind of mouth-to-air action.

I lean against the Mustang and take another look around the
marina. I am filled with anticipation and excitement. Soon I'll
be docking my yet-to-be-purchased boat at Two Palms Marina,
cleaning said boat in its boatyard, filling the gas tank at its Texaco

pumps, and purchasing sundries from the . . . and there stands Memphis outside his bait shop staring at me. We lock eyes. The Lighthouse takes two fingers, points them at his eyes, and then points them at me. The message is clear. I simplify the exchange by offering him one finger in return.

I climb into my rental and head back to The Windjammer Inn, stopping only for a cheeseburger-in-paradise and a milk shake. Gulf Boulevard is everything I've ever dared dream about, but the reality of buying not one, but three homes each worth over one million dollars in the span of three months, is surreal. I feel like I'm playing with Monopoly money. I question my actions and fear I might become another rags-to-riches-to-rags story if I don't practice some serious frugality going forward. A slight migraine ensues.

When I arrive back at the motel, my departure documents lay scattered on the bed: the rental car receipt and the airline ticket. The sight of them causes my migraine to kick into high gear. In order for me to return the car and fly out of Tampa International, I'd have to drive over that damn bridge again. *"FYI as you drive back to Tampa International."*

I pace the room.

There is no doubt in my mind if I travel the apex of the Skyway again, either an earthquake, a flock of geese, or a drunk driver will send me spiraling into Tampa Bay with my arms flapping, the radio blaring, and the top down on my rented Mustang. I didn't win all this money just to die an untimely death. I reach for the phone and cancel my AirTran flight out of Tampa and rebook it out of Sarasota. I then call Budget and inform them I will be dropping their car at Sarasota/Bradenton airport. These changes cost me a bundle and include stops at every airport along the East Coast, but that is fine with me because I'm not one to tempt fate.

∽

BACK IN my Massachusetts condo, The Hammer calls to inform me the bank is interested in my offer.

"Jason, I went to bat for you and hit a home run. Now it's your turn to act, young man. I need a nonrefundable deposit as soon as possible so the bank knows your offer is sincere. They also want to know how the balance will be paid and over what period of time. How much do you think you can put down?"

"One hundred dollars," I reply, just to give my little Hammer friend something to pound.

No. No. No. Jason, nobody puts down only a hundred dollars on a million-dollar offer. Get serious! Oh jeepers . . . don't tell me you're having a change of heart."

"Ms. Hammerstein, inform the bank I will overnight a certified check for the full amount. I expect the paperwork to be ready for my signature when I return in a week or so. I want to be moved in by the end of the month. Will that work for you, Ms. Hammerstein?"

"Yes! And please call me Phyllis."

Happy Hammer. "I can do that, and I appreciate your assistance with the bank. I have another favor to ask."

"Anything you need, Jason."

"Can I ship a few boxes to your office?"

"Certainly, I'll even arrange to have them brought over to Gulf Boulevard. This is so exciting. Oh, and I'm glad to hear you made it over the bridge in one piece. You seemed a little stressed when we parted."

No thanks to my realtor. "I ended up flying over the bridge instead of driving, the advantages of being a snowbird."

The Hammer laughs. "Well, I must say I misjudged you, Jason. I'm looking forward to getting to know you better."

Hmm, that sounds like a line being crossed. I thank Phyllis again and end the call before she resorts to panting.

Over the next day, I do research to find a boat to fit my needs. I decide on a Four Winns H260SS, with a 380hp Mer-Cruiser. After an extensive list of options, which includes a stainless-steel arch over the deck for my someday parrot to perch as we sing together in the open gulf, the price sets me back close to

$100,000. I place a rush order for the boat and advise the sales-man I'll need delivery as soon as possible to coincide with my return. Aside from a new truck and a few pieces of furniture, it will be my last major purchase before I settle into a life of seclusion and Internet porn.

I call my parents to inform them of my pending move. At first I wanted to tell them in person, but driving down to the cape and then back up into the wilderness of Maine is too much of a road trip for me. When I accompanied my dad to purchase his log home, we got so lost on the back roads of Maine that the female voice on his GPS system said, "Where the fuck are we?"

So on the phone to each of them in separate calls, I go into detail about the house, the beach, the privacy, and how I feel living on the island will arrest the aging process. Apparently, I am too convincing, because both of my parents want to visit.

On the phone with my mother I ask, "Just you and Dad, right Ma?"

"No silly. Bradley would love to see your new home, too."

On the phone with my father I ask, "Just you and Ma, right Dad?"

"Son, I don't go anywhere without Tranquility."

I tried. My parents decide on an extended stay over the upcoming holiday. It buys me about six months of solitude before Thanksgiving. I figure by late November, I might be in the mood for some company, even if the visit includes Brad and Tranny. On the other hand, I'm not too keen on having those two deposit quantities of toe scale and nose shale inside my brand new two-year-old home. However, I take solace in knowing if I notice these two starting to scratch or excavate, I'll simply force the festivities to the warm outdoors. That's the beauty of living in Florida.

I call a few close friends to give them an update on my plans, but I sense a shift has taken place amongst them. On the surface, they are happy for me, but their tones suggest there are levels of envy. I suppose some of them are looking at my good fortune, and then comparing it to their lame careers, failed marriages, or general ennui in the treadmill of life. I don't blame them. I guess I would feel the same. I tell each one I look forward to his visit as soon as I am settled. But the reality of that actually happening seems remote. I realize I'm not one of the guys anymore.

Over the following days, I list my furnished condo with a local realtor. I donate most of my clothes, and just about everything else I own, to Goodwill. The luxury of having a little coin in my pocket will allow me to purchase a new casual wardrobe fit for a beach bum once I am firmly planted on my sand dune. Finally, I call Sarah Holland and ask if she could arrange to have my car picked up and given to Theresa after I depart for the Sunshine State.

There isn't much left to pack. Some clothes, books, family pictures, and a stack of eclectic music ranging from The Beatles to Kings of Leon. And my chick-magnet DVD collection, which consists of the Three Stooges anthology, the ultimate six-season Sopranos compilation, *Casino*, *GoodFellas*, and the Godfather trilogy boxed set. Aside from the Stooges, I hadn't noticed the Mafia theme of my favorite movies until I was packing them in a box. I doubt there'll be any mobsters where I'm headed.

My cell rings. If it's Megan, I'm letting the monkey handle it. I'm not quite ready to follow through with her on the Malibu beach move, but it is coming. I check the number and recognize the Florida area code.

"Hello?"

"Jason, this is Phyllis Hammerstein. Good news! Your check cleared."

Funny Hammer. "The check was certified, Phyllis. Is the deal complete?"

I hear the sound of keys jingling. "Hear that Jason? I have in my hand the keys to a beautiful home on a beautiful island with your name on it. The deal is complete as soon as you sign the documents at the bank. Will you be arriving soon?"

"Within a week, I guess. I still have a few personal items to attend to, but I will be booking my flight soon. I'm packing what little I have left as we speak. Expect two boxes at your office."

"I'll keep an eye out for them. In the meantime, I've instructed the property management company to freshen up the house. I'll get over there myself and turn on the water, check the air conditioning, and make sure all the appliances are working. I'll even fluff the pillows for you."

Fluffer Hammer. "Again, I appreciate all you're doing for me."

"Well, Jason, you suggested we should be friends. I'm looking forward to it."

Sometimes, I don't think things through.

∽

It takes me another few days before I am ready to make the move. I send my boxes Federal Express down to Gulf Breeze Realty. I book a one-way airline ticket to Sarasota, which raises the eyebrows of a few terrorist-minded authorities. I am urged to report to the airport well before my scheduled flight. Before I leave, I meet with my lawyer, financial advisor, and broker to let them know where I'm headed.

"Do you have an address?" my financial guy asks.

"All I can tell you is Gulf Boulevard. No number and no mail delivery."

"What's your bank name so we can wire your monthly distribution?"

"I can't remember. It has a nice hunter-green tin roof though."

With all my affairs in order, I stand outside my condo for the last time. It is a warm spring day. The sun is brilliant; the neighborhood quiet. Stuffed in my carry-on are my laptop, cell phone, a set of clothes, toothbrush and paste, mouthwash, and enough Ativan so that I won't give a shit about being 35,000 feet up in the air without a parachute. My 2009 Honda Accord sits idle in the driveway. It served me well. I mailed the keys and title to Sarah Holland so she could arrange for the transfer of ownership to Theresa. I hope my gift will make her life a little easier.

The taxi I summoned pulls up to the curb. I climb in and instantly I'm overwhelmed by a musky scent of either bad incense or nefarious body odor. I immediately roll down the window. At the same time, another car is pulling into my driveway. It is Megan's car. I can't believe it. She steps out and stares at the taxi. The taxi driver eyes me in his rearview and asks in a high-pitched tone, "Logan?"

He looks like he is from one of those *stan* countries: Pakistan, Afghanistan, Kazakhstan, Iranistan, Iraqistan . . . *whatever.* The harsh smell torches my nasal passages as I slither down in the seat to avoid Megan's detection. I am nearly on the floor when the driver yells, "Hey, vat is dis? No getting sick in my cab."

"Just drive," I reply.

In a soprano voice, he yells, "No! No! No! You cannot do dis here. Get out! Get out!"

"Drive the fucking car, *Stan.*" I grab my money clip from my pocket, peel off a fifty, and lift my arm up over the seat to hand it to him. As the bill is tugged from my hand, I feel the car shift into gear and start to move. He starts mumbling something derogatory at me in one of those foreign *stan* tongues. *Like I give a rat's ass.*

As Stan puts distance between his taxi and Megan, I crawl up into the seat and steal a peek out the back window. I see Megan standing by my mailbox holding a phone to her ear.

And then my cell rings.

Monkey it or answer it? I fish the phone from my carry-on.

"Hello?"

"Where are you, Poopsie?"

"I'm driving around Malibu right now trying to get a feel for the area."

"Oh. I could have sworn I just saw you get into a taxi in front of your house."

"It wasn't me. I'm in California. You'd need a really powerful set of binoculars to see me from where you are," I chuckle.

"That's silly. You know I don't own binoculars. How come you haven't answered my calls?"

"Megan, I've been busy working a deal on the property. I told you I'd call when I'm ready for you to come out."

"Soon, Poopsie? *Please.*" I cringe at her ear-splitting whiny baby voice. It's like tin foil on a filling.

"What are you doing at the condo?" I ask.

"I'm being Mrs. Najarian again and picking up your mail."

Migraine ignites.

"Gotta go, Meg. I'll call you later today. In the meantime, pack light and be ready."

"I will! I will! I'm so excited! Hugs and kisses!"

I end the call. *Mrs. Najarian again?* Maybe I *will* puke in Stan's cab after all.

I look forward at the rearview mirror. Stan is giving me the stink eye. I am eyeing him back. He has all these strange artifacts on the top of the dashboard, which is covered by a shag rug remnant. The word Allah in a laminated sleeve hangs from a string around the rearview mirror. Attached to the instrument panel is a hack license displaying a smiling picture of Badi al Zaman. Secured to the sun visor by a rubber band is another picture of Badi staring lovingly into the sky. No doubt he had those seventy-two virgins on his mind at the time. Scattered on the front seat and floor, a collection of magazines and Internet articles adds to the clutter. I suspect much of the information has to do with the precise manufacture of things that go boom. Yes . . . I do profile.

I make it to Logan airport in one piece. When I step out of the cab after forty minutes in Badi's unwashed armpit of a ride, the smell of jet fuel is as inviting to me as the scent of cocoa butter. I'll have to burn the clothes I'm wearing as soon as possible. I lean in and pay the fare. Badi has some words for me when I don't tip. Screw him. He got pretipped with the fifty.

At security, extra time is spent trying to decide if Jason Najarian is indeed a terrorist as Memphis the Lighthouse had suggested. TSA officials want to know why I am traveling one way and carrying only a small bag. After a strip search and a complete inspection of my laptop and cell phone, I am given permission to proceed, less my toothpaste and mouthwash. Luckily I wasn't on any no-fly lists.

After four-plus hours in the air, or ten Ativan minutes, I land at Sarasota/Bradenton Airport. As I'm beginning to escape the calming clutches of my drug, the realization of living in Florida, on a barrier island, starts to wash ashore. I pinch myself to make sure this isn't simply another dream. Satisfied that I'm living in real time, I approach the counter at Avis rentals. The clerk is friendly and asks how I am doing today. My drug-induced reply refers to her big boobs. Or maybe it is just a thought. I can't distinguish between the two. The drug is slow to recede.

I manage to hand her my reservation. She looks it over, types some data into her computer and says, "Is it hot enough for ya?"

ᢁᣇᣚ

My first order of business is to meet The Hammer at the bank holding the papers on Gulf Boulevard. When I arrive, I meet some of the suits who try to sell me on their bank, sensing I am a wealthy boy after buying the house for cash, but I graciously decline. I explain to them they don't have a hunter-green tin roof. They look at me with a puzzled look.

After signing an endless amount of documents, the deed is passed through several hands until it ends up in mine followed by a round of handshakes. I am the proud owner of a $1.2 million home situated in a hurricane zone, with a tide of oil-polluted water drifting somewhere offshore.

"Would you consider buying the rest of the Decker property on Sand Key?" asks one of the bankers.

"I'll have to select more green M&M's before that is a possibility."

More puzzled looks as the bankers scratch their heads.

As we are leaving the conference room, The Hammer pulls me aside.

"You smell ripe, Jason."

Badi and his taxi. "It can't be me, Phyllis."

The Hammer lifts her arm and inhales. "Well it ain't me." She sniffs my clothes. "Sheesh, Jason, what did you fly down on, Dumpster Airlines?"

My next stop is at Pearson Marine to take delivery of my new boat. Of course it isn't ready. I meet with the sales manager, Big Sonny Pearson. He explains that due to the extensive list of options, the delivery date has been set back.

"Normally, it would take months to get a boat like this, but I managed to pull some strings."

The wonders of paying in cash. "How much longer?" I ask.

He scans some papers in a folder. "I'd say another week, two tops. In the meantime, we can loan you a Boston Whaler to get back and forth to the island."

"I appreciate that."

"Have you thought of a name for the boat? I'd like to put it on at no charge."

"I appreciate that, Big. How about—Laid Out and Candle Lit," I say, drawing an invisible underscore in the air.

Big Sonny rubs his chin. "That's a strange one. Where did you come up with that?"

"From a book I read."

"You know what it means?"

These are the moments I live for. I lean in closer to Big Sonny. "It means I'm lying naked on the deck, my wrists and ankles are tied to the cleats on the gunwale. A naked lady is straddling me and dripping candle wax on my lady pleaser. Laid out and candle lit." I left out the yapping monkey and the singing macaw.

Big Sonny chuckles. "Not quite my definition. Down here it means you're in a casket surrounded by church candles. Laid out and candle lit. In other words, you're dead."

"Hmm . . . not a good name for a boat then."

"No, sir."

I had given this some serious thought back at the condo. I played with several options like "All Green Ones," or "M&M

Delicious," but I settled on what got me here. "How about, 'Ticket to Ride' for a name?"

"Sounds like a winner," Sonny says.

We shake hands and Big Sonny summons a staff member to assist me with the Boston Whaler loaner. I'm about three miles north of Two Palms Marina, so the ride along the Intracoastal Waterway takes longer than normal, but who cares when you're on your way to paradise.

An hour later I tie off at my dock and walk along Gulf Boulevard. I am struck by how beautiful *quiet* can be. A slight breeze, birds announcing my arrival, and the distant melody of incoming surf. Not a person in sight. It is late afternoon and I am tired, yet at the same time excited. I climb the stairs to my wrap-around deck and enter my beach house through the unlocked screen door off the kitchen.

The drapes are drawn and the house is cool. Someone has set the air conditioner. A basket of Florida's finest citrus sits on the kitchen counter next to a set of keys. A note is attached from The Hammer thanking me and wishing me all the best. On the floor in the foyer are the two boxes I shipped down. I begin unpacking. When I'm done, I slip out of my condemned Badi-scented clothes and enjoy a long, hot shower. Refreshed, I flop naked onto the wicker sofa in the entertainment room. It is all too surreal. I have arrived.

After taking a few minutes to reflect on how lucky I am, I pad through the rest of the house. I flush the toilets, point the remote at the wall-mounted HD television, run the water in the sinks, and check the refrigerator. Inside I find a couple of deli sandwiches and spring water, courtesy of Gulf Breeze Realty. Upstairs I find fresh sheets on all the beds. Toiletries are stocked in the master bath. The Hammer has done me good.

I open the glass slider and step outside onto the upper deck. I inhale deeply. The best air I have ever taken in. My backyard faces due west so I am looking at the beginnings of the most spectacular sunset I have ever seen. A thread of lazy clouds turns the brilliant orange ball into a puffy quilt of complementary hues. Sailboats and motorboats are anchored just offshore to watch the event. I want to get a beach chair and cozy up to the shoreline, but I realize I don't own one. The to-do list is off and running.

I reach for my cell phone and tap in some numbers.

"Poopsie! I've been waiting all day. Tell me exactly what you are doing at this moment."

"I'm watching an unbelievable sunset."

"Isn't it kind of early for a sunset in California?"

Oops. I'm amazed at Megan's cognizance. "Out here, the sunsets start earlier and last longer due to the curvature of the planet."

"Oh . . . right. Did you buy the house? Tell me!"

"Yes." Screams from the other end. "I'd like you to come out as soon as you can get the time off. Don't do anything crazy like quit your job until you know this is where you want to be."

"Don't you worry. California, here I come. I'll book the flight online tonight. Where should I meet you?"

"Fly into LAX, Los Angeles. After you arrive, rent a car, and then call me. I'll give you directions to Malibu. Travel time is about one hour from the airport along the Pacific Coast Highway. One more thing, you like Michael Jackson?"

"Of course, but he's dead."

"He's our next door neighbor."

"Jason, cut the twine. He's been dead since he died."

"Yeah, well, how come the guy next door is wearing one glove and singing up a storm? Remember, Meg, the casket was closed."

"I read something about that at the supermarket checkout. Oh my God! Oh! My! God! I can't wait to get out there. Jason, I love you. Love, love, love, you."

"Remember, pack light. Call me with your itinerary. I guess I'll see you when I see you." *Or never see you again.*

I end the call. I have no doubt Megan will wink at the first surfer dude or muscle-head somewhere between LAX and Malibu and then get engaged.

The sun disappears beyond the horizon. I am officially on island time. I decide to have one of the sandwiches, courtesy of

Gulf Breeze, and then hit the sack. Over the next few days I will be busy on the mainland buying the supplies I need to embrace the solitude of the island. My life as a stress-free happy hermit is about to begin.

CHAPTER SEVEN

Island Beginnings

"Hermits have no peer pressure."
—STEVEN WRIGHT

I wake up still in paradise. No alarm clock. No clothes set out for the workday. No hurry up to get anywhere. I had fallen asleep with the glass sliders open, allowing the surf to serenade me. Some people purchase these soothing sounds to listen to, but I have a front row seat to the perpetual live concert that floats blithely, like a butterfly, into my room.

I pad out onto the deck. The morning air is cool. Early sunlight filters through the trees leaving warm spikes upon the sand and water. The gulf is glass still, like a cloistered pond deep in the forest, with the exception of repetitive two-inch waves that slap ashore.

A pelican glides effortlessly above the water line.

I wonder for a moment what time it is, but then realize I don't care. I slip on my boxers and make my way out to the beach.

I estimate there are about forty yards of beach from my elevated walkover to the shoreline. The sand is powder soft as I take my first steps. Closer to the shoreline, the sand hardens and is covered with seashells, seaweed, and small pieces of driftwood. A few brown palm fronds complete the image of a deserted island. It appears this end of Sand Key has escaped the erosion of islands farther south. Storms and tidal shifts have deposited sand rather than removed it. In another thousand years I might have fifty yards of beach. I can't wait.

As I stroll toward the shore, I watch several ghost crabs scavenging for leftovers deposited by the last tide. They work feverishly to beat the heat of the rising sun, but when they see me, they poop in their shells and scurry sideways until they disappear down holes in the sand. I must be the weirdest looking bird they have ever seen.

At the shoreline, I stand as the bathwater caresses my feet. Sandpipers peck at what the surf offers. Schools of minnows swim in perfect formation. As I gaze out toward the horizon, I notice a disturbance. The water splashes and then fins appear. I think sharks at first glance, and then one dolphin breaks the crest of the water before diving back in. Another follows and yet another. The pod consists of at least six. I cup my hands around my mouth and call out, "You guys play volleyball?"

One dolphin leaves the pod and heads toward shore. I am so excited; I start wading deeper into the water hoping to exchange a belly bump. I'm about ten yards from my new best buddy, when I step on something squishy.

My leap out of the water rivals that of a submarine-launched intercontinental missile. During my ascension, I manage to look back at where I was standing only to see a dustup of sand in the crystal clear waters. On my descent, I spy the sand-camouflaged stingray darting away. I land face first, regain my footing, and hastily make for shore. This is so cool. I can't wait to tell someone I have dolphins and stingrays hanging out in my backyard.

I lie down on the packed sand and close my eyes. I'm reminded from a *National Geographic* episode how killer whales often belly onshore to snatch unsuspecting seals. I question the odds, but realize for me, Murphy never rests. I get up and work my way back to the safety of the soft sand.

I rest again in a warm spike of sun, my fingers intertwined behind my head. My eyelids close. The day is heating up. I have things to do on the mainland, but no hurry. Hermits don't hurry. In the distance I hear Bob Marley singing *One Love*.

The sandpipers start rocking back and forth in rhythm. The ghost crabs climb out of their bunkers and form a conga line, pausing every so often to click their claws like belly dancers using finger cymbals.

"Jason!"

Bob Marley stands next to me. *"One love, one heart . . ."*

The dolphins swim ashore. The whole pod starts swaying to the beat. Even the stingray joins in by doing back flips along the shoreline.

"Jason!"

For some reason Marley turns and fades away. And then I feel the sensation of someone blocking the sun. I open my eyes and there stands Phyllis Hammerstein.

"Jason! Are you drunk?"

I lift up into a sitting position. The crabs are gone. The dolphins and stingray back in the gulf. My beach, once again, deserted.

"Drunk? I don't drink. I'm simply basking in paradise. What brings you out so early?" *My PMS kicks in—Do they want the house back?*

"Thought I'd bring you breakfast, being your first morning here on the island."

"Really?" Maybe this is merely southern hospitality, but if breakfast with The Hammer becomes a routine, I might have to look for a different property in the Caribbean.

"Really. I baked muffins and squeezed oranges and lemons. So why don't you shake the sand from your boxers and join me inside."

My gulf-drenched boxers are indeed covered with sand. I stand up, follow The Hammer across the walkover and rinse myself under an outdoor shower.

We share breakfast. The juice is fresh, the muffins delicious. The last person who baked me something was Megan. She had experimented with a brownie mix and ended up making regulation pucks for the National Hockey League. Of course I had to tell her they were the best brownies I'd ever eaten or I would have been utilizing the self-serve pump later that night.

"I like what you've done to the house," The Hammer says.

"I haven't done anything."

"My point." She walks over to a picture frame I had hung on the wall in the foyer. "Jason, why do you have eight green M&M's taped to the inside of a picture frame?"

I didn't think anyone would see it so soon. "New age art," I reply.

She grunts. "Weird. Well, at least it goes with the color scheme of the house."

I find this amusing considering the M&M's bought the house.

After spending an hour learning more details about Phyllis Hammerstein's personal life than I cared to know, and her yawning over my escapade with the stingray, I offer my thanks for breakfast and manage to nudge her out the door. I follow her by boat over to the mainland, part ways, and then begin to address my to-do list.

I find a Ford dealer and buy a new F-150 pickup truck off the lot. The salesman says it will take another two days to prepare the title and deliver the truck. He is so ecstatic with the quick cash sale that he offers to personally return my rental to Avis. Cash is king.

Next, I pay a visit to the First Federal Bank of Florida to set up a checking account. While filling out the paperwork, I say to the assistant manager, "I want to compliment you on your hunter-green roof."

The woman offers me a puzzled look, smiles, then reluctantly replies, "Thanks."

After the bank, I make a straight line to Home Depot and fill my rental pickup with power tools, a spade, a rake, beach chairs, an aluminum ladder, and a whole gaggle of supplies. What I don't take into consideration is that what has filled up the rental pickup, will overflow the eleven-foot Boston Whaler I have on loan.

So there I am, struggling to get across the Intracoastal Waterway looking as if I have just looted the local hardware store, post hurricane Katrina. I have a dozen bungee cords stretched across the boat like a spider's web in an attempt to hold everything in place. I almost make it intact over to Sand Key until a yacht comes too close, sending a wake that rocks my overloaded boat. The scraping sound is my ladder sliding into the drink. I watch helplessly as my new Little Giant six-footer slides off the boat and sinks to a depth of nine feet, according to the depth finder. I think about diving in to retrieve it, but I don't want to get adopted by a herd of do-it-yourself manatees.

After I unload the boat at Gulf Boulevard, I sit in a wicker rocker on the first level deck off the kitchen, holding a glass of fresh lemonade that The Hammer had left behind. Looking out toward the beach, I realize how cluttered it looks. I know I shouldn't mess with nature, but I don't want my beach to look like a scene out of the movie *Castaway*. I don't want my mother's boyfriend, Bradley, to offer up any of his wiseass comments like, "Where's Wilson?" or "Did the tide wash away your SOS sign?" It's not just his toe picking that annoys me.

I grab the rake, the spade, and two beach chairs and pad out to the shoreline. I set the chairs just a few feet from the water: one chair for my hermit butt, and one for my hermit feet. This will be my place of worship each day come sunset.

With rake in hand, I retrace my steps back to the walkover. From there, I pace back to the beach chairs, dragging the rake behind me. I repeat this task eighteen times until the width of my beach frontage is as smooth as a sand trap. Talk about pristine. I dig a hole on my not-yet-neighbor's property (they'll never know), and rake in all the debris. I stand leaning on my rake and marvel at my accomplishment.

A Great Blue Heron dinosaur lands nearby. The bird stands close to four feet tall. It walks gracefully, staring quizzically at my patch of raked beach.

"Well, whaddaya think?" I ask the bird.

The bird ruffles its feathers and shakes its head.

"Tough. Get used to it."

It is getting close to sunset so I hike back to the house, gather some food and drink, and return to the beach chairs, leaving unsightly footprints in my wake. The bird is still there. I offer it a chair. "Hey, take a load off those Q-tips." But the bird remains statuesque. I toss it some bread, but it ignores my offerings. I suspect it is a female.

Over the next hour, I watch another spectacular sunset as it falls seductively beyond the horizon. Boats drift unfettered in the gulf, while sun worshippers on board applaud nature's extravaganza. I can't wait to drift offshore in my boat, rocking gently as the sun relinquishes its grip on day.

As darkness ripens, I bid goodnight to the bird, grab the rake and drag it behind me as I make my way to the walkover. I leave the rake in its new home by the side of the handrails and pad inside the house. I know this will never get old.

∞

I PICK up the F-150 truck two days later. Then I head to Pelican Marina where I purchase a covered boat condo that comes complete with a boat-lift and two parking spaces in a secured, fenced-in area. I now have a berth for both my boat and my truck on the mainland.

During my return trip to Sand Key, the Boston Whaler, filled with food and supplies, is nearly capsized in the wake of another yacht. I steer into the onslaught of waves while my canned goods roll all over the deck. After a few minutes, the water calms and I find myself close to the spot where the ladder had sunk. I toss the Home Depot receipt into the Intracoastal Waterway just in case the manatees need to return it.

A week later, Big Sonny Pearson calls to inform me that my twenty-six foot Four Winns has finally arrived. His nephew, the technician, was testing the boat and would pick me up at my dock for a quick tutorial on how the boat operates. I quickly pull on a pair of shorts, a lightweight T-shirt, and sandals. Even though it is very warm, I need the T-shirt because the sun is intent on burning me to a crisp before I turn bronze.

I mosey down to the dock and sit with my legs dangling off the end as I watch the mullets jump out of the water. The lagoon is warm and crystal clear, so I can't figure out why the fish want to get out. I guess mullets enjoy diving into air like people enjoy diving into water. The grass is always greener . . . not that mullets would know the difference. But if one ever jumped up on the dock and wanted to hang out, that would be the perfect time for me to start drinking.

After a few minutes, the din of an approaching boat pierces the stillness of my hermit inlet. I feel guilty about the noise my new boat creates in this pristine lagoon and consider whether I should have purchased a canoe instead. But if I can't successfully get back and forth to the mainland in a small Boston Whaler, I'd definitely drown in a canoe. I'll have to ask nature for a variance from the laws of serenity.

Nephew Pearson brings my *Ticket to Ride* to dock and I jump aboard. We then cruise the Intracoastal Waterway while he teaches me how to navigate the helm. He explains all the controls and instruments, from bilge pump to trim gauge, before I feel confident enough to take over as captain. We then set course for the gulf. At times, the boat barely touches the water as I open her to full throttle. The wind combs my hair straight back. I doubt my someday parrot, perched on the overhead arch, would survive at these knots. Maybe I can teach it how to say, "Slow the fuck down," when it feels like it is in peril.

With my training complete, I bring Nephew back to my dock so he can return the Boston Whaler loaner to Pearson Marine. Good riddance. It isn't that the boat is bad; it's just that it is too small for open water. It's more suited for backyard pools.

With the *Ticket* secured to the dock, I can't help but stare at her beauty—my first boat. From bow to stern she is a looker. I gaze at her from the dock, from Gulf Boulevard, and from the barge landing Decker Development built across the lagoon. From every angle she has fine lines. Later, I plan to watch the sunset on the gulf, in the comfort of my boat.

It is midafternoon so I gather my laptop and head for the beach chairs. Even though I am a hermit-in-training, I still enjoy checking on the latest news from Boston. I especially want to keep tabs on the greatest sports city in America with the Red Sox, Patriots, Celtics, and Bruins all playoff contenders in recent years. The Boston papers have online sites so I can keep abreast of the news. Today's headline: Mob executions continue in Rhode Island. In sports, the Red Sox are trailing the Yankees in the standings, but there is still time. It's only late July.

I close the laptop, tuck it under my arm, and grab the rake. As I walk, I rake my footprints away until I reach the chairs. It is another beautiful Florida day. An onshore breeze keeps the conditions tolerable as opposed to the stagnant humidity on the mainland. Even so, the sun is hot. I lower myself into the chair, put my feet up, and inhale deeply.

My cell rings. I check the number and groan.

"Megan! How's it hanging?"

"Hey, Poopsie. What am I supposed to be hanging?"

"Nothing. It's an expression. Are you booked?"

"Yes! And I'm so freakin' excited. I'm flying out of Logan in three days! Cara is staying in my apartment while I'm gone, but I hinted that I may not be coming back!"

Cara is Megan's friend. I hate her—the only kind thing I can say about the woman is that she's a bitch.

"Have you met any more famous neighbors or movie stars? Shit, I hope I have the right eyeliner and lipstick for California. Talk to me, Poopsie, what have you been doing?"

"Well, I stepped on a stingray a few days ago. That was exciting."

"Oh my God. Didn't that Austrian guy die from wrestling one in his pool?"

Christ. "Yeah, something like that."

"Well, you be careful, Jason. We have a lot of Hollywooding to do. I don't want to be dragging a sick boy around. I just can't *wait* to get out there. When I see you, I'm gonna jump in your arms."

Prepare for a hard landing. "All right, Meg. Remember, call when you land at LAX."

Megan says she is blowing me a kiss. I let it fall to the sand and end the call.

I put the phone away and notice the heron is back. It is staring at me, obviously envious of my new laptop. I lift my feet and offer the chair. The bird takes a few steps back. Eventually, it is going to sit with me and watch a sunset. I have a gut feeling.

"I don't know if you're a male or female, but I'm naming you Harry because I need to talk sports with a guy. Do we understand each other, Harry?"

The heron moves closer. A friendship is formed.

∽

I AM cruising along the Intracoastal Waterway toward Pirate's Pass, which separates Sand Key from Englewood Island. The pass offers a clear run out to the gulf where I'm headed for today's showing of a sunset in paradise. On my way, I notice a boat idling in shallow water outside of the waterway markings. Someone is waving a white flag. I don't even have an hour on my boat, yet I am getting ready to play search and rescue. Maybe it is a beautiful damsel in distress who will fall in love with her rescuer. Hey, nobody said hermits can't get laid once in a while.

As I get closer, the excitement of saving a lovely woman goes overboard as quickly as my ladder did. There stands a heavy-set man waving a white beach towel. He is wearing a captain's hat, sunglasses, and a wildly busy palm-tree shirt that barely covers his flabby midsection that sags well below the waistline of his white Bermuda shorts. Black boat shoes and black knee-high socks complete the outfit. I pull up closer to the slightly bigger boat.

"Anything I can do to help?" I call out.

The man looks at me in frustration. "Somebody put a fucking sandbar in the middle of the waterway. Now my props are jammed."

The Intracoastal Waterway is notorious for being shallow, especially outside of the waterway markings. It's obvious that this captain had veered off course.

"Would you like me to try to pull you out?"

The big man nods. I notice the boat's name, *Wicked Pissa Hits.* I tie a boat line to my bow and toss him the other end. "Tie that off so I can pull you out." I then maneuver my boat so that the props remain in deeper water. My bow is to his stern. When I look up, the man has tied the rope around his waist and is bracing himself against the railing on the gunwale. Even if I take a picture, nobody will believe this.

"I think it would work better if you tied the rope off around a cleat. I'm afraid I might pull you into the water like that," I say. There is no doubt in my mind that if he did land in the water, the manatee population would increase by one.

I wait while the captain gets his end of the rope secure, and then I shift into reverse until the rope is taut. The cleats hold. I slowly power up until the props on the *Wicked Pissa Hits* emerge from the sandbar and the boat drifts free.

"Hey, fucking-A," the big man says, with a broad smile.

"Glad I could help."

He tosses me my line. "My name is Sal Santini. I live over there on Sand Key."

"Hey, Sal. My name is Jason. I live on the other end of Sand Key."

"No shit? You the guy who bought that house up there? *Madonn',* big fucking bucks they was asking."

"I got a deal," I say, wishing I had kept my mouth shut. Rule number three of the *Hermits Guide for Dummies*: Don't talk to people. "Why don't you start her up so we can make sure there isn't any damage to the props?"

Sal powers up. He lowers and raises the trims. The props seem in fine order. He walks over to the stern and says, "Hey, you're all right, kid."

I salute the captain and continue to the gulf to catch what little sunset is left. For some reason I have the gnawing feeling Sand Key just got a lot smaller.

~ PART TWO ~

CHAPTER EIGHT

Island Company

> "Life could be wonderful if people would leave you alone."
>
> —CHARLIE CHAPLIN

The following day I am back in the boat again, cruising the waterways. I just can't get enough of the *Ticket*. It is the weekend, Saturday I think, so there is considerably more traffic on the water. There are big boats, small boats, Jet Skis, pontoons, kayaks, you name it—if it can float, it is on the water.

As people pass me in their vessels, they wave. Not wanting to seem unsociable, I wave back. I know my *Ticket* is a nice looking boat, but it isn't *that* nice looking to garner all this attention. It makes me wonder why people are waving at me. Why am I so popular? Is everyone fascinated with the *guy* who bought that *house,* as the big captain suggested? But how would they know?

A large Bayliner, filled to capacity, approaches on my starboard side. The family onboard leans over to wave to me: men, women, children and even a drooling dog with a tail wagging furiously. I wave back. Back in Boston, the only time people waved to me was when they were standing on street corners holding campaign signs and begging for my vote. For about two weeks during election time, they all wanted to be my friend. But after the results were tabulated, these same folks resorted to the norm, which was waving their middle finger at me until the next time their candidate needed help.

By midday, I'm in need of some fuel, plus I want to find heron treats to entice Harry to pull up a chair and watch the sunsets.

It means I'll have to make nice with Memphis the Lighthouse, or travel miles out of my way. Reluctantly, I steer toward the canal leading into Two Palms Marina.

I set out two bumpers and dock near The Hammer's skiff. The marina is busy. A few young kids are working the outdoor bait tubs, and in the shop another person is ringing up sales on the register. I step inside and get behind a man and his son who are buying some fishing gear. The clerk is a pretty woman, early twenties, blonde, and sun-drenched. A huge upgrade over . . .

"What y'all want?"

I turn to see Memphis behind me, his hands on his hips, same clothes, same ugly, same stomach light drawing my eyes like a moth to a flame. *Why is this guy always sneaking up on me?*

"I'm in need of gas and some information. I thought the young lady might help me," I say, turning to look at her. She flashes me a smile. Cool.

"Ryanne, da fuel dock needs tendin' to." The young woman steps away from the register and heads toward the Texaco pumps, but not before I hear a frustrated "tsk."

"I hears yous bought dat house over on da Key," Memphis says.

"You hears right."

"Just so yous knows, dat don't make yous no native 'round dese parts, *Nar-Jar-Bin-Laden*," he says, while stepping behind the counter.

I am willing to bet Memphis the Lighthouse wouldn't wave to me if our boats passed. "Look old man, I'm trying to live the life of a recluse. Just sell me fuel and supplies and I'll be on my way."

He looks me over. "I can do dat, but only 'cause Ms. Phyllis has takin' a likin' to yous."

Damn! Just as I feared.

"Yous wantin' fuel and what else?"

"What do those tall gray herons eat?"

Memphis squints at me as he ponders my request. "I thinks dey eat snowbirds like yous." This wittiness brings a toothless grin to his face. The banjos start dueling again.

"Dat's funny," I say. "What else do they eat?"

Memphis shrugs. "I suppose glass minnows work. We sell dem as bait. But dem birds ain't needin' any of yous help to eat."

"I'm training one to sit and fetch. How much for a pound?"

As Memphis writes up the slip, I start humming *Dueling Banjos* to see if I can instigate a jig, or maybe entice him to break out some music spoons for his leg. I think he actually starts to twitch.

I drop cash on the counter, grab the bait, and pay for the fuel at the pump. Ryanne tosses me another beautiful smile as she takes my credit card. I wonder if she'd be willing to spend the rest of her life as my accomplice.

Back on the island, I realize my life is drifting aimlessly. That's not a bad thing for a recluse, but I've always been a creature of habit. I'm finding it strange not having a set routine. So I decide to create a schedule that starts each day with a workout. I've already gained several pounds during my first two months in paradise. That *is* a bad thing for a recluse. How many fat hermits do you know? I need to be in top physical shape in case the tortoise-riding naked lady shows up.

I also want to try my hand at trading stocks. So I put pen to paper and start jotting down a timetable for lifting weights, running on a treadmill, investing online, walking the beach, going mainland to shop or eat, boating, and, of course, watching sunsets. The schedule depends on near perfect weather, so if it ever rains for more than a few hours, I'll be totally discombobulated.

Driven by a surge of can-do adrenaline, I fish out a tape measure from my toolbox and start measuring the empty space off the foyer designated as a study on the blueprints. This room is the only one unfurnished. But I'll soon change that. My plan is to put a minigym on one side: bench, barbells, weights, and treadmill. On the other side, I'll install a television on the wall overlooking a desk, so I can watch the stock symbols scroll. I'll add a computer on the desk logged in to my discount broker's account for easy trading access.

I stretch out the tape measure from the lagoon-facing window to the wall separating the study and the entertainment area.

Eighteen feet. I'm about to measure the opposite side when a chime startles me—a ding-dong-ding sound.

I hurry through the house looking for faulty electronics. I check the smoke detectors, the kitchen appliances, and my music system. Everything seems to be in good working order. Perplexed, I start back toward the study when the chime sings out again. It is coming from a box above the front door.

Doorbell? Who puts a doorbell in a secluded house on an island? That's like installing a GPS system on a train. I add, *dismantle the doorbell*, to my to-do list.

I open the door to find the obese guy from the boat I pulled free from the sand bar standing there with a box in his hands. He looks different up close without his captain's hat and sunglasses. He has a thick neck and beefy hands. His black hair is combed back and his eyes are penetrating. He is hefty, mean looking, and intimidating, like a hit man ready to pull a gun on me. I dismiss my tendency to profile and blame it on having watched too many Mafia movies.

"Hey . . . how are you?" I say, having already forgotten his name. *Sam? Sid? Vito Corleone?* I welcome him into my abode. The big man steps inside and offers the package to me.

"This here is an expression of my gratitude. You like lobster tails?"

"I love lobster tails. But you didn't have to do that."

"Hey, somebody dumped a sand dune in the waterway. You pulled me out. End of story."

"I was just being neighborly. Are these Maine tails or local?"

"*La sfogliatella* from Providence, Rhode Island. The local tails here are no good, so I get a shipment sent down once a week."

I nod. Well, Maine is close to Rhode Island. "Forgive me, but I forgot your name."

"It's Sal. You best put those in the refrigerator with this heat. And just so you know . . . I ate one on the way over."

I chuckle. "I don't blame you. They are delicious, cold or hot. I prefer mine smothered in melted butter."

Sal grimaces, and then says, "Hey, to each his own."

"Would you like a drink? Water . . . juice?"

He dismisses the offer with a wave.

I place the box in the refrigerator and invite him on a tour of the house. We walk, single file, through the foyer, into the entertainment room, and out onto the first level deck.

"What's with the bowls of M&M's in every room?"

"My interior decorator thinks they add a festive color to the décor."

Together we stare out at the gulf. The warm, salty breeze embraces us like a fond memory.

"You married, Jason?"

"I was once, but she ran off with a pair of biceps."

"How about now? You got a girlfriend . . . or boyfriend?"

"No, with an emphasis on the latter. Why do you ask?"

"I'm looking at three beach chairs out there. And how come the sand looks so . . . immaculate? Like no one has ever dared step foot on it?"

"Two of the chairs belong to my feet and ass while I watch the sun go down. The other I reserved for a bird. As far as the sand, I rake the beach for exercise."

Sal raises his eyebrows in disbelief. "You rake the beach?"

It doesn't sound so rational when someone else says it. I simply shrug.

"I like the view here. Maybe if I'm in the area, I'll stop in and watch the sunset too."

No. No. No. I don't want playmates in my sandbox. This is not good for Hermitville. Plus, he is making it sound like he is doing me a favor. *How do I discourage this guy?*

We walk back into the house and through the kitchen, where he has to turn his bulk sideways to get past my center-island range. In the foyer, we shake hands and I thank him again for the tails. Something catches his attention beyond me. He walks up to the wall.

"What's this with the candy in the picture frame?"

Christ! "Those M&M's are special to me."

He shakes his head. "You're saving a chair for a bird. You rake the sand. You hang candy on the wall." He opens his arms wide, palms up. "And you've only been on the island what . . . a few weeks? *Madonn'*," he says, laughing.

Sal walks down the cedar steps, causing them to creak incessantly. He rests at the bottom, and then climbs into a golf cart definitely fitted with custom shocks. I watch as it gains traction on Gulf Boulevard before disappearing within the dense trees and foliage of the bird sanctuary.

Maybe I could build a wall on Gulf Boulevard. Warning: Stay Out!

As soon as Sal is out of sight, I race to the refrigerator, my mouth watering for a chewy lobster tail. I open the box and jump back, not recognizing what I'm looking at. Did they go bad in the heat? The tails look more like croissants with white powder sprinkled on top than crustaceans. Something white and creamy oozes out from the sides. *Guts?* It doesn't smell like lobster gone bad. I poke at it with my finger. It is soft and squishy. I'm not sure what these things are, but I'm sure they aren't Maine *or* Providence lobster tails.

∽

I sit in the beach chair, feet up, and wait. The sun is fading into dusk. Within a few minutes, Harry lands like a Harrier Jump Jet just a few yards from me. If I weren't looking, I wouldn't have noticed. That's how quiet and graceful the bird is. I open the bait bag and toss a minnow at him. At first he steps away from the catered meal, then surrenders to hunger and pounces on it. I toss another and Harry catches it in midair.

"All right now, Harry . . . sit." The bird ignores me.

I place a minnow on the chair. "Sit, Harry."

The bird stares back unfazed by my demands.

My cell rings. I look at the number. Hammer time.

"Hello, Phyllis."

"Hey, Jason, just calling to say I'm coming over tomorrow." I lean my head back and close my eyes. *What am I doing wrong?* "I did some food shopping and found a wonderful grouper recipe I'm dying to try out," she says.

"I was planning on buying some furniture for the study tomorrow. Can I take a rain check?"

"No, Jason you can't. We can cook this up when you return. And I hear your new boat arrived. When are you taking your favorite realtor out for a ride?"

"Soon. I'll call you tomorrow when I get back on the island." We say goodbye and I end the call. I look over at Harry. "From now on, you take all my calls."

∽

THE NEXT day, whatever day it is, I grab the measurements for the study and some notes on what type of equipment I want to purchase. I start down the steps on my way to the dock, when a golf cart emerges from the bird sanctuary. Maybe I should pile some tires on the road and burn them. That might send a message.

The cart pulls up alongside the sand walkway. An older woman with a cane steps out from one side, while a woman carrying a box eases out from behind the wheel. *More bad lobsters?* They haven't seen me, so I sneak back into the house.

It takes a few minutes for the older woman to scale my staircase due to the height of my pilings. When they reach the deck, the chime ding-dongs for the very last time, I promise myself. I open the door and feign my surprise.

"Hi, my name is Amber; this is my mother, Margaret. We live on Gulf Boulevard, but on the other end of Sand Key."

I extend my hand. "Nice to meet you both, my name is Jason."

"So you're the nutjob who bought this eyesore on nature," the old woman says.

"Mother, be nice to our new neighbor." Amber looks at me and frowns. "She gets a little riled up at times."

"When that oil sludge reaches here and fouls the island, it will be your payback, young man."

"Let's hope that doesn't happen for all our sakes," I counter, bewildered by the verbal assault.

"My mother is rather famous around here for her environmental causes. She's constantly writing letters," Amber says.

"I used to get more done till peabrain here illegally confiscated the keys to my golf cart," Margaret says, thumbing toward her daughter.

"Mother, you know you almost drove yourself into the waterway several times. I took the keys away for your own good."

"I did not, know-it-all. And I don't need anybody looking out for my own good."

To change the subject, I make the following observation: "You look a lot like Margaret Thatcher, Margaret."

The old woman grips her purse and gives me the stink eye. "Say that again, mister, and I'll come over here on a moonless night and take a chainsaw to your pilings."

"Mother . . . please. Jason is complimenting you. I'm sorry, Jason."

"No need to apologize. Can I invite you both in?" *Bad hermit move.*

"Give him the pie and let's go. I need to get my hair done," Margaret demands.

"Mother, it's Sunday. Your hair appointment is tomorrow."

"Tomorrow is my doctor's appointment. Monday I get my hair done."

"*Hellooo*, that's what I just said. We'll see the doctor on Wednesday."

"That's what I just said," Margaret argues.

I can feel my beard growing.

"The first thing to go is their ability to know what day it is," Amber says to me.

Uh-oh. I've already lost track of the days.

"That's because you never give me my medicine. If you gave me *all* my pills I'd be just fine," the mother seethes.

"She gets her medication, I assure you," Amber says. Exasperated, she extends the box to me. "I made a key lime pie for you."

"Oh, thanks. You didn't have to do that."

"She lies a lot. She probably bought it," Margaret chimes in.

"You were right there while I was making it, *Mother*."

Margaret turns toward the stairs. "Let's go, my hair appointment. Do I have to keep reminding you?"

Amber raises her arms in frustration. "Next time I'll come over alone." She tosses me a wink and a smile and catches up with her mother. I am receiving a lot of waves, smiles, and winks of late. I realize the women down here are much friendlier to me than in Massachusetts.

∽

LATER IN the day while on the mainland, I purchase everything I need for my minigym. I ask the salesman, who is the muscular type Megan fawns over, if he knows anyone who could get all this weight over to Sand Key for a fee. He informs me his brother has a boat and would be happy to do it. I offer one hundred dollars each, which brings a grin to the salesman's face. I leave out the part about climbing the twenty-two steps to my deck.

I also purchase a computer, a flat-screen television, and a teak desk to equip the investment side of my study. The store arranges to barge it over and install my system for an even larger fee. Again, I leave out the part about the stairs.

The best part of the day comes when The Hammer calls to cancel her intrusion. Something about an open house gone bad. So, I go about disassembling the doorbell from hell. After a few hours, I grill a rib eye and some veggies and head out to the beach chairs. I'm early; the sun still has an hour left. Harry is waiting. I guess that's what a few treats will do. I toss him more minnows and ask him to sit. He remains stubborn. This is not going to be easy.

I finish my supper and relax with my feet up. Harry manages to inch noticeably closer.

"Roll over, Harry." Nothing. The bird simply doesn't give a crap.

I watch as several Jet Skis zoom by me heading south. As I follow the young kids at play, I notice movement on the south end of the beach where it curves inland and out of sight. The heavy-set guy, Sal . . . *whatever*, is marching toward me, smoking a cigar and wearing those knee-high black socks again. His path follows the foot-high sand dune nature created parallel to the shoreline. The enormous weight of his depression causes the sand to fall back into the gulf. All by himself he is creating beach erosion. What took years for nature to create, Sal is undoing with one simple stroll.

Harry suddenly takes flight.

CHAPTER NINE

Island Conversations

"If everything seems to be going well, you have obviously overlooked something."

—STEVEN WRIGHT

"See . . . I told ya I'd come by," Sal calls out as he approaches.

Lucky me. "That you did, Sal."

I lift my feet off the chair as Sal stands in front of me. It is a total eclipse of the sun. He grabs the chair and positions it toward the sunset. I sense a situation is about to unfold. He turns and lowers himself into the seat. I hold my breath. The metal frame expands and sinks inches into the sand, but it holds.

"Boy, this here is beautiful," he says, stretching out his legs, flicking cigar ash on my sand.

"Yeah, I think so."

"So, what's your take on the pastry, Jason? You like?"

Pastry lobster tails? What a fraud. "They were different. But to tell you the truth, I thought we were talking real lobster tails."

"No shit? Like the clawed thing in the shell? There's no way that could be. *Fuggeddaboutit.* I'm allergic to shellfish. My doctor says, 'Sal, stay the fuck away from shellfish.' So, I stay the fuck away."

And I'm supposed to know that how? His reply makes me realize I haven't given much thought to finding a doctor or dentist, so maybe Sal might have some references. "Who's your doctor? I'm gonna need one sooner or later," I inquire.

"His name is Doctor Jack over in Sarasota. I call him Jack the Knife."

"Really? And your dentist . . . is his name Danny the Drill?"

Sal seems unfazed by my lame humor as he stares out into the gulf with a vacant expression. A thin smoke line lifts lazily from his cigar.

"As a kid, I was raised on Italian pastry," he reminisces. "Cannoli, pignolo, biscotti, bomboloni, I could eat six or more at a sitting. It made me the man I am today."

I look at him. *Is he a comedian or just a moron?*

The horizon has captured half of the sun.

"If you like, I can run in and get you one," I offer, hoping to reduce my inventory.

He waves me off. "I've already ate my share today," he replies, patting his portly stomach. "Hey, where's your bird?"

"He took off a few minutes ago. Seen one sunset, seen them all, I guess."

"If you're into birds, you should get yourself one of them talking ones. African parrots, I think. I hear they talk up a storm."

I nod. *How did he know about my plans for a singing parrot?* "Yeah . . . I've been thinking about one for a while."

"So tell me, what do you do for a living? How do you pay for all this?" Sal asks.

Preferring to keep my windfall private, I've prepared a mental script to address the inevitable curiosity. Whether it is believable is another question.

"I'm up to my ears in debt since I bought this house. I sold what I owned up in Boston, cashed in an inheritance from my grandmother, and came down here to find myself. For income, I write letters to Nigerians to scam them out of their nairas."

Sal looks at me. "No offense, but you're full of shit."

The inheritance or the Nigerians?

"Your accent confirms you're from Boston, but my guess is you're part of the M&M family. Like a trust-fund baby. By the way, I'm from Providence. So we're fucking neighbors up there and down here. Go figure."

"Providence? Man, there are a lot of headlines coming out of there lately."

Sal doesn't respond. Instead, he stares pensively into the gulf, polluting my air with repetitive smoke rings.

"What do you do for a living, Sal?"

The big man pauses before answering, as if he is searching for the right answer. "I'm in the music business. I'm a producer. I own a company called, Wicked Pissa Hits."

"Like the name on your boat?"

"Yeah, like that."

I get the sense Sal is done exchanging pleasantries. I want to know who he represents and what songs his company produced, but his tone has changed. It makes me feel like he is hiding something or maybe he isn't who he claims to be.

We sit quietly as the sun flickers from behind clouds gathered on the horizon. It isn't a clean sunset, but it is just as beautiful. I am savoring the different hues while contemplating who the guy next to me really is, when Sal taps my arm.

"Check this out," he says, motioning toward the curve of the beach where he emerged from earlier. I lean around him and notice a woman jogging toward us. You've got to be kidding me. If this keeps up, how far behind could a Starbucks be?

"She's my neighbor," Sal says. "She moved in a few weeks after I arrived. *Madonn'*, I bet she can suck a watermelon through a screen door. Anyway, since day one she wants to know all about the island. Tells me she's an Indian looking to get her tribe recognized. You know what that means don't ya? She's gonna build a casino next door to you."

I stare at the woman as she approaches. Petite, long dark hair, toned. I do what comes natural and suck in the gut. Damn, how I wish I installed the minigym a month ago.

The woman stops in front of us just as the sun snaps out of sight. She bends over, resting her hands on her knees in an effort to catch her breath. I am jealous of the sweat that flows freely across her body.

"Jason, this here is Running Bush. Running Bush, this is my friend, Jason."

Friend? I question to myself.

"You have friends, Sal?" The woman steps in front of me. I stand. She extends her hand. "Hi, I'm Fiona Tallahassee. I'm wondering if you can help me."

"Sure," I say taking her hand. My eyes are suddenly weighted as they fall to her breasts.

"Good, cause there's a beached whale sitting next to you. We need to get it back in the water."

"Whoa!" Sal interrupts. "Hey, don't you have a fucking casino somewhere needs your attention?"

Fiona starts to laugh and punches Sal softly on the arm. I smile, and even Sal cracks a grin. She gestures toward Harry's someday chair. "May I?"

"Please," I say. Fiona lowers her sculpted masterpiece into the seat. As she turns, I notice the ink on her back. It's a colorful snake, coiled and angry, just below her shoulder. Why a beautiful woman wants to display a serpent ready to attack befuddles me. On my left is the largest guy I have ever seen, and on my right is the most beautiful woman I have ever seen, without first logging onto a website. I watch her settle in gracefully, serpent and all, and realize she is well above my pay grade.

"Wow, you have a stunning view here," Fiona says, burying her bare feet in the sand. "Hey, how did the sand get so smooth around here?"

"He rakes it," Sal offers with a smirk.

I am becoming an embarrassment.

"Really? That's so cool," she says.

Later, when left alone with just thoughts of Fiona, I'll check the *Hermits Guide for Dummies* to see if a departure can be made from the rules of hermitology.

"Let's hope it stays this way," I say.

"You mean the oil, right? What an environmental disaster that is. If it ever reaches these beaches . . ." Fiona says, letting the thought pollute the moment.

The boats watching the sunset begin to ease back to shore.

"I'm hoping it does," Sal blurts. "It makes for a lucrative business opportunity for me. I'm thinking Santini Oil Recovery and Beach Renovation. I could make a killing. I'd hire Jason here to rake."

Fiona leans around me. "You're a sick fuck, Sal." To me she says with a smile, "Excuse my French, Jason."

"No, I'm an opportunist," Sal insists. "Tomorrow, I'll bring Toast with me and he'll explain how the government causes these disasters in order to create business opportunities that turn into jobs."

Fiona rolls her almond eyes.

"I don't have any more chairs," I whine.

"So go out tomorrow and buy more, mister M&M," Sal says. And it isn't a suggestion.

Screw it. Later tonight, I'll send a blanket e-mail inviting the free world.

"You guys sit out here every sunset?" Fiona asks.

I want to say just Harry and me and that Sal is an anomaly, but before I can . . .

"Yeah, me and Jason," Sal replies.

Christ. One time he sits out here with me and he's a regular.

"Mind if I join? I love sunsets on the beach. It's so romantic," Fiona says.

"Sure," I say. "The more the merrier." This is my nonhermit mouth talking on orders from my little head.

Fiona claps her hands softly and rapidly to express her excitement. Sal starts to lean forward. I sense another situation about to develop.

"Getting dark, time to go," he announces. After rocking back and forth a few times, he lifts up onto his feet. The problem is my beach chair remains attached to him like a dog stuck in the act of procreation. My first impulse is to pour water over the chair to loosen its grip on Sal's extensive back side. Before I can, he starts pushing on the chair to escape. After a few seconds of pounding and punching, he says, "Get this fucking chair off me."

I can hear Fiona's hushed amusement at the sight.

I grip the chair and steady my feet in the sand as Sal steps forward. With a thump that rivals a cork escaping a wine bottle, Sal is freed.

"What the fuck?" he says, lifting his arms in the air. "Fuckin' death-grip chairs?"

I want to reply, *"No, a lifetime of Italian pastries."* But I'm lacking in the intestinal fortitude department. Instead I say, "I'll look for some new chairs, built better, when I hit the mainland tomorrow."

"Ya, you do that." His chubby finger points at me.

Sal starts to walk home. I turn to Fiona expecting to find her sitting on a turtle, naked, reading a book. No such luck.

"I better leave, too," Fiona says. She lifts out of Harry's some-day chair. Unfortunately, it doesn't stick to her. "Thanks for the invite. I look forward to sharing some sunsets with you," she says, followed by a sexy island wink and smile.

"Sal, wait up. Can I walk back with you or will we set off the rumor mill?" she calls out as she jogs toward him.

Sal stops and looks back. "What rumors? I already got plenty of women banging down my door."

"Yeah, but from the inside," she replies.

I watch as the two of them walk away toward the bend in the beach. I'm thinking Beauty and the Beast, or Bluto and Olive Oyl. After they turn the corner, I look for Harry to swoop down and reclaim his spot, but it is too late—dusk has yielded to night. The no-see-ums are chomping at the bit. All that is left is me and one boat adrift on the gulf and manned by a guy holding binoculars as he surveys the beach. Is he picking out a spot to watch sunsets? Maybe I should start charging a fee.

I rake the sand around the chairs, and proceed back to the house, dragging the rake behind me. When I reach the walkover, I hear the boat power up and speed off toward Pirate's Pass. I don't like being spied on.

MURPHY'S LAW states if you plan to watch a sunset with a beautiful woman, it will rain. When I wake up the following day, dark clouds threaten to unload a jihad of storms over the southern gulf region. It will be the first rainy day in weeks, so who can complain except me? My first concern, as the rain begins to fall intermittently, is that my boat is going to get wet. It takes only a second for me to realize my concern is the lingering contagion of irrational thought left over from my marriage to Megan.

I hurry to beat the deluge forecasted by the ominous black clouds. As no-luck would have it, I am in the middle of the Intracoastal Waterway when the sky opens up. Being from New England, I'm used to gloomy and misty days that drag into a week as storms anchor off the coast. We were lucky if the rainfall added up to a quarter of an inch. The first wave of giant raindrops pelts the *Ticket* and me and creates a puddle on the deck that easily exceeds the total yearly rainfall in many countries of the world. The horizontal rain is biting. The visibility is reduced to zero. I am instantly drenched. My shirt, shorts, and sandals are soaked. I would've been drier if I had swum to the mainland.

I manage to navigate to the boat condo and tie up under the metal overhang. The rain slapping against the roof creates a deafening roar. I reach for a package of terry cloth towels from the small storage bin allotted to each berth. I peel off my wet clothes, stand naked, and use half the cloths just to dry off. The worst part is putting the wet clothes back on. Thankfully, I ventured out commando style, so I only have to suffer through putting on a clingy T-shirt and shorts. I run back through the tempest and climb into my truck.

I drive down to the Port Charlotte Mall. My first purchase is a T-shirt and shorts so I can stop feeling like I'm in the rinse cycle of a washing machine. I find the nearest restroom and make the change. Next, I search out a specialty shop that sells beach chairs. Surprisingly, they offer wide-body chairs. I don't think any chair is wide enough for Sal, but I purchase three tropical chairs with palm-tree prints, and one wide body with an appropriate orca print.

As I stroll through the mall, I come upon a crowd of people gathered around some kind of show. I hear laughter and a squawking bird. I push several little kids aside and make my way to the front of the crowd. Two women are showing off the many vocal talents of a pair of parrots: one green and one gray. They are singing and talking and drawing oohs and aahs from the crowd. On a table close by is literature regarding the adoption of parrots. The company name is Talking Feathers. I ask one of the women, "Do either one of these birds know the Nantucket limerick?"

She isn't sure so she asks me to belt out a few lines. I decline. We continue talking and I learn most of their birds were rescued. "Given the economy, people tend to rid themselves of pets when times get tough," she explains. "And then we have the DEA which confiscates parrots when they go on drug busts. I guess drug dealers prefer talking parrots as much as they do pit bulls."

I find it interesting, and sort of an omen. I take one of her business cards and tell her I'm in the market for a talking parrot. She tells me she has a large collection and invites me to her store in Fort Myers.

I'm about to gather up the chairs from the specialty store and leave the mall when my cell rings. It is Megan. The end is near.

"Hey, Meg."

"Jason I'm so freakin' excited. I'm jumping on a plane tomorrow morning. I'll be in your arms by dinner. Make a reservation at the most expensive restaurant."

Spend my money, why not? "I can't wait for the expression on your face," I say.

"So, what's new out there . . . how's the weather . . . what should I wear?"

Megan is so excited her sentences are running together. "It's summer out here, too, Megan. Wear what you're wearing."

"Have you met any more movie stars?"

I'm standing in front of a newspaper kiosk. Mel Gibson is on the cover of some magazine and it appears he is yelling at someone on the phone. "Yeah, I'm standing next to Mel Gibson on the beach."

Megan screams. I have to pull the phone away from my ear.

"I loved him in *Legal Weapon*."

"*Lethal Weapon*, Megan."

"*Whatever* . . . can I talk to him? Did you tell him your wife is coming out?"

Wife? My neck hairs stiffen. "He can't talk now. He's on the phone."

"Interrupt him, Poopsie. Tell him I'm his biggest fan."

"I can't. He looks like he's yelling at someone. I don't want to piss off our new friends."

"All right, I understand. But at least invite him to dinner. Oh. My. God! Me and Mel Gibson at the same dinner table!"

"I'll ask him. What time do you arrive?"

I hear papers shuffling. "Ten after four in the afternoon, Pacific time."

I calculate that I'll be watching the beginning of tomorrow's sunset, Eastern time. "OK, don't forget to call me once you arrive."

"I will, Poopsie. Hugs and kisses. I'm so excited I'm shaking!"

We say our next-to-last goodbyes and I end the call. Some might feel I'm being too cruel to my ex-wife—my mother for example—but I look at it as one extreme *Punk'd* episode. And nobody deserves a good punking more than Megan O'Mally.

I pick up the new beach chairs and head back to the island.

CHAPTER TEN

Island Farewell

"The biggest mistake of my life was marrying you."
—MEGAN O'MALLY-NAJARIAN

The following day, the weather clears and life returns to normal in southern Florida. Well, almost. I have two deliveries scheduled, which means it's going to be a rare busy day at my lagoon.

The first boat to enter is riding low in the water due to two rather huge crewmates, who resemble *Saturday Night Live* characters, and an assortment of gym equipment. The water is practically lapping at the gunwales, as the Hans and Franz lookalikes steady the boat next to the dock where the *Ticket* is tied. I offer some assistance, but they respectfully decline as if they are concerned I might hurt myself. Both men step from the boat and slap high fives to each other—a prerequisite of body builders. In only minutes, they have unloaded an assortment of weights, a bar, a reclining bench, barbells, and a number of boxes that hold parts for the assembly of the treadmill. Hans and Franz perform another high five over their accomplishment. I decide the time is right to piss them off.

"Hey guys, the path to the house is over here," I point. "I'm on pilings, so there's a few stairs to climb."

Hans turns to Franz. "Glutes!"

Franz replies, "Glutes!"

Another high five.

They remove their muscle shirts, flex to invisible mirrors, and then lift an assortment of weights and equipment onto their shoulders. They follow me to the stairs. I offer my assistance again but Hans, or maybe it is Franz, simply hands me the delivery receipt to carry. I lead the way up, burdened by the weight of the paperwork, listening to the grunts and farts behind me, as the men struggle up twenty-two steps in the heat of midday. When we arrive on the deck, the two men covered in sweat high-five their arrival.

"You guys need a towel or something?" I say, hoping to avoid having a trail of steroid-sweetened sweat beads sully my floors.

"Yeah, that would be good," replies Hans or Franz. Without pausing to rest, they hurry down the stairs, hoist the balance of the equipment on their shoulders, high-five, and struggle back up to the deck. I toss each of them a towel, which I will later burn. They dry off, high-five, and begin snapping the towels at each other, something I haven't witnessed since the gay-pride tournament at my old racquetball club.

An hour later my minigym is operational. Hans and Franz test my bench by lifting over three hundred pounds. Show-offs. I'd be lucky to start with ten pounds at each end of the bar. Pleased with their impromptu workout, they high-five each other, then offer a high five to me. I decline, claiming carpal tunnel syndrome.

I thank the muscle-heads, pay each one hundred in cash, and escort them back to their boat. As they navigate out, another boat enters carrying Phyllis Hammerstein. When she is close to the docks, a second boat makes the turn in. I assume it is the delivery of my desk, television, and computer.

"Busy port of call," Phyllis says, tossing me a line. I tie her skiff to a cleat.

"Deliveries," I say. "What brings you out?"

"It's a beautiful day, so I thought I'd drop in on my favorite recluse."

I offer her a hand knowing she will either bite it or slap it aside, but instead she grasps it firmly, places a foot on the gunwale, and allows me to pull her onto the deck. She manages to land too close to me. Like almost in my arms. The Hammer adjusts her bosom. I think about a small island retreat in the South Pacific.

"You're looking good, all tanned. Gaining some weight, too," she says.

"Well, I plan on working it off. I just had a weight bench installed. You think you can spot me?" I joke.

"Spot you? You're standing right in front of me."

Christ. "This must be my office arriving," I say, changing gears.

The boat with a crew of one, ties off next to Hammer's skiff. I am getting good use out of my someday-neighbor's docks. The kid starts unloading the computer, printer, flat-screen TV, desk, and chair. When he is done he produces a clipboard and says, "Sign here."

"Hold on," I say. "The salesman assured me you would deliver and set up."

"Dude, we're short-staffed. I ain't about to lug all this stuff by myself."

"Wait just a minute, young man," Phyllis says, stepping in front of me. "You work for Coastal Electronics?"

"Yeah. So?"

"Do you know who Ace Palmer is?"

"Of course, he's the owner."

"Damn right he is. I sold Ace a gulf-front on Boca Grande a few years back. A real sweet deal, too. He's been kissing my ass ever since. So if you want to avoid the unemployment line, mister, I suggest you deliver and set this stuff up, *now.*"

Who let the dogs out? Woof . . . woof, woof woof. Having Phyllis next to me is like having a pit bull at the ready.

The kid mutters a few words under his breath—*bitch* being the most prominent. I suspect The Hammer is about to nail him, but instead she sneers, "Yeah, and I'm all of that!"

I feel bad for the kid. He is well out of his league going toe-to-toe with this five-foot titan, plus he appears shell-shocked at her transformation from ball-peen hammer to sledge. So I diffuse the situation and offer my assistance. "Why don't you take the computer equipment up to the house, and I'll help you with the heavy stuff in a minute."

The kid reluctantly picks up the printer box, and stomps away in the direction I point.

I turn to Phyllis, "Youth. Whaddaya gonna do?"

A calmer Hammer says, "I'm sorry about the cancellation the other day. I really wanted to cook you up some grouper. So to make up for that . . ."

In the distance we hear, "Holy shit!"

"The kid just came upon my stairway to heaven," I say.

". . . I'd like to invite you to be my partner in a golf tournament this weekend."

Hermits don't play sports, especially golf. It says it right on the first page of my guide. "Thanks, Phyllis, but you don't have to do that. I'd embarrass you. I'm a terrible golfer. I'm the king of chili dippers."

"Jason, if you live in Florida, you have to play golf. I'm sure you're just underestimating your ability."

"No, really, I suck. I've spent a lot of time at the driving ranges. I can't hit long and I can't putt. I have no control over where the ball ends up. Even Tiger Woods couldn't help me find the hole."

"I don't think Mr. Woods is the right guy to be showing you where the hole is."

Hammer humor. "Good one, Phyllis, but you know what I mean."

"Have you ever golfed on a course before?"

"Are we talking miniature?" I smile.

"No, Jason, real golf with a set of clubs and a fairway."

"A few times—I think my best score was in the nineties. My friends did way better, though. They nicknamed me *ninety-nine* that summer."

Phyllis steps back and raises her eyebrows. "Are you sandbagging me, Jason?"

"No, why?"

"Not many weekend warriors around here *ever* break a hundred. I'm impressed. Why the nickname?"

"They called me ninety-nine because of my score in the nineties for nine holes. Is that considered good down here?"

Phyllis raises both hands to her mouth. I can't tell if she is laughing or getting ready to expel her brunch. When tears well in her eyes, I realize she is trying desperately to control a fit of giddiness. The kid returns and Phyllis quickly morphs back to pit bull status.

"Dude, those stairs are like from hell."

"I'll help you as soon as I see my friend off," I say.

I walk Phyllis back to the skiff and untie her lines. "I still want you to consider playing, Jason," she said between giggles. "I'll call you with the details. At the very least, it will give you a chance to meet some of the locals."

I've already met the only local I need—Harry. I hem and haw, but finally acquiesce. I am failing miserably at becoming a hermit.

"Hey dude, I need to get back today," the kid whines.

I push the skiff away before The Hammer can jump out and devour the kid.

☙

I<small>T TAKES</small> another hour or so for the Coastal Electronics' employee of the year, with my assistance, to complete the office section of my war room. I hand him a hundred—it would've been double if he hadn't whined so much—and then escort him back to the dock. When his boat leaves, stillness returns. The wake flattens out. Fish resume diving into the air. And once again, from over the dunes, I can hear the gentle surf coming ashore. I amble into the house, pour a glass of lemonade and step out onto the deck to appreciate the seascape for the first time since the early light of dawn. Something is off. In the brighter light, the sand has taken on the appearance of the moon's landscape. The pelting rains from the previous day have left my beach with golf-ball sized dimples. A fresh raking is in order.

I grab the new beach chairs, along with a beach bag of assorted goodies, and head out to the beach. It is late afternoon and still hot and humid. An onshore breeze has created a chop in the gulf, and cooled the shoreline somewhat. I set the new chairs out. The wide one is for Sal, another for his friend, another for Fiona, one for me, and one for someday Harry. I dig a hole on my some-day neighbor's property, drop in the Hans and Franz towels, soak them with lighter fluid, and light a match. It is close to where I burned and buried my clothes after Badi's cab ride.

I begin raking up and down the beach until my sand is the smoothest in the neighborhood. When I'm done, Harry swoops in. I dig out a minnow and toss it his way. "Sit," I command. But Harry doesn't move. Maybe he is a deaf heron.

I settle into my chair for the impending sunset. I pull out a few M&M's and a bag of Cheez Doodles and open my laptop. Nothing is newsworthy out of Boston. Nationally, BP officials are cautiously optimistic that the well gushing out all the oil will be capped soon. The Red Sox, fraught with injuries, are falling behind both the Yankees and the Tampa Bay Rays. My horoscope says I take great pleasure in surrounding myself with friends. *Right again!* Cheez Doodle dust begins to mount on my keyboard. I'm about to peruse the personals section on Craigslist when my cell rings. It's Megan. Buckle up.

"Hey, Megs! Are you here in LA?"

"Yes, Poopsie, I'm finally here. This is soooo wicked pissa. It seems like famous people are everywhere. I'm like stargazing at the airport! There are signs everywhere for shopping. My sister told me to check out Rodeo Drive, but I'm not into cowboy stuff. I'd rather spend my time at the mall where the movie stars go. I can't freakin' wait!"

I shake my head. "Okay, plenty of time later to shop. Did you rent a car?"

"Yes, I'm standing here with the keys in one hand and my luggage in the other. Now what? I really wish you would've met me at the airport."

"But that would've ruined my surprise," I say. "Find the rental and drive out to Interstate 405 north. Then look for Interstate 10 west. Follow it to the ocean, then turn north onto the Pacific Coast Highway. Overall, it should take less than an hour to reach

Malibu. Once there, look for Paradise Cove beach, pull in and call me. I'll walk you in from there."

"Oh, I'm so psyched, Poopsie! I'll tell you right now, I'm never going back. I'm gonna be humongous out here, I can just feel it. Parties every night, rubbing elbows with everything Hollywood. Are we having dinner with Mel?"

"Yeah, and Harry Potter may pop in. I'm playing chess with him right now on the beach."

"Get out of town! Let me talk to him, *please!*"

I toss Harry the heron another minnow. "Okay, hold on." One Mississippi. Two Mississippi. Three Mississippi. Four Mississippi. "Megs, he says he wants to keep it a surprise. In fact, there are a ton of surprises awaiting you, so hurry up."

"I am! I am! I can't wait to see you and all our new friends."

"And I wish I could see the expression on your face when you arrive."

"You don't have to wish much longer, Jason. Okay, I found the rental. The Hertz guy just loaded my luggage in the trunk. Boy, I'm really surprised by one thing."

"What's that?"

"I can't believe all the Puerto Ricans working out here."

⌒∞⌒

SHORTLY AFTER I end the call with Megan, Harry spots movement at the south end of the beach. Sal, Fiona, and a skinny guy are headed my way. They look like a comic strip walking together. The fat and skinny guys are the comic part, and Fiona I want to strip. When the intruders are too close for Harry's comfort, he takes flight. I don't blame you, pal.

Sal lets out a puff of cigar smoke and says, "Jason, this here is Toast. Toast, Jason." I reach for his hand and we shake. Toast is a thin man, with curly locks and a pointed nose. He is hairy: chest, arms, and legs, with growth sprouting from out of his embarrassing Euro bikini.

"My name is Aubert Mainard. I have the distinct misfortune of living next door to this beast," Aubert says, nodding in Sal's direction. Sal flops into his new wide-body orca chair. Fiona brushes up next to me.

"Why do you call him Toast, Sal?" I say.

"Hey, I can't call him Al, 'cause the frog misspells it A-U-B-E-R-T. If I call him Au, it sounds like I'm belching. *Au*. So I call him Toast here 'cause of his political views. If I was under the Eiffel Leaning Tower, I'd call him French Toast." Sal starts laughing.

"You are a grand imbecile, *mon ami*," Toast declares, claiming the chair next to Sal.

Fiona places her hand on my shoulder as she laughs. The electric current from her touch jolts my system and washes ashore a mighty fine piece of driftwood. The problem is I have taken a liking to dressing commando style, so there is no restraining order in place to rein in my excitement. Luckily, my condition avoids detection, and I am able to sit in my chair and place the laptop . . . on top. It reminds me of those guys who can balance and spin plates on the tip of a stick. I bet if I got the laptop rotating fast enough, the video would go viral on YouTube.

"So, Toast, Jason wants to know who caused the oil spill," Sal says, smiling at me through smoke rings.

"It is a proven fact the war criminals, Bush and Cheney, conspired to dump the oil in order to raise the price worldwide. There are pictures, held back from the public, that show these men in scuba gear near the site of the explosion."

"No kidding?" I say.

"I'm certainly not, sir. They are also profiting from the cleanup. I tell you, these men and the organization they belong to are still running this country. Obama is nothing more than a figurehead."

Sal taps my shoulder and winks. "What about September 11, Toast?" Sal asks.

"It's the same story, no? Your president was trained to fly aircraft. And it was aircraft that flew into the building. Here we have men taking premeditated actions to enrage the American public into war, while blaming innocent Muslims."

I lean over to Toast. "If you're implying President Bush flew the plane into one of the towers, wouldn't he be dead now?"

"Think parachutes and remote control. It's more than a theory, *mon ami*. The truth will be exposed."

I lean closer to Sal and whisper, "Okay, I see your point. But I think Burnt Toast is more appropriate."

Sal nods and laughs.

We sit back and watch as the sun dips slightly beyond the horizon. A dozen or so boats drift on the gulf. One boat in particular catches my attention. It is the same boat from a few nights ago. Two men are onboard; each dressed in black T-shirts and black baseball caps. They appear to be watching the sunset, but at times they look through binoculars at where we sit on Sand Key. It concerns me. *Who are they watching and why?* I turn to Fiona.

"You see that boat out there," I say pointing.

Fiona rests her hand on mine. The electric jolt returns and in no time the laptop begins to wobble in my lap.

"Which boat," Fiona says, looking out into the gulf.

My heart is racing. My driftwood struggles to get a peek at what the fuss is all about. My mouth goes dry with anticipation. I'm foot tapping the sand to some love song I can't hear. Only three women in my life have sent such a sexual charge through me with just a mere touch. Unfortunately, Megan was the first, then Tina, my hair stylist, and now Fiona. As is my bad luck with women, all three had looks beyond my reach leaving me fearful of rejection. In time, Megan's touch blew a circuit when she cheated on me. I had to leave Tina's hair salon, because it was just too embarrassing having uncontrollable driftwood lifting the barber's cape. And now, sitting on my beach, Fiona appears out of nowhere sending my heart into overdrive.

"Never mind," I say. Odds are those guys are simply eyeing Fiona with high-powered glasses. I can't blame them. She is beautiful.

Her hand is still resting on mine when I decide to lean closer. To hell with rejection, I am too old to worry about it. I toss the hermit guide to the wind and look at her. She feels my stare and returns the glance with a smile.

And then my cell rings. Megan. *The biggest mistake of my life was marrying you.*

"Hey, Megan."

"I'm here, Poopsie. I just changed into my floss bikini, just for you. Come and get me. And bring your movie star friends with you."

"I'm waving my arm, Meg, can you see me?"

"No, Jason, the beach is crowded. Come up to the parking lot."

I stand up and start waving my arm in the air. "Can you see me now?"

"No, Jason, for chrissakes, I'm standing here practically naked. Come get me."

Sal asks, "Who you waving at?"

I cup the phone. "My ex-wife."

At the same time, a boat with several women cruises lazily in front of us. I continue to wave my arm. "Can you see me now? I'm wearing a green bathing suit."

"No, Jason. I'm looking everywhere and I don't see you."

The women on the boat return my wave. That prompts Sal, Fiona, and Toast to wave at who they think is my ex-wife in the passing boat.

"Jason, please get your fucking ass up here."

"Meg . . . can't . . . see . . . mistake," I purposely stutter.

"Jason, you're breaking up."

"Big . . . mistake . . . ever . . . mar . . . me."

"Jason! Jason! I can't friggin' hear you. I'll call you right back."

I snap my cell phone in half, spike it into the sand and do the best end-zone dance one could imagine. I pump both fists into the air. I fall to my knees and scream the immortal word of William Wallace, *"Freedom!"*

When I compose myself, I notice Sal, Fiona, and Toast sit mesmerized by my performance. I pick up the pieces of the phone and deposit them in my bag. I then sit in the chair feeling the stares of all three.

"What the fuck was that all about?" Sal finally says. "They coming out with a new color M&M?"

CHAPTER ELEVEN

Island Regifts

"I'd kill for a Nobel Peace Prize."
—STEVEN WRIGHT

I stand on the upper deck surveying the gulf, a glass of orange juice in my hand. Thick cumulus clouds and heavy humidity embrace the early morning seacoast like a drunkard grips his indulgence. It is unlikely the trio of invaders from the south end of Gulf Boulevard will occupy the vacant beach chairs at the shoreline. Tonight's sunset will most likely be cancelled due to inclement weather.

I have a few things to do on the mainland. As a result of my spontaneous, irrational exuberance at the image of Megan turning in circles on a California beach, trying desperately to redial me, and hearing whatever people hear when a phone on the other end is suddenly in pieces, I am in need of a new phone. Additionally, the *Ticket* needs fuel, my mail awaits me at Gulf Breeze Realty, and I decide today would make for a nice trip down to Talking Feathers in Fort Myers to have a chat with some birds.

But first, it is time to start my workout routine while watching the business reports. I have decided there are two sand paths to follow in becoming a bona fide hermit. I could become gaunt, grow my hair wildly, add a Taliban-style beard, and write manifestos all day. Or, I could create a lean and mean recluse who enjoys a life of solitude. I choose the latter path because I want to be a happy and healthy hermit.

I press the remote for the television, bringing the Fox Business report into my war room complete with talking heads and a stock-symbol scroll at the bottom of the screen. I then start my bench-press routine with twenty-five pound plates on each side. It is pretty easy at first until I hit a brick wall during my third set. At some point, the fifty-plus pounds multiplied tenfold. I replace the bar and switch to dumbbells for three sets of hammer curls and lateral raises. When I finish, I am sweating profusely and seeing stars in my eyes. I manage one last set of overhead triceps extensions before crawling off, wheezing in pain, to a corner of the room to rest in the fetal position. I think I call out for my mother several times, but I'm not sure.

When I am able to focus again, the talking heads are discussing fertilizer stocks. I hear about food shortages worldwide and the need to ramp up production of phosphates. A few stocks are mentioned as bust-out plays for the balance of this year and into next. I crawl to my computer and press the on button.

I do my due diligence on the recommendations and decide to invest in one—Mosaic Company, because it is based in the United States. I'm a homer at heart. While reading the research on this company on the Yahoo finance page, I notice a sidebar news thread about human waste being used as fertilizer in North Korea. I click on the story.

It seems human excrement is one of North Korea's hottest consumer products. In fact because it is hard to keep up with demand, human manure shops are opening up in markets across the country.

You have to be shitting me!

The story continues about households using human excrement as fertilizer. "The polite thing to do after enjoying a meal at a friend's house is to use the bathroom before leaving."

I think, why not? The ultimate regift. So I picture a North Korean named Choe Yong-nam, for example, finishing a meal of rice and Rottweiler stew at his neighbor's shanty, when the urge to regift moves him. He asks for directions to the drop zone, and begins to walk down a corridor until he comes upon a framed picture of Supreme Leader Kim Jong-il on the wall. There he takes a left, followed by a right that leads toward a poster of the Dear Leader taped to a door leading out of the dwelling. Once outside, he negotiates a path bordered by miniature wood sculptures of Kim Jong-il, until he reaches a life-sized plastic statue of Our Father, the same Kim Jong-il, overlooking several buckets marked: Fertilizer only—in Korean of course. These are the regift potties.

And these folks possess a nuclear bomb.

It makes me ponder. Maybe I could bridge the gap with our adversary by reaching out with some humanitarian aid. A small gesture—as only an individual hermit can reach out to a hermit nation. I rise from the chair and shuffle over to the bathroom, my overworked muscles twitching and my progress still wobbly. It takes a few minutes to muster up a sizeable donation, but in the end, there it floats. One man's clogged septic system is another man's fertilizer. I see the Nobel Peace Prize in my future.

I don a pair of rubber gloves, grab a large ziplock bag, and make the transfer. I then seal the bag and place it in a box along with the gloves I carefully ease out of. To pack the contents securely, I fill another ziplock with pink Styrofoam shipping peanuts left over from the packages I had delivered, and write on the bag: Dried Shrimp. I figure my new friends can eat while they apply the fertilizer. I tape up the box and go back to the computer in search of a shipping address.

The best I can find is a dude named Hong Dong-San and he resides in the capital city of Pyongyang, which sounds like a sex toy to me. *Hey honey, do we have any batteries for the Pyongyang?*

I fill out the international shipping documents, pay the shipping fee with a credit card, and print out a label from DHL— the only delivery service to North Korea. For a return address, I decide to use Bradley's, he of Harvard's faculty and my mother's boyfriend. I figure if good comes from this, Bradley, the toe-picking liberal, will embrace it like Al Gore embraced creating the Internet. But, if the shit hits the fan, there is no better person than Bradley to catch the fecal blizzard that would ensue.

Feeling sore, yet energized, I gather up Hong's package, my money clip, the boat and truck keys and head out. My first stop is the watering hole for the *Ticket*. I ease the boat into Two Palms Marina hoping Memphis the Lighthouse is preoccupied. A young kid stands sentinel by the Texaco pumps, texting on his phone. I maneuver in, toss him a line and hand over my credit card. He hands me the pump. As I watch the gallons of fuel accumulate (I swear I have a hole in the fuel tank), two men emerge from the bait and tackle shop. One is smoking a cigarette, while the other, who looks vaguely familiar to me, is rolling back the wrapper from a candy bar. Both men are dressed in black. *Who wears black in this heat?*

I ask, "How you guys doing?" Remembering that Sal wears black socks, I reach the far-fetched conclusion these guys are associated with Sal's music business in some way. Maybe they're security or part of his entourage. The guy with the cigarette ignores me. Candy man nods slightly.

"I've seen you boating around Sand Key. You guys interested in island property?"

Candy man stops in midchew to stare at me. A second later, cigarette man nudges him and both men disappear into the store.

∞

I DOCK at the condo and transfer to the truck. Since leaving Two Palms Marina, all I can think about are the men in black. I decide to ask Sal, next time we share the same view, if he has associates roaming the area. If not, these guys are certainly sketchy and a threat to the peace and serenity of the island.

My next stop is at Gulf Breeze Realty to collect my mail and leave my humanitarian aid for pickup. When I enter the office, I'm greeted with winks, smiles, and waves from the staff of forty- and fifty-year-olds. I sense my weight-training program is already working. Maybe after a few more workouts, I'll catch the eyes of women closer to my age. Phyllis jumps up from her desk to greet me.

"Jason, so nice of you to drop in," she says.

"Hello ladies," I say sweeping the room. "I still think I should set up a mailbox at the post office instead of having my mail delivered here. You're too kind."

"Never you mind," she says, handing me a few envelopes. "It's closer for you and no trouble for me. Have you been practicing your golf game?"

"Yeah. I've been driving balls into the gulf, but the dolphins keep throwing them back at me." The office staff chuckles.

"Isn't he a hoot," Phyllis says, grabbing my arm and pressing it close to her breasts.

"Hey, I was wondering if you could hold this package for pickup," I say, showing her the box. Phyllis grabs it from my clutches and reads the address.

"Oh my word . . . *North Korea?*"

I shrug. "Humanitarian aid."

"That's so sweet, Jason. I learn something new about you every day. Seems kind of light though," she says, weighing the box in her hand.

"Well, it's just some shit I had hanging around."

"Who is Bradley . . . ?"

"He's a professor at Harvard. An old acquaintance of mine up in Boston. I'm sending the gift in his name. Actually, it's a regift," I add sheepishly.

The staff nods and giggles. There are plenty of professional regifters among them.

"No problem," she says while placing the package on her desk.

"Thanks a whole bunch. I appreciate what you do for me. I'm sprinting to the Sprint store next to buy a new phone. By the way, have you seen a couple of guys dressed in black checking out property on Sand Key?"

The office falls silent. I have the attention of all the agents. *Sales call!* The Hammer's eyes widen. "No, I haven't." She scans the office and is satisfied that the other agents haven't beaten her to a potential sale. Ever the salesperson, she hands me her card and says, "If they're doing more than just kicking sand, you send them my way, you hear? And by the way, you already have a phone."

I take the card. "I *did* have a phone, but I dropped it on the sand and two ghost crabs crawled off with it. I think the bastards are running up minutes on me."

She shakes her head, punches my arm and pushes me toward the door. "Have a nice day, Jason, and stay out of trouble."

"Don't forget my shit," I say, pointing to the package.

"I won't forget your *shit,*" she promises. I wave goodbye to the staff and return to my truck.

A few miles farther south on the Tamiami Trail, I stop at a Sprint store. In a previous dream, I remember the words Sprint 4 G speed painted on the shell of a sleeping turtle. I figure if I purchase a Sprint phone, maybe the naked lady sitting on the turtle will appear at my doorstep.

A young man greets me as I step up to the counter. Before I have the words out that I need a new phone, the guy is shoving the latest model in my face.

"It's the latest smartphone by HTC called EVO 4G with an Android platform, 4.3-inch screen, one gig of memory, plus an eight megapixel camera." He pauses to catch his breath. The guy lost me at smartphone, but I fake my interest as words like WiMAX technology and Snapdragon processor fly over my head. When he is done, he hands me the phone to hold. "Do you currently own a phone?"

"Yeah," I say. "A Samsung flip. But it flipped out and went to pieces."

"Dude, that's like so . . . two years ago. You deserve the latest technology of a smartphone."

"My phone was pretty smart. I punched in some numbers and within seconds I was talking to someone on the other end."

"I'm talking connectivity," he says. "The EVO will bring the world to your palm."

"I'm kind of just a string and can type of guy," I say.

"On this phone you're on the Internet instantly with thousands of apps to choose from. You can download movies, books, games, bank accounts, stock market, GPS, all on the phone . . . it's endless, man."

"Why would anyone watch a movie on a 4.3-inch screen?" I ask the Sprint salesman.

Walk with me for a moment. The need for useless technological innovation is driving me nuts. At times the industry seems to force advancements on society that we really don't need. Would life end as we know it without the ability to text? And what about 3-D televisions? My prediction is they will bomb as badly as satellite radio. Who wants to sit in front of a sixty-inch, high-definition television to watch a two-hour movie with sunglasses on? I suppose the first few times it might be cool watching bullets zoom past my head, or experiencing an explosion that rocks my living room, but over time, even that wears thin. On the other hand, the porn industry might be able to save the 3-D technology. I can envision naked women reaching out for me, or me to them. In fact, if they could perfect a beautiful ass that wiggles off the television screen and falls into my living room, I'd go down to the local optometrist and have my eyes permanently adjusted for 3-D viewing.

"Everybody watches movies on these devices because of the resolution. Think of the convenience of just pressing a button and your favorite movie or song is downloaded," he adds.

There is no way I need this phone. I'm sure by the time the phone is obsolete—I'm guessing in several months—I still won't have all the features figured out. "I just need something simple. Do you have any cell phones with a rotary dial? The numbers on my last phone used to stick."

The guy smiles. "You're not serious, right?"

"Here's the deal," I say. "I'll take one of these EVO phones because it sounds like Eve and that's a woman's name, and it was a woman I saw sitting on the Sprint turtle."

"Huh?"

"And can I regift to you my busted Samsung?"

I am off to Fort Myers with my new "smartiephone" which, when fully charged, will intimidate me to no end. I try to find Talking Feathers without the GPS, but I get lost on College Parkway. So I take the phone off charge and tap in the number from their business card to get directions. Funny, it works the same as my old "dummiephone."

"You're real close," says a woman named Caprice. "Turn onto Kenwood Lane and travel south until you see the huge live oak on your left. Take that left. We're located half a mile down the road near Olive Garden."

"Did you say live oak as opposed to what . . . a dead oak?" I ask the parrot keeper.

"That's the tree's name. Live oak."

I'm confused. "So, let's say I had a live oak in my backyard and it died, would I call someone to cut down my dead live oak? It just doesn't make any sense."

She laughs. "From your accent, it sounds like I'm talking with someone from New England. A beautiful region of the country, by the way, that suffers from rotaries—silly roads that go in circles. I had a friend once who spent several weeks on one of those circles. It just doesn't make any sense."

"Touché," I say. "I'll be pulling in momentarily."

Talking Feathers is a small pet shop filled with birdcages of every size and shape imaginable. Some are constructed from bamboo, others from metal, and several furniture-like pieces made out of oak, dead live oak I surmise. A few of the cages hold parrots. Other birds are perched freely on small tree limbs in the center of the store. As I introduce myself to Caprice, several parrots say hello and one offers a wolf's whistle—the little flirt. Caprice claims she remembers me from the mall as she lifts a bird onto her shoulder. We talk together and to the birds as she explains in detail about each one. After meeting all the parrots except one, I motion toward an African Grey set aside.

"Is that one sold?" I ask, walking over to the cage.

"Well, no. He came in about a month ago. He's a very smart boy. When he's motivated, he can talk better than some people I know."

"But . . . ?"

"But, he's a rescue from the DEA. His previous owner, some drug dealer from Miami, filled his vocabulary with expletives. I'm having a difficult time finding a home for him because once he's motivated to speak, well, you can't have children in the same room."

I start to laugh. "What's his name?"

Caprice pulls me aside and whispers, "His name is Montana, and apparently he has the movie *Scarface* memorized. His name is also his key word. As soon as he hears it, he responds. Here, watch. Hey, cutie boy, want a treat?"

The parrot stares back, unfazed.

"Now introduce yourself starting with his name."

I move toward the cage. "Montana, how are you today?"

The bird inches closer to me and says, "*Hey, fuck you, mang.*"

I turn to Caprice with a huge grin on my face. "I'll take him."

In order for Caprice to sell me a parrot, she first has to approve my home to make sure it is fit for one of her babies, even if he is a foul-mouthed fowl. I explain that I live on an island and rarely mingle with humans, but she insists on a visit, so I make an appointment to meet her at my boat condo in a couple of days. I leave thinking how much I'm going to enjoy watching all my Mafia movies again with Montana perched on my shoulder.

I drive back home feeling like I had a successful day. I regifted a Poopsie poop, and by the way, I make a note never to let anyone call me that again. I regifted my busted dummiephone, and I purchased a parrot who will ignite shock and awe at any social gathering, should I ever fall victim to one.

By late afternoon, the skies are still cloudy, guaranteeing that I'll be sitting at the shoreline alone with my laptop, a sandwich, and Harry the heron. I think of Harry and Montana together and wonder if they will get along. Wouldn't it be great if the three of us could sit and play poker: Montana chomping on a Cuban cigar and Harry with his poker face?

I tie off at Gulf Boulevard and head toward the house. As I emerge from the thicket of cabbage palms and buttonbushes, I notice a figure sitting at the top of the stairs. I freeze. I don't have a clear view, but it looks like a person wearing a black garment. There are no boats in the lagoon and no golf carts parked out front. I step back and lower myself behind a cluster of mangroves.

Chapter Twelve

Island Bloom

"I can resist everything except temptation."
—Oscar Wilde

"Jason, what are you hiding for? I heard your boat coming in."

I stand up and step out from behind the flora. "Fiona?"

She is standing now at the top of the staircase, looking down at me, hands on her hips. A smile so engaging it reaches out and hugs me. She is wearing a black two-piece swimsuit, with the bottom half covered by a sheer sarong wrap. Her raven hair is pulled to one side in a ponytail that wraps seductively over her left shoulder and curls along her collarbone. From behind her ear, a pink hibiscus flower in full bloom accentuates her beauty.

"It's me. Are you going to dance and break your phone for me?" she giggles.

I start up the stairs. "No, not today. I just bought a too-expensive smartiephone that hopefully prevents me from doing dumb things." I wave the phone in the air to show her.

She looks beyond me toward the lagoon, and then turns her attention to the gulf. "What a view from here. I mean, I could really get into this."

Music to my ears. I reach the top of the stairs and join her on the deck. I have no idea why Fiona is here, so I ask the one pertinent question any guy would in the company of a visiting goddess.

"You need to borrow a cup of sugar or something?"

She pouts. "No, Jason, I'm here to see you. It doesn't appear we'll enjoy a sunset today, so I thought I'd drop by and see for myself what Sal keeps calling, 'Jason's sand castle.' He thinks you're an off-the-wall, trust-fund baby."

My defense mechanism, constructed after my lottery windfall by a million hermit thoughts and glued together with my PMS (Pessimistic Magnet Syndrome), questions why such a beautiful woman would take an interest in me. Since meeting her on the beach, Fiona is an arm's length fantasy in high definition: realistic looking, but untouchable. Or maybe I'm just too jaded by the likes of Megan.

"Yeah, he already ran that accusation by me. I assure you I'm not a baby."

"But the off-the-wall part works, right? You rake the beach, put out a chair for a heron, and rumor has it you have an infatuation with M&M's." She is smiling ear to ear.

I shrug. "Guilty as charged, Running Bush."

"Oh really?" She playfully punches my arm. "How about I call you . . . Dances with Phone?"

"I guess I'm not gonna live that down any time soon."

"No, sir. You own it. *Freedom!*" she mocks.

We laugh and gradually fall quiet; the sound of the surf suddenly becomes as loud as an approaching marching band. She leans against the deck railing and stares at me. I try returning her gaze, but I can't. My eyes find excuses to wander: a passing sailboat, a pelican swooping down, a breaking wave. I feel like I am wobbling in the breeze. Thankfully my smartiephone occupies one of my hands, but I have no idea what to do with the other. Sitting with Fiona during sunset, with Sal and Toast as company, was comforting. Being alone with her on my deck is intimidating.

The fragrance from her hibiscus bloom wafts within the space between us.

I take a deep breath in anticipation of saying something, and then realize I have nothing to say. My jaw becomes tight, my mouth dry.

"Well?" she says.

Did she ask me something I didn't hear? Women hate men who don't listen.

"Well . . . what?" I reply, tentatively.

"Are you going to invite me in, or does the hospitality start and end on your deck?"

Christ! I'm such an idiot. "I'm sorry. Come on inside."

We enter through the squeaking screen door that leads into the kitchen. Her first comment is how spacious it is.

"Sal had a hard time squeezing through here on his walk-through," I say.

"*Duh,*" she replies.

I find her remark funny. As I proceed to the foyer, Fiona remains in the kitchen, running her fingers along the appliances as if auditing for dust.

"I used to love to cook," she says in a voice that suggests she is longing for a different time in her life.

I read somewhere when a woman tells a man she loves to cook, she's planting a seed within him. Hopefully she doesn't require any North Korean fertilizer. I step back into the kitchen. "Why don't you cook anymore?"

"Long story short, I'm always on the road. The Eastern Council of Indian Affairs has me traveling back and forth along the panhandle, into Alabama and Louisiana, and up to DC to meet with politicians. After all these years, we still have to fight for our rights with the white man," she smiles.

I throw my palms in the air. "Hey, leave this white guy out of it. I saw what you did to Custer."

"That was a different tribe, and a different time, Jason."

"And in case you haven't noticed, we elected a black guy for president. So you're fighting with the black man now, kemosabe."

"You're an incorrigible boy," she says, smiling.

"Boy? I'm twenty-eight. How old are you?"

"I'm thirty," she replies with authority, as if I needed to respect my elders.

"Cougar," I mutter.

"*Huh?* Cougar? I'm aghast at the accusation. Are you implying I'm on the prowl, Mr. Nar . . . *whatever your name is*? And I doubt a difference of two years falls under the definition. Do you really think I'm on the hunt?" she says. Her head tilts playfully to one side.

Driftwood. "I think you're here to melt my stash of M&M's. Let me show you the rest of the house."

Fiona follows me into the foyer where most of the rooms can be seen at a glance. I point out the view from the east-facing windows toward the lagoon where the *Ticket* is docked. I explain the functionality of the first-floor layout, and touch on the majestic dead live oak staircase in front of us that leads up to fantasyland. "Let me show you the war room," I say.

She starts to walk with me then stops. "Oh . . . look, just like Sal mentioned. A framed set of green M&M's on the wall."

I shake my head. A monkey duct-taped to the wall reciting messages from my smartiephone wouldn't garner a fraction of the attention my tribute to the winning M&M's does.

We enter the minigym. "This is my exercise and investment area. I can work out while I dabble in the stock market."

"Pretty neat," she says. "I like the treadmill and free weights. Hey, I'm coming over here instead of the gym on the mainland. Mind if I try the bench?"

"Be my guest. But please don't hurt yourself."

She lies on her back and reaches for the bar. "How much are you lifting?" she asks.

Not knowing what to say, I fabricate a number. "I'm pressing ten reps of one fifty through three sets," I reply, as I step around to spot her.

"Really? I figured you for more," she says.

Dammit! I try to recover. "I just started my routine so I'll be adding more weight soon." I watch as she lifts the bar and does ten reps without breaking a sweat. Even the hibiscus remains in place.

"Not enough weight," she says, resting the bar in place. "Normally I do one twenty-five."

If I were at my computer, I'd type WTF. Two muscle heads and a petite squaw are putting me to shame. I suspect the lingering effect of Angelo's sandwich shop is to blame.

We quickly leave the war room and enter the living room which is furnished with wicker chairs, a sofa, and two rockers, all ready for the entertaining I'm not planning on doing. On the wall, my sixty-inch, theater-quality plasma television. I figure this room will impress her, but instead she says, "I like all the bowls of M&M's." She reaches for the closest one and grabs a handful.

We sit in chairs opposite each other. Fiona begins tossing candy in the air and catching it in her mouth. This chick is so cool, but at the same time, my freakish PMS suggests lesbian tendencies abound. I kick the PMS aside.

"So you're really a Native American Indian?"

She mouths the rest of the candies. "Yes. My family belongs to the Apalachee Nation, which at one time lived along the Florida Panhandle. Tribal enemies and the encroachment of Spanish settlers forced my ancestors to migrate to Alabama and eventually settle in the swamps of Louisiana. Today we're trying to gain recognition back here in Florida, and that's where I come in. So what's your story? Are you hiding out from your ex-wife?"

"Nope. I'm a hit man. This is where I relax between assignments."

Fiona freezes. Her eyes widen, her smile forgotten. I think I scared her. Sometimes my humor needs a filter, or at the very least a proofreader. "I'm only kidding. I decided to leave the cold of New England for the sand, surf, and sun of the gulf of Florida."

Fiona relaxes. "No girlfriends? You're just a rich boy living alone in this huge beach house?"

"Except for the ex-wife, who is probably still shouting obscenities at me from a beach in Malibu, I currently have no interaction with the opposite sex. *Freedom!*"

"Malibu? I thought you were waving at her as she passed in the boat?"

"Optical illusion. My ex is three thousand miles away."

Fiona adjusts in the chair by tucking her legs beneath her. This leaves an opening that seduces my eyes. I need a distraction so I think of Bradley picking his toes across the room. When that doesn't work, I think of Hong Dong's elation at receiving my regift.

"So what do you do for intimacy?" Fiona practically whispers.

I don't think bringing up porn at this point would be advantageous, so I say, "When the need arises, I drive up to Sarasota International and let the TSA guards feel me up."

Fiona bursts out laughing and quickly covers her mouth. Her body shakes and her toes wiggle. Every move she makes is sexy.

"Oh, God, that was funny," she says. "Can you elaborate on the other night for me? I still love it. *Freedom!* Just like in the movie, *Braveheart*. Even though I didn't show it, I was laughing my ass off on the inside."

I proceed to tell her the story of Megan O'Mally, from the lap dance in college to her most recent journey to California. She listens intently. At times Fiona giggles, other times she shakes her head in disbelief. When I finish, she grabs another handful of M&M's.

"I can't believe what she did to you. No wonder you live alone," she says.

"With respect to her, you're hearing just my side, but . . . she was bat-shit crazy. At times she even slept upside down from the ceiling."

Fiona laughs and then chokes on a candy. How can a woman choking still look beautiful? She quickly recovers and clears her throat. I offer water, but she refuses.

"Stop making me laugh, the candy goes down the wrong pipe." She puts more in her mouth and says, "Do you think she'll come back gunning for you?"

"I have a new phone number and Megan has no clue where I live. She'll never find me. Anyway, I suspect she's already met a surfer dude, and the wedding invitations are in the mail."

"Why send her to California?"

"She wouldn't go to Somalia, so, I thought . . . California. Probably because one time I placed a bet on the New England Patriots and lost on the point spread. So I said aloud, 'Now that I know the score, I wish I could fly out to California and bet the game again because they're three hours behind us.' And she said, 'That's a great idea! Why hasn't anyone thought of that?' So the West Coast made sense."

"You're something else, Jason," she says, shaking her head. "Is there more of this sand castle to show me? Where do those stairs lead?" she points.

I wave her off. "Just a few bedrooms on the second level. Hey, you want to watch some Three Stooges?"

"I'd rather see the upstairs. Don't worry if your bed isn't made, or your laundry is piled in a corner, I'm not judgmental," she says, standing up.

I'm uneasy about bringing Fiona into my bedroom. Why? I don't know. "My underwear sticks to the wall," I warn.

"Nice try."

Reluctantly I stand and escort her up the stairs. I show her the two spare bedrooms that will only be used when my parents visit. I show her the bathroom shared by both bedrooms. I stall even more by displaying the extensive closet space throughout the second floor, along with the craftsmanship of the banister railings.

"What's through that door?" she says, pointing down the corridor.

"The master bedroom," I say.

She skips ahead and pushes open the already slightly ajar door. Fiona gasps as she stands in the middle of the room. "Are you shitting me?" she says, turning in a circle. "There's an echo in here."

She slides over to the cavernous walk-in closet and nods her approval. Then she hurries over to the other side and starts exploring the master bath.

"Teak? You have two pedestal sinks and a tub made out of teak?" Apparently she is still stunned.

"As of this morning I did. Is there a shower stall in there, too?" I ask.

"Ye-ah. Floor to ceiling, all glass."

"Good, I can't afford to have things go missing."

Fiona steps from the bathroom, spreads her arms, and twirls like a ballerina. "Your home is so awesome, Jason. Maybe some-day . . ." she says, leaving the thought lingering in the air like dandelion dust on a breezy summer day. She walks over to the king-sized platform bed, which I make every day by the way, mili-tary style, and sits on the foot end. Once again she appears to be overwhelmed by her surroundings. She sits motionless, look-ing down at her hands, absentmindedly caressing her fingertip. I don't know whether to sit next to her, or wait for an invitation. I'm about to ask her if she is all right, when suddenly she bolts to her feet.

"Look at the view!" she exclaims, rushing over to the glass sliders that open to the upper deck. She steps outside, soaks in the vista, and leans against the railing facing the gulf. I move to join her when she abruptly turns and heads back in.

"You've got company," she says with a half-smile, thumbing me toward the beach.

"Company?" The word is an affront to my hermit lifestyle. I step outside and notice a boat anchored a few yards offshore. A woman stands in the midst of my beach chairs, gazing up at the house. What grabs my attention is that she is topless.

"Is she your ex-wife?" Fiona asks with a smile.

I turn and join Fiona inside. "No. I told you she's in Califor-nia. I've never seen that woman before. Give me a few minutes to find out what's going on. Sit on the bed again. Do some comfort-able things. I promise I'll be right back."

I hurry from the room, down the stairs, and out the screen door. From the walkover I call out to the interloper, "Can I help you?"

The woman notices my approach and proceeds to walk across my impeccably raked beach to confront me. On first impression, she appears to be one of those free-spirit types, who seek out deso-lated beaches to sunbathe nude, except there isn't any sun today to bathe nude in. I grab my rake.

"I'm pretty sure nudity is illegal here," I say, keeping the weight of my gaze from dropping below her chin.

"Hi, my name is Jenna Decker. I built the home you live in."
She extends her hand, we shake and she jiggles. I'm taken aback.

"That house?" I say pointing, as if there are a dozen houses to
pick from. Fiona stands on the upper deck watching.

"That's the one—Decker Development. We had plans to build
out this end of Gulf Boulevard, but . . . let's just say things didn't
go as planned. My husband Cyrus ended up in jail for bribery, the
bank took all our assets, and now I'm left with very little."

"Yes, I remember my realtor telling me now. I'm sorry to hear
that."

She glances around the beach. "Why is the sand so different
here?"

I display the rake. "It's a hobby of mine."

"That's weird."

This coming from a woman standing topless before me. "Are you
here to look at the house?" I ask, wondering where this conversation is headed.

"I spoke with Phyllis, your realtor, and she told me a little
about Mr. Jason Nigeria."

"Najarian."

"Rumor has it you're a well-off young man. You were able to
purchase this beautiful house that I designed and built, practically
at cost."

"Only because of the threatening oil slick," I say, somewhat
defensively.

"So, I was hoping you might find it in your heart to help a
woman down on her luck."

Here we go. Palms up. I thought I'd left this behind in Massachusetts. "Ms. Decker, I don't know what you've heard, but I'm
barely making ends meet."

"I need these girls fixed." She cups her breasts, lifts them
up and lets them fall. "See how gravity has a greater influence
on my right tata? Look at them. One hangs lower than the other.
I need breast work, Mr. Nigeria. I can't start a new life out of
balance."

I drop the rake and run my hands through my hair.

"Please hold them. Feel what I'm talking about." She grabs my hand and before I know it, I'm holding a double D. I jerk my hand away and step back, embarrassed.

"Look, I'm real sorry your girls aren't twins, but I can't help you."

Jenna Decker, former vice president of Decker Development, stares at me, dumbfounded. "I thought you might take pity on my situation. Instead, you dismiss me. You're cruel. I hope you rot in hell, Mr. Nigeria." With that, she kicks sand at me and returns to her boat.

I watch as she speeds off, making sure she doesn't return to steal my beach chairs. When she enters Pirate's Pass, I notice Harry has landed behind me.

"I can't sit with you now, Harry. I have a beautiful woman waiting in my bedroom. I'm sorry."

Harry shakes his head and flaps his wings, obviously perturbed.

"I know, bros before hos, but give me a break this one time. I'll double the minnows later."

Harry takes flight. A crazy topless woman and a heron are pissed at me. I grab the rake to smooth out the area tainted by the double Ds, and then head back to the house.

"You're not going to believe this," I say entering the kitchen.

"Fiona?

"Fiona?"

I know this game. I had a girlfriend once who liked to sneak into my condo, play possum under the covers and then surprise me naked when I entered the bedroom. She ended up working for a party-favors company as the girl who pops out of cakes. I hurried up the stairs, two at a time.

When I enter the bedroom, the bed is still made. "Fiona?" She is not on the deck, not in the bathroom, and not hiding in my closet. Deflated, I head downstairs to see if she is adding more weight to the barbell. Nothing. I look out on the deck and down Gulf Boulevard. Fiona is nowhere in sight.

I drift back into the living room and slump into a chair. How disappointing. I felt we were close to something romantic. At least it appeared that way. Did I read her seducing looks incorrectly? On the coffee table is a spread of M&M's. At least she could have put them back in the bowl before leaving.

I have no way of contacting her. I don't know what house she rents and I don't have her phone number. *Maybe I should run after her?* The M&M's appear in some order.

One minute she is looking down at me from the deck, the next she is gone. The friggin' Decker woman changed my course from fantasy world back to Hermitville.

Freedom? I look closer at the M&M's. Fiona had spelled out the word freedom with a question mark. Now I have two women and a heron pissed at me.

CHAPTER THIRTEEN

Island Foreplay

"Golf is a good walk spoiled."
—MARK TWAIN

I am floating on my back just offshore, the gentle movement of the gulf swaying me like a mother rocks her newborn. A flock of Sandwich Terns hovers above using their wings to fan a cool breeze down on me. Fish float to the surface to have their bellies scratched. The sky is cloudless. The only sounds are born from nature. Everything seems perfect until Lou Bega parachutes from the sky singing "Mambo No. 5." It startles me awake.

A little bit of Fiona in my life . . .

I sit up and the first thing I notice are two men dressed in black standing on the deck laughing as they urinate over the edge.

"Hey!" I call out.

A little bit of Fiona by my side . . .

Fiona is sitting in a chair tossing M&M's in the air. I'm about to climb out of bed and talk with her when the Decker woman comes charging out of the bathroom.

A little bit of Fiona's all I need . . .

She arrives at the side of the bed and taps my shoulder. At the same time, Fiona shifts her legs in the chair leaving a peephole between her thighs that activates a flashing neon light, shaped like an arrow with the words *Open for Business.*

A little bit of Fiona's what I see . . .

"Hey, Nigeria," Decker says, interrupting my bliss. She leans slightly backward and places a twelve-inch carpenter's level across her breasts. "See! I can't get the fucking bubble in the center! My tatas are off."

A little bit of Fiona in the sun . . .

Montana appears on the bed and says, *"Big Pussy swims with the fishes."*

"Jason!"

The naked woman lying on the other side of my bed rolls over and says, "It's that woman again."

The men in black are still relieving themselves off the deck. How much did they have to drink?

A little bit of Fiona all night long . . .

Fiona stands up and starts to slip out of her swimsuit, slowly and seductively.

"Jason? Are you awake?" the voice from downstairs calls out.

"Nigeria, whaddaya think of this?" Decker has rolled a bandana under her gravity challenged breast, and tied it off around her neck. "I got a center bubble, *finally!*"

Montana moseys over to the other side of the bed to stare at Decker's breasts. *"Bada Bing,"* he squawks.

A little bit of Fiona here I am . . .

"Hey, Jason. Golf this morning, remember?" the downstairs voice gets louder.

The naked woman nudges me. "Get up, Jason. Get up."

I watch Fiona start to drift away as her swimsuit bottom slips down to her ankles.

A little bit of you makes me your man.

I open my eyes to an empty room and hear noises downstairs. I climb out of bed and pad out of the bedroom to the top of the stairs. "Who's down there?"

"It's me, Jason. Let's go, it's almost tee time," Phyllis calls back.

I yawn and then try to rub the sleep from my face. "I don't drink tea." Why is she making tea in my kitchen? I shuffle back into the bedroom and head over to the shower. *Did she say golf?*

Showered and dressed, I walk into the kitchen to find The Hammer sitting at the counter, eating a muffin with juice, while reading the newspaper.

"Did you say tee time as in golf?" I mumble.

"Today's the day, champ. You and I are partners against Moira and Bernie Segal from Coral Bay Realty." She checks her watch. "We're teeing off at Oyster Creek in one hour."

I pour a glass of orange juice. "Did I not emphasize that I suck at golf?"

"As long as you have a pulse, we're good. We could wear blindfolds and have one arm tied behind our backs, and still beat the Segals."

"You said miniature golf, right?"

"No, Jason, eighteen big-boy holes. This is going to be so much fun. I love beating Moira."

How do I get myself into this crap? Hermits don't play golf. Hermits don't do anything but hermit. "I can't play. I don't own clubs."

"Not to worry. You can use my husband's TaylorMade set. You guys are about the same height. He won't be using them. By the way, your doorbell isn't working. I'll have property management come out next week."

I look at her fingers and still see no rings. "Whoa, let's not giddy-up past that factoid. You're married?"

She checks her watch again. "It's time we hit the road. I don't want to lose a stroke off my score for being late." She rinses out the glasses and grabs her keys. "I'll tell you about Murray, my late husband, on the way."

"Oh, shit . . . I'm sorry."

It is a warm sunny morning as we travel across the Intracoastal Waterway toward Two Palms Marina. The din of the outboard keeps us from conversing, so I'm left to speculate about Mr. Hammer. Had Phyllis married an older guy, maybe for money? Had there been a tragic event in her life? Or did she just nag him to death? Inquiring minds want to know.

After we dock and pay a good morning to Memphis the Lighthouse—Phyllis did, not me—we climb into her car.

"My husband was a stubborn *meshuggenah*, may he rest in peace," she begins, as we drive down the crushed-shell road leading out to highway 775.

And this is why I won't get married. Women generally outlive men by quite a few years, and they spend all of those extra innings bitching about their dead husbands.

"Murray always had to have the best of everything. He felt a man was only as good as the toys he acquired. My husband had to live in the best house, drive the best car, own expensive golf clubs, captain the best sailboat . . ."

"Own the best power tools, right?" I interject. "My father thinks the same way."

"No tools. Murray hired out for manual labor. Anyway, everything he purchased he clamped onto like a hungry gator on a wading deer. Nobody could touch his toys. *Nobody.* So three years ago, Murray and his buddies enter the annual Tarpon Tournament over in Boca Grande. They found a sponsor and bought these funky-looking uniforms. They looked like a bowling team wearing paint-splattered spandex. Of course Murray went all out and bought a really expensive rod and reel. He was sure of winning the tournament. Catch a fish, weigh it, throw it back. Go figure."

I thought of my dad fly-fishing up in Maine.

"Long story short, Murray, the novice angler, hooked a big one. Unfortunately for him, the tarpon had other plans. The fish jumped out of the water and pulled Murray's rod right out of his hands. Now what's a sane fifty-six-year-old man do once that happens?"

"Buy another rod?" I reply.

"Exactly, but not my Murray. He sees a tarpon making off with his toy, so he jumps into the water after the fish. They told me he surfaced once with his hands on the fishing rod screaming 'I got it!,' but was soon pulled back under. It was the last anyone saw of him."

"That's terrible, Phyllis."

She waves me off. "I'm pretty confident Murray never let go, so I'm thinking the fish was so fearful of what he was towing that he tried to outswim Murray, but instead dragged my husband across the gulf to someplace in Central America. My guess is he's living over there in some fancy tree house." She winks at me as she pulls into the Oyster Creek parking lot.

I carry dead Murray's golf bag filled with TaylorMade sticks over to the clubhouse where we meet up with the Segals. Moira and Bernie are dressed in wildly colorful golf attire as are most of the members and guests. The Segals look to be in their mid- to late-fifties, and tell me how they are also in the realty business. But it is Phyllis Hammerstein who draws most of the attention. Everyone seems to know her. "She's quite popular as the reigning number-one realtor in Sarasota County three years running," Moira explains, with a hint of venom. My immediate problem is I fear people are looking at me like I'm The Hammer's date.

The golf course is a par 72, shaped like an "M"; five holes down, four holes up, four holes down and five holes back to the clubhouse. It is crowded. Parties of four or more walk the greens and golf carts buzz the pathways. People linger around waiting their turn. Our party waits for the green to clear. Opposite the first hole is the ninth hole. I can see one person holding the flagpole while the others circle the hole.

"How are you feeling, champ?" Phyllis asks.

"Like a fish out of water. Where are the little windmills I'm supposed to putt under?"

Phyllis reaches into dead Murray's golf bag and lifts out a driver. "Here, par 4. Tee it up and whack the shit out of it."

I watch as the Segals take turns launching straight drives down the fairway. I hope Phyllis doesn't have any money riding on this. I step to the tee and try a few practice swings. When I think I am ready, Phyllis comes up behind me and runs her hand down my leg to open my stance. *Oh God and people are watching.*

I swing, whoosh, and hit the ball dead on. I marvel at how fast the ball leaves the tee and how efficiently, without assistance from any wind, it changes course in midair to resemble a banana. There is a woodpecker's knock heard, when ball meets tree bark, followed by squirrels scurrying away. From there, my drive ricochets off a golf cart, between holes eight and nine, before coming to rest in the rough.

"Nice start," Phyllis quips.

"Hey, I warned you."

The rest of the front nine fares no better. At the fourth hole, my slice whizzes past an onlooker on the sixth hole, prompting Phyllis to suggest I call out foreplay before I tee off. "Some old biddies might come running over, but think of all the lives you might save."

On the seventh tee, I swing so hard I lose my grip on the club. It travels farther and straighter than the ball, prompting Bernie to ask sarcastically, "Is that considered one or two shots?"

How about one shot to your nose? I wouldn't mind giving old Bernie a fist sandwich, because I'm pretty sure I could outrun him should he be a tough guy.

At the halfway point, I have lost a dozen balls. The Segals are giddy with the thought of finally beating Phyllis. After nine holes and with the clubhouse in sight, I want to call it a day and end my ordeal. I feel bad about my play, but The Hammer won't hear of it. She exposes the soft underbelly of her hardened exterior by pulling me aside and telling me it isn't my fault. It's all bullshit, but I appreciate it. She takes the driver from my hand and speaks to it.

"Murray, for chrissakes, let the boy use your clubs."

With dead Murray less angry, I do better on the back nine. Not enough to rally for a win, but I score lower than the front nine. My total is an embarrassing 118. Phyllis has the best score at 89, Barry shot a 95 and Moira a 98. The combined score by the Segals bested Phyllis and me. At least The Hammer can continue to claim individual superiority over her archrivals.

On the ride back, Phyllis eases my humiliation by addressing my potential and the need for a few golf lessons.

"Maybe my own sticks, too," I add.

"Maybe," she chuckles. "I guess Murray wasn't too happy with me loaning out his clubs."

Thankfully, she doesn't ask me to partner up again. When we reach Two Palms Marina and climb aboard her boat, she notices Memphis pumping gas, which appears to jog her memory.

"I forgot to tell you. Those guys with the black clothes you told me about in my office?"

"Yeah?" *The same guys who took a leak off my deck.*

"I asked around in case they were looking for a realtor. Turns out Memphis has been renting them a boat. He said both men produced licenses from Portsmouth, New Hampshire, but later he overheard one of them say he couldn't wait to get back to Philly to eat a real steak and cheese. Memphis doesn't think they're here to buy property, that's his gut feeling anyway. He thinks they're visiting someone on the island."

"And this is the gut behind his headlamp?"

"Stop it. Memphis is a nice man once you get to know him. He also said they speak with a foreign accent, and that one of them is as mean as a squall. I'd keep my distance if I was you."

This news troubles me. The fact that all of a sudden I find myself surrounded by men with countenances that resemble vendettas is pure caffeine for my PMS. I've weighed whether there is a connection between Sal and the men in black, but I can't connect the dots. Are they associates or enemies? Did Sal screw somebody in the music business and now these guys are here to settle a score? Does Sal even produce music? Maybe my imagination is simply out of control.

∽

BACK ON the island, I remember I need to call my parents and give them my new phone number. I call my dad first, but he doesn't answer so I leave a message. Next, I call my mother. Bradley answers the phone and tries to chitchat with me. I try to make it seem, with one-word replies, how oblivious I am to his existence, but he doesn't pick up on it because he's an airhead. When I can take no more, I ask him, "Hey Brad, what's your take on North Korea?"

"North Korea? Well, I suppose that's another example of how the United States bullies a sovereign nation. We have no business denying them the right to have nuclear power for peaceful purposes. Instead, we starve their population with sanctions. We, as a populace, should rise above our government and extend a peace offering to the people of North Korea."

"I agree. Is my mother around?"

I hear the knucklehead call out her name. What I would pay to see Hong Dong show up at Harvard University and take a dump in Professor Bradley's loafers.

"Jason, where have you been? I've been trying to contact you."

"Hey, Mom. Sorry, I forgot to call and give you my new number."

"I thought something was wrong. Megan called me in a tizzy about a week ago. Were you supposed to meet in California?"

I hate lying to my mother, but hey . . . "California? Is that where she went?"

"Yes. She told me how upset and scared she was stranded on a beach in Malibu. The poor girl was crying. What's going on with you two?"

"Nothing is, and you know very well Megan only produces alligator tears. She wanted to see the house, so I told her to meet me at Malibu *Resort* on North Redington Beach, Florida. I'm telling you, the woman never listens."

"Oh . . . I can see the confusion. Well, at least it turned out all right. She called me back a few days later to let me know a handsome lifeguard had literally swept her off her feet. They're dating now."

What did I tell you? "Great news," I beam.

"Should I tell her where you live and give her your new number if she calls again?"

"No, Ma. If you do that, I will sell the cape home with Bradley in it, and make you move in with Dad and Tranquility."

"Oh my . . . I get the message, Jason."

"Good." I give my mother my new smartiephone number and tell her I'm looking forward to her visit in a few months, preferably sans the Bradmeister. She says she can't wait to see me and totally ignores the sans part.

After a couple of cheeseburgers-in-paradise for dinner, I gather my laptop, a bag of Cheetos, a pocket full of M&M's, and a bag of stinky minnows for Harry. Fiona has been on my mind all day. Would she show up for the sunset or have I seen the last of her? The damn Decker woman dropped a double D in my hand like it was a sack of gold coins, and I am sure Fiona witnessed the squeeze play from the deck. What a conundrum. How many hermits enjoy the company of a beautiful and seductive woman in the bedroom one minute, and then get accosted by a pair of beluga whales the next? I start to leave for the beach to secure a good seat for the sunset when my smartiephone starts singing the tune *Right Round*. It also shows me my dad is on the other end. This smartiephone has potential.

"Hey, Dad."

"Hi, Jason. It's Tranquility. How are you?"

Tranny always speaks slowly like she is perpetually living in the Spicoli van from, *Fast Times at Ridgemont High*. I usually find myself two sentences ahead of her.

Tranquility: "How's things . . ."

Me: "Where's my dad?"

Tranquility: " . . . down in Florida?"

Me: "Is he out fishing?"

Tranquility: "Is it hot enough . . ."

Me: "If he is, tell him I called earlier to give him my new cell number."

Tranquility: " . . . for ya?"

Me: "Bye."

Tranquility: "Yes, he's out fishing. Do you want to leave a message?"

Me: End call.

It is shaping up to be a fantastic sunset. I shuffle across the walkover, grab the rake and find my seat. I look south along the beach hoping to see Fiona coming around the bend. Nothing. I look for Harry. Nothing. *Is Fiona still upset? Is Harry sitting in a chair with someone else on another island?*

I look south again. Nothing. Alone with my thoughts, I'm left to feel for some reason this is the calm before the storm.

CHAPTER FOURTEEN

Island Update

"Never look back unless you are planning to go that way."
—HENRY DAVID THOREAU

The sun has a good hour remaining before it melts into the horizon like a snowball on a fire pit. A plethora of boats have dropped anchor just offshore, in the front-row seats. Some captains are cooking up supper, while others relax in chairs and raise toasts to the sun's slow departure. I flip open the laptop to check the latest news from Red Sox Nation. Thoughts of Fiona tug at me.

The front page of the *Boston Herald* details the grisly murder of a man found just over the border from Rhode Island. In the subhead, the authorities speculate the ongoing mob violence plaguing the Ocean State has spilled into Massachusetts. I think about Sal and the men in black, and wonder if the violence has also spread to Gulf Boulevard. It is a pebble in my shoe that I can't liberate. If I can muster the nerve, I will confront Sal tonight about his music business, the men in black, and whether he is associated with any of the bad tempers raging up north.

I surf to the sports section and start reading about the successes and failures of the struggling Red Sox. Suddenly, a swooping pelican catches my attention. I watch as the bird dives beak first into the gulf and then spreads its wings and heads southward. As my gaze follows, I notice company rounding the bend.

The three of them walk in a single line led by Toast, then Fiona, and bringing up the rear is Sal, puffing on his cigar and carrying a book. They look as if they are headed to tribal council to see who gets voted off the island. My vote is to jettison the Abbott and Costello duo and keep Fiona. *Hands?* I lift my arm into the air for effect. Toast thinks I'm waving to him and waves back. What a dork.

Being creatures of habit, each sits in the same chair as they have since the first day of their invasion. Fiona to my right, Sal in the orca chair to my left, and Toast to Sal's left. Greetings are exchanged and Sal immediately shares a joke that lacks political correctness. As the two boys laugh, I turn to Fiona.

"You disappeared the other day." Fiona is wearing a one-piece swimsuit that doesn't reveal much. It is rather conservative. In fact for southern Florida, it's the equivalent of a burqa from one of those *stan* countries. Still, she looks stunning.

"Two's company, three's a crowd," she says. "I thought I should leave in case you wanted to bring your mermaid up to the house."

"I assure you, I don't know that woman. She came ashore rambling about building my house and needing money for a breast augmentation."

"Uh-huh. You're telling me a woman you don't know just appears and drops her rather large cantaloupes in your hands? You must be one special guy," she says, smiling.

Damn Decker woman. "It was *one* cantaloupe in *one* hand."

Fiona touches my knee. The jolt returns. "Relax, I found it hilarious. I was watching from the deck when she grabbed your hand. I've never seen a man pull away from a breast as fast as you did," she says with a giggle.

Sal leans over. "What's so funny?"

Detour. No need to share Fiona's visit. "What are you reading there, Sal?"

He lifts the book. "It's called *Hangman*. I sent away for it thinking it was filled with them hangman games. Instead, it's a book, book."

"No pictures?" I ask.

"No fucking pictures, or games, or nooses. Nothing to hang. So I have to start reading it 'cause they won't take it back."

I shake my head in sympathy. "Imagine, you buy a book and end up having to read it? What the fuck is wrong with this world?" I find myself slipping easily into a vocabulary of expletives in the company of Sal. Drinkers keep company with other drinkers; profanity mongers keep company with other profanity mongers.

Sal nods and tucks the book back in the sand.

As much as I want to turn my attention back to Fiona, I am curious to see if Sal has seen or heard of the latest news about the Mafia war in his home state. I open my laptop, shake off my nerves, and take a deep breath.

"Hey, Sal, check this out." I scroll down to the story and start paraphrasing. "Sounds like the Mafia war spread from your state into mine. The cops found a body in a motel room in Plainville, Massachusetts. The guy, a reputed mobster, was murdered execution style. The article reads two bullets to the head." I turn to Sal for a reaction. He seems to be ignoring me. I continue reading.

"The body was identified as Joseph Di Matteo, aka Joey 'The Nose,' aka Joey 'Ravioli,' aka Joey 'Banana Nose,' a capo working for the Raymond 'Junior' Gulioti crew out of Providence, Rhode Island."

I turn to Sal again. "Don't you just love these Mafia names?" I ask, smiling.

Sal remains impassive, staring instead at the sunset. A tic appears on his face, and then another. *Is he apprehensive about something? Did I strike a nerve? Maybe his music business is in danger?*

"The article goes on to report that the violence is related to what authorities feel was a hit gone bad, several months earlier, on Gulioti's only son. Since then, several different families, stretching from New Jersey to Rhode Island, have gone to war in retribution resulting in the execution-style murders of eleven men. The FBI crime task force has become involved and is looking for several characters of interest, one being Angelo Triscaro, aka 'Angie T,' and another, Salvatore Scalise, aka Sally 'Two Scales' Scalise."

I pause here as a troubling thought takes shape. *Could Salvatore Scalise be sitting next to me? Holy Shit! What are the odds?* I continue reading.

"Both men have been known to associate with the crime factions in Rhode Island and their names surfaced during FBI investigations. 'With everything that is going on, I'm not sure these guys are even still alive,' said one FBI agent speaking on the condition of anonymity."

I try to rationalize that Salvatore is a common name, but my PMS is in full throttle as the man next to me seemingly morphs into a Tony Soprano type. To mask my uneasiness as my imagination runs amok, I try to lighten the moment with Sal.

"That's a lot of a-k-a's, and one has the same first name as you, Sal," I say.

"It's a popular fucking name," Sal mumbles.

I take a deep breath and look at Fiona to see if she shares in my uneasiness. She has a wry smile on her face and I'm guessing she is imagining her breast in my hand. Hey, I can dream.

"I like your laptop," she says, changing subjects. "Is it the new Panasonic?"

I close the computer, never to report the news again. I am relieved to step away from the topic of mobsters. Even though Sal looks the part, as I am known to profile, there is no way he could be associated with the mob. How could I possibly move to a deserted island and end up next to a Mafia guy wanted by the FBI? It sounds implausible in my mind, but my PMS continues to pulsate. I turn to Fiona.

"It is. I bought it before I moved down here. I hated giving up my old one because it used to go down on me all the time."

After a moment, Fiona laughs, her hand covers her mouth. I like a woman with a sense of humor. Toast lets out a geek giggle like the ones people type in e-mails: hee-hee. Sal is unmoved. Something definitely seems wrong with him. *Is he mad at me? Did I insinuate something when I read the article aloud?* I hope he is just a normal guy in charge of a music business. If I did say something to upset him, I will apologize and buy him a real Hangman puzzle game book. In the meantime, my curiosity with the men in black prompts my next inquiry.

"Hey Sal, do you have an entourage hanging around the island? Like maybe a couple of guys in the music business looking for talent down here?"

He turns to me. "What the fuck you talking about?"

"I've noticed a couple of dudes hanging around Two Palms Marina and out on the gulf, too. Rumor has it they're visiting someone on the island. Each time I see them, they're dressed in black T-shirts, black pants, and a black cap in this fucking heat." Not unlike your black knee socks, but I don't let that escape my mouth.

"No fucking clue," Sal replies.

"Okay, just thought I'd fucking ask," I say.

I turn my attention to the gulf to see if the black-clad, Johnny Cash wannabes are looking back. I can't find them.

We sit quiet for a while as the sun continues to set. I can hear music from a few boats offshore. Conversations are carried onshore with the breeze. If I were alone I would take pleasure in the solitude, but with three other people in close quarters, it becomes uncomfortably silent. Sal seems distracted since I gave him the update from his home state. Maybe he is troubled by the thought of returning. Living on Sand Key can certainly make going home a depressing thought, especially if he found himself embroiled in a Mafia conflict. I wonder if the Mafia has their hands in his music business like they do with waste collection and construction. If so, Sal has reason for concern, as do I should trouble come ashore on Sand Key.

I want to break the silence with Fiona by asking her out to dinner. I need to know if her overtures have any validity. I am having a hard time thinking this beautiful woman has eyes for me, but the heat can have a strange effect on people. If Sand Key survived a nuclear holocaust, instigated by someone who sent poop to North Korea, and her choice was limited to Sal, Toast, or me, I'm confident Fiona would take up residency with me. But I don't want to discuss a personal relationship with her while these two guys are within earshot. Instead, I speak over the din of nature and address Toast.

"So tell me, Toast, what brings you to the island?"

Normally Sal would answer any questions asked to anyone, but not this time.

The wiry Frenchman sits up in his chair. "My business allows me to enjoy the magnificent beauty of this moment for several months a year. I like to rent off-season, like Sal here, to avoid the crowds so I can become one with nature." He spreads his arms. "There is no better place that soothes the eyes and cradles the senses."

He sounds like a commercial. "Yeah, I live here, too. What do you do for a living?"

"I write romantic passages for greeting cards. American women love the French flavor for words. The beauty is I can write here on Sand Key, or create my sentimental expressions from a loft in New York City. I just hope Bush and his band of bandits fail in their attempt to ruin what we share here."

"Yeah, I'm sure George Dubya is formulating a plan back at the ranch to destroy Sand Key. Him and Cheney."

"And Rumsfeld, too," Toast adds. "There are many neoconservatives bent on running your country. They understand that by poisoning the gulf and oceans with oil, people will cocoon because the oil will be rationed and too expensive and nature will no longer be inviting."

I don't like Toast. I don't like the French. I was good with the name change to Freedom Fries. People with outlandish philosophies and outrageous conspiracy theories make me want to barf. They're akin to the dangerous religious zealots on the right. I vote we jettison Toast off the island now. *Hands?* I put my arm in the air again for effect. Toast thinks I'm seeking permission to speak.

"Yes, *mon ami*?"

I'm about to engage in what would be a moronic debate with him when Fiona comes to my rescue.

"Aubert, can you give us an example of your writing?"

Sal moans. It is the first mutter we've heard from him in over thirty minutes.

Excited, Toast lifts out of his chair. "This is from a selection of messages I recently had published."

He clears his throat and takes several deep breaths as if he is getting ready to narrate to the world the medical procedure for curing cancer. *Drama queen.*

"My love, like the wings of a bird, drifted through life without purpose until I found safe harbor in the arms of a beautiful woman. And that woman is you."

He stands there expecting an ovation.

"That's so romantic, Aubert. Well done," Fiona says.

"Here's another."

I roll my eyes.

"My love for you is placed not in my heart, for hearts can break, but rather in a circle because circles go on forever."

Fiona purrs and then applauds.

"So you're the twit who writes all the crap regular guys would never say?" I say, rhetorically.

"What is this *twit*. Is it done with a phone?" Toast inquires.

"One more, Aubert," Fiona pleads.

Sal lets out a fart that pushes his orca chair another six inches into the sand. I look at him, flabbergasted, but he continues to stare out into the gulf, his cigar smoked to a soggy nub. Here I sit with a squaw, a free-farting, tough-guy, possible Mafia-guy-type music producer, and a sappy, obnoxious, French greeting-card writer. I feel like I am the only normal one sitting at the Chalmun's Cantina in Mos Eisley. All that is missing is Megan dressed in a Chewbacca outfit.

When the air clears around Sal, Toast offers another gem.

"There is no age too young for love, because love doesn't come from your mind, which knows your age, but from your heart, which knows no age."

What? Even Fiona has trouble with this one. "Will I find that card in the pedophile section?" I ask. Fiona punches my arm.

Toast, happy with his performance, twirls in the sand and reclaims his seat. The sun has thankfully set, and the boats start heading inland. I search for anyone dressed in black, but find no one. Maybe they went back to Philadelphia for a cheese steak.

"Hey, I almost forgot. Tomorrow we'll be joined by my new friend, Montana. He's a real cool character. I think you guys will like him."

"Great. I look forward to meeting him," Fiona says.

"The more the merrier," Toast adds.

We watch in silence as the remaining boats disperse. Sal is the first to call it a night and lifts out of his seat. From nowhere he proclaims, "I wanna go fishing."

I point to the gulf. "There's the water."

"I wanna go fishing 'cause I've been putting it off too long."

"Well, you own a boat, and there's plenty of fish. I even got some bait for you," I say, as I lift Harry's bag of minnows. "What else do you need?"

"You," Sal says, chomping on his unlit cigar.

"Me?" I'm reminded of poor Murray and the tarpon takedown. "Why me? What about Toast?"

"He can't swim."

I look at Toast and he nods in agreement. *Off with your head, Frenchie.*

"What about . . ." I turn to Fiona and she is already giving me the stink eye. With my thoughts of mobsters and Sal's possible connection, I'm hesitant to be alone with him. On the other hand, this could be one of those "offers you can't refuse" deals. If I decline his invitation, I may piss him off, and this island is too small to have a Mafia/music producer annoyed with me. "Fine, Sal, I'll be happy to go fishing with you."

The big man grunts. He grabs his unread *Hangman* book and proceeds to leave. Toast jumps up to follow. Fiona rises to join them, but not before she brushes by me and plants a kiss on my cheek.

"Stop that!" I say.

She smiles and blows a second kiss.

"Listen, because of you I'm already seeking medical attention for that four-hour thingamajig in my pants."

"Maybe I can fix that," she says, raising her eyebrows while raising my hopes. She giggles and then turns to catch up with Abbott and Costello.

I watch as the three of them round the bend and disappear. Fiona does not look back. I've heard if a woman looks back one last time before she climbs into a car, or goes into her house, or rounds the bend on a beach, it is a tell on how interested she is. I waver between excitement and disappointment. There is no doubt she knows how to flirt, but I need some sort of confirmation. At this point, I'd accept smoke signals from her teepee if they were clear enough about her intentions.

I slump into the beach chair. Dust to dark is enveloping the area like a fog bank drifting onshore. I'm left to the soothing sounds of small waves slapping against the sand. A gentle breeze caresses the evening heat. My thoughts swing like a pendulum between my interest in Fiona and my anxiety over Sal. The no-see-um bugs hover above waiting for the right moment to attack. I hear the whooshing sound as Harry drops anchor.

"Hey, Harry. You still mad at me?"

He turns away and looks out to the gulf. Something tells me Harry might be a Harriet.

"Look what I have for you." I open the bag and toss him a minnow. He edges closer. All seems forgiven. We are friends again.

It is when I toss him a second minnow that I notice the red laser dot dancing on my arm.

CHAPTER FIFTEEN

Island Litter

"Knowledge is knowing a tomato is a fruit; wisdom is
not putting it in a fruit salad."

—MILES KINGTON

My first instinct is to slap at it, as if it is some kind of exotic
insect that has already sucked in so much of my blood, it looks
like it has been dipped in red dye. My second instinct, born from
my extensive library of crime movies, is to hit the deck.

I fall to the sand in one quick motion and try to find refuge
beneath a beach chair, as if the flimsy sand seat will repel bullets.
My sudden dive frightens Harry, prompting him to take flight.
Whoever is targeting me, I wish for them to leave Harry be.
Thankfully, the heron escapes without injury.

I wait. My heart races. Nervousness and humidity cause me
to sweat. The sand I retreat to adheres to my body like a million
leeches. My position is clearly vulnerable on the beach as I lie
with only a laptop propped in front of my head. Where is my
smartiephone when I need it?

I try to assimilate the reasons why someone would target me.
*Is it jealousy over winning the lottery? Have I already made enemies
during my short time in Florida?* I think of Memphis the Lighthouse
or even the Decker woman. It doesn't take much to push some
people over the edge. *Could it be something to do with Sal?* But Sal
has already left the scene. Somebody is messing with me, and that
makes me panic-stricken. I can't find a reasonable explanation for
my predicament, and I can't reconcile why someone would find
cause to assassinate a hermit in training.

I peer over the laptop in the direction I feel the laser origi-nated. Darkness envelops the area. A red laser would be easy to pick out. To the right of my house is a modicum of dune grass and buttonwood shrubs that grow steadily in height along Gulf Boulevard until the foliage melds into the bird sanctuary. It offers an excellent vantage point for someone with a gun and a vendetta. *Why is this happening to me?*

Unless one of my neighbors from the southern end of Gulf Boulevard has reason to venture out into the evening in their golf cart, the shooter could keep me pinned down as long as needed. I resort to mental telepathy to make my smartiephone, which is resting comfortably on the kitchen counter, call 9-1-1.

I consider powering the laptop, but on an ink-dark beach the illuminated screen would reveal my position like a bonfire. I try to focus on the shrubs looking for gaps where someone could be aiming from, but the darkness has turned the landscape into one black blur. No red dots appear.

I can't stay here all night. It's time to see if I am facing a gun, or some mischievous, soon-to-be-dead kids from the mainland. If this is a juvenile prankster with a laser beam, I will bury him alive on my not-yet-neighbor's property.

I maneuver the laptop down to my side and lift it into the air. No red dots appear. I put the laptop down and roll over to the rake. I leverage it under a beach chair, and then lift the chair into the air from my prone position. Still, no red dots. Satisfied, I relax. I wait another five minutes then grab the laptop, the bag of minnows, and the rake, and proceed to crawl in the direction of the walkover. As I do, I drag the rake behind me to make sure I leave the beach sand immaculate. I am a perfectionist, even in the face of death.

At the walkover, I dart across until I reach the house. Once inside, I grab the smartiephone, punch in 9-1-1, and slump to the floor.

"Englewood Police Department."

"I'd like to report a laser beam."

"Come again?"

"Someone was pointing a red laser at me like from a gun."

"Did you see the gun?"

"No, it was too dark."

"Did you see the person?"

"Still too dark."

"But you're sure it was a laser beam from a gun?"

"Hey, I've seen my fair share of movies where the bad guys use lasers to aim."

"Have you seen your fair share of kids using these devices to cause mayhem?"

Hmm. The other possibility. "I suppose it could've been kids." This realization seems to calm me.

The officer asks for my name and address to report the incident. I answer, wishing I had seriously considered other possibilities before calling.

"What number Gulf Boulevard?"

Good question. "I don't have a number. I'm out here on Sand Key. North end."

"Do you feel you're in immediate danger?"

I assess the situation. "Not now, officer."

He puts me on hold. By this time, I just want to hang up. It had to be kids, right? This is paradise. Mafia types, killers, or people with bad tempers don't reside in paradise. I feel embarrassed wasting the officer's time. He comes back on the line. "I'm sending a boat out to check the area. Did the laser come from the Intracoastal Waterway side or the gulf side?"

"Intracoastal. I was on the beach facing my house when I noticed it on me."

"All right. We'll have an officer out there to take a look. In the meantime, stay inside for the rest of the evening. Some kids like to take their Jet Skis out to the barrier islands and cause mischief, Mr. Na-gyration."

"Najarian."

"Right. I'm sure that's all it is. If you need further assistance, call back."

"Thank you, officer."

I'm sure the police are right. Some kids probably pulled up to the docks while our foursome sat watching the sunset. When it was dark enough, they had a few laughs by targeting me with a laser pointer. Just kids having fun.

For the first time since moving in, I lock all the doors.

∽

THE NEXT morning, after a restless sleep, I head downstairs to work out before my meeting with Caprice and Montana at the boat condo. I've been doing my weight-lifting exercises for six days, one day on and one day off, but I still look the same in the mirror. *Why is it taking so long?* It's the seventh morning of reps and treads, and the result is still a lack of breath and excruciating pain. I limp over to the kitchen, grab a muffin, and wash it down with orange juice. I gather up the keys and head out.

Another gorgeous summer morning embraces me on the deck. All I can hear are songbirds and a gentle breeze filtering through the trees. Instead of going directly to the dock, curiosity guides me to the row of bushes and palms where I guess the red laser beam originated. I stand over the flora and look down the beach at the four chairs. This has to be the spot, yet nothing seems out of the ordinary. No broken branches or cigarette butts. No footprints in the sand. I shrug my shoulders.

I resume my pace to the dock and step aboard the *Ticket to Ride*. Whoever played laser tag last night left my boat intact. Good thing, because you should never mess with a man's boat. I power up the engines and ease into reverse. Once I clear the dock, I push the throttle just beyond idle and set course for the slow ride out to the Intracoastal Waterway.

I notice the calmness of the incoming tide. Birds dart playfully from one tree to another. Fish jump out of the water for a few seconds to dry off. Everything is as nature intended, so it is easy for me to instantly notice the distraction of a candy wrapper floating in the water near the mangrove roots next to my dock. I drift over, reach out with a pole and remove the litter. *Kids.*

∽

I PULL into the boat condo and see the bird van parked in the visitor's lot beyond the security gate. It is hard to miss with its colorful vehicle wrap of parrots and palm trees advertising Talking Feathers. When Caprice sees me securing the boat, she slides open a side door and brings out a large bamboo cage with an African Grey parrot perched inside. She joins me on the dock and we exchange greetings. Montana appears irritable, moving back and forth on his perch.

"Why's he pacing?" I ask Caprice.

"It's just nerves. Greys are inquisitive, yet sensitive birds. Right now he's out of his element and that causes him to be a little flustered. You'll notice a quick change once we find a suitable location in your home that offers him stimulation and security."

Caprice is a wealth of information with regard to parrots, as she should be, so I start peppering her with questions about care, feeding, and bonding. I want Montana to be a happy hermit parrot so he will someday speak the words I can't, like, "Hey Brad, stop picking your toes."

We board the boat and secure the cage to a seat. Although southern Florida has a multitude of barrier islands, this is Caprice's first adoption off the mainland. The whole concept of boating to get home intrigues her. I power up the *Ticket to Ride* and tap the throttle into reverse.

"I love your boat," Caprice says.

"Thanks." I point to the overhead arch. "I bought this for Montana so he would have a perch to sing pirate songs from as we cruise the gulf. Yo ho, yo ho, a pirate's life for me."

Caprice laughs. "He wouldn't last very long up there, even at a moderate speed. You're a funny guy, Jason. You *are* kidding, right?"

Not really. "Of course."

Caprice sits next to the cage as I maneuver out from the condo canal toward the Intracoastal Waterway. I'm disappointed at the realization that Montana will never sit atop the arch and parrot pirate songs with me. I never envisioned a moderate headwind turning him into a feathered Ferris wheel, or even blowing him off the arch like a hat from my head. *Bummer.* The arch was a waste of money. Another instance where I didn't think things through.

A tapping noise catches my attention as I approach the end of the canal. I know nothing about the inner workings of a boat, so I look around the deck for objects left unsecured. Everything seems tight. The noise stops.

"Why did you name the boat *Ticket to Ride?*"

"I'm a Beatles fan." White lies save time.

Caprice smiles. "Me, too."

I push the throttle forward and raise the bow.

"How far is it to your home?" she calls out.

"Twenty minutes, cruising speed. Less if I open her up."

The noise returns. A steady drumming.

"Take your time. This is fantastic."

I bring the bow back down and shift into idle. I'm determined to find the source of the rattle. I leave the helm and follow the racket to the stern near the engine area. As soon as I arrive, the noise stops.

"Is something wrong?" Caprice asks.

The noise starts again. It is coming from the seat shared by Caprice and Montana. "Do you hear that noise?" I ask. "Sounds like its coming from around here."

The drumming stops.

Caprice looks around. She stands up, checks her seat, checks the cage, and sits down. "What noise?"

"Like a knocking noise," I say.

"Oh, maybe you're hearing Montana," she says. "He makes this repetitive sound when he's nervous or feels threatened."

On cue the bird starts spitting out a tat-tat-tat noise.

I point at the bird. "That's it. What's he mimicking, the engine or something?"

"Well, taking into consideration his upbringing, I don't think he cares about the engine noise. My guess is Montana is shooting us with a machine gun."

<hr>

AFTER A tour of the house, Caprice selects a corner of the open-air living room that offers a view of the gulf to the west, and a view to the flat-screen television to the east. We situate the cage on an end table until later when I will install hooks in the ceiling beams so that Montana and his habitat can hang like a wind chime. Caprice is happy. I am happy. Montana remains pissed.

I insert the *Best of The Three Stooges* DVD, Volume One, into the entertainment system to keep Montana entertained while I escort his former keeper back to the mainland. At the front door, the bird lets out a squeal of .223 caliber-sounding rounds from an imaginary M-16 assault rifle that sprays the walls and door, and instantly kills Caprice and me. I look at the bird and see he is bopping his head from side to side as if to declare, "Yeah, I'm bad."

Caprice turns to me and says with a smile, "Have patience."

I drop Caprice back at her van and promise to give her a weekly update on Montana's progress. I add if she doesn't hear from me in any given week, she should come by the house just in case Montana switched to live ammunition.

After leaving her, I drive into town, do my weekly food shopping, and satisfy my list of hardware needs. I stop in at the bank to grab some cash and get my monthly ass-kiss from the branch manager—a million dollar checking account pays more than simple interest—and then I stop in at Gulf Breeze Realty to say hello to Phyllis. After a few hugs, she morphs into The Hammer.

"So what do you want, I'm busy here," she says, lifting her glasses while reclaiming the seat behind the desk.

"A friend . . . well, really an acquaintance . . . or better yet a neighbor . . ."

"Jason, shut up and talk to me."

"Okay, a guy I know asked me to go fishing with him. I don't have any gear, so I was wondering if I could borrow one of your husband's fishing rods for the day."

The Hammer lowers her glasses and gazes beyond me for a moment. "We never found the really expensive one he bought."

"Oh. I thought Murray had others."

The Hammer returns her focus back to me. "He does, but after the golf club debacle, I promised I'd ask him first before loaning out his stuff."

"You're asking your dead husband?"

"Yes, my dead husband. Murray is real particular about his toys. If I let you use the fishing rod without getting permission, he'll arrange for you to hook a great white shark so large and ornery, it'll swallow your boat whole. Then what? I'm left trying to sell your house again to a flock of annoying snowbirds. Catch my drift?"

I nod, reluctantly.

"I'll call you later after I talk with him," she says with a wink.

Did I move to Hermitville, or did I take a wrong turn and end up in Weirdville? This is a valid question I ask myself as I cruise south on the Intracoastal Waterway. My next stop is Two Palms Marina for fuel. If I am indeed stuck in Weirdville, Memphis the Lighthouse is the mayor.

I drift close to the Texaco pumps, hand the attendant my credit card, and ask the young man to fill the tank. I then jump onto the cement dock and head to the store in search of advice on what kind of bait to use, even though I have no clue what Sal and I will be fishing for. Seeing that Sal is taking me out in his boat, the least I can do is buy the bait. The woman behind the counter suggests shrimp and goes into detail on how to hook them. She explains the best way to keep shrimp bait fresh all day and what kind of fish I can expect to attract. I'm fascinated until I feel a presence behind me. I turn slowly to see Memphis, hands on his hips, same headlight dangling from his neck, same oil-stained overalls. *Why is he always sneaking up on me?*

"Yous guts someone pissin' in yous boat," he says, devoid of the normal antagonistic tone he usually reserves for me.

"What?" I reply, my defenses alert. First, I don't understand him, and second, I don't trust him.

"I says, yous guts a guy pissin' in yous boat. Two guys with dem girly type shirts. Das headed out by now," he says turning away. "I has the boy hose it down, 'cause dat ain't right what dey dun."

I stand by the counter for a few seconds looking at the woman for a translation. "Did he just say someone was peeing in my boat?"

"I think so," she says, nodding.

I thank the woman for the bait education and hurry back to the *Ticket*. Sure enough the fuel pump boy is standing in my boat, holding a water hose, and rinsing the deck.

"What's going on? Did you spill fuel?"

"No sir," the teenager replies. "I'm sorry, real sorry."

"Tell me what happened," I say, climbing into the boat.

"Two guys walked up as I was fueling her. They talked in like a different language all laughing and stuff. Then one guy whips out his dick and starts pissing all over your groceries and seats. There was nothing I could do while holding the fuel nozzle, mister. When they were done, they got in one of our rental boats and headed out."

I am infuriated. "What did they look like?" I ask, powering up the boat.

"Flowery shirts, shades, I've seen them around here before, except they're usually dressed all in black."

I stare at the kid. *The men in black? What did they want with me?* It was time to find out.

"Get out of the boat, kid." I coil the hose and fling it onto the pier. I step behind the wheel and hear something crunch beneath my sandal. I reach down and find a candy bar wrapper. Pressing it into a ball, I toss it on the dock.

"Don't leave your garbage on my boat," I say.

"I didn't mister. One of the guys threw it in there."

I think for a moment. I fish from my pocket the wrapper I snagged earlier from my lagoon and toss it at the kid. "Are those two wrappers the same?"

The kid unfurls each one and says, "I can't tell."

I push forward on the throttle and speed through the no-wake zone, leaving waves crashing against the cement barriers. When I reach the end of the canal, I slow my approach into the Intra-coastal Waterway. There are about a dozen boats heading in different directions. I latch on to one heading south and push full throttle.

As I get closer, I can see two men in Hawaiian-type flowery shirts. One is at the helm while the other holds on to the railing on the port side. Both are focused south and have no reason to anticipate my approach. We pass the inlet to Hermitville lagoon as I gain on them.

When I reach their wake, the guy from the port side happens to turn and notice me. He immediately pushes on the arm of the man behind the wheel to get his attention. He thumbs in my direction. Both men stare back at me. I give them the finger.

Their boat slows and I'm able to approach carefully on the port side. We idle together in the middle of the waterway, not more than ten feet apart. Both men look at me while conversing in what sounds like Italian. They chuckle while giving me the finger. I give it back again. We are having a finger-off.

"You guys piss in my boat?"

The taller one spreads his arms. "Hey, how you say . . . not having a pot to piss in, *si?* So I used your boat." Both men bend over laughing at this.

I grab my grocery bag and pull out a container of six vine-ripened tomatoes I originally planned to use in a few salads. The first one I toss splits the two men and smashes into the star-board gunwale. On my second toss, I aim for the tall guy, but he ducks and the tomato splatters all over the helm. Both men continue to laugh at my assault. The next toss hits the shorter guy in the middle of his back as he turns to avoid my red grenade. This prompts the taller guy to laugh even louder as he points at the shorter guy with the splattered tomato dripping down his flowery shirt.

I am frustrated my efforts for revenge have turned into a carnival act. Here I am in the middle of the Intracoastal Waterway under the midday heat, tossing tomatoes at two guidos who, for some reason, have a bug up their ass for me. I grip another tomato, soften it with a squeeze and hurl it toward the taller guy's face.

Smash.

The laughter halts. It is a direct hit. Tomato puree slides down the man's face. Chunks are lodged in his nose, mouth, and shirt pocket. It appears I'm in trouble now. Maybe my bravado wasn't such a good idea after all.

The shorter guy starts laughing until the taller guy removes his sunglasses and stares him down with a vicious gaze. Slowly, he wipes the mess from his face and flips it overboard.

"*Vaffanculo,*" he says pointing at me. With his other hand, he reaches into a duffle bag stowed under a seat cushion and removes the largest freakin' handgun I've ever seen.

CHAPTER SIXTEEN

Island Quandaries

"What happens if you get scared half to death twice?"
—STEVEN WRIGHT

But the massive gun is without a clip. While the tall guy roots in the duffle bag in search of my cause of death, I toss another beefsteak at him. He leans to one side, off balance, the gun in one hand, the found clip in the other, to avoid another tomato pasting. In the few seconds he is too wobbly to load the handgun, I manage to push the throttle forward and then fall to the deck.

The *Ticket to Ride* lurches out of the water, bow rising up, engines screaming, before she levels off as the hull slaps against the water. The boat is flying, literally going airborne off the slightest wave. If anyone is watching, it must look like the largest remote-controlled boat ever, because no one is standing at the helm. The captain is out of sight, flat on his belly, in fear of the business end of a gun for the second time in twenty-four hours.

I lift my head high enough to see the other boat in pursuit. The short guy is talking on the phone as he steers the boat. Worried I'm about to dry dock on an island, or ram into on oncoming craft, I peer over the helm to get my bearings. Luckily, the *Ticket* is still within the channel markings heading south. I grip the wheel while glancing over my shoulder. I'm confident I can outrun these guys, but what difference does it make? The candy wrapper suggests they know where I live. Preparing financial reports for Sam Steinberg back at the rope company is sounding pretty good at the moment.

Up ahead is the southern tip of Sand Key, but before I reach it and escape through Gasparilla Sound on my way to the gulf, I pass the ferry landing on my starboard side. On a dock near the launch stand three people waiting to be transferred to the mainland: the friendly woman who delivered a key lime pie to me weeks ago, her crazy mother, and Fiona. The woman smiles and waves as my boat speeds by, but Fiona fails to notice me because she is preoccupied on her phone.

And then my smartiephone starts playing *Right Round* in my pocket. Is Fiona calling me?

I fish it from my pocket and answer the call without looking.

"Hey."

"Hey yourself, *asshole.*"

I pull the phone away to look at the number.

"Megan?"

"Can you hear me now, Jason? That was real cruel what you did to me in California."

"Listen, I can't talk now. I'm being chased by a couple of gun-toting men in a boat."

"Yeah, right. What make-believe celebrity is starring in this bullshit? Are you being chased by Vin . . . *whatever*, the guy with the gasoline name?" Megan asks, sarcastically.

"Diesel. Vin Diesel." I look back at the boat pursuing me and notice it has slowed as it changes course. *Are they headed back to my house?* "How did you get this number, anyway?"

"I asked Mom, who by the way has way more class than you, but she promised not to give out your number. So she suggested I call Dad and guess what? You forgot to include him in your conspiracy. It was a simple process of examination."

"Elimination, Megan." I hate her use of mom and dad as if we are still married.

"Are you threatening me, Jason?"

I'm entering a narrow section of the Intracoastal Waterway at high speed. The distance between lands is so close that one could stand on Sand Key and have a conversation with someone on the mainland. No-wake signs are predominant along the thicket of mangroves on one side, and the cement barriers protecting waterfront homes and docks on the other. I blow right past the marine police boat hiding in a cove.

"No, I'm not threatening you. Look, let's have this conversation another time, right now . . ."

Blue lights reflect off the instrument panel. I turn to see the police closing in on me. I pull back on the throttle.

"Better yet, Jason, I'm gonna find out where you live. Then I'm coming to you and we're gonna live happily ever-fucking-after. You owe me that, because I'm your ex-wife."

The line goes dead. Either she has ended the call or I've just entered into a wonderful cell dead zone where Megan can't reach me. But the cops can. I slow to an idle, allowing the police boat to approach from my port side. We each set out bumpers. The men in black are nowhere in sight.

"Did you see the no-wake signs, sir?" the female officer asks.

All twenty of them? "Yes, but I'm being chased by two men, and one has a gun. They urinated in my boat back at Two Palms Marina, so I chased them down. That's when one of the guys pulled a gun on me."

"Really," she says, nodding her head in sympathy. "Unfortunately for you, I get that story every week. Where are these characters now?" she asks, surveying the waterway.

I point north. "They changed course a few minutes ago."

The officer nods as if she expected my answer. It is followed with a look of disdain—the you're-so-full-of-shit look. "License and registration, please."

I hand over the documents.

She clicks on her pen and starts writing me a ticket. *Who gets written up on the water?* I try pleading my case again. "Officer, I'm telling you the truth. My life is in danger." I gaze beyond the stern wishing the men in black would make an appearance.

"You were speeding through a no-wake zone. It really doesn't matter who, if anyone, was chasing you. I need to see your life vests, sir."

I lift a seat cushion and remove the vests stowed below.

"You should be wearing one, Mr. Na-jarine."

"Najarian."

She hands me the ticket. "A no-wake zone means you reduce your speed so as not to create a wake. Understand? Follow the rules of the waterway for your safety and the safety of other boaters."

I stare at the ticket. "One hundred dollars?" I ask, incredulously.

She pushes off from my boat, lifts her bumpers, and moves away. I can't believe it. I'm out a hundred bucks along with my groceries covered in guido piss.

I cruise just offshore of Sand Key, parallel to the beach, until I reach the four unoccupied beach chairs sitting within a stretch of manicured sand. Hermitville looks lovely from the gulf. I steer toward shore and anchor in about three feet of water.

I spy on my house through a set of binoculars. Nothing seems out of the ordinary. No movement. The afternoon breeze is gentle, the water calm, and the symphony of nature is as clear as if I had on headphones. From where I stand on the *Ticket,* the slap of my spring-loaded screen door, opening or closing, would reverberate like a clap of thunder. I wait.

After thirty minutes, I leap overboard. I make my way past the chairs and through the smooth sand, leaving unsightly footprints along the way. I cross the walkover and climb the stairs to the deck. From the top step I can see the lagoon filtered through the trees. The docks are vacant. I step out of my sandals, shower off the sand, and then enter the house. The Three Stooges are still yucking it up in the entertainment room; Montana seemingly hanging on every word. In need of an upgrade from the tomatoes, I step into the kitchen and grab a knife. Not that a knife would ever win in a gun battle.

On the balls of my feet, I inspect the house, yelling out an all clear in my head after each room is inspected, the result of watching too many cop shows. When I'm done upstairs and the danger is alleviated, I flop on the bed. *Who are these guys? What do they want? Where did they come from?* Instead of throwing tomatoes, I should have asked them their purpose—then throw the tomatoes. I'm frustrated, angry, and fearful. This is not what I expected in my island paradise. Maybe I should enlist the help of others.

I think first of The Hammer. She has connections all over town, plus Phyllis could scare a shark away from chum, but I don't want to call on her just yet. Enlisting Phyllis would be like having my name called out over the public address system to report to the principal's office. My only other option is to share my dilemma with the sunset crew, specifically Sal. I still feel the men in black have a connection to him. My troubles are compounded with the thought of Megan who can't comprehend the *ex* part of ex-wife. I guess it didn't work out with the lifeguard.

I make my way downstairs and walk over to Montana. "Hey, Montana, how goes it? You like the Three Stooges?" He scratches his head and fluffs his feathers. Had he jumped to the bottom of the cage, spun in a circle while saying woo-woo-woo like Curly Howard, it would've brightened my day. Instead, he just looks at me without mimicking a word. At least he isn't shooting me anymore.

I check the docks again, no visitors. Maybe the men in black with flowery shirts had returned to Two Palms Marina to wash off the tomatoes. I hurry out to the beach, rake behind me, footprints erased, and wade out to the *Ticket*. I bring her back through Pirate's Pass, cruise the waterway, and steer back. For the moment my adversaries are nowhere to be found.

I toss the urine-tainted groceries in a green trash bag and store them for a trash run the next day. I follow that with a thorough washing of the *Ticket*. It's too late in the afternoon to make another mainland run just for supper, so I'm left to raid the freezer.

I eat a microwave meal in silence on the lower deck—no television, no music. Montana is perched next to me in his cage. I try to alleviate my concerns by talking to the bird, but he just offers back a blank stare. I open the laptop and catch up with the latest news. On the front page of the *Boston Herald*, cautious optimism is abound after the broken well in the gulf is finally capped. I stare out into the gulf, thankful the currents didn't drag the sludge to my paradise. When I notice Sal, Toast, and Fiona appear at the bend, I grab the cage to join them.

"Isn't he the cutest," Fiona gushes. "What's his name?"

"Montana," I say. "Usually, it serves as his key word to talk, but so far no luck."

Toast starts tapping on the cage. It annoys me and I'm sure it annoys the bird. "Hey, Toast, don't do that. What if I came over to your house and started banging on the walls?"

"Parrots are supposed to talk, *mon ami*. Maybe he's a mute? Have you heard him speak?"

"Yes, of course. It's why I bought him. He supposedly knows all the quotes from the movie *Scarface.*"

"No fucking shit?" Sal injects.

"Fucking shit," I reply. *Who's the parrot now?* I look at the bird to see if the sound of his favorite words might inspire a few syllables, but he remains tight-beaked. Montana seems to have an affinity for Sal as he edges closer to him. Birds of a feather . . . I guess.

"He's so handsome, I don't care if he can talk," Fiona purrs in baby talk.

"He can talk," I say, somewhat defensively.

"I think you got taken, Jason," Toast boasts, while reclaiming his seat. I look over at him and picture my fist in his face.

Sal leans closer to the cage, "Hey, Montana, show me your little friend."

Montana turns his head, eyes wide, eager to listen. This has Sal laughing. "Too bad he can't fucking talk."

"He can fucking talk," I insist. *Christ!*

After a few minutes, the interest in Montana wanes and the subject of our nightly rendezvous takes center stage. The sunset is filtered by a thread of clouds, which creates all kinds of red and orange shades. It is simply spectacular.

"So what's newsworthy since we last got together?" Fiona asks the group.

"I just read that BP capped the well. The oil flowing into the gulf has stopped," I report.

"Finally, some good news. We lucked out here," she replies.

"Don't hold your breath," Toast warns. "Bush and his oil company buddies will knock that cap off as soon as they can get down there. They need to keep the price of oil artificially high."

"Aubert, that seems a little absurd," Fiona says.

I'm a little blunter. "Toast, you're so full of shit that even if you had a *grande Frenchie* enema right here, you'd still be full of shit."

"Thanks for that visual, Jason," Fiona complains.

I notice Sal's mass jiggle with amusement.

Toast puts his hands up, then points to himself. "Remember where you heard it first."

We sit in silence for a while. Fiona reaches for my hand and holds it. I just can't figure out this woman. The sun is almost set when I finally work up the nerve to share the day's events.

"Somebody is trying to kill me," I blurt out.

Fiona starts laughing. Sal looks at me with a scowl. Toast appears hopeful.

"What the fuck you say?" Sal asks.

I start spitting out what transpired beginning with the laser beam attack the previous night. I mention the men in black, even though they switched to flowery shirts. When I get to the part about them urinating in my boat at Two Palms Marina, Fiona laughs again. I don't think it is funny. I let go of her hand.

I go on to describe the boat chase, the tomato paste, and the cannon that was pointed at my face.

"I don't think the tomato thing was very smart," Fiona advises. "These guys were probably just messing with you. I doubt they meant any harm."

Fiona's lack of empathy is irritating to me. I turn to Sal. "What do you think, Sal?"

The big man adjusts his bulk in the chair. "You got gambling debts?"

"None."

"You owe anybody money?"

"No."

"You banging someone else's broad?"

"No. I'm a hermit here."

"A hermit *crab* if you ask me," Toast mumbles.

My fist is inching closer to his face.

"I don't know what the fuck then," Sal says, resigned. "It seems these guys want your ass for something."

I lean back in my chair. "You sure these guys aren't associated with you in some capacity?"

Sal turns his weight toward me. His sudden move reminds me of a spooked elephant I had seen on an *Animal Planet* episode.

"Associated with me? Are you fucking right in the head, Trust Fund? What makes you think your friends have anything to do with me?"

I want to delve into my profile mode and mention the similar black clothes, or the Italian references, but I refrain. A spooked elephant is not as dangerous as a mad elephant on a stampede.

"Nothing does, Sal. I was hopeful these guys were part of your music empire, like an entourage, but I guess not. Hey, maybe these two are the missing Mafia men the FBI is looking for. What if they are down here to take someone out?"

No one comments on my inquiry. Instead, I've apparently sent each of them into a stupor. Sal is staring out into the gulf, Fiona is staring down at the sand, and Toast is staring at something he found while flossing. My words were meant as a joke, but apparently received as an option.

Finally, after deliberating for several minutes, Sal breaks the silence. "Do me a favor," he says, attempting to lift out from the chair. "You see these guys coming at you with hardware, tell me so I can get the fuck out of the way."

"So, I guess I should call the cops," I say.

Fiona grips my arm and chimes in. "Jason, you don't want to do that. Bad idea. Just lay low and this will blow over. These guys are probably local thugs. You bring the police in and tell them about urine and tomatoes . . . you'll end up sounding crazy."

I recall how the boat cop looked at me with skepticism.

"And maybe piss these guys off even more," Sal adds. "Next time they take a dump in your boat." Sal's warning causes Toast to laugh and I fantasize how much damage I can do to him with a floss stick.

Sal points at me and says, "Tomorrow, you ain't got no problems 'cause we'll be out fishing." He then turns to Toast and lightly slaps the Frenchman's head. "Let's go before these fuckin' bugs take me for a three-course meal."

Fiona stands up. She takes my hand again and looks into my eyes. "Be cool, okay?" She leans in and kisses my cheek. I want to sweep her off her feet and take her back to the house. She'd look great lying next to me in bed.

She squats down in front of the cage. "Bye, bye, Montana, you handsome boy." She pops back up, waves at me, and skips a few paces to join the other two for the walk back to the southern end of Gulf Boulevard. I watch as they retreat down the beach. Fiona never looks back.

After the sunset crew turns beyond the bend, I expect an incursion of red laser beams to cover my body like the stars emerging in the ceiling above me. I am overwhelmed with a wave of paranoia. *Is someone after me? Is someone after Sal? Are the men in black the Mafia guys I joked about?* To add to my increasing anxiety is the mistake I made in agreeing to go fishing with Sal. Maybe if I gouge myself on the remaining fake lobster tails, I can come down with food poisoning and avoid my alone time with Sal.

I start to pack up for the safety of my home when Harry swoops down. The heron looks at Montana. Montana returns the gaze.

"You birds wanna play poker?"

The heron takes a few steps forward to inspect the feathered beast in the cage. When Harry is too close for comfort, Montana pulls out his gun and starts shooting.

Startled by the sound, Harry stumbles back, spreads his wings and takes flight.

"*Pelican, fly. Come on Pelican,*" Montana squawks.

I raise my arms in the air. "He talks!" I walk several paces in the direction of my departed guests and bellow, "My bird talks!"

Rather than continue my conversation with a deserted beach, I lift the cage, the rake, and head back to the house. No red dots appear, but why tempt fate?

Back in the house, I place Montana's habitat on the end table. A few sunflower seeds follow as a token of my appreciation for his vocal outburst. I walk into the kitchen.

A shadow.

Pain.

Black.

CHAPTER SEVENTEEN

Island Sympathy

"There's a fine line between cuddling and holding someone down so they can't get away."
—AUTHOR UNKNOWN

Somewhere in the vague distance I hear my name. A female voice calls out to me. She is getting closer and louder like the whistle of an approaching locomotive. Occupying a seat next to her is a dark cloud of pain in the shape of my face. The train is traveling at a high speed when the engineer suddenly slams on the brakes in the middle of my kitchen.

"Jason." She hovers over me. Close to my face. Dabbing me with something wet. *Is she the naked lady on the turtle?*

"Jason. Jason, I'm here for you. What the hell happened?"

My eyelids lift slightly and a flood of artificial light pours in. I can't feel half my face.

"That's it, Jason. Look at me."

Dark hair. Four eyes, two noses. A few blinks, a reset, and her face comes into focus. Fiona. And then the pain arrives at the station. "Fuck me," I moan. Part of my impish mind wonders if she might take my first words as an invitation.

"Did you walk into a wall or what?" she asks, brushing my hair with her hand. She is sitting on the floor beside me, my head on her lap. Her other hand grips a facecloth spotted with blood.

"My face hurts. It's numb."

"You have a bloody nose, but I think it's still in one piece. You also have a fat lip and some puffiness under your eye. Does it hurt when I touch you?"

I nod. "Was I robbed?"

Fiona looks around. "I can still see the juice glasses," she says, smiling. She helps me lean against the wall, then walks around and takes a quick inventory of the first floor. "Nothing I can see is missing. Montana is safe. All your electronics are where they should be. Why? Do you think someone was in your house?"

"No, this always happens when I brush my teeth. Of course someone was in my house. I remember walking into the kitchen and then wham, lights out. What are you doing here by the way?"

Fiona is standing by the freezer door wrapping ice cubes in a different face cloth. When she is done, she slithers back down beside me and gently holds the cold compress against my swelling face.

"After I got home, I felt bad about laughing at what happened to you today. So I thought I better drive over here and apologize. Forgive me, please. I just didn't think you were serious. But now . . . now you definitely need to call the police."

"It's too late at night now. Maybe after I get back from my fishing trip with Sal tomorrow," I say, regaining my footing. I'm still a bit woozy, and my face feels like a pincushion, but I'm able to shuffle over to a stool at the kitchen counter. "What if Sal is right, though? If I call the cops, these guys might come down harder on me. *Christ!* Why me? What did I do?"

"Nothing," she says joining me. "Obviously, these guys are thugs. You were just in the wrong place at the wrong time. Believe me—I think this will go away."

"How do you know?" I ask.

"Look around. No damage, nothing stolen. If it was those guys in black, I think they served a plate of payback for the tomatoes you threw at them."

"They were in my house."

"I know," she whispers, while putting her arm around me.

We are silent for a time. The only sounds are the ticking of a wall clock and the cracking of sunflower seeds from the birdcage.

"Montana spoke after you guys left," I say.

"Really? What did he say?"

"He called Harry the heron a pelican, just like in the movie."

"Wish I was there to hear him."

I look up at the suddenly raucous clock. It reads just after nine o'clock which is late for island time. I'm tired and my face is throbbing with pain. I need a shower, a soft bed, and my doors locked. Tomorrow I'm scheduled to meet Sal at Two Palms Marina at sunrise. I wonder if my swollen face will be reason enough to cancel.

"Thanks for coming over, but I need to hit the sack so I can get up early for the fishing expedition I was suckered into with Sal. Are you gonna be all right getting home in your golf cart?"

"Maybe I don't want to go home," Fiona replies.

Pain? What pain?

I look into Fiona's eyes. "Excuse me? I think the knockout blow to my face caused a little hearing loss. Can you repeat that?"

"I'd like to stay here tonight and keep you company. If you don't mind," she says—her smile mischievous.

"I thought that's what I heard. Sure, why not. You can take the bed upstairs and I'll take the couch."

She inches closer to me, softly touches my swollen lip with her finger, and then kisses my cheek. After a few seconds she whispers, "Upstairs, together."

Sounds like a plan.

I shuffle through the first floor and make sure all the doors are locked. I dim the lights and grab a snack for Montana. Fiona joins me at the cage.

"He really is a handsome bird," she says.

I place the sunflower seeds in his dish. "I'm taking this pretty woman upstairs, Montana. You be a good boy tonight."

"So say goodnight to the bad guy."

Our jaws drop and then we burst out laughing which sends a spike of pain across my face.

"That sounds so real!" she says.

"I told you he could talk. Good boy, Montana."

Fiona adds, "Montana, you're way too smart."

The gangster parrot bobs his head up and down. *"The only thing in this world that gives orders is balls."*

Now I'm red with embarrassment to accompany the pain. Tears from laughing fill Fiona's eyes. I pull her away before a litany of f-bombs roars out from his beak. When we are at the foot of the stairs, Montana squawks, *"I got ears ya know. I hear things."*

By the lack of an overnight bag, she isn't prepared to stay the night, which makes me feel her decision was impetuous. *Is there a sympathy lay in my future?* Ask me if I care. All that matters is Fiona is standing in my bedroom, wearing only a sundress and sandals, arms crossed over her breasts, and still giggling over Montana's mimics. I take her hand and lead her out onto the deck.

The night sky is clear and the breeze is fresh and invigorating. In the ink-dark canvas above me, it is as if a million faint lights beg to have a wish bestowed upon them. They twinkle and pulse and I try to wish upon a few in an effort to keep Fiona in my arms. In that moment, on the deck, under the stars, we are the universe.

"Ever see so many stars?" I ask.

"Yeah, at the other end of the island," she replies.

"Humor me, I'm trying to romance you," I whisper.

"I'm sorry. Wow, I've never seen so many stars before," she says with a wide grin. "This is really romantic, Jason. You don't have to try so hard."

She kicks off her sandals and cuddles closer as a warm breeze slips between us. We stand as one taking in the salt-laden air as the humidity of the evening seals us together. My hand drifts around to her back and slides down over her bottom. That prompts her to lift up the sundress enabling my hand to rest on the soft cheeks of her buttocks. After a second, she steps away from my embrace, lifts the sundress over her head and slips back into my arms.

I can't tell you how long we stand as one. Why measure time when you hope the moment is fixed for eternity? But we do begin to wobble, and giggle, and touch noses, and tickle each other, until Fiona asks me to carry her over the threshold into my bedroom. I gently lower her naked body onto the bed.

"You're swelling," she says.

I look down at my shorts and notice the bulge.

"Not there, your face. Well, there too," she says, and then reaches out for me.

I cup her breasts as she lowers my shorts. Although the evening air is warm and humid, it is no match for the heat emanating within our two-foot space. The earthquake called Fiona is enticing my volcano to explode.

"Do you have an extra toothbrush?"

Why do women do that? Ask the most inane questions at the most inopportune times? I recall Megan had a master's degree in asking questions right before an orgasm. Like, *Did you take all the trash out?* or *I think I left the dome light on in my car.* These questions were always incorporated at the precise time when my eyes were bugging out and my muscles were teetering on spastic paralysis.

"Yes, I do." It comes out sounding like a pervert breathing heavy over the phone.

"Let's take a shower," she suggests while climbing off the bed.

So we take a shower and play with the lather and explore each other. We share a towel, and then stand over the sinks and brush. I find I like watching breasts bounce with each stroke of the toothbrush. *Brush harder, woman.*

Fiona seems perplexed to be without whatever she needs next. I think she wishes she had planned better. Maybe she wishes she had included a hairbrush, perfume, or some degree of cosmetics. It certainly isn't makeup; she is a natural beauty, which keeps a small section in the back of my mind pulsating in suspicious mode.

We work our way back to the bed. The dance begins as we both navigate uncharted waters. Our hands roam freely. Touching, squeezing, caressing. Too hard, too soft, just right. In minutes we have a rhythm that seems too natural for just our first time. We roll on the bed from side to side, end to end. The cover sheet is pulled away; the pillows already on the floor. Sweat and passion cover our bodies. We find comfortable positions to pleasure each other until we become so sensitive to the touch that climax is a mere tongue stroke away for both of us.

"I want you inside me," she whispers.

I think safe sex, but it is a fleeting thought because I have no baggies.

I change positions and look into Fiona's eyes. I push aside the wisps of hair pasted to her moist skin. With her legs in the air, her feet caress my face as my body leans into hers. I knock at the door, enter slightly, and then exit. When my teasing is too much, she grips onto my backside and lifts her body upward bringing me fully inside her. We both moan. Her grip is tight. We rock together, back and forth, each plunge eliciting more sighs of pleasure. For our first tango, we are an amazingly fine-tuned dance machine. After a few shudders, Fiona climaxes. If a tsunami horn went off in my bedroom, I wouldn't hear the warning because Fiona screams at the top of her lungs.

Now, bear with me for a moment. I saw the movie where Meg Ryan fakes a climax in a cafe. As a guy, it traumatized me for many years. *How would I ever know if the woman I was with was faking it? Should I care?* Maybe not, but I do. Over time, I knew exactly when Megan started counterfeiting her zenith. So I find myself staring into Fiona's contorted face for any tic or sign that indicates she is writing me a bad check. Her body spasms are in tune, her toes raking my face are suddenly curled, and her switchblade fingernails leave a mark on my skin. I conclude it has to be the real deal. She has experienced a powerful release and it allows me to blow the top off the volcano and set free the flow of lava. There is no doubt mine is as real and as equally potent.

I think we could have gone a few more rounds, Fiona and me, but several factors preclude us from enjoying the pleasures of each other all night. For one, I need to lie still and apply the ice pack to my face to get the other swelling under control. Plus, I have to get up early to fish. I desperately want to call in sick, but there's a certain amount of planning that goes into fishing, so I don't want the big guy angry at me. After we snuggle a bit, we call it a night, but I find sleep elusive.

Fiona lies next to me, resting on her side, her breathing steady. *Is she the naked woman in my dreams? Have I found the perfect woman in paradise?* I stare at the ceiling wondering how many people get chased with a gun, punched in the face, and laid by a goddess in the same day. With the adrenaline of sexual anticipation drained from my body, the pain from my bruises takes center stage. The ice is numbing, but I can still feel the pin pricks as if some indistinguishable force is using my mug as a voodoo doll.

In need of more ice, I slip out of bed and head downstairs. I flick on the light switch near the front door which illuminates the deck, the stairs, and the dock area. I unlock the door and step outside. I can see the docks and the *Ticket to Ride* is the only boat at rest. At the foot of the stairs is Fiona's golf cart. An armadillo waddles across the road. Near some bushes, a ruckus between other critters is under way.

I walk down the stairs. I know I have to buy a golf cart sooner or later, so I'm curious what model she tools around in. When I reach it, I see a woman's bag on the floor of the passenger's side. Did she forget it? Was she too preoccupied to retrieve it in the heat of the moment?

I scurry back up the stairs, lock the doors, switch off the lights and ease cautiously into the kitchen. No fists await my arrival this time. I open the freezer, wrap more ice in the towel, and gulp down a bottle of water from the refrigerator. I take a second one in case Fiona wakes up thirsty. I then head back to bed to see if I can get a couple of hours sleep before the smartiephone alarm goes off. As I pass Montana's cage, I whisper, "Hey Montana."

And he replies, *"Hey, fuck you, mang."*

Never wake up a parrot that can mimic all the lines from *Scarface*.

CHAPTER EIGHTEEN

Island Fishing

"Men and fish are alike. They both get into trouble when
they open their mouths."

—JIMMY D. MOORE

The smartiephone on the nightstand chimes in with my wake-up
call. I reach over and slide the screen off. With one eye open, I
notice I have four text messages. A couple of finger taps and I am
looking at three from Megan and one from Phyllis. I touch Phyllis's message and read that she has left the fishing rod I'd asked
to borrow over at Two Palms Marina, in the care of a Pattie Ann
Everett, whoever she is. The other messages from Megan I leave
for the monkey.

I swing my feet over the side off the bed and sit touching
my bruised face. *What a dream,* I think. Out of all the times my
dreamweaver imagination has swept me away to strange yet comforting adventures, last night's escape to make love with Fiona,
right here in my bed, was by far the best. It seemed so real.

I stand up, scratch the jewels, and stretch.

Amazingly, I can smell a hint of her scent. I inhale deeply. It
is as if the dream is a reality and she is lying next to me. And the
action . . . I feared my stint on the disabled list, due to the lack
of female companionship, might require a refresher course. Yet, I
must say, my performance rivaled any seasoned porn star. I know,
it was my dream and my imagination, but I really banged one out.
It was worthy of an Oscar nomination. If my talents were filmed
in high definition, I would have . . .

"Up so early?" she purrs.

I spin around, eyes wide open, my testicles banging into each other like two dice at a craps table. "Fiona?"

She lifts up on her elbows. "Wow, Jason, who did you expect?"

"No, no, I'm sorry. At times my mind drifts off to unusual and wild excursions, so I thought maybe last night was another figment of my imagination."

"Typical male," she says, rolling off the side of the bed.

"I'm sorry, Fiona. Everything we shared last night I can remember like it happened a second ago. It will be burned in my . . ."

She waves me off. "Save it. I was talking about the wet spot I ended up in. Typical."

"Oh." I raise my hand. "I'll volunteer for the wet spot tonight."

Fiona smiles. "Chivalry is alive, but I'll have to take a rain check. Tonight I'm in Tallahassee for business. I'll be flying out late morning." She walks over to me and takes my hands. "When I get back tomorrow night, we can spend the remaining days of my working vacation in your bed."

The remaining days part drains me. I don't want to lose the woman I've begun to fall in love with. I want her to stay here with me, in Hermitville, forever.

"Why leave?" I ask. "I can give you everything you've ever wanted right here on Gulf Boulevard."

She lowers her head. I sense a need, a want, but there are other driving forces within her.

"I just can't quit on my responsibilities. My people are so close to gaining government recognition as a tribe. With that come the riches that will lift many from a life of poverty. It will document our history, and allow us to be the proud people we once were. I just can't walk away now. Do you understand?"

"No," I say. She punches my arm.

"Plus, I'm high maintenance, Jason. Over time, I doubt you'll want a woman as complex as I can be."

"My boat is high maintenance *and* complex, yet I still love riding around in her."

She looks up and stares at me blankly. In the early morning predawn darkness of my bedroom, I swear tears are welling in her eyes. We stand together, naked; a light breeze cradles us. I don't want to let go of her.

"You're swelling again," she whispers.

I feel my face for renewed puffiness.

"Down there, Jason," she says.

"Oh, yeah, look at that."

"Let's take a cold shower," she says. "The last thing you want to do is keep Sal waiting."

We kiss and hug goodbye on the deck. Me, reluctantly on my way to meet Sal at Two Palms Marina, and Fiona, hanging around the house until the sun is higher in the morning sky when she will go home and pack for the short flight to the capitol building. It almost feels like the old days, married to Megan, while living at the condominium. We would kiss at the doorway as I left for work before she did. How romantic. Well, maybe not. More like pedestrian, until I was killed in the crosswalk by a cheating Megan and her steroid bubblehead.

I barrel down the stairs, my keys jingling, the early morning stillness pervasive. I step past her golf cart, noticing a film of dew on the fiberglass. I think of her handbag. I stop, lean in and lift the bag. It weighs a ton. I look up at the deck to see if she wants it, but she has stepped back inside. Fiona has a tendency to never linger or look back. Too bad, because for me it is a huge turn-on to catch a woman sneak one last look.

I stand there wondering what in the hell weighs so much in her bag. A running outfit, cosmetics, and the usual inventory of personal items a woman might carry around all day, would only equal a fraction of the weight I just lifted. It felt like a bag of rocks, or a ten-pound weight from my barbell set. I want to take a peek, pull the zipper, satisfy my curiosity, but the rational side of the ledger rules against it. So I remain stumped how a woman could forget her bag, a designer bag on closer examination, filled with stuff that is so heavy. But then again, women stump me all the time. I turn away and head for the dock.

∽

Iᴛ ɪs close to 6:00 ᴀ.ᴍ., dawn has surrendered to a rising sun. As I idle along the canal leading into Two Palms Marina, I notice Sal, to my disappointment, at the gas pumps filling up. He is chomping on a cigar, wearing his captain's hat, a canary-colored polo shirt, and red knee-length shorts that band around his belly. Just below the shorts are his black knee-high socks. He doesn't look Mafia in this scene, and that eases my anxiety somewhat.

We exchange a wave, either of acknowledgment or of the mandatory on-the-water-salute variety. He steps to the bow, chews his cigar over to the corner of his mouth, and says, "Take my spot, berth 14."

I nod and continue forward until I reach Sal's mooring. I drop the bumpers and maneuver the *Ticket* against the floating dock. A young kid comes over with a Two Palms Marina shirt on and asks for my lines. I toss them and he ties me off.

"Thanks, kid. Hey, you know where I can find Pattie?"

The kid turns and points toward the snack shack behind the bait shop. "She's over there serving up some breakfast."

I thank him again, hop onto the dock, and follow the wafting perfume of bacon and eggs.

The Two Palms Snack Shack is open only for breakfast and lunch. And it is smaller than small, with five stools at the bar and three picnic tables under umbrellas. There are string lights everywhere, a couple of tacky five-foot tall plastic palm trees covered with colorful lights, and a few speakers inside the shack. I guess the locals come here to drink beer and listen to music at night. Maybe dance a jig to *Dueling Banjos*. Two stools are occupied. A woman with a small towel slung over her shoulder chats with a customer. A pencil grows out from behind her ear. I proceed to belly up to the bar.

"Hello, young man," she bellows as I reach the counter. "What can we do ya this fine morning?"

"Phyllis Hammerstein said she left a . . ."

"You must be that Jason fella who bought the house on Sand Key?" she says, pointing at me.

"Guilty."

"My oh my. You're the rich boy from up north. Single and whatnot, right? Just as handsome as Ms. Hammer said you was. Hi, I'm Pattie. Glad to make your acquaintance," she says, reaching her hand over the counter.

I shake her hand. "You call her Hammer?" I ask.

Pattie leans in closer. "You ever have a long conversation with that woman, and I love her to death, but you come out the other side feeling like a nail driven into a two-by."

"Yeah, I've been there," I laugh.

"There you go, then. Can I whip you up some grits or you just passing through?" She says this while stepping behind a wall and returning a second later with Murray Hammerstein's fishing rod.

"Thanks, but I'm on my way out to the gulf to feed the fish. I'm hearing a twang uncommon to these parts, Pattie. Where're you from?"

A big grin. "I'm from Texas. I moved here for the hurricanes 'cause I was tired of them tornadoes."

A huge paw lands on my shoulder. "We fishing or eating?" Sal says from behind me.

"Good morning, Sal," Pattie says. "Are you boys going out deep or just a stone's throw?"

"Wherever the fish are hanging out, sweetie," Sal says. To me he says, "Let's go, Trust Fund, I ain't got all day." I nod to Pattie and join Sal for the walk over to his boat.

As we pass the bait tubs I slow my pace and say, "Sal, let me pay for the bait."

"We don't need no bait," he replies, without losing stride.

What? Are we gonna sweet talk the fish on board? "If you already bought the bait, let me reimburse you."

"No bait. Instead, we're gonna put M&M's on the hooks. Make you feel at home."

"You're a funny guy, Sal."

He stands behind the helm, filling the skipper's area with his bulk. For the life of me, I don't know how the captain's hat remains on his head, because we are flying through Pirate's Pass into the Gulf of Mexico, but the hat barely budges.

We cruise in silence as the day brightens. The gulf is flat and the temperature is rising. A few clouds linger in the sky, carefree, without direction. We are a few miles offshore when Sal pulls back on the throttle, slowing the speed. He is gazing into the depth finder when he summons me to the helm.

"See that? That's a small school of fish. When we hit one that fills the screen from here to here, we fish." He shifts the throttle to neutral, setting the boat adrift. He then taps a button on the console and Dean Martin starts singing through the speakers. I retreat to the rear cushion seat, holding my borrowed fishing rod, waiting for the excitement to begin. I notice there is no fishing gear on board. No rods, no bait. Maybe this excursion isn't about fishing. Maybe Sal has a couple of strippers hidden below deck and they are waiting for the sun to warm the day before the show begins. Or, maybe Sal is in cahoots with the men in black to kill me, for reasons still unknown, and they are lingering below waiting for his signal. My eyes are glued to the steps leading down to the galley. My imagination is out of control. I knew this was a bad idea.

Sal lifts the ice chest cover, grabs a couple of bottles of orange juice, and then joins me. He hands me one and says, "What the fuck happened to your face?"

I expected him to ask, but I don't want to share the actual details until after I call the police, so I let the bullshit fly.

"I was cruising in my boat and this fish jumped out of the water and slammed into my face. It had to be like two feet long," I say, even though the spread of my arms exceeds four feet. "I had to tackle the . . ."

"What the fuck happened to your face?" Sal asks again. This time the question is followed by a Luca Brasi stare that implies if I don't tell him the truth, I'll be swimming with the fishes instead of fishing for the fishes.

"All right, this is embarrassing, but after you guys left last night, I went into my house and wham, I walked right into a fist. I didn't see who suckered me and I wasn't robbed, but I have my suspicions."

Sal nods. "That shit ain't supposed to happen on the island."

"It does now. My guess is the punch belonged to one of the guys in black. The goons I was telling you about."

Sal guzzles half the juice, and then stares at the bottle. I wait for a response, but Sal appears mesmerized by the label. I look at my bottle. There is nothing special I can see. Is he reading the calorie count? I doubt it. *What is he thinking about?* My gaze returns to the galley steps. Suddenly, my imagination shifts into overdrive and concern for my safety begins to percolate with a rapid thump in my chest. *Is Sal weighing whether to kill me? Is he about to signal for the men hiding below deck to do the job?* I look for the shoreline, but it has fallen out of sight. *Can I swim away?* Not in these shark-infested waters. Fear escalates within me.

What do I know about Sal Santini? Only that he came here from Providence, Rhode Island, and he looks an awful lot (I am profiling again) like the men involved in the ongoing Mafia war. *But how do I fit in? Who would want me dead?* I should've given greater weight to these concerns before agreeing to this trip. Instead, here I am out on his boat, under the guise of fishing, completely defenseless. My panic directs my eyes to search for ropes, tarps, or concrete blocks, the materials needed to dispose of a body at sea—items I might've been oblivious to when I first stepped on board. I survey the surrounding area for other boats. There are a few, but well beyond the sound of a plea for help. My hands grip the fishing rod. I am gasping for air.

I turn to Sal who is still staring at the orange juice bottle. He is waiting—anticipating something. A pulsating beep emits from the helm. *Is that it? The kill-me signal?* My eyes dart between the galley steps and Sal. *Are they going to drown me or shoot me first?* I'm sweating bullets. I've never been so scared in my life. Suddenly I miss the cold winters of New England.

I can't bear the rising tide of anxiety anymore. I stand up and yell, "Sal! Why are you doing this?"

He looks up at me, and then points to the bottle label. "It says here, made from concentrate, so I wanted to see what the fuck happens if I concentrate. Maybe the pulp does funny things and makes more juice, ya know?"

Wide-eyed and mouth agape, I fall back into the seat. *Is this nutjob being funny, or is he a moron?* And then I recall the day I pulled Sal off the sand dune, when he wrapped the boat line around his waist. My mental checkmark selects moron.

"Jason, I need to tell ya something," he says, then gulps the rest of the juice. The back of his hand wipes his mouth. He adjusts his weight on the cushion. I remain skittish to every move he makes.

"This is between you and me, and it don't leave this boat, *capisce?*"

I nod. "Yeah." I notice my hands are still trembling.

"These fuckin' guys that are giving you the hard time? I thought about it last night and I think they're here for me. Some people back home know about my place down here. It only takes one fuckin' rat. So I think these guys are hanging around, maybe waiting for the paper."

"What paper? The *Boston Herald?*"

Sal looks at me as if I am the idiot. "The fuckin' *paper,* like in a contract. They can't take me out unless the boss signs off on it. Since you mentioned these guys were visiting from up north, I've been trying to call in a few chips, get some information, but nobody's answering their fuckin' phone. It's like everybody I know up there is dead."

I assimilate what he has to say. "So let me get this straight, your boss at the music company is trying to whack you?" I think *whack you* sounds cool as I say it.

Sal shakes his head. "You're such a fuckin' civilian, you know that, Trust Fund?"

The helm emits a steady beep this time. Sal jumps up. My heart spikes. I watch as he settles into the captain's chair and adjusts some buttons on the depth sounder screen. Although somewhat relieved that my demise appears to be just another chapter in my book of imagination, I still keep one wary eye on the galley steps.

"Time to fish," Sal commands. He lights up a new cigar, tilts his head back, and blows the first few puffs skyward, as if the smoke will rise and hitch a ride on the nearest passing cloud.

With no bait for my fishing rod and Sal seemingly without gear himself, I watch as he opens a couple of storage bins. The first item he removes is a spool of line with what looks like a foot-long pipe secured to the end. He unwinds some slack from the spool and lowers the pipe overboard.

"We gonna beat the fish to death?" I ask.

"Naw, first I'm gonna take their picture," he mumbles through his cigar.

After about three yards are unwound, he clips several bobbers on the line, which is definitely thicker than standard fishing line. The bobbers will keep his jig device at a certain depth.

"Do you have a jig I can use?" I ask, eager to test my fishing skills using Hammer's rod.

Sal inserts a stick through the center of the spool. He pulls out a lot of slack as the spool spins freely. "Here, hold this with both hands; let the line run while I find us a better position."

I hold the stick as he powers the boat slowly away from the bobbers. The slack disappears and Sal hollers for me to keep unwinding line, so I pull on the spool to supply additional slack. After about five minutes, Sal shifts the throttle into idle. The bobbers float on the water maybe one hundred yards north of where we have drifted.

From another storage bin, Sal removes a battery and wire cutters. He snips the line and peels it into two. With the clippers, he splices the wires.

"Ready, Jason?"

For what? "I guess so."

"Smile fishes," Sal yells, as he connects each wire to a battery terminal.

Like an idiot, I look out toward the bobbers expecting a picture flash to go off, but instead the gulf belches a giant bubble as if a monstrous fart needed airing. I hear a splash and see Sal tossing the spool of line overboard. He then steps to the wheel and powers the boat.

"Jason, go below deck and get the nets," he orders, turning the boat around and heading back toward the bobbers.

Below deck? My angst comes ashore again as I envision the men in black waiting for me. I don't want to go down the steps. In fact, for a second, I think about hitting Sal over the head with the battery and commandeering the *Wicked Pissa Hits* back to shore.

"What nets, Sal? Look, I'll take the helm and you go below deck. You know what you're looking for."

"Get the fuckin' nets, Trust Fund." It is followed by a wind-blown, off the gulf, Luca Brasi stare down.

Shit! I wobble over to the steps, lean in, and don't see anyone below. I step down one level, then another. I see the nets hanging on the wall. I jump over the final step and land on the cuddy floor. Straight ahead of me is a bed, and on that bed is enough firepower to thwart a small army. I see Uzis, assault rifles, handguns, knives, and a few other large metal objects that are foreign to me. I wonder if Sal has grenades in the refrigerator and a Stinger anti-aircraft missile launcher in the commode. The man is well armed. I feel relieved. None of this could possibly be destined for me, for it would be quite the overkill.

I grab the nets and scurry back upstairs. Sal is slowing the boat as we approach the bobbers. At first I can't believe my eyes, but sure enough, dozens of fish have floated to the surface. Groupers, cobia, mackerel and others I can't readily identify. Even some jellyfish seem like they were stunned to death. Sal leaves the helm and grabs a net. He leans his bulk over the gunwale and nets a fish.

"Oh, this here's a fuckin' huge one," he says, as if he is fighting the fish while reeling it in. He empties the net on the deck and reaches in for another. "Scoop, Trust Fund, scoop," he yells.

We do this for fifteen minutes or so. Sal reaches in, scoops a fish, checks the horizon like a cat burglar might check the neighborhood before breaking in, and then dumps the catch on deck. After we have netted twenty-three fish, Sal is tired and wheezing, so he decides it is time we move. I am also motivated to move by the sudden appearance of sharks circling the death zone. Call me Chief Brody from Amity Island, but when sharks are in feeding mode, no boat seems big enough.

Sal steps behind the wheel, pushes the throttle forward and sets course for Pirate's Pass. As we cruise back to shore, he asks me to bring the nets below. I do as he asks, replacing them on the wall. I then stare in awe, for a second time, at the arsenal spread out on the bed. I lift an Uzi and think of Montana's machine-gun mimic. Should I buy a weapon? Life is getting crazy. I replace the gun and bolt up the stairs to join Sal on deck.

"Jason, put the fish on ice." He points to a latch in the deck's floor.

I pull the panel up expecting to find nuclear-tipped torpedoes, but it is a fish well, filled with ice. I push the fish into the hole and replace the door. I then step over by the helm. "That's an impressive gun collection you have below deck," I say, unsure if I'm being nosey, but it isn't like he is trying to hide anything.

Sal looks at me. A sly smile emerges. "I was a fuckin' Boy Scout at one time. Always be prepared."

After we dock at Two Palms Marina, Sal distributes his catch among the locals. I hear him bragging to Memphis the Lighthouse about how several of the fish put up a real nasty fight. Memphis pats Sal on the back and the two men share additional fish stories. Pattie from the snack shack wanders by and Sal offers her several fish. After the gas attendant fills the tanks, Sal gives the kid a fish. When he is done playing the conquering hero, he asks me what I want. I wonder if Phyllis has a recipe for stunned-to-death fish. I settle on a couple of groupers, and he tosses them onto the deck of the *Ticket to Ride* with a thump.

I back out of Sal's berth. As I am turning to head out of the marina, Toast appears and yells out from the pier.

"Hey, how was the fishing, *mon ami?*"

Sal displays a thumbs-up and says he'll bring some fish by his house.

"And don't forget to bring a few for Fiona," Toast says. "I think I just saw her driving toward the ferry landing with her dude friend in her car."

Dude friend in the car? I check the time on my smartiephone. It flashes 1:10 P.M. Something isn't right.

CHAPTER NINETEEN

Island Congestion

"No doubt exists that all women are crazy; it's only a
question of degree."

—W.C. FIELDS

On the boat ride back to Gulf Boulevard, I struggle with the fact Fiona may have lied to me. *What was she doing in the middle of the day with a guy in her car when she was supposed to be in Tallahassee for a meeting on Indian affairs?* Fiona Tallahassee in Tallahassee—it suddenly appears too contrived. *Is she really the person she claims to be? Is anybody on this island who they claim to be? Does she really have to leave soon to represent her people, or is escaping the island a calculated move?* I start questioning everything about Fiona, from her flirtatious moves at sunset, to the fact she showed up right after the knockout punch. *And what the hell was in her bag that weighed so much?*

Then again, maybe Toast was wrong. Maybe it wasn't Fiona he saw in the car. My mind is so preoccupied with this conundrum I almost miss the turn into Hermitville lagoon. In fact, I can't remember crossing the Intracoastal Waterway from Two Palms Marina. I shake off being in autopilot and guide the *Ticket* to the dock. With the engines off, the quietness of my paradise seems deafening. I grab a boning knife from the storage bin and fillet the two groupers, leaving the carcasses in the water for the hordes of scavengers eager to clean up.

When I'm done rinsing off the boat, I enter the house cautiously. It saddens me it has come to this. I never had this problem in Massachusetts. As I open the kitchen screen door, the salt-beaten springs squeal as if being tortured by an empty oil can. I step inside ready to clobber any intruder with my grouper fillets. The door slaps shut sending a sharp announcement that ripples throughout the house like the undulation from a rock tossed in a pond. The only sounds I hear come from the soft hum of the air conditioner and the rustling from Montana's cage. I place my smartiephone on the kitchen counter, the fillets in the refrigerator, and then secure the rest of the house. All is clear.

I slump onto the sofa and kick off my sandals. Next to me in his cage, Montana seems content breaking apart sunflower seeds and spitting the shells onto the floor. As I was checking the house for unwanted guests, I also kept an eye out for any notes Fiona may have left, but there were none. *Why leave a note when she was gallivanting with some dude instead of being where she said she'd be?* The woman was becoming enigmatic to me. One minute I thought I knew her, the next I didn't have a clue. I thought being a hermit meant never being frustrated again, or harboring a jealous streak.

I step into the kitchen to wrap the fillets for the freezer when my phone vibrates on the granite countertop. I look at the number accompanied by the image of a skull and bones. I assigned that icon to Megan's digits after the last time she called. I thought about ignoring her disturbance and sending it to the monkey again, but how much could the poor fella take? I grab the purveyor of bad news and tap the screen.

"Yeah, Megan."

"*Yeah Megan?* That's the way you answer when your wife calls?"

"You're not my wife, Megan. You're a tax lien."

"Why do I always have to remind you, Jason, that we were once happily married?"

"You're right. There was that one day, foggy as it is."

"Really? Did you forget all the romantic trips down to Cape Cod, or the week we camped in Acadia National Park, or the crazy sex we had at that apple orchard before the owner chased us off—you running back to the truck with your pants down to your ankles?"

In a moment of weakness I smile, but quickly regain my composure. "It turned out to be a bad dream. I've awoken from it, but apparently you remain in a coma."

"You're always the sarcastic guy. That's what I love about you. Even though you left me stranded on a beach in Malibu surrounded by gawking men and jealous women, I still love my Poopsie. That's why I'm not going to press charges against you for abandonment."

I laugh. "I gave you money and sent you on a vacation. How's that abandonment?"

"You left me there exposed under the hot sun without tanning lotion or any Evian to drink."

"You had the whole Pacific Ocean to drink."

"I'm not going to drink the same water fish go to the bathroom in. You know, Cara (Megan's whore friend) says any jury would find in my favor because your stunt was premedicated."

"Premeditated."

"*Whatever,* Jason. You built up my hopes of becoming Hollywood elite, and then it all came crashing down when I was traumatized to find out California and your movie friends were all lies. I'm the victim here."

"Didn't the victim fall in love with some lifeguard within seconds of her arrival?"

Pause. "That's beside the point," she finally says in an agitated tone. "Chipper came to my rescue. I needed a friend. Cara says I should sue you for everything you have, Jason."

Chipper? "You want to sue me? Hey, bring it on."

"I don't want to *bring* it on," she replies, switching to her baby, I-want-something-voice. "I want to *turn* you on. You need me, Jason. I'm the best thing that's ever happened to you."

Every woman I've ever dated has said she was the best thing that's ever happened to me. What's up with that? And how do they all know?

"Nobody can get my Poopsie more excited than me. You know it and I know it."

Fiona flashes in my mind. Then I picture her with some face-less dude.

"So tell me where you're living in Florida and I'll catch the next flight down. The best sex you'll ever have is just a few hours away."

I check the wall clock and calculate when Fiona is supposed to be back. But she is already back. *Did she ever leave?* I'm getting depressed.

"Megan, listen to me. Write this down if you have to. I don't want you. We are over. We've been over. Can't we simply hate each other like normal divorced couples?"

"Poopsie, I love you and I know once I'm in your arms again, you'll love me. Just give me a chance, please. *Please.*"

It is my sudden lottery windfall Megan is in love with. I don't need a degree from MIT to figure that out. "All right, Megan, I guess we can give it one more try."

"Oh, Poopsie! I love you! You won't regret it. I'll be the wife you always wanted. Where are you living? Miami? We'll be the sexiest couple on South Beach."

"Not quite. I'm living on a private island south of Key West."

"Really? An island? Are you like surrounded by water?"

"Yes, I'm looking out and there's water on all sides of the island."

"That sounds so beautiful. Is there nightlife and rich people like us?"

Like us . . . Christ. "Yes. I think you'd fit in real well."

"Okay, I'm freaking. Tell me how to get down there. I want to jump into your arms so bad. You better meet me this time as soon as I arrive."

"I will, I promise." My fingers are crossed. "All you have to do is catch a flight into Miami, then drive down to Key West. Once there, look for a Spanish-speaking captain with a boat, there are plenty, and tell him you want to head out about 90 miles due south from Key West until you reach the island."

"This is so exciting. What's our island's name?"

I pause for a moment, and then say, "Abuc."

"Abuc? Is that like French? I've never heard of it. Is it like an exclusive resort island? Do the residents flock to Miami?"

"Every chance they get."

"Good, cause I want us to be *the* nightlife in Miami. I can't wait, Poopsie! Dad said you were in Florida, so I know you're being straight with me this time, right?"

"Of course. Remember, find a boat heading south that will take you to Abuc."

A banging sound from the front of the house startles me. I walk over to the window and see Phyllis hammering her fist on my door. Beyond her, the Gulf Breeze Realty skiff is docked next to my boat.

"I gotta go, Meg. The tour boat is taking us treasure hunting today. I need to be fitted for scuba gear." I love bullshitting the gullible and Megan is as susceptible as they come.

"Jason! So cool! I'll call you as soon as I . . ."

I tap end call on my smartiephone screen. *Say hello to Fidel.*

I walk over to the door figuring Phyllis is here to retrieve Murray's fishing rod. When I open it, a blast of midday heat overwhelms me as Phyllis storms in.

"I can't believe they haven't fixed your doorbell yet," she complains, opening up her planner and scribbling a note.

Actually the island's maintenance company had been by and the guy had fixed the doorbell. I just unfixed it after he left.

"I'll make sure he's out here . . . holy cow, Jason, what happened to your face?" she says after finally making eye contact. We are standing in the foyer, just under the disabled doorbell.

"I was on the beach, under a palm tree, and I looked up just as a coconut was falling. It caught me smack in the face."

"There are no coconut palms on Sand Key, Jason."

"Oh. I wonder what it was then."

Phyllis gives me a smirk reserved for wiseasses. "I just happened to be on the island checking on a couple of rentals for listing when I saw your boat. I thought I'd save you the trip of returning the fishing rod. How was your excursion with Mr. Santini by the way?"

"It was a blast."

"Really? I heard you went out in his boat. I don't like that man, just so you know."

"What's not to like about Big Sal?" I ask.

"Don't get me going on him," she warns. "I've had a few run-ins with him. If you ask me, I think he's a gangster."

The boat full of guns might justify Phyllis's assessment. "Ah, he's harmless," I lie. "He told me he's in the music industry. That's a tough business to be in, so maybe he needs to have an edge all the time."

"He's rude, obnoxious, disrespectful, and devoid of manners. You could do a lot better, Jason, when it comes to finding a fishing buddy. Thankfully, he doesn't live here full time, although this current stay has exceeded all his previous visits. God, I hope he doesn't plan to retire here."

For exotic entertainment, I am thinking a cage match between a diminutive, fleet-moving realtor, and an obese, sloth-moving music producer. As long as The Hammer avoids his grasp, she probably wins by tiring him out.

"Figure this one," I say. "I get along with you and Sal. Memphis gets along with you and Sal. And you get along with Memphis and me. I think we should all get together and throw some shrimp on the barbie. Are you in?"

"Not in this lifetime."

At the same moment Phyllis is writing off my inane suggestion, Montana squawks for some attention.

"Oh my word, you bought a parrot?" she says, leaving the foyer for the living room. I follow her as she approaches the cage. "Isn't he the cutest? Does he talk?"

"He does, sometimes, but only after hearing his name. Montana, this is my friend Phyllis. Can you say hello?"

Montana glides along the perch until he is facing Phyllis.

"Say hello to my little friend." He follows that with a round of gunfire that kills Phyllis and me instantly.

"Wow, that's impressive," she says. "What was all that noise?"

"He was shooting us."

"You fuck with me, you fuckin' with the best."

I cringe as soon as the f-bombs land. Phyllis takes a step back; her eyes wide open, her hand over her mouth. After a few seconds she uncovers her smile. "Did you teach him that, Jason?"

"No, he came preloaded with that software. I apologize. I never know what he's gonna say. His original owner thought it would be funny if the bird mimicked quotes from the *Scarface* movie."

"Well, I think he's hilarious, but I'm afraid you're looking at a targeted audience," she says chuckling. "That's not to say I wouldn't love to have him talk up a storm at my office some afternoon."

"No problem. He's a cheap date. A few sunflower seeds and you can own him for the day."

"Tempting. Now where's my fishing rod? I'm sure somewhere Murray is getting anxious."

We walk out of the house toward the boat docks. Emerging from the Gulf Boulevard bird sanctuary is a golf cart. Normally, any odd movement on the island causes a disruption of the perpetual serenity, so Phyllis and I are fixated, like deer in headlights, as we gawk at the approaching disturbance. I squint down the road until I recognize the driver as the key lime pie woman.

"Oh, it's Amber," Phyllis says.

When the golf cart arrives, Amber steps out and hugs Phyllis. I step away from the women to retrieve the unused fishing rod and place it in the skiff. I'm sure Murray will be happy to have it returned in the same condition as he had left it.

The women are yapping girl talk when I step off the dock. Three people together without a sunset constitutes island congestion. So I start to slowly slip away when Amber calls out, "Jason, I have something for you."

Another pie? She says her goodbyes to Phyllis, and then begins rooting through the back of her golf cart. I wave to Phyllis as the skiff putters away. After pushing a few things aside, Amber retrieves a pot of marigolds and brings them to me.

"I thought you could use some color for the deck."

I am genuinely appreciative, so I invite her into my sand castle for a cold drink.

We sit in wicker chairs on the gulf-front porch sipping tall glasses of lemonade and watching the graceful sailboats navigate the late afternoon chop. Closer to shore, wind-surfers and Jet Skis traverse the turquoise waters. Amber settles in as she slips out of her sandals. Earlier I escorted her through the house without the Mafia bird causing an incident. At one point, she stopped to grab a handful of M&M's from one of the dozen candy dishes throughout the house. I really think M&M's are a chick magnet.

"Your house is so beautiful, Jason," she says, summing up all she had seen.

"Thanks." Amber is a good-looking woman I'm guessing in her midthirties. Even better looking without her mother around. She has blonde hair, a slim frame, and fair complexion. She's the type of woman who wears a big hat and expansive sundresses to protect her from the sun while she lives on a sun-drenched island.

"What's with all the M&M's? Were they on sale?"

"It's my vice. The candy and I are sort of bonded together."

"Interesting. Well, I saw you yesterday speeding through the Intracoastal Waterway. You really should slow down and enjoy the scenery. Not to mention it's a no-wake zone. I'm just saying," she says, smiling.

"I know. I know. I've got a hundred new reasons to slow down. But I was being . . ."

Amber leans forward and wrinkles her forehead. "Why is the sand so perfect in front of your house?"

I lean forward. "Sheesh, I don't know. Maybe it's the wind."

"No seaweed, no shells, no footprints. Must've been hurricane force winds, or maybe it's the rake I see leaning at the edge of the walkover. You rake the sand, don't you? My neighbor mentioned the new guy on the island rakes the sand."

I suck at not being noticed. "And your neighbor is?"

"Fiona Tallahassee. She's renting down the road from me. As soon as I met her, I knew she'd make a great islander. We really hit it off. She jogs along the beach a lot, not that she needs to. The woman is a natural beauty. Have you seen her around the island?"

"Yeah . . . I've seen a lot of her. She seems like a very nice woman."

"She's a doll. I wish all the seasonal renters were like her— quiet, unassuming, and so friendly. I'm gonna miss her when she leaves in a week. My brothers, well stepbrothers, are in love with her. I think the imbeciles are stalking her."

In a week? More competition? I adjust in my chair and gulp down the rest of my lemonade. "I've met your mother, but I didn't know you had brothers. Do they also live on Sand Key?"

"Heavens no. They're staying on the mainland. We happen to share the same mother and that's all we have in common. To tell you the truth, I really can't stand them," she adds in a whisper, as if her brothers could hear from the mainland.

A stiff afternoon breeze massages us as we sit looking out toward the gulf. Several windsurfers are struggling in the gusts. In the distance, majestic sails ripple on boats as they race across the white caps. It is all so beautiful, but I can't keep my mind off Fiona. Is this thing we shared together going to be reduced to a three-week stand?

"And then there's my other neighbor who is the *complete* opposite of Fiona," Amber continues. "I call him the antichrist of islanders. I'm sure you've seen the rather large man named Sal who's sinking our end of Sand Key into the Intracoastal Waterway?"

"That's mean," I say, smiling.

"I suppose, but you live next door to him for a time and let me know how it works out for you. The man is vulgar and terribly inconsiderate. One time he got very angry with me for asking him to lower his music late at night. This is an island, Jason. I asked him nicely and he just stared at me like some Mafia guy who wanted to kill me. I explained to him this is an island and he should respect the rules of island etiquette. So what does he do? For the next week he opens up his window facing my patio, sticks his fat patootie out while I'm sitting there, and rips the nastiest farts in my direction. I mean air-horn loud farts, Jason. I swear he's frightened away the sea turtles from nesting on the island. At one point my mother grabbed a shotgun and was headed out to confront him. I had to rein her in. A few days ago, my mother had my stepbrothers pay him a visit and read him the riot act. I guess they're good for something," she laughs.

"No kidding?" I say. I didn't share with Amber that I'd been a witness to one of Sal's patootie blasts at sunset.

"Somebody should put a contract out on that guy. And his sidekick, that little French weasel. I don't trust him at all either. Every time we cross paths, I feel like he's undressing me. But, Fiona seems to get along with them. I guess men act differently around beautiful women."

"Maybe they're just jealous that you can live here year-round and they can't. Rest assured, when the season is over, the island will be ours again." After I say that, Amber's eyes seem to flutter. I quickly change the subject. "So you said Fiona leaves in a week?"

"That's what she told me a few days ago. Her one-month rental is up."

A thousand scenarios are spinning in my head. I just don't know which one carries the most weight. When I see Fiona again, if I see Fiona again, I have a few significant questions that require answers. Amber tilts her head to one side and sighs.

"Have you ever been married, Jason?"

"At one time, but I managed to escape from the abduction and find my way back to earth."

Amber giggles. "Tell me one thing that was wrong with her."

I ponder for a moment and then say, "My ex-wife thought AT&T was a place to get drinks because they always advertised about having the most bars."

She giggles again. "All right, what about a girlfriend?"

"None that I know of. What about you?"

"I was married once, but he lost interest in me. So I immersed myself in my writing and ended up in this truly beautiful place. We are so blessed to be here. I think the true quintessence of where we are on this island should never be left for just one person. It should be shared, don't you think Jason?"

It is time I jolt Amber out of her dreamy comfort zone. "So, back to your stepbrothers. Are they older or younger than you?"

"They're younger. Both of them are like fish out of water down here. Their visits always turn into hell week for me—taking my mother to the mainland so they can hug, kiss and fight, while I ease to one side to avoid being included in their mayhem. Every time they arrive, I can't wait for them to drive back home."

"Sounds like your typical family reunion."

Amber grunts. "Yeah, real typical. A couple of hooligans who think wearing black clothes in ninety-degree heat is considered being cool."

CHAPTER TWENTY

Island Secrets

"I don't use drugs, my dreams are frightening enough."
—M.C. ESCHER

My mind trips on the words, black clothes, as I stare at Amber in disbelief. Her brothers, or stepbrothers, are the men in black— my tormentors, with the big guns and small bladders. And if I were a betting man, I'd say the owners of a red laser and a sucker punch. Small world.

I'm about to enlighten Amber about my bonding with her upstanding siblings, but I hold my tongue as she continues her story.

"Just last night, Frankie, the older of the two misfits, told me he scared the crap out of a guy he said was hanging out with Fiona. I screamed at him, 'Why would you do that? Fiona is my friend! She's a guest on the island!' and he smiled back and said, 'Because I could.' Can you believe that?"

He hit me when I wasn't looking, the coward. "Yeah, I believe it. But I doubt he scared the crap out of the guy," I say. "My guess is he probably just landed a sucker punch." I want to point out my black eye as proof to see if Amber would connect the dots, but I wait, thankfully.

"So after I threatened to tell his father that his boys were caus- ing problems down here for my mother again, he tells me the other guy started it by throwing tomatoes at him. 'Tomatoes?' I said, doubting every word he was telling me. 'Who would be so irrational to start throwing tomatoes at you?' I asked him. He insisted the other guy did it and even showed me a stained shirt he'd just purchased. I still didn't buy it, though. The slob probably spilled marinara sauce on himself. Can you picture someone lame enough to start throwing tomatoes at a stranger?"

I stare off into the gulf as if to ponder the question. Her story is conveniently devoid of the peepee caper, and the subsequent cannon pointed in my face, which I am not about to interject into the conversation in an effort to protect the innocent—being me. I shake my head no and agree no one would be that lame.

"Now you know what I have to put up with when these two visit my mother. Thank goodness they're driving back home tomorrow."

My first thought is of revenge fading away like a flickering light bulb. Not that I could do anything beyond tossing tomatoes, but hey, I can think retaliation like Sal might, and feel good about myself. My second thought is of Sal. It now appears Amber's stepbros have no connection to his music business. Instead, it is simply a case of my bad luck having crossed paths with these cretins because, as they spied on us from a boat during sunsets over the gulf, I was a little too affectionate with Fiona for their liking. The good news is Sal has nothing to worry about. His arsenal can be stowed away for another day or for bigger fish. I'm eager to tell him his concerns are all for naught.

"Tomorrow, huh? Not soon enough, I guess."

"No, not soon enough," Amber repeats, as she stares at me for a few seconds and then tilts her head to one side. "Hey, how did you get that shiner by the way?"

"You won't believe this, but as I was speeding through the Intracoastal Waterway, someone threw a snowball at me."

We talk a little longer and Amber enlightens me on what to expect as a year-round resident on Sand Key once the seasons turn over. Aside from the yearly threat of a hurricane, she explains how damn nippy living by the shore can get—like fifty degrees ice cold. I give her a look of incredulity and explain where I'm from, fifty degrees in the winter is considered a heat wave prompting people to run amuck screaming global warming.

She also warns me that for a couple of months, the Gulf Coast will seem desolate, but after the New Year, the snowbirds begin their invasion and steady commerce picks up again. I am fine with that. It will give me some time to hone my hermit existence. All I have to do is make it through Thanksgiving when my parents and their leeches pay a visit.

I walk Amber back to her golf cart and thank her again for the marigolds. Although I am eager to experience the seclusion of the island—when the sailboats, the Jet Skis, and the sunset sit-downs go into hibernation, it is also good to know Amber is balancing Sand Key from the opposite end of the island. I anticipate being alone which means in my heart I have already written off Fiona as a resident of Gulf Boulevard. In fact, I don't even know if I'll ever see her again.

After Amber disappears down Gulf Boulevard, I rush into the house and peer out toward the beach to see if the chairs are occupied. They are empty and the gulf is lacking an audience of boaters. The only activity is a shrimper pulling nets. But it is still early. The horizon displays a line of puffy clouds that stretches for miles and will make the sunset spotty at best. Maybe this will act as a deterrent. I look toward the bend of the beach and see only a flock of birds nesting on the sand. I bring Montana out onto the deck and wait.

It appears everyone on this island has secrets. It's a toss-up whether Fiona shows up after her nontrip, or Sal makes an appearance after an exhausting day of blowing up fish. I wonder if I will have the intestinal fortitude to uncover some secrets by questioning Fiona about the trip she never made to Tallahassee, instead spending the day, I assume, with some guy. I don't want my jealousy exposed. With Sal, I am eager to share what I've learned about the men in black. They are only here as visitors and are leaving tomorrow. Big Sal has nothing to worry about, but I still feel secrets remain that I need to unearth about him. If it is only Toast who ambles around the bend, I will lock the doors, turn off the lights, and call it a night. I settle into the wicker chair, lift my feet up, and wait.

As expected, the sunset is a no-show. A few boats drop anchor in the gulf only to leave disappointed. Nobody shows up at the beach chairs. Dusk overcomes the area in expeditious fashion. *Is it the lack of sun or a noticeable change in the seasons?* The onshore breeze remains warm and is accelerating my need for sleep after a long day. I feel like it is time to eat, but I am too tired to move and too comfortable to think of food. I do have a craving for a handful of M&M's. I look at Montana and wonder if I can train him to fetch.

As I struggle to stay awake, my mind sets about creating a timeline on how I met the people who invaded Hermitville. Why? Blame it on the salt air. It all started when I yanked Sal's boat off the sandbar. For some reason he felt the need to express his gratitude by delivering obesity-creating pastries. Then he noticed the beach chairs and to my surprise, the big man came promenading along the sand dunes the next evening. Then Running Bush, aka Fiona, appeared out of nowhere sprinting down the beach. I think I was in love at first sight, but I quickly wrote it off as unattainable. The next day, I was in love a little more as Fiona joined Sal and me for our sunset by the gulf. Soon after, Toast appeared, but who gives a shit about him. It was my fascination with the big man and my driftwood for Fiona that matter.

I hear footsteps climbing up the stairs. *Who could be visiting at this hour? Fiona?* My heart starts pounding. A figure emerges as a silhouette in the darkness.

"Hey, asshole," Megan appears in the doorway.

"How did you find me," I ask.

"She probably drifted in with the tide," Fiona says.

"Like fucking seaweed," Sal adds.

"Who are these losers?" Megan demands.

Along the walls of my deck, a dozen singing bass nailed on wood plaques erupt at once with their mouths yapping and their tails flapping to the tune of the fish fillet commercial.

"Give me back my fish life. Give me my life. Ooooh."

At the far end of the deck, the men in black juggle tomatoes. Sal starts laughing as he points at the singing fish.

A shape shifter opens the screen door and enters.

"Give me back my fish life. Give me my life."

"This is Fernando," Megan says proudly, "the boat captain from Key West. He took me over to Cuba, or for a moron like you, Abuc. We had some delicious mojitos and fell in love."

Sal stands up and levels the Luca Brasi stare at Fernando.

"What if it was you hanging stunned on this wall?"

"I think we can work this out amicably," Fiona suggests.

The men in black resort to throwing tomatoes at each other.

"If it was you on this plaque you wouldn't be laughing at all."

Amber grabs both her stepbrothers by the ear and drags them along the deck.

"Give me back my fish life. Give me my life. Ooooh."

"Can you shut those freakin' fish up?" Megan complains.

"I kinda like the fish," Fiona says.

"Well, then keep that your little secret, bitch. I've got business with my husband."

"Husband?" Sal and Fiona say in concert.

"Give me back my fish life. Give me my life.

"I'm not her husband. We're divorced. We're over. Megan, what the hell do you want?"

"I want my share of the lottery, Jason. In payment for the years I toiled as your wife and ex-wife."

Montana is pacing in his cage, spitting sunflower shells and enjoying the show.

"What if it was you hanging stunned on this wall?"

The naked lady appears on the deck, her thick-rimmed glasses balancing on the end of her nose. Her long strawberry blond hair hangs down across her breasts. "It's time for you all to leave," she announces.

With that, Sal fires two shots into Fernando's head.

"If it was you on this plaque you wouldn't be laughing at all."

"Nice double tap, Sal," Fiona admires.

Megan looks down at Fernando's body. "Oh, real pissa. Now how the fuck am I supposed to get home?" she wails.

Phyllis Hammerstein begins dragging Fernando's body from the deck. "Where to?" she asks me.

"Bury him next door, in my not-yet-neighbor's sand."

Phyllis nods and proceeds to drag him down the stairs.

"Let's go. The party's over," the naked lady says. Fiona and Sal start to shuffle toward the door. Fiona winks as she brushes in front of me. "Hey, how come you never made it to Tallahassee?" I ask.

Fiona shrugs her shoulders.

When Sal walks by, I say, "Sal, nothing to worry about with those men in black."

He also shrugs his shoulders.

Megan is the last to walk past me; she stops, places her fists on her hips and says, "When I find out where you live, I'll know where you live. Hell has no fury like a woman scorched."

It starts to pour; a sudden torrential bucket of rain pelts the house with the force of an open fire hydrant. The noise reverberates along the empty deck. I look left, then right and realize I am sitting alone. And apparently awake. Montana stands quiet on his perch. The soft light from inside the house is enough to see that his eyes are closed, his head tilted forward.

I lift out of the chair and step over to the deck railing. A scattering of sunflower shells, littered on the deck, stick to my feet. There is nothing to see. It is pitch dark and even darker with the rain. I pad into the house and grab a flashlight.

I never take anything for granted and that's why I subscribe to Murphy's Law. I also suffer from an abnormal amount of idiosyncrasies. So it is completely normal for me to shine the flashlight on the floor of the deck in search of Fernando's blood. The memory purge is already under way. Of course there is no blood. I have simply returned from another trip along the outer edges of my mind.

As quickly as the rainsquall blew in, it stops. All that remains are the intermittent drops falling from my roof. The gulf is quiet and still, as if the downpour has pounded it flat. There is no breeze to carry the scents of warm rain, salt air, or flora perfume. It has become so silent that I can hear the faint wail of sirens from well off on the mainland.

CHAPTER TWENTY-ONE

Island Paranoia

"Life is a bitch and then you die."
—AUTHOR UNKNOWN

The next morning, the sun is out and another late summer day blossoms in southwest Florida. After eating a light breakfast and cleaning Montana's cage, I reluctantly enter the exercise room, which I have neglected for several days. Okay, call it a week. I jump on the stationary bicycle, point the remote at the television and begin spinning. A reporter from WINK News on channel 11 is standing in front of a yellow tape that reads, CRIME SCENE: DO NOT CROSS. It is draped across the entrance to the Portico Inn in Englewood, just a short boat ride across the Intracoastal Waterway from Sand Key. After a couple of seconds, the live shot shifts to a split screen with an incident recorded earlier. It is night—the lights from police and emergency vehicles pulsate off the surrounding buildings. EMTs are pushing two stretchers, each carrying a black body bag. The caption at the bottom of the screen reads: *Breaking News: Two men found shot to death in local motel room.*

I switch to another station. The local channel 7, WZVN, is also live on the scene, but from a different angle of the motel. The reporter is reading from a notepad about two dead men who were apparently on vacation visiting relatives in the Englewood area. The police have no suspects or motives. There was no sign of a struggle and both men had occupied the same room. He goes on to report that police suspect foul play, with one detective describing the scene as an execution. The identity of the two victims is being withheld pending notification of the families. The only information leaked by the motel manager is that the men were from out of state.

I stop spinning. The story ends, so I quickly switch to a third local news station. WBBH channel 2 has an eye-in-the-sky helicopter hovering over the motel as a reporter's voice reiterates some of what I've already heard. Again, there are no names or motives offered. I learn the bodies were discovered in room 114, around 10:00 last night by the night manager after he'd responded to an anonymous complaint about rats in the room.

Could the men in black be in those black body bags? How ironic. Although I have stopped spinning with my feet, my mind is spinning at full speed. *Does Amber know yet? What kind of trouble were these guys into that warranted their demise? Is Sal involved?* I'm still having a difficult time reconciling Sal the music producer as Sal the Mafia assassin, even considering his propensity for violence and a boatload of weapons.

Given my nasty exchange with Amber's stepbrothers, I wonder if the violence bestowed on them would somehow find a path to me. *Holy crapola!* Once again the life of a hermit remains well beyond my embrace. After contemplating what action I should take, I grab the keys to the *Ticket* and cruise out to the Intracoastal Waterway to make my initial visit to the south end of Sand Key in an effort to stick my nose where it doesn't belong.

The pier at the entrance to the lagoon was built to accommodate a ferry/barge for the delivery and pickup of passengers and vehicles. It is the same dock where I'd briefly eyed Fiona holding a phone and Amber waving at me, as I raced along the waterway to escape the tomato caper. I turn into the inlet, throttle down, and let the wake carry the boat forward. The landing is vacant of people and goods, with the exception of a pelican perched on a piling. Several golf carts are parked to one side while the owners visit the mainland.

I drift farther down until I reach three smaller docks separated by the encroachment of mangroves into the lagoon. Tied to the third dock is a familiar boat, but I pay little attention to it not knowing exactly where I have arrived. With only a dozen or so homes on the south end of Gulf Boulevard, I have to be close to someone I know.

I pull into the first slip and cut the engine. Water laps against the wooden structure. I secure the boat and walk the length of the dock. Above the dense vegetation and frond-laden trees, I can see the peaks of several houses. I continue until I'm on a crushed seashell path that leads to a small home built on pilings and decorated with a multitude of colorful flowers displayed in containers and hanging pots. Along the porch is a series of wind chimes that add a melody to the serenity at the slightest breeze. The home is weathered, beaten both by sun and salt, yet it is as inviting as an island home can be. Underneath the structure is a golf cart, a kayak hanging from hooks on the pilings, a barbeque grill, and a walk-in storage shed. I can see the semipaved surface of Gulf Boulevard, and beyond the road, more palm trees and thick flora. At ground level, the gulf is out of view, but I can hear it, smell it, and almost taste it.

I have no idea whose property I'm trespassing on until I recall Amber telling me about her patio and the house next door where Sal resides. Sure enough, the adjacent home of similar construction has a window overlooking her yard where Sal supposedly tooted his flatulence. The close proximity of these structures suggests they once belonged to one family. But my guess is the current residents curse the intimacy of their location each day.

I continue along the trail, the weight of my gait crushing more shells, until I reach the bottom step of the deck. A metal sign bolted to the house at the left of the entrance reads, "Beware of Turtle." On the opposite side, strings of colorful seashells hang from the porch ceiling like beaded curtains in a fortune-teller's doorway. I bound up the stairs between the numerous potted plants and stand on the open-air porch. In front of me is a screen door offering a view inside the house. With the windows raised and the main door wide open, the lack of security suggests someone is home. But this is island living—carefree and unconcerned. I rap on the wooden screen and announce my greeting.

I listen for a reply, a rustling, footsteps, but all I hear is the gentle melody of the wind chimes surrounding me. I try another couple of knocks and one more hello, but they fall on the emptiness of an untenanted house. I conclude that if this is Amber's home, it is conceivable she is on the mainland with her mother identifying the bodies of her stepbrothers.

I turn when I hear noise coming from the house next door. Sal Santini emerges onto his porch carrying a couple of bags. I watch as he descends the stairway and hurries along the path toward his boat. Now I'm no sleuth, but I find it awfully curious that he seems to be in a hurry, as if making an escape. I leave what is now confirmed as Amber's porch and make my way over to the cover of a bushy needle palm separating the properties. I spy on Sal as he returns from his boat less the bags. He bolts up the stairs and goes back inside the house. I don't have a good feeling about this. Sal hasn't mentioned a trip or a move. *Is this a hasty retreat or simply housecleaning?* His actions seem suspicious to me on the same day two dead men, who I suspect are Amber's brothers, are making headlines.

Rather than speculate, I decide to mosey out from behind my concealment and offer Sal my assistance. He emerges a few seconds later with more duffle bags—one over his shoulder and one in each hand. After he walks by the bush, I step out and call his name. As I say it, I realize it is a stupid thing to do.

Sal stops in his tracks. The bags slip from his hands and fall to the path. I see his arm move into the shoulder bag, and then suddenly the big man whips around with a handgun pointed in my direction. Back in Massachusetts, Carlos, the warehouse manager at Winchester Rope, tossed small items such as paper clips at me every morning. In Florida, people prefer to point guns at me. Maybe I should've moved to an uninhabited island in the South Pacific.

"Whoa! Time out, Sal," I shout. I throw my arms in the air to surrender.

"What the fuck, Jason?" Sal spits back. "You stupid or what sneaking up on me like that?"

"I'm not sneaking, Sal. I was just over at Amber's, checking in on how she's doing. Did you hear about her brothers?"

The gun is still pointed at me—my hands are still in the air. He looks beyond me to Amber's house.

"Yeah, too bad. You the one who popped them?" he chuckles.

So it is true. The men in black are dead. How did Sal already know?

He lowers the gun, places it in the small of his back, and reaches for the bags on the ground. I slowly lower my hands.

"I heard on the news they were executed," I say, the statement lingering in the late morning humidity. Sal lifts the bags, turns, and continues to the boat. I dare not move. Since the day I first met Sal, he has been a bit peculiar, a little mysterious, somewhat threatening, and a whole lot of unpredictable—especially now that I know he subscribes to the gun-of-the-month club. On his way back toward me he says, "So?"

I stand in the pathway as he shuffles by, no eye contact and no invite inside for a cold drink. He enters the house. Here's where I extend my nose firmly where it doesn't belong. I should have referred to my *Dummies Guide to Hermit Living*, and retreated to my end of the sand dune. But I didn't. When he exits with more bags, I start asking him questions like a contestant with all the answers on *Jeopardy*.

"Sal, can I help you?"

"No."

"Are you moving out or something?"

"No."

"Are you leaving the island for a while?"

"Maybe."

"Are you coming over to watch the sunset later?"

"Yeah." That last answer is thrown over his shoulder as he reaches the boat. He unloads the bags, leans on a piling, and removes a cloth from a back pocket to wipe his brow. The humidity does not seem to mix well with the years of Italian pastries secured to his midsection like layers of concrete. After a few deep breaths, he regains his footing on the path.

Alex, I'll take "Killers Among Us" for $1000.

When he is a few feet from me, I take my life in my hands and blurt, "Did you kill those guys, Sal?"

He comes to a sudden stop like an eighteen-wheeler would— if it could. Instantly, the bad-guy Mafia stare is all over me like a bunch of football players falling on a fumble.

"I'm just asking . . . based on our conversation on the boat," I add, tentatively.

He peers down at me. Sweat pours freely from his face. I'm not sure if he is debating whether to shoot me or snap me like a twig. It is the longest minute I've experienced since the day I stood at the altar and waited for Megan to finish, "I . . . I . . . I . . . I do."

"Don't you have something to rake?" he finally says.

"I spoke with Amber yesterday. Her stepbrothers were no-bodies. They were just down here creating a little trouble while visiting their mother, and now they're headline news. I think you're paranoid, Sal. They weren't here for you."

He sighs. As he is pulling out the cloth to revisit his brow, he says, "This is bigger than you, Trust Fund. There are rats every-where right now and each one is talking up a storm—some to cop a plea, others to cover their ass. Those guys over there," he says pointing at Amber's house, "they was rats. I don't know what degree of rat they were, but they were down here to rat."

"How do you know that? I mean, what are the odds your neighbor would have brothers spying on you?"

"Fuck the odds. It's instinct. I know it when I see it. Like when you pulled me off the sand bar, I knew you was a civil-ian. These guys—fucking rats. Maybe they held the paper on me, maybe they was just putting me back on the map. Either way, they had to go."

I take a step back from him and replay what I think sounds like a confession. Yet he doesn't seem fazed by his admission. It is as if it slipped out and he doesn't know it, like a person running a stop sign inadvertently. Sal Santini is a killer.

Grasping for something to say to keep Sal from realizing what just spilled from his mouth, which of course once he does, will put me in great peril, I utter, "How did the music business get so out of hand, Sal? Is this like an East Coast versus West Coast type of thing?"

He looks at me strangely. "Huh?"

I shift gears. "So what's with all the bags? Are you going back to Providence to straighten things out?"

Sal turns and looks at his boat. "No. I'm thinning out. Putting some stuff into storage. I may leave in a few days, I need a vacation."

"You are on a vacation."

He stares at me again. It isn't his Mafia glare this time, although it is still unnerving. It is as if he is coming to some kind of decision about what to do with me. My problem is I have no idea of the infestation that clutters his mind.

He extends his large paw and it falls on my shoulder. "Can I trust you, Trust Fund? You're about the only guy I can turn to right now."

Suddenly I miss the frigid temperatures of New England.

"I don't know, Sal. I'm still trying to fill in the blanks. What if somebody really has that paper on you and I happen to be standing near you when they arrive. Will they take me down, too, or do they need like a special override or an addendum for that?"

Sal removes his hand from my shoulder. "You know, Trust Fund, you've eaten too many of them M&M's. Your mind is like on a sugar high; your imagination on overdrive, *capisce*?"

I nod to the killer before me. I sense an argument might be detrimental.

He reaches into his pocket and removes a set of keys. "Take these—one for my Escalade and one for the boat. It's a duplicate set in case something unforeseen might happen." He motions for me to follow him to the steps, where we sit.

"In the car you'll find a Dean Martin CD. Open it up to the bio on Dino. There'll be three numbers noted in pen—one at the beginning, one in the middle, and one in the end. It ain't obvious, so study it carefully. You know where Stor-Mor Public Storage is in Englewood?"

"No idea."

"Then find it. My stuff will be in bay 17. Those numbers on the CD will open the combination lock. Start at zero then go right, left, right, got it?"

"Why are you telling me this, Sal?"

Another wipe of his brow. He doesn't answer me at first; instead he seems to be studying the sandy pathway at the foot of the stairs. I wait.

The song of the cicadas responds to the day's heat. Two chameleons run in circles around the base of a palm tree.

"I fucked up," he says.

"Are you referring to Amber's . . ."

"Up in Providence. I was given a job, but it didn't go as planned. How the fuck was I supposed to know the boss's son was a finook?"

This is like trying to put a brick through a key hole. "So let me get this straight, your boss at the music company had a son that what . . . finooked? Is that like a fishing term or something?"

Sal rakes his face. "How can anyone be so civilian? No, it means his son was playing for the other team—like a homo, except he was as tough as nails like his old man, the head of the family. Go figure. Anyway, I fucked up. So I had to come down here and wait it out while people I trusted tried to make things good. You know, explain it like it was all a mistake. But instead, a war broke out."

"Are you telling me you're the cause of all that Mafia stuff happening in Providence?"

Sal nods.

"Holy shit! No wonder you're paranoid." I immediately start surveying the area for assassins hiding in the foliage. I shift my seat slightly away from Sal in the hopes I can escape from being collateral damage.

"So I came down here, stayed under the radar and waited. Problem is most of my connections are dead now. I know there's a contract on me—important people want me dead. So don't tell me I'm paranoid when I'm being cautious."

"You killed the boss's son? The Mafia boss?"

Sal nods.

"And you killed Amber's brothers because you think they were here to kill you?"

"They admitted being here."

"Of course they did. They *were* here. But not for you."

"I put the barrel in the big guy's mouth and the little guy sang a tune."

"Sal, what if he just said what you wanted to hear to save his brother?"

He shrugs. "I would've killed them either way."

I stand up to leave. Sal says, "Sit down." I sit down.

"What I'm telling you is between you and me, *capisce*? I need to trust you for the time being until I figure out what my next move is. I'm expecting a call today from a friend up north who ain't dead yet. He's got his ear to the ground, finding out stuff. I suspect the boss handing out the paper will keep sending mechanics down here, and I'll keep making trophies out of them."

"What do you mean by trophies?" I ask.

Sal reflects for a second as if he might answer my question, but instead he says, "But that gets dangerous, so I need to move around until I figure how to go on the offense. *Capisce*? Kill or be killed. So you and me—we got this trust thing now. If they get to me, you go to the storage unit and dispose of all the bodies."

"What?"

"I'm fuckin' with ya, Trust Fund. There'll be instructions inside on what to do. You only go there if I'm dead, *capisce*? If you go there prematurely, I'll kill you prematurely. Deal?"

"*Deal?* I'm not liking the terms, Sal."

He shrugs as if he doesn't care about my concerns, and then extends his hand to seal our agreement. Out of fear for my life, I shake it and say, "Just so I understand, you've been hiding down here the whole time?"

"Yeah."

"And there's no music business?"

"No music business."

"And you're a . . . *hit man*?"

"Now you know, Trust Fund."

CHAPTER TWENTY-TWO

Island Anxiety

"I try not to worry about the future, so I take each day
just one anxiety attack at a time."
—TOM WILSON

I rise slowly from the porch step and survey the best escape route
to my boat. It appears the conversation with Sal has concluded,
leaving two options lingering in the humidity like the sweat beads
along his upper lip. He could either trust I will keep his secret
and let me leave or he could suffer an anxiety attack of second
thoughts and kill me on the spot. I am not prepared for this predicament, nor have I read anything about Mafia confessions.

I feign a stretch to conceal my intensifying fear. The sudden
enlightenment of Sal's occupation and his murderous endeavors
causes my heart to pound like a drum, and my shorts to rise into
an uncomfortable wedge. I have shown this killer my home, sat
with him during sunsets, and spent a day bomb-fishing on his
boat. Being an ardent profiler, I should've recognized the clues:
the Italian lobster pastry, the general mobster-type demeanor, the
arsenal of weapons. And the boat name – *Wicked Pissa Hits*. Talk
about a double meaning. I had hoped over time my new friendship with a music producer might pay dividends in the form of a
few autographs from some famous singers. Instead, the man has
graded his accomplishments on the stern.

My anxiety level soars into the stratosphere. *How does one dis-
engage from a hit man?* I want to move, but my feet feel like they
are cemented in place. If I could summon the courage to simply
walk away, it would mean turning my back on him, whereby I

am sure I'd soil my shorts in anticipation of a slug tearing into my back. Or I could walk backward toward the dock watching to see if he made a move with his gun, as if I could outrun or dodge a bullet fired in my direction. Suddenly, Sal rocks in place on the top step and frees the cloth from his pocket. I nearly empty my bladder.

I sense the longer we remain without words, the greater the chance Sal will change his mind and turn my trust into dust, so I ask him, "Is it hot enough for ya?"

He wipes his brow, his face, and then lets the cloth linger around his flabby neck. When he is satisfied he's soaked up enough perspiration, he stuffs the cloth into his pocket and reaches for the porch railing. I keep a keen eye on his hands. Any movement toward the small of his back and I'll ask God's forgiveness for ignoring Him all my life.

Sal grunts as he lifts his bulk upright. He brushes the sand from his pants, farts, and says, "See you at sunset." He turns and heads inside the house, the butt end of the gun reaching out from the crack of his ass.

My mind is already in the boat setting course for Massachusetts, but my heart, ever the cool dude, has other plans. Even though I promised Sal, under duress I might add, that I would keep his secret, I'm enraptured with the idea of saving Fiona. If what Sal predicted about bad guys on their way down to try to kill him comes true, the proximity of Fiona's presence on the island might put her in harm's way. She could be standing on the ferry dock when assassins riddle the area with machine-gun fire, like my gangster parrot is prone to do. Or she could be jogging along Gulf Boulevard near Sal's house at the exact moment hired killers launch a grenade attack. The scenarios are too numerous. I need to rescue Fiona—remove her from the imminent danger—be her Caucasian knight in shining armor.

I retreat onto Amber's property, turning my head every second or so, maybe more, to focus on Sal's whereabouts. I study the doorway and windows to see if he is sizing me up through the scope of a rifle, or holding a clacker to detonate a concealed claymore mine, which would send out hundreds of fragmented steel balls to disintegrate me and ruin my already shitty day. I quicken my pace.

When I arrive on the dock, I reach in my pocket for the keys. I have to root out mine from the sets Sal gave me. I power up the *Ticket* while replaying in my head why I'm in possession of his keys. One is for his Escalade and the other for his boat. A Dean Martin CD is in the car. There is a code inside the CD flap. I'm supposed to look for three numbers to unlock a combination. First left, then right, or maybe right, then left, and it is located at a storage facility. Bay number . . . *shit!* I power the boat in reverse, clear the dock, and shift into forward steering deeper into the inlet in search of Fiona's rental.

It wasn't like a blood-brother type ritual. Sal and I didn't carve up our palms and press them together to forever bond his confession as sacred between us. But I did agree to keep his secret. He needed to trust me. I guess in Mafia speak, that probably means I better keep my mouth shut, but Fiona's well-being trumps whatever trust Sal has burdened me with. It's not like I'm going to the police—I simply want to rescue my damsel in distress, even though she isn't quite in distress yet.

As I steer through a bend in the inlet, I glimpse the backside of Fiona just as she disappears into a thicket of mangroves and shrubs where her dock meets land. At the waters end of the mooring, a tall man leans against a piling, smoking a cigarette, while observing my approach. He is wearing cream-colored pants with a matching sport jacket over a mint colored T-shirt—a Sonny Crockett wannabe. *Is this the dude Toast had seen with Fiona? Is he the reason she lied about going to Tallahassee?* Maybe there isn't a damsel to rescue.

As I drift closer, the man comes into focus and my first thought is he looks like one of those Decepticon robots from the *Transformers* movies. His physique makes me wonder if he had recently transformed from the shape of an M1 battle tank. Draw a square and place a circle on top and it would be an artist's rendering— broad shoulders, big arms, expanded chest, tree-trunk legs, and a small pecker. I'm not sure of the latter, but the thought brings a smile to my face. Am I jealous? Of course I am. Why do I always lose women to men who look like they belong on the cover of bodybuilding magazines? The anxiety of the day, mixed with the simmering heat, and a dash of woe-is-me, has turbocharged my erratic imagination.

I toss a bumper over the side as I approach the dock. The mass of muscle looks at me, cigarette in mouth—a fierce drag in process. I cut the engine and ask, "Fiona around?"

"Who wants to know?"

"Who's on first base." It's like I can't control myself.

"What?"

"What's on second."

Exasperated, the machine man pushes away from the piling and peers down at me. "What are you, a wise guy?"

No, he lives a few docks down. "I need to speak with Fiona. It's important."

He points his stogie-sized finger at me. "I decide who speaks to Fiona and it ain't you because I don't know you."

"I don't know is on third." A part of me clearly harbors a death wish.

The man inhales another lungful of smoke, balances the re-maining butt on his thumb, and then flicks it at me. I dodge the missile and give the creep my best Sal Santini-inspired Mafia intimidation stare. He doesn't appear to shake in his Top-Siders, so I up the ante. I point back at him and declare, "Only I can save Fiona, now go get her."

Sometimes I should just keep my mouth shut. If I provoke the machine man, he could easily jump into my boat and turn me into a human accordion.

He starts laughing. "Only I can save Fiona?" he mimics. "You're a funny little man. Now turn around and go back to where you came from."

Where I came from is my neighbor's house who just happens to be an assassin. If this guy has stolen Fiona from me, I wonder if Sal would offer a discount rate on his professional services now that we share his secret. I puff out my chest and demand to see Fiona again.

"I said, leave now or I'll throw you from here to the mainland," the machine man barks.

I have no doubt he can deliver on that threat, so my next mistake is to flip a feisty middle finger in his direction. It is the equivalent of lighting a fuse. The man turns red with anger as if instantly sunburned. He starts shuffling his feet, looking for the easiest way to get down into my boat without soiling his *Miami Vice* outfit. I grab the only thing I can to defend myself, a spare bumper, and hold it like a baseball bat. Suddenly, a cool breeze materializes in the form of an angel's voice.

"Jason?"

I look over to see Fiona walking barefoot onto the dock, flashing a brilliant smile. She is wearing a brightly colored, palm-print bikini, which contrasts beautifully against her tanned skin. From the corner of my eye, I notice machine man retreat a step, so I drop the bumper.

"What are you doing over here?" she asks.

"Can we talk?"

"Of course. Here, throw me your line."

She catches my toss and ties the *Ticket* to the dock as the machine man looks on. I step onto the gunwale and then the dock and stand between Fiona and the Decepticon. He looked big from my boat, but is even bigger standing next to me. As I size him up, he flexes his pecs beneath the tight T-shirt which I've come to believe is some kind of physical disorder among bodybuilders— the result from years of steroid injections. I give him a look of indifference knowing muscles are no match for an obese assassin with guns. I turn to Fiona. She reaches out and takes my hands in hers.

"What do you want to talk about?" she says.

I start to say something, but the moment is awkward. I want to be alone with her to see if I am still relevant. Plus, I have to rescue her from the impending doom of the soon-to-be gunslinger convention on Sand Key. I can't say all this if the machine man behind me is her new love interest. I look at Fiona and roll my eyes in his direction.

She looks at me confused and utters with a smile, "What?"

I roll my eyes again, arch my eyebrows repeatedly, and tilt my head to draw her attention behind me. She still doesn't get it.

"Jason, just spit it out."

Maybe I need a PowerPoint presentation, complete with graphs. I clear my voice and lean in close to her. "Who's the guy?"

She smiles. "Jason, this is Thomas Hawke. Thomas, this is my friend, Jason Najarian."

I turn slightly to my left, acknowledge his presence with a nod, and turn back to Fiona. No handshakes are exchanged or expected, for just moments earlier I had planned to kill him with my bumper.

"What is a Thomas Hawke?" I ask her.

Sensing a testosterone confrontation, Fiona wraps my arm around hers as we begin to walk across the dock toward the island.

"I'm so happy to see you. Did you miss me?"

When I am far enough away from the machine man to speak above a whisper, I ask again, "What is a Thomas Hawke?"

"Thomas is my bodyguard. The Indian Affairs Commission thought it best I be assigned some protection. Unfortunately, not everyone agrees with our agenda. So, Thomas travels with me when the venue is published and people know I'll be in attendance. Usually Tallahassee, and especially when I'm staying in Washington. He's really a nice guy when you get to know him."

I don't want to sound like a lawyer doing a cross-examination in court, but I need to know how *much* of a nice guy she thinks he is. "Did he go with you yesterday to Tallahassee?"

My phone vibrates. I lift it out of my pocket and see the incoming call from my father. This is not a good time to hear how thrilled he is to be with Tranquility. Nor do I care about the size of the fish he probably just reeled in. I'll leave it for the monkey and get back to him later.

"No, Tallahassee was cancelled yesterday," she says. "Instead we drove over to Orlando to meet with a contributor. I was going to tell you all this tonight when I came over. Assuming you still want me to spend the rest of my vacation with you?"

A pleasant vibe comes ashore. It is the same feeling I had when I realized the lottery numbers matched, but not as intense. My problem has solved itself. Well, one at least. I turn toward the machine man and smirk. "Tommy Hawke? *Really?*" I say, feeling confident about my situation.

"Hush . . . we don't call him Tommy. He's sensitive about the correlation."

I wish she hadn't told me that.

We walk a little farther until even a strong breeze can't carry my voice. It is time to save Fiona and break Sal's trust a mere hour after Sal expected it to last forever.

"Did you hear about Amber's brothers?"

"No . . . well, she told me they were here to visit her mother."

"First of all, these are the guys I mentioned who dress in black—the goons who harassed me. Yesterday, Amber paid me a visit and told me about her stepbrothers, how much trouble they are, and how she dislikes them. But she never mentioned their interaction with me. I think she's clueless about what these guys have been up to."

"Why would Amber's brothers harass you? They're down here to visit their mother."

"My guess is they are infatuated with you, and when they saw you take an interest in me, that's when the trouble started for me."

"I find that hard to believe."

Which part? "Anyways, it's not important anymore. This morning they were found murdered in their hotel room. It's all over the news." .

Fiona takes a step back, her eyes wide with surprise. "We need to go see Amber."

"I already tried. No one answered. She's probably on the mainland dealing with police business. But it gets worse."

"Please don't tell me you're involved, Jason."

In some perverted way, I take it as a compliment that the woman I am falling in love with would think I had the stones to bump off two bad guys. My resume would not live up to her expectations, though. Tomato throwing or wielding a boat bumper would certainly fall at the bottom of Sal Santini's preferred weapon list.

"No, I'm not involved. But . . . can you keep this between us?"

Fiona says yes, but her head is shaking no. I look to my left and then my right. I turn toward the machine man to make sure he hasn't transformed into a giant bionic hearing aid.

"Keep what, Jason?" she exclaims.

"Sal."

With a confused look she replies, "Sal what?"

I lean closer and whisper. "Sal killed them. He's a hit man."

Fiona pauses for a moment and then starts to laugh. "Okay, nice." She looks beyond me as if someone is hiding in the shrubs. "You got me. The joke's on me. Where's fat Sal hiding?"

"Fiona, listen to me. Sal is a hit man. The Mafia is after him. He believes Amber's brothers had some kind of paper contract on him, so he went and killed them last night. He admitted this to me just an hour ago. And he also said that more bad guys are probably coming after him."

She looks into my eyes for the truth, biting her lip. "I've been down here a month and never once felt Sal to be that kind of person. I don't believe it. It must be some kind of misunderstanding."

"I assure you it isn't. Sal confided in me and made me promise not to tell anyone."

"But why you?"

"I haven't figured that out yet. Maybe we bonded while bomb-fishing. Anyway, he's still coming over for sunset, so this is not a matter open for discussion."

"This whole thing makes me very upset, Jason. I only have a few days left on the island, so I wanted it to be special. I feel so sad for Amber and her mother. And Sal . . . I don't know what to make of this. I'm scared."

I remove my knight's helmet and slide off my horse. "Me too. This is why I think it best you move into my place for the rest of your time on the island, sans the tomahawk guy of course. I'd feel a lot better knowing you're safe. You said you wanted to spend time with me before you leave, so make it full time. I can offer raked sand, a foul-beaked parrot, and plenty of M&M's. What more could you want?"

Fiona smiles, but it is forced. The news has troubled her. Her focus is everywhere but on me, as if she is calculating her next move. I wait for a reply, but she seems immobilized by a state of indecision. I suspect she will opt to stay by Amber's side, as a concerned friend would, in an effort to comfort her.

"Look, think it over. Whatever you decide, please stay clear of Sal's house." I kiss her cheek and start for the dock where I dread walking past the machine man to get to my boat.

After a few steps she calls out my name. I stop and turn.

"I'll pack my things and be over later."

I nod.

Her appearance brightens. She hurries back to her cottage and I turn for the dock. As I make my approach, the machine man has another cigarette in his mouth, his jacket is folded over a rope line, and he has donned a pair of mirror sunglasses. I dislike not seeing where someone's eyes are darting, and I hate even more seeing my reflection approaching me.

On the dock, the machine man folds his arms over his chest to accentuate his biceps while I attend to the cleat to release the boat. As is my warped proclivity for stupidity, I start humming the old war chant of the Atlanta Braves baseball team—the one where thousands of people respond with a tomahawk chop.

The machine man doesn't pick up on it at first. I throw the line in the boat, step onboard, and start the engine. After I've cleared the dock, I turn the volume of my chant up to that of a scream, and accompany it with my own version of the chop. The machine man points at me and says, "Get back here."

My proclivity for stupidity has its limits. I stay the course.

When he realizes I'm not about to turn my boat around and confront his wrath, he displays a series of body gestures; a flip from under his chin, a slap of his outstretched arm, and an assortment of middle fingers all to send me an ominous message.

He yells, "How about I give you another black eye?"

I push the throttle forward to expedite my escape. And then I think—another black eye like the one I have? Or another black eye like the one he already . . .

CHAPTER TWENTY-THREE

Island Tension

"We're all in this alone."

—LILY TOMLIN

When I arrive back at my house, all appears calm. Paradise at the northern edge of Sand Key has been unaffected by the tumultuous events going on at the southern end of the island. Murder and mayhem have engulfed Sal and Amber, and I fear Sal's continual pilgrimage to the sunset seats could endanger the peacefulness of Hermitville, like a sudden earthquake rattles a beautiful day. But how do you tell a hit man to screw off?

This is what I get for sticking my nose where it doesn't belong. I merely wanted to express my sympathies to Amber for the loss of her brothers, even though the news set off a muted Mardi Gras-type celebration within me. Instead, I had unwillingly assumed the role of a confessional priest to an assassin, along with that of a crypt keeper to his secrets in some mysterious storage unit. Thankfully, I convinced Fiona to escape to the safety of my arms. But then there was that parting comment by the machine man. The dichotomy of events has my mind spinning as I welcome an exhaustive collapse onto the couch. And then I feel my smartiephone bounce in my pocket, and I'm reminded of my father's call. I fish out the phone and tap in his number.

"Hi, Jason . . ."

"Hey, Tranquility, I didn't know you had caller ID so deep in the sticks."

". . . how's the weather in the Sunshine State?"

"My dad called earlier, is he around?"

"I bet it's warm, huh?"

"Is everything all right with my father?" I assume it is or Tranquility's opening indolence would've been more on the side of urgency rather than the weather. But who knows with her.

"And how come they call it the Sunshine State? I've watched the weather station on television, Jason, and it sure gets sunny in other states, too."

The duo of Megan and Tranquility would cast perfectly for the female version of *Dumb and Dumber*. "My dad, is he around?"

"Oh yeah, we get caller ID up here. It's really cool to see the picture of the person calling. I'm looking at you now, Jason. Smile."

I rake my face. "Tranny, I need to speak with my dad. He called me."

"Yes, your dad is doing fine."

If my smartiephone hadn't cost so much, I'd heave it into the gulf right about now. "Here's a clue: Find my father and hand him the phone you're holding."

"Do you want to speak with him?"

She reminds me of a new ketchup bottle that won't spill its slurry no matter how many times I whack it. "As much as I love mindless banter, Tranny, I need to speak with my father."

"I'm handing the phone to your dad now. I can't wait to see you on Thanksgiving. Save some sun for me."

Yes, I'll put some sun in a jar and save it. These are minutes wasted I'll never get back. If I don't already have enough on my mind, the realization of a Tranquility and Bradley visit on Thanksgiving strengthens my nascent headache. Having them both here will definitely offset the effects of a dozen Ativan taken in one gulp. I will have to beg Fiona to attend if not just for balance.

"Hello son, I think I've blundered."

The admission surprises me. My father is never wrong, and he isn't shy about letting me know that. But I've often wondered how long it would take for him to realize the age difference, or intelligence gap, or the bush under her arms, would wear thin. Had it reached that point?

"Dad, look, she's young and a bit naive. You knew that going in. As much as the sex is probably great, she's still a space cadet."

"What the hell are you talking about?"

My dad's anger surprises me. I sit up and realize I might be holding a tennis racket on a football field. "What are *you* talking about?" I counter, hesitantly.

"Your mother says I screwed up."

I sigh. He is dumping Tranquility. "Look, I'm sure Ma is jealous and she's prone to offer opinions that get under your skin, but . . ."

"Jason, are you high on something?"

"No, Dad."

"Then let me get out what I have to say without you blabbering. Megan called me a few days ago and wanted to know exactly where you are living. She told me she had something that belonged to you."

My head falls into my idle palm. My skin begins to crawl. I sense a shit storm forming over the gulf.

"So I told her you bought a place on Sand Key off the west coast of Florida. She wanted to know if it was also called Abuc or something, but I had no idea. I told her all I knew—Gulf Boulevard on Sand Key just south of Sarasota. She seemed happy after I told her. She also mentioned how difficult it's been to find you, and that finally she could return what was rightfully yours. I didn't know what the hell she meant, so I called your mother and she explained the situation to me. You should've let me know, son, that you didn't want Megan back in your life."

My headache has evolved into a migraine. *Do I have enough time to sell the property and flee from both the hit man and the crazy ex-wife?* "Did she happen to mention when she was coming down?"

"Well, not exactly, but her parting words suggested she was catching the next available flight."

"Shit."

I pace the living room trying to figure out how the arrival of hurricane Megan might upset the relationship I have cultivated with Fiona. I could call and caution her about coming down—bad weather, rabid manatees, North Korean invasion—but I feel certain my efforts would be ignored. By calling my father, Megan appears to be on a mission and her obsession with becoming my wife again is squarely in her sights. I hoped by now my antics would've demonstrated I didn't want her in my life. Yet something wicked this way cometh. I have underestimated her penchant for my financial windfall.

I stop in front of Montana's cage in a lame attempt for guidance, but all the gangster parrot offers is, *"Why don't you try sticking your head up your ass? See if it fits."* What a team player.

"Jason?" I hear the faint call from the deck beyond the front entrance. I rush across the room, open the door and see Fiona. She is standing with luggage in both hands. She looks troubled. Her smile is mislaid. Without a word, I reach for the bags and Fiona hurries back down to the golf cart for another suitcase and her handbag. I meet her halfway up the staircase, take the additional bags, and follow her up and into the house.

"You're right," she blurts.

"About what," I say, lowering her belongings. The designer bag still weighs a ton.

She puts a hand to her forehead. "As I was leaving, I saw several men rummaging near the properties as if they were looking for something or somebody. I was so scared driving through the bird sanctuary wondering if I'd even make it here. Maybe I should just leave the island now and go to the motel where Thomas is staying. I'm so scared, Jason. I feel something bad is about to happen."

I take her in my arms. "You're safe here. If something happens at the south end, it won't affect us. Maybe the guys you saw were police looking for clues related to Amber's brothers?"

"Maybe so, but you said Sal is coming over here for the sunset. What if he brings trouble with him?" She pushes away from me. "If what you told me is true, I really don't want to be near that man again."

"I understand, but he is coming over with Toast, just like every night. If we don't join them, he'll get suspicious. It's not a good idea to be on Sal's bad side at the moment."

Fiona slumps onto the couch. "Why don't we just leave a note on the beach chairs telling them I had an emergency on the mainland? Some excuse like that. Then we load my luggage on your boat and go. We can have a quiet dinner in Sarasota and then get a room."

I sit down and take her hand in mine. This is my opening to see if she really harbors feelings for me. "I don't want you to leave tomorrow night. I'd like you to stay with me. Live with me. Grow old with me."

Fiona looks into my eyes with the same lost expression I've seen before. It is as if she wants to jump into my arms and accept, but is held back by a straitjacket of circumstances. *What is holding her back? Is it her lifetime commitment to the Indian affairs job? Is it my laid-back lifestyle in contradiction to her political aspirations? Or is it as I suspected—she is just too good looking for me.*

She sighs. "I need a sugar fix." She grabs a handful of M&M's and walks out onto the gulf-front porch. I follow in her wake carrying Montana in his cage.

The beach chairs are empty, it is still too early to meet for sunset, but a few boats have started to anchor offshore. We sit and Fiona immediately snuggles up to me and wraps her arms around my neck. She exposes her tongue with a glob of colorfully melted chocolate. I know this is her way of changing the subject. I won't get an answer and my pride won't allow me to ask for one again.

She seductively swallows the chocolate and then our lips meet. The kiss is soft at first, tentative, playful, before she presses hard and passionately. I am confused. Call me old-fashioned, but I can't reconcile how someone can display such desire and then simply walk away a day later. I compare her disingenuous affection to that of Sal's impassive ability to murder. These two have similar characteristics.

After a period of quiet embrace, our eyes closed, our breathing in sync, the onshore breeze carries with it the sound of laughter. I look beyond Fiona and survey the beach. The hilarity comes from Toast as he attempts to lift Sal before they reach the chairs. His effort is futile, of course: an ant can't lift a boulder, but he tries and falls to the sand in amusement. Sal drops his book and offers Toast a hand. He is also smiling and appears absent of any regret for the murders of Amber's brothers or the fear of an imminent reprisal from the mobsters up north. I realize at that moment I want an annulment to our pact. Sal can keep all his secrets and find someone else to trust. I want out.

"Is that them?" she whispers. I hold on to Fiona like a kid holds on to the string of a helium balloon, fearful if I loosen my grip she will float away forever.

"Yep, they're here."

"How about we climb in bed and hide under the covers until I have to leave for Tallahassee," she purrs.

Tempting, but Fiona is as confusing to me as Sal is threatening. Fearful of my Mafioso neighbor, I don't want my absence from the sunset to be construed as a flight from his predicament until I am able to tell him otherwise. I don't need to be added to his hit list. And I don't want to wake up one morning to find a dolphin's head in my bed.

"I can't. Sal more or less confessed to me the murders of Amber's brothers as well as some Mafia guy up north. I can't just disappear. I need to act like I'm his trusted friend until I figure out an exit strategy. If I don't join him, he'll come looking for me wondering why I didn't spend his last two sunsets together before he departs the island."

Fiona disapproves. "I can't believe you're spurning me for the likes of a callous and overweight . . . killer. If you're right, then that's what he is, Jason, a cold-blooded killer. I think you should make love with me, and not war with him."

I squeeze her tighter. It may be my last opportunity to hold her in my arms.

"I'm sorry," I say, expecting her to get up and demand I take her to the mainland, but she remains in my embrace. My heart is torn that I will soon lose this woman, but I'm reminded it was probably never meant to be. I am certainly in over my head with her. But, hey, what else is new.

Sal and Toast arrive at the chairs. After adjusting his bulk and placing the book he never reads in the sand, Sal takes a glance back at the house. He can't see Fiona and me through the porch screen, but I can see him and from his scowl it appears he's not happy I'm not there to greet him. I need Fiona to make a decision. But first, I offer her an invitation I'm sure she will also ignore.

"Any chance you can escape from your job and visit me on Thanksgiving?" Of course, I realize too late Thanksgiving isn't a popular American Indian holiday.

"I'd love to," she says without hesitation.

Her reply surprises me. I assumed once she left for Tallahassee, I would never see her again.

"Great. I look forward to introducing you to my parents."

"I can't wait," she whispers.

I hate being this perplexed.

"Sal and Toast are in the chairs. It looks like another beautiful sunset shaping up. You can stay here and I'll be back after sundown, or you can join me. It's your call."

Fiona pushes away and looks down at the shoreline. "I'll come with you, but if I get killed in a Mafia shootout, I swear I will never speak to you again."

I place Montana and his cage in the sand, and then sit down next to Sal as Fiona slithers into the chair to my right. I exchange greetings with both men as if this get-together were as normal as any other, but Fiona has arrived with an attitude and refuses to say a word, which causes Sal to lean over in her direction.

"Hey, where was ya? We came by and you wasn't there?" Sal inquires.

Fiona ignores him. She remains distant, her gaze bonded to the horizon. I'm sitting between them hoping Fiona says something. I am fearful her continued silence will reflect back on me and signal to Sal I have shared his secret. I need a diversion.

"So Sal, what's tonight's joke?" I ask.

Sal leans back, his face begins to brighten. He is more than eager to share another crass joke from his endless library of witticisms. He lights up a cigar and delivers the gag to an attentive audience of two. When the punch line arrives, Toast bends over in laughter. Sal joins him with a belly laugh between blowing smoke rings. When he looks at me, I say, "Good one, Sal." When he looks beyond me, he is no longer amused.

"What the fuck, you catch the bird flu? You ain't talking neither, like mountain bird over there?" Sal complains to Fiona.

"It's not mountain, Sal, it's Montana. And he does talk," I interject. "Wow, what a sunset, huh?"

Fiona turns her head toward Sal and finally says, "Have you no sympathy for Amber's family? We should be talking about how we can help her, not sharing disgusting jokes. Her brothers are dead, *Sal*."

I cringe as Fiona piles too much emphasis on his name.

"Fuck them," he roars. The two words hit the beach like the Normandy invasion. His anger is so loud I notice a few people out in their boats turn toward the shore. Sal shifts in his seat, lowers his cigar, and points his finger at Fiona. I can clearly see the Mafia resemblance once unwrapped.

"They got what they asked for. Whoever punched their ticket deserves a medal." He places his hand on my shoulder. "Ask Trust Fund here. All the shit they put him through."

Will I never stop being the center of attention? "Wow, look at how orange the orange color is," I say, pointing toward the sunset.

Fiona sits stunned. She has retreated from Sal's outburst by slumping in the chair and folding her arms across her breasts. She is pissed and I am regretting my suggestion that she join me at sunset. I have no doubt she will demand I take her to the mainland as soon as we get back to the house.

The four of us sit in an uncomfortable silence for what seems like forever. The tension is palpable. Sal and Fiona are fuming, and Toast is oblivious to the exchange as he harvests words for a greeting card nobody would ever voice. The sun has nearly set, the beach is isolated. Some of the boats have begun to pull anchor. It appears there will be no payback against Sal tonight.

Suddenly, Fiona lifts from the chair and storms off. I turn and watch her angry gait kick up sand on the way to the walkover. I then look at Sal. He appears apathetic as he puffs more smoke into the air. But then he squeezes out of the chair and in a furious display throws the cigar into the gulf. Without saying a word, he picks up his book and begins to lumber down the beach toward home. Toast jumps out of the chair and follows in his footsteps.

I sit alone as the theater empties. It is just Montana and me as I contemplate the chaos that surrounds me. I don't know what to do, what to say, how to act. I want Fiona in my life and Sal out of it, but I fear neither will happen. I stare out at the water and focus on the floating Cuban Cohiba. I dread leaving the beach to face Fiona's wrath. *Will she blame me for not taking her side against Sal? Will she admonish me for hanging on to his secret?* Sal's discarded Cohiba drifts lazily with the current. I remind myself to collect his litter or I will find the brown matter deposited by the tide days later and confuse it for a re-regift from North Korea.

As I start to get up, I notice that Sal has reversed course and is stampeding toward me. Toast remains in place farther down the beach, so whatever Sal's intentions are it is between him and me. As he gets closer, I realize what a bowling pin must feel like as the ball barrels down the alley.

"Did you fucking say something to her?" Sal says. He is angry and I notice the hand that isn't holding the book is now a fist.

"What are you talking about?"

"Fiona—she wasn't right in the head tonight. Did you say something about me? Something maybe that was supposed to stay between us?"

"Of course not, Sal. I wouldn't do that. You trusted me to keep a secret and I'm obligated to do so." I hate lying, but I hate dying more. I have to convince Sal I am still on his side.

"I always tell the truth even when I lie."

Stunned, I can't believe Montana has picked this moment to speak. I try to pretend I didn't hear what he clearly said, but the thought that he might mimic my conversation on the porch with Fiona makes my jaw drop. Montana heard it all, and now I fear my gangster parrot could turn state's evidence and become a gangster rat.

Sal leans to one side to look at Montana. "Your fucking bird does talk."

"Yeah, Sal, my fucking bird does talk." I turn toward Montana and give him the stink eye.

"Hey, I'm talking to you."

Montana's sudden need to express himself, along with my assurance of solidarity, places Sal at ease. His large mass relaxes; his fist unclenches. Luckily, dusk is quickly fading to dark so this confrontation is nearing the two-minute warning.

"So whaddaya think?" Sal asks.

"I think the bird doesn't have a clue what he's saying."

"Not the bird . . . Fiona. She on the rag or what?"

"I think she's genuinely upset with the news of Amber's loss. I wouldn't take her reaction tonight any other way."

Sal looks up at the house. "You tapping that, Trust Fund?"

"Yeah, right, me? Come on, Sal, we're just friends. She's sad about leaving, so we decided to get together tonight and have dinner on the mainland." More lies, more secrets, but as long as Montana bites his beak, I just might survive.

"Yeah, monthly rentals end tomorrow," Sal confirms. He turns to see Toast sitting in the sand, halfway to the bend, waiting for him. "He'll be here another two weeks," he says, tilting his head toward Toast. "So after tomorrow, it's just you and him watching the sunsets."

I doubt that. "Sounds like fun. So, you're still headed up north to try to fix things?"

He takes a step closer. "The call I mentioned came in this afternoon. I was warned a team of two is already in place down here, but we know they ain't no more," Sal winks. He pauses for a moment and stares into the thickening dusk. "They'll probably send more, though."

"These are the guys with the paper, right?" I'm talking to an assassin like I might talk to a banker processing a loan.

"I'll find out who has what contract and take care of business on my terms. Ain't no one gonna fuck with Sal Scalise."

"Who's he?" I'm confused.

"You make sure there ain't no pillow talk with Fiona, *capisce?*" he says, while pointing a finger into my chest.

"There isn't any pillow or talk, I promise you. But if you want my two cents, I still think you rubbed out the wrong guys. If I'm right, you still need to be careful."

"Rubbed out?" Sal repeats with a grunt. "You got more balls than a bowling alley, Trust Fund."

I'm not sure if this is a compliment or a threat. He turns and starts walking down the beach to join Toast. "And I don't want your fucking two cents," he shouts out indiscriminately.

Sal's frame slips into the darkness turning him and Toast into shadowy figures. When they are around the bend, I reach for the cage and rake, and proceed back to the house, smoothing the sand behind me as I go. I have only a few minutes to plan my defense in an effort to convince Fiona to stay with me. It won't be easy. In the short time that I've known her, I haven't seen her so angry.

When I walk into the kitchen, my phone is beeping from the counter. I reach for it and retrieve the message pending. It is from Megan and she is calling to say that she knows exactly where I live and that she will be paying me a visit soon. *What else could possibly go wrong?*

I place Montana and his cage back on the hook and scold him for almost getting me killed. I think he flips me the wing. I then walk over to the foyer in search of Fiona and notice the outside lights are on. Then I realize all of her bags are gone.

"Fiona?"

CHAPTER TWENTY-FOUR

Island Shadows

"Sometimes things aren't always what they seem."
—AUTHOR UNKNOWN

I open the front door and step outside. From the deck, I peer down at the foot of the staircase and notice her golf cart is gone. It is as I dreaded. I scan Gulf Boulevard, but all I can discern are the shadows of nature leading down to the bird sanctuary. The incoming tide plays an undulating melody that whistles through the flora. The breeze is slight, the air refreshing, and the sky is beginning to illuminate with sparkling dots of distant worlds. All seems perfect in paradise with the exception of a growing void in my heart. I realize I can't appreciate the moment with the knowledge that Fiona has just up and left.

But I expected as much. I am a mere rest stop in the highway of her life. She jogged in, gassed up, had a bite to eat, and moved on as quickly as she arrived. It is an exodus on her part without a hug, or a good-bye. I doubt she ever looked back.

I inhale deeply and hold the essence of nature within me in an effort to heal my inner wound. I close my eyes and give Fiona one last chance. I count to ten. When I open my eyes, she is still gone.

I dim the exterior lights and retreat to the living room where I slump in a chair and grab the remote. I surf around for a movie, but after a while nothing holds my interest. I'm not hungry and I don't have the motivation to lift weights, so I decide to call it a night. But before doing so, I call Megan to strongly suggest she cancel her plans to come to Gulf Boulevard. The last thing I need is her prowling around in my zip code.

My first attempt goes to voicemail, so I hang up and send a text. In it I explain that recent events on the island have made it a very dangerous place. I tell her people have been killed and fish bombed. I explain how I've been chased by gunslingers and my home was invaded by a gang of ruthless thugs—I have a wicked nasty black eye to prove it. I tell her if she shows up, I can't guarantee her safety. I urge her to stay put and I will come up to see her as soon as things calm down. I tap the send button hoping to buy myself some time.

My last chore before retiring is to slide in a Three Stooges DVD for Montana's late-night viewing pleasure. I consider it similar to a Rosetta Stone language instructor. In an effort to clean up some of his vocabulary, I've begun playing the adventures of Moe, Larry and Curly in the hopes that by Thanksgiving my gangster bird won't drop any f-bombs on my parents, but Bradley and Tranquility are fair game. So that Montana can tell the difference, I hang an eight-by-ten framed picture of my parents together in better days next to the television while the Stooges yuck it up.

I grab some sunflower seeds from the cabinet. Montana understands this routine and says, *"Me, I want what's coming to me."* What a gangster!

I retreat to the bedroom where the scent of Fiona seems to linger like dust webs. I take a shower and wash away the events of the day, from Sal's revelation to Fiona's separation. Refreshed, I open all the sliding doors in an effort to waft away her memories. I climb into bed and open a book. Eventually, the night air sweeps me away on a cloud of slumber. I don't know how long this jaunt lasts, but it is rudely interrupted by a banging noise. I toss a bit under the covers, not sure if the noise really exists. The book slips off the bed with a thud as my eyes open to total darkness.

The banging returns, clearer now.

Startled, I rise from the bed, slip into a pair of shorts, and pad to the top of the staircase. Is Montana making the noise? The

DVD has run its course, so the house is completely still. I wait. My body is tense, ready for something, yet prepared for a false alarm. When the noise fails to repeat, I relax, writing it off to roving island critters.

Another bang.

I nearly jump out of my shorts. I run down the stairs and maneuver slowly through the darkened living room using LED specs on my electronic equipment like runway lights. I crawl into the kitchen, reach up for the counter, and retrieve the biggest and sharpest blade I can find from the wooden block of knives. I then work my way toward the front door where the banging has resumed.

When the current series of knocks concludes, I ease closer to the door to listen for voices. I hear none, so I run my hand up the wall until I feel the light switch. My finger leans against the toggle as I assess the situation. If this is a visit from Sal's paper-holders, I am screwed. If it is Sal himself seeking sanctuary, I am screwed. If it is the police with an arrest warrant for not ratting on Sal, I am screwed. If it is Megan making an early arrival—she never did answer her phone—I am screwed. There is no good reason for me to turn on the lights other than I simply can't control myself. I lift the switch and flood the deck with light.

I quickly hunch down away from the door to avoid any gunshots and listen. From the other side I hear a faint female voice say, "Yippee."

"Fiona?"

I stand up and peek through the window. Fiona is standing on the deck looking back at me. She smiles. I unlock the door and let her in.

"I was knocking forever," she says. "I think you need a doorbell."

I am silent as she brushes by me. I close the door, lock it, flip on the foyer light then switch off the exterior lights. I turn and face the enigma standing by the staircase. Fiona places her designer bag on the floor and sits on the second step. She is wearing the same bathing suit from earlier when she fled the beach. I look at the wall clock that reads almost midnight. *Where has she been for the last four hours?*

"Did you get lost?" I ask.

She smiles, and then lowers her head. "I'm sorry. I was so angry at Sal," she says, looking up at me. "I had to get away, but I acted like a petulant child. I blame it on being a hot-blooded Sicilian."

"But you're an Indian."

"I know, go figure. So I drove back down Gulf Boulevard and caught the last ferry over to the mainland. But then I had second thoughts. I didn't want to leave you and I didn't know your cell number. I was sure you would be angry with me if I left without saying a word. And how could I visit on Thanksgiving if you're mad at me, right? So I begged the ferry master to take me back to the island. He agreed, but not on the ferry. I had to wait for him to take me back on his boat. He was kind enough, though, to drop me off at your dock. I came back here, Jason, to say I'm sorry for leaving abruptly, and I'd like to spend the night with you if you'll still have me."

It is a perplexing situation at best. I am eager to accept Fiona back into my arms, but I question how hastily she can simply disappear. What if the ferry master had said no? Her return has my PMS needle encroaching on the danger zone.

"Where are the rest of your bags?" I inquire.

"I stowed them on your boat. Is that being too presumptuous?" She stands and shuffles over to me. "Look, I'm sorry. I owe you an apology and believe it or not, I plan to apologize to Sal tomorrow. As messed up as that sounds, I want to leave here on good terms with everyone. Sal may be the mobster you say he is, but he never did anything bad to me. Right now, though," she coos leaning against me, "I want to show you how sorry I am, but first, can you put that knife away?"

I look at the knife, and head back to the kitchen to replace it. At the same time, Fiona finds the closest bowl of M&M's in the living room and scoops a handful. Back in the foyer, we embrace. With Megan, I learned quickly I was only as good as the sizeable chunk of money in my checking account, so I am a bit suspicious as I wonder what Fiona wants from me. Maybe it is my perpetual stash of M&M's. Hey, that candy won me millions; maybe it found me a beautiful woman, too.

After a few minutes, I switch off the foyer light and we start blindly up the stairs. Fiona calls out into the darkness, "Goodnight, Montana."

The gangster bird replies, *"You know what? Fuck you! How about dat?"*

And that Tony Montana mimic sends Fiona into a fit of giggles.

I can't call it make-up sex, because we weren't really mad at each other. Instead I'll refer to it as clear-up sex because I misinterpreted Fiona's feelings for me based on her bluster toward Sal. And she misconstrued my silence on the beach as support for Sal's anger toward her. There's nothing like a tryst under the sheets to put an end to a convoluted day.

My roller-coaster feelings for her once again reach an apex. For the second time we played nice in the shower and naughty in bed. At times it was like a gentle harp soliloquy, and at other times, a percussion explosion of crashing cymbals. The comforter was kicked off the bed, our clothes were flung haphazardly, and the pillows were nowhere in sight. We jostled, rolled and wrestled until the train whistle blew. Exhausted, we melded together, breathing in rhythm, like the final two pieces of a puzzle. Needless to say, I liked the way she apologized. I hope she doesn't plan on doing the same for Sal. And at some point we fell asleep.

It is a sense of balance that, once disturbed, sends out a distress call to the far reaches of the mind that holds the file marked, "Check this out immediately." For that reason, I find myself suddenly awake in the middle of the night. The bed is out of balance because Fiona is no longer in it. I feel first with my hand, and then my foot, but the other side of the bed is unoccupied. I roll over and look at the clock display: 3:47 A.M. I manage to navigate my eyes to the bathroom where I notice the door open and the light off, just as I left it. To make sure she isn't tinkling in the dark, I crawl out of bed and shuffle over. It is vacant. I rub the stubble on my face, and head over to the sliding doors to see if Fiona is taking in the star-filled evening. The deck chairs are empty. I step outside, lean on the railing, and see the vague foamy caps of the incoming tide brushing against the shore. A thought occurs to me. Maybe she is a closet chocoholic and is in the living room devouring the bowls of M&M's. I'm about to turn and pad downstairs to check this inclination when a shadowy shimmer catches my attention near the beach chairs. I don't focus very well this early in the morning. In fact, I never even knew this hour existed, so I have to squeeze my eyes tight several times before zooming in on the dark beach where I think I see shapes move.

And there it is, another shape shifter, and it appears to be close to the ground. The center of the object blends with the darkness, but on each side of the mass there is movement and it looks like sand is being kicked aside like a dog digging a hole. Or more likely it is a sea turtle, like the one from my dreams, which has come ashore to lay her eggs. Prior to purchasing the house, I was informed of the many rules protecting sea turtles and one stated that no exterior lights on the gulf side were to be turned on during the nesting season. I can't remember what months were designated, but late September makes sense. Dolphins, stingrays, an Indian girl, and now sea turtles—if this isn't Shangri-La, it is damn close.

The mass seems to rise up as the wings become idle. Maybe the turtle is leaving. I have to find Fiona and share this moment. I want to ask the turtle if he has seen the naked lady. As I race through the bedroom and down the stairs, I think about buying the supplies needed to build a protective cage around the nest to shelter the eggs from island varmints. Then nature calls, so I enter the bathroom while calling out Fiona's name. She doesn't answer. Well, it's hard for her to speak with a mouthful of candy.

When I come out, I call her name again. No answer. I start to think, *here we go again*, but when I switch on the kitchen light, her designer bag lies on top of the counter. A woman would leave her lover, her career, and even her lust for chocolate, but she would never leave her bag. So where is she? I check the other rooms, whispering her name so not to rile up Montana. When I'm sure she isn't in the house, I head toward the screen door leading out to the beach. Just as I step outside onto the deck, I hear the thump of bare feet crossing the walkover. I squint to focus. The footsteps get closer and as they do, Fiona emerges from the cloak of darkness completely naked.

"What are you doing out here," I ask.

She turns and points into the blackness. "I left my sunglasses on the beach earlier, when I abruptly left. But I found them." She raises her hand and shows me. I'm taken aback with her beauty, even in the shadows, and I wonder if she is the naked lady on the turtle. *Did I simply screw up the hair color?* "Did you see the turtle?" I ask eagerly.

"What turtle?" she asks.

The one you always sit on. "The sea turtle nesting in the sand near the chairs." I look beyond her to confirm the shadowy shape shifter, but it is too dark to decipher from the lower deck. "I saw it from upstairs."

"Oh yeah . . . the turtle. I did notice something crawling into the water. That must have been it." She kisses me on the cheek and proceeds into the house. I follow. She stops for a drink from the refrigerator, drops the sunglasses in her bag, and urges me seductively to follow her upstairs.

Most of me obliges, guided by a lustful sensation, but the microscopic population of asexual thoughts in my head remind me that I raked the sand earlier after everyone left, and there were no sunglasses to be found.

CHAPTER TWENTY-FIVE

Island Emotions

"When you come to the fork in the road, take it."
—YOGI BERRA

The next day, and the final day of Fiona's extended vacation, along with Sal's self-imposed anonymity, I awake to the squawking hunger call from Montana's cage. Fiona is in the bathroom; I hear the shower running. I'm glad there won't be another search and rescue mission for her. I step out on the deck to a beautiful morning. My eyes are drawn to the sand where I see Fiona's footprints from her late night excursion leading out to the beach chairs and back to the walkover. *But why? Who needs shades at night?* The search would've been much easier in the morning. Close to the beach chairs the sand is disturbed. I assume it is the area where the sea turtle has laid her eggs.

Fiona pads onto the deck wearing only a towel and hugs me from behind. As soon as I feel her touch, the ill feeling of separation anxiety begins to seep into my heart. She's given no indication she has changed her mind about staying in Hermitville. My gut is convinced, once we say our good-byes, it will be final. I bring her around to my side.

"Look at the mess you made in my sand," I say pointing.

She stares at the beach like she is looking at evidence from a murder scene.

"That wasn't me, that was your turtle," she finally says.

I steal a kiss and grab a hug. "Yeah, like turtles need to look for sunglasses."

We get dressed and have breakfast. Our final day together will be spent on the mainland doing assorted errands before joining Sal and Toast for a final sunset. We've planned a champagne farewell on the beach followed by another night of raucous behavior under the covers.

I feed the gangster bird some gangster seeds and leave for the dock with Fiona. I jump aboard the *Ticket* as she unties the lines. She hands me her bag and tosses in the ropes. I help her aboard and return the bag. As I do, I notice it is much lighter. A spike of optimism arises. Maybe she has moved some of her personal care items into the bathroom. I can't wait to look in the cabinets.

We dock at the boat condo and transfer to the truck. My first stop is at the hardware store to buy wire fencing and stakes to protect the turtle eggs I assume have been deposited on my beach. Next, Fiona needs to check her itinerary with Thomas, so we stop by his motel so she can confirm their travel plans. I stay in the truck to avoid the machine man and hope those plans result in her staying longer with me. Our last stop is at the food market. And that's when the day takes a turn for the worse.

I push an already filled carriage along as Fiona tosses in items like a basketball player shoots free throws. It's nice having a woman's touch when it comes to buying groceries. I have the steaks, pasta, and deli meat down pat, but she introduces me to the health-food section, which I always thought was reserved for sick people.

"If I'm going to visit, you need to have better food in the house," she declares, as she steers me down the organic aisle. *This coming from an M&M addict.* So I let her toss things in the carriage I would never eat, like a bottle of Natural Celery Root, Sprouted Quinoa Trio, and my favorite, Holy Crap Cereal. I assume the latter contains blessed fiber, hence the holy crap part. I'm sure these products will eventually collect dust in my kitchen, but they will also act as a reminder that she is coming back.

In aisle ten—chips, dips, and hundreds of other snack foods— I reach for a normal bag of chips, but Fiona replaces it with a container of raisins. I'm about to protest when I notice Amber coming down the aisle.

We lock eyes, and I think for a second she is about to turn and leave, but she stays in the aisle and waves at me. I signal Fiona and she rushes ahead to embrace Amber. The women hug and talk for a few seconds before my carriage reaches them.

"I'm sorry to hear about your brothers," I say, which is a bold-faced lie. But it comes out sincere. Amber shrugs her shoulders.

"They had it coming someday, either here or up north. They were both trouble, but my mother is taking it badly," Amber says softly, tears welling in her eyes.

Fiona reaches out and holds her hand. "Do the police have any suspects?" Fiona asks.

I look at Fiona and wonder if she will rat out Sal to Amber. Women stick together, no matter what the circumstances. If she does, then I'll end up paying the price.

"Oh, I already know who killed them. I told the police who," Amber says.

Fiona and I stand as still as statues, waiting for the next shoe to drop.

"As soon as I got the call, I knew it had to be Sal Santini, the fat fuck living next door to me."

Fiona turns to gauge my expression, but I maintain eye contact with Amber. I'm thinking Sal can't get out of town fast enough, and if I had his cell number, I'd advise him to leave immediately.

"What makes you think Sal did it?" I ask. "And why would he?" I am walking a fine line of pretending I don't know anything when I know everything. Or at least I think I do.

I can tell my question angers Amber by the way her face suddenly flushes. I like her as a friend so I don't enjoy playing this act, but I like me better so I have to play as dumb as possible.

With steely eyes Amber replies, "A few days ago, Sal was walking in from his boat with some fish. I was sitting on the porch when he raised them in the air to brag. I wasn't impressed so I looked away, then he said, 'Your brothers will sleep with these soon.' You guys are aware my mother and I have had our run-ins with Sal, so while my stepbrothers were down here they shared some heated words with him. I figured it was all bluster on Sal's part. He's just a fat-fuck music producer, or so he says."

I gulp.

"So I never expected this to happen. The afternoon after they were found murdered, I sought out Sal on the island. He was leaving in his boat as I was pulling in. I yelled across the docks, 'Did you do this?' and Sal looked at me with a smirk that made my skin crawl."

"Oh my God," Fiona says.

I shake my head in make-believe disbelief.

"So I called my stepfather and told him the whole story. He was devastated and infuriated. I informed him that I loaded my shotgun and was waiting for Sal to show up so I could kill the bastard for the pain he caused my mother."

"No Amber, you can't do that," Fiona says. "Go to the police and tell them what you think."

"I did, but all they said was I don't have enough evidence. Well, it's enough evidence for me and my family."

I am convinced Sal is a moving target. If I'm right about Amber's brothers being just thugs, then Sal has two other people with paper still stalking him, plus a next-door neighbor aiming a shotgun in his direction. I'm feeling very uncomfortable about sitting next to Sal on the beach later today.

"And if I don't get him first, I'm sure my stepfather will. He'll be flying in today to arrange for the bodies to be sent back. He advised me not to do anything because he was bringing in some of his associates to handle Sal. But I want vengeance to be mine."

This time Fiona and I exchange a worried glance. She steps forward and hugs Amber again. "Please think this through, Amber. You need to put your emotions aside and let the authorities handle this. If there is anything we can do," Fiona says, trailing off.

Amber looks at her, then at me. "There is one thing," she says. "Do you know where Sal is now?"

"I have no idea," I say.

"Not now, anyways," Fiona adds, "but he's supposed to be watching the sunset at Jason's house later today."

My stomach falls to the floor, followed by my heart, and then my balls. I can't believe Fiona just offered up that information. I stare at her, daggers spitting from my eyes. Amber thanks Fiona and continues shopping. After she has moved far enough away, I whisper-scream at Fiona, "Do you know what you just did?"

Fiona looks surprised. "What?"

"You just turned my beach into the O.K. Corral."

Fiona waves me off. "You really think Amber is going to shoot Sal? *Pa-leeze.*"

"What about her family entourage headed this way?"

Fiona smiles. "Well, I guess we'll just have to pop some popcorn and watch the festivities from the comfort of your bed. And even better, I won't have to apologize to Sal. It's a win-win."

I can't get out of the market fast enough. Not only am I fearful we will bump into Amber again in the checkout line, where I have no doubt Fiona will offer to hold Sal down while Amber exacts her retribution, I am also nervous about being considered complicit. How many people have seen me with Sal? How many have seen me with the men in black? Put one and one together and I'm the common thread. When will someone at Two Palms Marina tell the police the men in black pissed in my boat and that I sought retaliation?

We load the groceries in the truck and head back to the boat. When I arrive, my cell rings. It is The Hammer. If anybody in southern Florida has inside information to share about anything, it is Phyllis Hammerstein.

"Hey Phyllis," I say as cheerily as possible. Fiona overhears and asks me to say hello as she loads the bags into the boat.

"Mr. Najarian," she says all businesslike. "Do you have a sister?"

A sister? I thought the call would be about the murders. "No, why."

"Because my clerk, Lilly, took a call from a Megan Najarian yesterday. She told Lilly she's been looking for you and she has some valuable property you vowed to keep until you died. Lilly assumed she was family, Najarian not being a common name and all, maybe a cousin? Anyway, when Lilly asked how she found our number, Ms. Najarian said she Googled Gulf Breeze as the realtor who sold the property on Gulf Boulevard. She then added that she was flying in today to visit you and would be appreciative if we could assist in getting her over to the island. She asked Lilly to keep it a secret because she wanted to surprise you, but she never asked me, so that's why I'm calling you. I know you hate surprises."

I am getting nauseous. My PMS is kicking into high gear. I can feel the hairs on my neck spring to life.

"She's not family," I say. "Look, if she does arrive at your office, tell her Sand Key is under quarantine. Blame it on the red tide or something. Convince her to turn around and go home."

"So you do know her?"

"Yeah, I do."

Phyllis starts to laugh. "Oh, I'm thinking this is gonna be fun," she says. "A secret from Jason's past. I'll bring her over as soon as she arrives."

"Thanks, Phyllis. See if I ever borrow anything from you again. And Fiona says hello."

"Oh great, say hi and tell her I have the recipe for the grouper dish I've been promising. I'll get it to her before she leaves."

"Yeah, whatever." I press the end-call button and hang my head. I have the sudden urge to bury myself in my not-yet-neighbor's property to escape this calamity.

"Bad news?" Fiona asks from the boat.

"It was Phyllis with the latest weather report. It seems there's definitely a shit storm brewing on the horizon."

On the way back, I stop into Two Palms for fuel. "Fiona, please stay in the boat and ward off anyone who might be in need of a urinal while I pay the bill inside."

"Aye, aye, Captain," she responds.

As I enter the bait shop, I see Sal and Memphis the Lighthouse sitting in chairs at the rear of the store. Memphis notices me first and immediately gives me the two fingers indicating he is watching me. I tell him what he can do with his two fingers with my one finger. It is beginning to be a ceremonial greeting between us. Sal looks up, sees me, and waddles up to the counter where I am handing the clerk my credit card.

"Hey Trust Fund, how's it hanging," he says, pounding my back with his paw.

"I'm buying gas, Sal. How's it hanging with you?"

He shrugs, winks at me and says, "Things are coming together."

That is an understatement. After the clerk hands me my receipt, I motion for Sal to join me in privacy. We step over to a display of fishing rods. I look around satisfied that no one can hear us.

"Look Sal, you need to leave the island like right now. I ain't kidding. Get in your car and go wherever you are planning to go."

Sal laughs. "You sound like a guy I knew who ain't around no more. So what's this all about?"

"Amber is pissed. She's coming after you."

Sal laughs harder. "Fuck her."

"And she told me her family arrived looking for revenge."

"Fuck them."

"And I still think those professional paper holders are close by and looking for you."

"Fuck 'em all."

"Stop fucking everybody, Sal, you're being an asshole! This is serious," I urge him.

"Fuck you, Trust Fund."

"Sal, you're not hearing me. You need to get out now before something goes down. I mean it. I'm talking to you as a friend." Okay, so I lied.

Sal sizes me up, and then surveys the store. For a moment I'm sure I've managed to crack his thick skull with some common sense, but then he says, "Where's Fiona? She never showed up at her house last night."

"She's staying with me until she leaves for Tallahassee."

"So you are tapping the bitch. Who woulda thought?"

I stare him in the eyes for a moment—my anger rising. "Hey Sal, fuck you. And one more thing, fuck you."

I push past him and exit the store. Once I'm on the boat and seated at the helm, Fiona approaches and rests her head on my shoulder.

"Everything all right?" she asks.

"I just swore at a Mafia hit man. Is Sal following me?"

Fiona scans the dock. "No, why, is he here?"

I power the boat and quickly pull away. "Any chance you know how to do one of those last will and testaments on line?"

CHAPTER TWENTY-SIX

Island Situations

"You can get much farther with a kind word and a gun
than you can with a kind word alone."

—AL CAPONE

I dock at Hermitville lagoon and hastily gather the bags while keeping an eye on the inlet opening for anyone following me. On the ride home, Fiona expressed her opinion that I was merely talking Sal's language meaning I had nothing to worry about. Maybe so, but I seem to have a propensity for pissing off people on Gulf Boulevard, and after last night's little situation on the beach with Sal, I'm left wondering if the camel's back had been broken in the bait shop.

"If you're so concerned that Sal is mad at you, let's do what I suggested and have dinner on the mainland. Afterward, we can spend my last night in a hotel. We don't need to waste any more time with Sal or Aubert," Fiona reminds me.

It appears there will be no change of plans in the offering. Fiona is leaving tomorrow. I feel the pressure of each situation bearing down on me: Megan's invasion, Amber's revenge, Fiona's departure, and Sal's volatility. I start to wish for a foot of snow and my old office back.

But, if I play my cards right, I could escape the next twenty-four hours with just a broken heart. As depressing as that would be, it's better than broken bones . . . or even death. I need a plan to divest myself of Sal's trust. I need to stall Amber's payback until Sal is gone from the island. If Megan shows up, I need to scare her so bad that she abandons her fixation with my money. And with Fiona, I reluctantly need to let her go. Only then can I get on with my hermit existence. At least I hope I can.

"I'll make a deal with you," I say, as we scale the steps. "If Sal shows up, I'll go down there, sit with him, gauge his mood, apologize if I have to, and watch the sun go down. I can do that knowing he's leaving tomorrow. If he doesn't show, it means things have changed for the worse at which point we leave the island as fast as we can."

"Whatever," she sighs. From her facial expression, Fiona is not on board with my idea, but she appears resigned to the fact I know too much about Sal's situation. My absence from sunset could cause me problems. I realize I can't get through this day fast enough because of Sal, but I want my remaining time with Fiona to drag by.

After putting away the groceries—I hide the organic foods deep in a cabinet to avoid the embarrassment of inquisitive eyes—we sizzle two steaks on the outdoor grill and settle in for an early dinner. Fiona has a handful of M&M's next to her plate. I watch as she slices a piece of steak, stabs some vegetables, and chases both down with a few pieces of candy. I've never seen anything like it. I speculate whether I can corner the market on M&M's, forcing her to stay with me forever.

As the minutes tick forward, I find myself staring at the clock, then out at the beach. It is late afternoon, but still too early for sunset. Fiona relaxes in the rocker on the porch and flips through a magazine she purchased at the market. I pace inside the house trying to generate a strategy that won't result in me soiling my pants. When I glance over at Montana's cage, I notice he is watching me intently.

"What, Montana?" I call out to the gangster bird.

"Chi Chi, get the yeyo."

I have come to learn this means he's hungry. "Go get it yourself."

"Go home. You stoned."

I wave the befuddling bird off. I walk over to the front door to see if there are any uninvited boats at the docks.

From the other side of the room, *"You know what? Fuck you! How about dat?"*

The moorings are clear of enemy combatants. Only the *Ticket* rocks gently with the incoming tide. The sunlight has fallen low enough to escape the tree-lined lagoon, leaving the first hint of twilight. My thoughts are seized by worst-case scenarios involving Amber, her family, or the mysterious paper holders Sal claims exist. The more I think about it though, the more I believe Sal has created the illusion of people coming after him so he could justify the assassination of the men in black.

"Fuck Gaspar Gomez!"

"Hey angry bird, how about I put you in a slingshot and try to score some points?" I say, pointing at Montana from the foyer.

"You think you can take me? You need a fucking army if you gonna take me!"

"Or maybe I call Caprice to arrange another rescue."

A wing shoots up in my direction. I swear he just flipped me the bird.

I escape from the f-bomb barrage and enter the kitchen to check my e-mail. I see nine in my inbox, many of the spam variety offering fake Rolex watches or erectile-dysfunction cures. The first legitimate mail I find is from my father and it has an attachment. It is a photo of him grinning ear to ear while holding a rather large lake trout. I assume Tranquility snapped the photo because some of the picture is blocked by a finger. Last month, my mother e-mailed a photo of her oil painting of Cape Cod Bay, or at least I think that's what it was. It might've also passed for the salt flats in Utah. My parents seem intent on justifying the millions I spent on them by sending me photos of their hobbies.

The only other nonspam e-mail is from Megan, which really is a degree of spam in itself. The subject line reads Bermuda. Hope springs eternal. I click it open and read the following:

> *"hi poopsie, in bermuda w/cara and girls. havin a blast lol. the water is pissa warm and so is the sun. miss u. getting wasted @ bar but not 2 much LMAO cuz long drive back to boston. c u soon. Meg"*

My hope bubble bursts when I realize Megan's mind has constructed a highway between Boston and Bermuda. She tried to be clever with me, but sadly I am convinced she has already landed in Florida and found her way to Gulf Breeze Realty where The Hammer is ready to welcome her with open arms.

Fiona enters the kitchen and leans on the doorway. "Your friends are coming."

I step past her onto the porch and glance out at the beach. Several boats have anchored offshore and more are cruising into the gulf from Pirate's Pass. The sun has lowered in a cloudless sky and promises a magnificent setting. Sal is walking along the shoreline in a confident stride, a cigar in one hand, and a book in the other. Toast falls in behind him. There is no sign of Amber, no sign of Amber's family, and no sign of Sal's imaginary men coming to kill him. Maybe I have overblown the urgency of the situation.

"Are you joining me?" I ask Fiona.

She stomps her foot playfully. "Do I have to?"

"I'm anxious to see what the turtle left us."

Fiona pauses for a moment. "The turtle . . . right. Let's go take a look."

She grabs a sleeve of paper cups along with a bottle of Moet. I venture back into the gangster's lair for his cage. Montana never speaks when his habitat is on the move, but I'm sure his gun beak is locked and loaded. We stroll out from the kitchen and down to the walkover. Sal is standing, stretching, surveying the beach and puffing billows of smoke into my clean air. He sees us approaching and waves. All appears normal in Hermitville.

As Fiona hands out the cups, I meander behind the beach chairs to confirm what I saw last night. The sand is certainly disturbed and a slight mound created just as a giant turtle would leave it after digging a hole and then covering it up. The problem is the location. Unless the turtles could fly, the creature would have had to crawl around the chairs leaving a distinctive path in its wake. I didn't see one.

"Jason, come toast with us," Fiona calls out.

I drag my foot over the mound to smooth out the sand. Maybe it was an island critter I noticed in the starlight, digging for ghost crabs.

"Come on, Jason," Fiona insists.

But why would a varmint cover the hole after digging?

Mystified, I reluctantly join Fiona, Sal and Toast. Fiona hands me the bottle of champagne. My first inclination is to launch the cork in the Frenchman's face, but at the last moment I point it skyward. Cups extended, I pour the bubbly. When we are ready to salute our last sunset, Fiona raises her hand.

"Guys, I want to apologize for my actions yesterday. Sal, I'm sorry we had words. It was uncalled for on my part. And storming off was rude." She steps forward and taps cups with him. "Are we still friends?"

Sal grunts. He shifts his enormous weight, his eyes dart in all directions, and then he finally mumbles, "Sure, Running Bush." It appears to me he is not accustomed to receiving apologies.

The four of us raise our cups, tap, say cheers, and wish for long and healthy lives. Fiona suggests we all meet back here on a regular basis and that makes me cough up some of the champagne.

Sal whacks my back. "You need for me to drink that for you, Trust Fund?"

"No, wrong pipe."

We settle into the chairs just as the sun touches the horizon. Toast insists on making individual salutations, but I do my best to tune him out. My attention is on the boats that sway gently in the gulf.

Toast falls to one knee in front of Fiona and starts one of his nauseating sonnets. It is like greeting-card karaoke. She smiles and that makes me jealous. I want to put Sal's book to good use and throw it at the French weasel. Instead, I lean closer to Sal to take the temperature of our relationship. "Hey, sorry about the dustup back at the bait shop. You kinda pissed me off," I say.

Sal doesn't reply. My heart moves up-tempo.

"We good, Sal?"

He won't turn toward me; he keeps his attention on the horizon. "We'll see what's good when I get back." His reply is curt and it makes me uneasy.

Toast shifts from Fiona to me. He is about to start a verse when I lash out, "Get the fuck outta here." I follow my outburst with a kick of my manicured sand in his direction. In the company of Sal, I am becoming Sal.

Toast falls backward and responds with a string of angry French words that go on without pause. His hands move rapidly as if he is signing to a deaf person.

"Press one for English," I sneer.

Sal is laughing. He waves Toast back to the empty chair and urges him to share some of his rhymes with him. Fiona places her hand on my arm and gives me a quizzical look. She can be calm because she has nothing to worry about, the Godfather has forgiven her. I, in turn, have to worry about Sal's unpredictability. I have to live in a state of anxiety until Sal's return. I lift up from the chair and stroll the few yards to the shoreline. I step into the warm early autumn water. As I look out over the gulf, I wish I were alone again. I want Sal to go away and never come back. I want Harry to fly back in. And as much as it pains me, I want Fiona to leave. If she doesn't want me, I don't want her.

The sun is nearly half gone and I urge it to fall faster. Music blares from the flotilla of boats facing westward. Laughter spikes between muted conversations. These are happy people on the water, partying people, without the worry of a hit man being pissed at them. I am pleased to see one boat begin to exit the gulf before the sun has fully set. Soon they will all pull anchor and that will prompt the assassin and the French twit to vacate my beach, hopefully for the last time.

Fiona watches me as I walk back to my chair. Sal is enthralled with his cigar; his book rests on the sand. Toast has retreated to his earbuds and is moving to the beat like a bobblehead doll. When I'm seated, she asks if I am all right. I don't have an answer. Instead I think about taking her over to the mainland, when the boat that had peeled away early catches my attention. It is speeding directly at us.

There is nothing abnormal about a speeding boat on the gulf. At any second the operator will turn sharp to the portside toward Pirate's Pass sending a wave of water toward shore. At any second he will turn.

Any second.

I lean close to Fiona. "Are you watching that boat?"

She nods.

The boat slows, but continues on a direct course toward the beach.

Fiona grips my arm.

"He'll turn any second," I say.

"He's not turning," she counters.

She is already lifting up from the chair when I say, "I think you should get back to the house."

Fiona is on her feet and headed quickly toward the walkover. With her seemingly out of harm's way, I turn my attention to Sal.

The boat's bow continues to point directly at us.

"Sal, I think we have a situation," I warn, keeping my eye on the incoming intruder.

Sal has discarded his cigar. In his lap rests his book. When I look at him, I can't tell if he is planning to get up and leave, or start reading. He opens the cover.

I glance quickly over my shoulder at Fiona's progress, but she is nowhere in sight.

The boat is less than twenty yards out. The person behind the helm is nondescript. If there are other passengers aboard, they are hidden. If this is an assault, they are within range to do damage.

Again I look at Sal. The book is opened and to my surprise it is not meant for reading. Imbedded in the pages is a handgun and Sal is gripping his piece.

I stand up, ready to run. Sal is lifting out of his seat.

The boat closes in. Ten yards out.

I urge him to duck, take cover. As I do, I notice a hooded figure approaching quickly from the south end of the beach carrying what looks like a rifle. I turn to grab Montana's cage.

The explosion is deafening.

The quick, piercing blast startles me, and I stumble backward almost knocking over the cage. When I regain my balance, I see Fiona standing behind Sal holding a plastic bag. It is smoking, and so is the back of Sal's head.

She waves the bag at Toast, prompting him to fall out of his chair. He gets up screaming and starts running away, earbuds dangling and arms flailing, down the beach toward the hooded figure.

As she brings the bag around, I see the end of the barrel pointed at me. I immediately lift my arms in the air. The first image that flashes in my mind is of a black widow spider killing off the male after mating. I am sure Fiona is going to eliminate me for a number of reasons, starting with the obvious, being a witness to the slaying of Sal—to the far-fetched, being a lousy lover. I look in Fiona's eyes, which have suddenly turned murderously cold.

CHAPTER TWENTY-SEVEN

Island Mayhem

"Killing is what I do for a living."
—FIONA TALLAHASSEE

The boat drifts ashore; the hull scrapes the sand. I glance at the camo-clad person on board, but the masked man remains indistinguishable. The beaching of the vessel cues Montana to start shooting indiscriminately.

"Put your hands down," Fiona says softly.

She drops the gun on the sand behind Sal's orca chair. The plastic bag falls into the uncovered hole. I look at Sal's hunched body. The force of the shot has pushed him out of the chair and onto his knees. He looks as if he is praying at the altar of the Gulf of Mexico. The book has fallen open on the sand and the gun remains in his grip. There is a gaping hole in the back of his head with a lot of something leaking out. I resist the urge to vomit.

"Jason, put your damn hands down!" Fiona demands.

Montana continues to shoot. It's becoming unnerving, and for his sake I hope nobody shoots back.

I lower my hands, unsure of her next move. I take some solace in the fact she isn't holding the gun any longer, but the man in the boat has me just as terrified. Most of the sun watchers are cruising leisurely back toward Pirate's Pass, and some are looking in the direction of the blast, but the man on the boat returns their curious concerns with a friendly wave of his hand. Farther down the beach I see Toast reach for and then tackle the hooded figure.

Fiona shuffles over and stands in front of me. "I really love this place, Jason. The water, the sand, your home . . ." She shakes her head as if disappointed.

"Fiona . . . why?" I stutter.

"What, Sal?" She looks at him and chuckles. "I'm a mechanic, Jason."

"You, too? I thought mechanics just fixed cars?"

She smiles. "I solve problems. Killing is what I do for a living."

I can't get any more traumatized than I already am. Hearing Fiona and killer in the same declaration just doesn't reconcile with me. Out of the corner of my eye, I see the man on the boat lean against the gunwale and point something in my direction. In the terrifying couple of seconds that follow, as my eyes water and my oxygen depletes, it becomes clear to me. Fiona can't kill me after what we shared. Instead, she will have her paper partner do it. My heart pounds furiously. I can barely focus. Tomorrow's headlines will eulogize me as collateral damage.

"Fiona, please, don't mechanic me," I manage to mumble.

"Stop it, Jason."

Beyond Fiona, Toast is dragging the figure around the bend when the hood falls off. It looks like Amber and she is resisting him the whole way as they slip out of sight. With them gone and the gulf free of boats, I am alone on my beach with two professional assassins and a wannabe gangster bird.

She reaches for my hands. "I'm sorry to involve you. I really tried to wrap this up earlier, but my facilitators kept getting killed." She is amused by this. "I almost walked away from this job. In fact, I just got paid the front money a couple of days ago over in Orlando, three weeks after they commissioned me. And just so you know, I didn't want this to happen here either," she says with a wave of her arm that canvasses the beach. "I tried to take Sal out last night, but he never showed up at his house."

My eyes dart between Fiona and the man on the boat. Montana has emptied his clip of mimicked bullets. All is quiet except for the gentle waves lapping the shore.

"So I had to do it this way, tonight, before he left the island, not knowing where he would be later on."

"You used me," I say, pointing toward the house. "The time we spent together up there . . . was that part of your job description?"

Fiona steps closer. *Knife? Poison needle?* I step back.

She frowns. "Jason, please, I want you to know that what we shared the past few weeks was real. I like you very much, *Trust Fund*." She smiles. Her eyes soften.

But is it me she likes or my M&M's?

"Each time we were together, I envisioned coming back to Gulf Boulevard someday to settle down after I'm done doing what I do. So that makes you my new fantasy, Jason. Just like you said, we could grow old together on this beautiful island."

"So you're not planning on killing me?"

"Of course not."

"Then why are these red dots bouncing all over me?"

Fiona looks at my arm and then turns to the man on the boat. "Frankie, cut the shit," she snaps.

The man on the boat laughs, then pulls in the gun and says, "We gotta move."

"Frankie? He sounds like Tommy Hawke," I say.

Fiona shrugs.

"So was this whole Indian tribe stuff part of your act, too? You're really not an Indian, are you?"

"No, I'm not. But I did grow up a Cleveland Indians fan," she says. "Does that count?"

I shake my head in disillusionment. "Did he give me this black eye?" I ask, pointing at Frankie.

Fiona nods. "For some reason he doesn't like you much," she whispers.

I walk a few feet away from my manicured sand and pick up a piece of driftwood from my not-yet-neighbor's beach. I toss it at him. It is not something one should do in the company of killers, but I never think things through anyway. The stick bounces off the boat and falls into the water. It is harmless, but it is enough to tap into his killer instinct. The machine man jumps off the boat and comes after me, gun in hand.

"Jason!"

The greeting carries down from my deck like a meteorite crashing to earth. Frankie stops in his tracks while Fiona and I turn toward the familiar voice.

"Look who I have . . . your wife!" Phyllis sings out. From behind The Hammer, Megan steps into view, smiling and waving.

"Your wife?" asks Fiona, incredulously.

At this point, I welcome the machine man to put me out of my misery.

"She's not my wife. She's my ex-fucking-wife."

"Hello, Fiona!" Now Phyllis is waving. Both women are excited as they start to navigate the steps leading to the walkover. I can't believe what is happening. The woman I am sleeping with just killed a Mafia hit man. Her abettor is just about to put a beating on me. And now Megan has invaded Hermitville. At any moment, I expect Sal will stand up and fart, just to add to this mayhem.

Fiona turns to the machine man and gestures him back to the boat.

"This is the ex-wife you told me about? The whack job?" Fiona asks.

I nod.

Fiona seems to contemplate for a moment, and then says, "Look, if you want, I'll take her out right here, right now, no charge, for the inconvenience I've caused you."

I look at Fiona and realize she is not joking. I'm grateful the sudden turn of events will keep this murderess from meeting my parents on Thanksgiving. But then I consider a *what if* scenario when I think of Bradley . . .

"Jason! Yes or no?" Fiona is in my face.

"No, Fiona. How the hell are you going to explain Sal to them?" I'm panic-stricken.

She waves me off. "Don't worry, I'm invisible. These jobs never come back on me. The evidence always points elsewhere."

Phyllis and Megan are giggling with anticipation as they step off the walkover. Unbeknownst to them, they have just entered the Twilight Zone.

Fiona dashes up to greet Phyllis. They hug. They gab. Phyllis introduces Megan and then reaches into her portfolio to show something to Fiona. Megan steps away and starts walking toward me. She is wearing a green sundress and carrying her sandals. Her brunette hair rests on her shoulders. She is tanned and toned and ready for battle. Megan is pointing her finger and smiling like she caught me with my hand in the cookie jar. I look at Sal and wonder who is better off.

She throws herself against me. A few hugs and kisses ensue. Then she steps back.

"Poopsie, you mischievous little devil, you. First Malibu and then Abuc. Did you think I could be fooled a second time? I figured out that Abuc stood for Abaco, and it was one of them alphabet islands in the water near Mexico. You tried to send me on another wild goose call," she says waving a finger at me. "But all is forgiven. I'm here for you. We're together again."

I place my hands on her shoulders to grasp her full attention. I look at Fiona still conversing with Phyllis a few yards away, and then at Frankie who is pushing the boat back into deeper water.

"Megan, you need to get out of here now. These people are killers," I whisper.

Phyllis and Fiona start moving closer.

She scoffs at me. "Jason, you never give up. I'm here to stay, so get over it. I like this place," she says looking around as dusk settles in. "Kinda uninhibited here, I don't see any other houses. Are there any nightclubs on the island?"

"Is that Sal?" Phyllis asks, as they join Megan and me.

I don't know what to say or do. I am fearful if I open my mouth I will swallow what follows a red laser dot.

"Yes, that's Sal meditating," Fiona chimes in. "Dare not disturb him."

"Sal Santini meditating?" Phyllis questions.

Luckily our distance on the beach, along with the waning light of day, keep Sal's condition inconspicuous. If either Phyllis or Megan notices the gaping hole in his head, I am sure the machine man will be ready to take no hostages, starting with me.

"He looks like one of those statues from Easter Island," Phyllis adds.

The women giggle.

The engines on the boat rev. It is the machine man's signal to move.

"Time for me to get going," Fiona announces. "Megan, nice to meet you. Phyllis, thanks for the recipe, I'll call you soon hon. Jason . . . to the good times." She steps between Megan and me and plants a kiss on my lips, tongue and all. When we part, she winks.

"So long, gang," she says, and then skips toward the shoreline.

Phyllis waves farewell. I manage to flap my hand in a relieved kind of way.

"I do adore that woman," Phyllis gushes.

Fiona splashes into the water next to the boat. The machine man reaches over the side and lifts her on board. They reverse into deeper water, turn starboard side and speed off. The most beautiful woman I have ever met is now a feather in the wind. I watch the boat slip into the night. Fiona never looks back.

"What was all that about?" Megan inquires. "What good times?"

I turn to Phyllis. "We need to call 9-1-1. Sal is dead. Fiona, or whatever her name is, killed him."

Megan chortles. "Here we go again."

Phyllis looks over at Sal. "That Sal? Fiona did what?"

"Phyllis, he's kidding. This is another lame attempt to play hard to get. I told you what lengths he's already gone to," Megan says.

"Oh my word, are you serious? Fiona?" Phyllis is shaken as she stares at Sal.

"Yes. She's a mechanic. And I don't mean the car-fixing type."

"Really? Both of you?" Megan laughs. "What is this, a movie set? Are they filming now? Where are the cameras?" Megan turns in circles searching for a hidden production crew. When she finds none, she walks over to where Sal has crash-landed on his knees. She stands in front of him, pokes him, and stares into his face. "He looks real, I'll give you that," she calls out.

Phyllis reaches for her cell phone and taps in 9-1-1. There is nothing left to do except wait. I step over to the hole where Fiona, *the turtle,* had hidden her weapon of limited destruction. The gun inside the plastic bag is huge. It reminds me of the one owned by the men in black. *Does everyone carry giant handguns in Florida?* No wonder her fancy designer bag weighed so much.

Her designer bag!

I look on the sand, around the chairs, near the cage, but I don't see it. She must have left it in the house. My existing state of paranoia burps up guilt by association. I don't want to be considered an accomplice in her crime spree. As far as I know, nobody has a suspicion that Fiona and I were carrying on in the penthouse suite except Sal, and dead men ain't talking. Before the police turn Hermitville into a crime scene, I have to remove everything from the house that suggests my relationship with Fiona exceeded merely watching sunsets.

Phyllis is talking animatedly on the phone. Megan is still inspecting Sal, aka the corpse. Darkness is settling in. I run up to the house, somewhat awkwardly without my trusted rake in hand. I open the screen door and enter the kitchen. Her bag is on the counter. What to do? My hands are shaking. I open the bag. Inside is a collection of seashells and a note. I pull the note out and read it.

> *"Dear Jason,*
> *I had a wonderful time with you during my stay on the*
> *island. You really helped me complete what I came down*
> *here for. I couldn't have done it without you. What we did*
> *together will always be our secret. Until we meet again,*
> *Love, Fiona"*

I reach out for the counter to steady myself. If the police had found this note, I'd be looked at as her collaborator and thrown in a small southern jail cell until a false confession was beaten out of me. I rip the note into small pieces and flush the remains down the toilet. I empty the seashells onto the counter, reach for a paper grocery bag and stuff her designer bag inside. *Is there anything else? Anything Fiona owned?*

I race upstairs and check the bathroom. Nothing. I look around the bedroom. Nothing. I am confident there is no reason to think she ever placed a foot in the house. Other than depleting my M&M inventory, Fiona has left no lasting impression. There is a sad commentary to all that, but I choose to ignore it for now.

I double-step back downstairs, grab the bag and head out to the beach. Phyllis is approaching on the walkover.

"I just got off the phone with my friend, Sheriff Williamson. He's sending over a team from his department and he's also notified the marine patrol, along with the highway patrol."

I nod. "What the hell is she still doing down there?" I ask, pointing at Megan.

"She's been talking to and poking Sal for the last five minutes. The man is dead, what's wrong with that woman?"

I roll my eyes. "You're the one who brought her over here."

"She said she was your wife, Jason. What was I supposed to think?"

"Ex-wife, Phyllis. As in former, prior, extinct, defunct, invalid, void . . ."

"All right, all right, my bad. What's in the bag?" she asks.

The bag. "It's from Montana's cage. I need to empty it."

"On the beach?"

"Um . . . the ghost crabs. They like the sunflower shells. I guess we should wait in the house for the police. I'll send Megan up."

"Okay." Phyllis heads up the stairs toward the deck.

I jog down to the beach. Megan is standing next to Sal's corpse, somewhat confused, with her hands on her hips. It is getting darker by the minute. Montana is squawking impatiently for something to eat.

"Megan, go up to the house. It's getting dark."

"This looks so friggin' real, Jason. How did you do it?"

"Megan, the man is dead. He's been murdered. In a couple of minutes the beach will be crawling with cops. Now please, go up to the house and stay with Phyllis."

She smirks at me. "I'm gonna figure this one out, Poopsie. You wait and see." She steps around the chairs and heads toward the walkover.

I grab the rake, run onto my not-yet-neighbor's property and dig a hole. I drop the bag inside and cover it up. I realize I am altering a crime scene, obstructing justice, and probably aiding and abetting, but I can't take the chance of doing the time if I didn't do the crime. I recall Fiona's words, *"The evidence always points elsewhere."* Well it ain't gonna point at me.

I lift Montana's cage and walk over to pay my last respects to Sal. His eyes are closed, his mouth agape. His mass of weight seems to be collapsing slowly into the sand. Sal has no one to blame but himself. He lived a life that made this outcome inevitable.

"See Montana, take a good look at him. That's what happens to gangsters."

Montana slides along the perch in his cage to get a better look at Sal. He bobs his head a few times and then ruffles his feathers.

"Well, you stupid fuck, look at you now."

And that's when the police boats appear in the gulf.

CHAPTER TWENTY-EIGHT

Island Investigation

"Better to remain silent and be thought a fool, than to speak and remove all doubt."

—RUSSIAN PROVERB

The police respond to Phyllis's 9-1-1 call by converging on Gulf Boulevard from the gulf side and through Hermitville lagoon. As I stand next to the departed Sal, I see blue lights piercing the night sky, and then two patrol boats emerge from the mouth of Pirate's Pass. They hug the shoreline with one boat shining a spotlight that scrapes along the beach in search of the reported murder victim. I don't want to be a shadow the police shoot at first and ask questions about later, so I use the night as my cover and hurry back toward the house with Montana.

When I reach the walkover, I notice the lagoon area is lit up with pulsating blue lights that bounce off the trees like a spinning strobe light. As I reach the steps to the house, I am abruptly awash in a bright light. I turn toward the source and the light is blinding—I can't see a thing. It feels like I just made it over the prison wall and can almost taste freedom, but then the guardtower lights catch up to me. I respond in a manner I've become accustomed to this evening. I lower the cage and throw my hands in the air.

The spotlight fondles me for a few seconds, and then slithers back to illuminate the shoreline. One of the boats has come ashore on my not-yet-neighbor's pitch-black beach, and four police officers wielding flashlights disembark. Hermitville is under siege.

I keep my hands in the air—the one false move theory—but Montana begins firing.

"Stop it, Montana," I whisper. I doubt the police can hear his machine-gun beak from their position on the beach, but why risk it? When he doesn't stop, I kick the cage.

Montana shrieks, like only a pissed-off gangster bird can. It is a loud enough noise to summon the spotlight back on me. My hands are still in the air, and when I look down at Montana, his wings are in the air.

"You're gonna get us killed," I scold him.

"You think you can take me? You need a fucking army if you gonna take me!"

And then he starts shooting again. This time, even louder.

Suddenly, one officer, who had started combing my beach, barks out something that causes the rest of the flashlights to run toward him. The spotlight follows. They locate Sal.

My first thought, as the police surround the corpse and the lights brighten the crime scene, is the embarrassing condition I left the beach in. One chair is tipped on its side, the rake lies out of place, and the sand has an unsightly hole surrounded by a profuse amount of uneven footprints. I feel bad about it. I should have raked the sand before leaving the beach. It would've left a good first impression with the officers, not to mention making it easier to draw a chalk line around Sal's final resting place.

At the risk of being shot, I lower my hands. I can hear footsteps stomping up the stairs from the other side of the house. Below me, police are barking out orders. I hear pounding on my front door. I lift the cage, quieting Montana, and proceed up the stairs and into the kitchen.

Phyllis is standing by the front door as several uniforms enter. The first officer bends over and gives Phyllis a peck on the cheek. The other four officers fan out into my house and appear to be waiting for orders. Within seconds, two are sizing up Megan and I can see a twinkle emerge in her eyes. I place the cage back on the ceiling hook and turn to see Phyllis and an officer approaching.

"Jason, this is Sheriff Williamson," Phyllis says. We nod to each other.

"Jason is the owner of this house and an eyewitness to the crime," Phyllis continues, but the sheriff is summoned to the beach by a crackle of clatter over his shoulder-mounted radio. I escort him to the deck steps leading to the walkover and switch on all the exterior lights.

The sheriff leaves the house accompanied by one officer, while the other three stay behind to foil any attempted escape. I am unofficially confined to the house with Phyllis and Megan.

"You never told me you had a parakeet," Megan says, as we wait in the kitchen sipping drinks. Beyond the huge officer, who is blocking some of my view of the activities on the beach, I notice that another boat has arrived. It appears an effort is being made to shift the corpse onto a small barge. I doubt the sheriff found any volunteers willing to lug nearly 400 pounds of dead weight along the beach, over the walkover, up the stairs, down the stairs and out to the docks in the lagoon. I think the plan is to tip Sal from his praying position onto a floating device and let the tide do the heavy lifting.

"It's a parrot. And why would I tell you?"

Megan shrugs. "I would think you might tell me before I move in. What if I have a bird allergy?"

Move in? I look across the counter at Phyllis to plead my case, but she is oblivious. Her head is down and in her hands she twirls a mug incessantly. She is clearly jolted by the events as I am, but unlike her, I knew what the end game was; I just didn't know who all the players were.

"Hey, Phyllis, are you okay?" I ask.

She looks up. "How did she expect to get away with this?"

It is a rhetorical question and Phyllis is mumbling to no one in particular. I have an opinion, but I also have to be careful to filter all of my statements to keep my secret relationship with Fiona a secret. Any connection to Fiona and me under the sheets could prove detrimental to my status as an innocent bystander. It is bad enough I am the eyewitness to a murder that took place on my beach and in one of my chairs. If the investigators find out I was also romantically involved with the perpetrator, my testimony would be considered tainted under the assumption I might be protecting her. And then the conspiracy theory would take root that I was an accomplice. I need to keep that poop far away from the fan.

"She gets away with this because she's a professional. Fiona admitted to me on the beach that she did this stuff for a living. It's a job to her, and I have no doubt her escape was well planned. I doubt we'll ever see her again."

Phyllis shakes her head, unwilling to accept the outcome.

"You mean she's a professional, like in a hooker?" Megan asks. "That's why she said, 'to the good times' to you. Unbelievable, Jason, you've been screwing around with a prostitute!"

I ponder whether Fiona's gun might still be on the beach. "A few minutes ago, Megan, you thought you were walking onto a movie set. Do me a favor, slip back into that demented state of mind," I beg.

"We shared lunch a few times, we shopped together, and I even invited her over to my house for dinner once," Phyllis sighs.

It is not the time to play one-upmanship, but I am confident my activities with Fiona trump hers.

"She was an excellent renter and everybody at the office liked her. I can't believe this: it gives me the willies. I must say, I've never been bamboozled like this before."

"Hey, it happens to the best of us," I say. "Just ask Megan."

"Don't ask me, I don't even own any bamboo," Megan replies.

After the photographs are taken, the body removed, the evidence secured, and the crime scene shuttered, Sheriff Williamson returns to the house. His step is brisk and his actions immediate. He gathers his remaining officers in the kitchen, removes a pen and pad from his pocket, and grabs a chair.

"My name is Sheriff Tyson Williamson. Kindly excuse me for being blunt, but I have to move quickly to determine who committed this grisly wrongdoing, and why the victim met his demise on this beach tonight. This situation therefore requires the full cooperation of all parties present. Now, I've known Ms. Hammerstein here all my life, so I'm gonna rule her out as a person of interest. But as far as you two go," he says, pointing at Megan and me, "I have an itch that needs to be scratched."

Megan displays her hands like a fiancée showing off her new diamond. "Check out these fingernails, Sheriff. I have excellent scratchers."

He scowls at her and I swear it resembles Sal's intimidating Luca Brasi's glare. Megan slowly returns her hands to her lap.

"Now Phyllis, for the record, you arrived on the beach after the crime took place, but while the suspect was still there?"

"That's correct, Tyson. I gave Megan here a ride over to the island. When I arrived, Jason and Fiona, the woman I told you about, were on the beach standing a few yards away from Mr. Santini. There was a boat drifting just offshore. When I saw Fiona, we started talking like nothing was wrong. I did notice there was something strange about Mr. Santini, but it was getting dark and I didn't dwell on it. Fiona was leaving and I wanted to see her off. It wasn't until after she climbed aboard and sped away that Jason told me what happened."

The sheriff's attention turns toward me. "Ms. Hammerstein has informed me you're a stand-up guy, Mr. Najason."

"Najarian," Megan corrects. "Mr. and Mrs."

"You two are married?" The sheriff asks, surprised.

"Yes."

"No!"

"Well, I'm glad we could clear that up," the sheriff says. I hear snickers from the other officers.

"Kindly explain to me in detail, sir, what you witnessed on the beach tonight."

I start by explaining how the sunset gatherings began. How a few of us islanders would meet for an hour or more and watch the sun go down. I left out everything I learned about Sal and everything I shared with Fiona. When I was done, it sounded as innocent as neighbors getting together on the beach. When I began detailing the events of the evening, I made sure I sounded as shocked as possible. I explained about the boat speeding toward shore. "Fiona apparently dug up a gun buried in the sand and then fired at Sal for no reason. After she shot him, she and the man on the boat threatened my life. That's about when Phyllis showed up."

I offered an ambiguous description of Fiona, as if I never really paid much attention to her. In truth, part of me was still enamored with her, and that part didn't want to be considered a rat. With the machine man there was no hesitancy. I described him in detail. I closed my statement with, "Sal was a nice man, and Fiona was a sweet woman. What happened tonight has left me traumatized." My intent was to remove myself from their sullied pasts.

Megan claps her hands softly. "So, we showed up just in time to save your life. You owe me now, Poopsie!"

The sheriff asks, "Did you happen to notice how the gun ended up buried on your beach, near your chairs, and a stone's throw from your house? From your testimony, the suspect never wore enough clothing to conceal such a weapon."

"No idea, Sheriff."

"What about the boat? Make, model, name, numbers? In what direction was it headed?"

"A white and blue Sea Ray is all I could make out, and due south it appeared."

"And why didn't you inform Ms. Hammerstein upon her arrival that a crime had taken place?"

"When Phyllis called out my name from the deck, Fiona warned, 'If you say one word, I'll kill you and them on the spot.' What was I supposed to do?"

Phyllis gasps. The sheriff leans back in the chair.

"Does that shiner of yours play any particular role in the circumstances surrounding tonight's events?" he asks me.

"This?" I say, pointing to my eye. "No way. I'm embarrassed to admit I slipped and fell while on my boat."

Megan sits straight up. "That's not what . . ."

"*Fuck Gaspar Gomez.*"

"What the hell was that?" the sheriff says, turning toward the living room.

"Uh . . . that's my parrot. He has this . . . unique vocabulary. It's best we just ignore him." I'm fearful the gangster bird will start singing about Fiona and me sitting in a tree.

The sheriff stares at me for a moment and then leans over to one of the officers.

"Radio the marine patrol and add a white and blue Sea Ray to the APB. Tell them we're looking for a male and female, considered dangerous. Send them over the descriptions we have with images to follow ASAP. Spread it as far south as Naples and alert the highway patrol boys south to Interstate 75. I want eyes at RSW airport, too." The officer exits the house to coordinate the search from the sheriff's boat.

"Just so I understand, you're telling me you and your neighbors frequented the beach in front of your house to watch the sunset? Is that correct?"

"Yes," I say.

"And other than that, you never socialized in any way with any of them?"

"Well, I went fishing once with Sal, the dead guy."

"I loaned Murray's fishing rod to Jason," Phyllis interjects.

The sheriff smiles at her. "I hope Murray doesn't find out."

"Ms. Hammerstein spoke briefly with me on the phone about her relationship with Fiona. Did you, sir, spend any personal time with the suspect? Was she ever in your house?"

I thought it was best to remain silent and risk looking like a fool. I shake my head no.

"She was just a neighbor then, nothing more?"

I nod, fearful Megan will mention the parting remark by Fiona about "the good times." If she does, I will sacrifice it all and turn Megan into the second murder victim of the night.

The sheriff closes his pad and returns the pen to his pocket. "I'm gonna ask you all to come down to the station and fill out some witness statement reports. I know it's late at night, but we need your immediate cooperation in this matter. Phyllis, if you could accompany one of my men to your office so we can get your files on this Fiona woman, I would be grateful. You mentioned you have a copy of her license on the rental agreement?"

Phyllis nods.

"Good, in the meantime, do you have a problem, sir, if my men have a quick look around your house? It would mean a lot to me if I could bypass getting a warrant at this hour."

The request makes me very nervous. I've watched enough television to know about forensic investigations, so I am sure there is a long dark strand of Fiona's hair hiding somewhere in my house eager to get me in big trouble.

"Yeah . . . I guess you can, but what would that accomplish?"

The sheriff looks at me sternly. "Putting aside the kind things Ms. Hammerstein has told me about you, I would be remiss not to include you on my short list of who fired that weapon tonight. So, what I'm trying to do, sir, is eliminate you as a person of interest even though you're the only witness to the crime."

Sheriff Williamson directs the officers to search the house. They slip on gloves and head off in different directions. It will not be a turn-everything-upside-down type cellblock toss, but more like an easing around to make sure I am the stand-up guy Phyllis claimed I was.

"Is that your boat at the dock—the *Ticket to Ride?*" the sheriff asks.

"Yes," I say.

The sheriff stands up and clicks his shoulder radio on. "Officer McArdle, kindly do a sweep of the boat docked down there before you return."

"Wait . . . what about Toast?" I call out excitedly.

The sheriff looks at me strangely and says, "Not for me, thanks."

"I'll have some. Do you have grape jelly?" Megan asks.

"No! *Toast,* you know." I look at Phyllis. "Aubert what's his name. He was on the beach tonight too. He saw what happened."

Phyllis shakes her head. "He wasn't on the beach when I arrived, Jason."

"That's because as soon as Fiona fired the gun, he ran away. He saw what happened. He can eliminate me as a person of interest."

Sheriff Williamson sits back down and looks at Phyllis for confirmation.

"His name is Aubert Mainard and he's renting the unit next door to Mr. Santini. Unit number sixteen," Phyllis says.

"Then I think we should be talking to this boy," the sheriff says. He calls over two officers and directs them to pick up the Mainard fellow at unit sixteen for questioning. As they are leaving, one of the officers places an Oprah Winfrey magazine on the counter. "Found this on the deck, Sheriff," he says. When Megan sees the cover, she lunges for it, causing the sheriff to slap her wrist.

"That's evidence, young lady," he scolds her.

"But it's the big O! I haven't read that issue."

"Is this yours?" he asks me, while searching the magazine for an address label.

There is only one answer. "Of course it's mine."

Megan purrs. "Poopsie, reading that magazine makes you *so* sexy."

The sheriff shakes his head in dismay and drops the periodical to the counter. "I think it's time we head back to the mainland and wrap this up." He pushes back on the chair. The remaining officer drifts back into the kitchen from his search of the second floor without any damning evidence of my relationship with Fiona. We are about to leave the house when the sheriff's radio crackles.

"Sheriff, I found something on the boat you need to see."

CHAPTER TWENTY-NINE

Island Departures

"The only reason some people get lost in thought is because it's unfamiliar territory."

—PAUL FIX

On *my* boat? In a matter of seconds, I go from being somewhat curious to outright panic when I speculate what the officer has found. My jaw seems frozen and I'm overwhelmed with fear and exhaustion.

Fiona's luggage!

I think the worst. *How will I explain away Fiona's clothes or multiple passports, or any other personal items stuffed in her suitcases and stowed on my boat after I just spent the last few hours making every attempt to distant myself from her?* I shiver at the thought there may actually be a piece of paper somewhere in her bags titled "Contract to Kill" stating for a certain amount of money, Fiona is to put a bullet in the back of Sal's head. Found on my boat, it would make me look like an accomplice in her getaway. Hundreds of scenarios flash in front of me in rapid succession, but what stands out in high definition again is her words, "The evidence always points elsewhere." *Could she have planted something incriminating in her luggage?* My PMS conjures up a different note thanking me for killing Sal and promising the check is in the mail.

As the sheriff herds everyone through the front door, I glance back at my house for what I fear will be the last time. I look at Montana and feel bad he will end up homeless again. As I follow Phyllis outside I hear him squawk, *"I always tell the truth, even when I lie."*

We descend the stairs single file. The sheriff leads the way followed by Megan, Phyllis, me, and an officer in tow. I guess he is bringing up the rear in the event I decide to make a run for it. My heart pounds faster and my legs gain weight with each step I take. I shuffle along as if I'm wearing leg irons. When we reach the wooden slats that lead to the well-lit mooring, I peer around the line of people and see Fiona's three brightly colored suitcases piled at the end of the dock next to an officer standing sentinel. What I ate for supper with Fiona just a few hours earlier is in the process of making a U-turn.

The parade comes to an abrupt halt when the sheriff reaches the dock. He sweeps the deck of my boat with his flashlight, and then leans close to the officer to say something I can't decipher. The sheriff proceeds to lift the smaller of the three bags and turns around to single me out.

"Are these yours?" he asks.

In a split second, I try to visualize the luggage I carried up the stairs for Fiona. I remember they were heavy, but I can't recall seeing any name tags because I was more in tune with her unpacking the bags and moving in. If I answer no to his inquiry, I will open up a can of worms labeled: Then why are these on your boat? If I answer yes, I might be playing right into Fiona's plans. "The evidence always points elsewhere." I close my eyes and put all my trust in a woman who assassinates people for a living.

"Yes. They belong to me," I blurt.

I can't breathe. I sense the officer behind me is reaching for his cuffs.

Megan turns around. "Really, Jason? That luggage is yours? You have no friggin' fashion sense whatsoever."

The sheriff drops to one knee and begins to unzip the first bag. He pulls back the cover and reaches inside.

I want to dive in the water and disappear. It is dark enough that they will never find me. With any luck, some manatees will come along and guide me to a safe harbor.

The sheriff turns to me with a quizzical look.

Or maybe I could swing around real quick and grab the gun from the officer behind me. Then I could tie everyone up with dock lines and make my escape to Abuc.

He lifts his hand a few feet above the suitcase and pours out a handful of sand.

Sand? I think.

"Sand, Mr. Narjarsamin?" Sheriff Williamson questions.

"Najarian," Megan insists. "*Na-jar-re-in.* Jason and Megan."

Phyllis turns to me and smiles. "Are you trying to smuggle sand off the island?"

The sheriff reaches for the second bag and opens it. More sand. And in the last bag, even more sand. It appears to be a continuation of Fiona's ruse.

He stands up, wipes his hands together and says, "Enlighten me, sir. Why do you have suitcases filled with sand on your boat?"

I shrug. "Traction for my truck?" It's my first thought and admittedly a lame one.

Everybody is suddenly staring at me. I can even feel the eyes of the officer behind me boring into the back of my head. Little do they know this is yet another cog in Fiona's elaborate scheme to disguise her intentions while on the island. She has played me like a fiddle. Regardless, part of me remains infatuated with her.

The sheriff shakes his head in disbelief and says to the officer, "Put the man's bags back on his boat. We don't want him getting stuck in any snow."

"Wait . . . it's supposed to snow?" Megan asks.

Phyllis and one of the officers leave Sand Key in her skiff to retrieve Fiona's information from her office. The rest of us board the police boat for the ride over to the mainland. During the jaunt, I manage to overhear on the police radio that Aubert Mainard has been located and officers are bringing him in for questioning. Another report provides an update on the search of Fiona's rental unit. I am grateful my DNA never made an appearance in her beach house. Several other reports site the Sea Ray in question, but each turns out to be a false identification.

It is close to 2 A.M. by the time we arrive at police headquarters. We are asked to sit on a wooden bench in the front lobby facing an officer whose job it is to answer the phones. She is also surrounded by a collaboration of television screens that monitor the activities of the facility. A few other officers are moving about in a caffeine-induced frenzy. Not only do they have the events of tonight to deal with, this small-town force is still reeling from the double murder of Amber's stepbrothers.

As the early morning drags by, Phyllis, Megan, and I are interrogated separately. When it is my turn, I enter a small room with a table and three chairs. Video cameras are attached to the walls at each corner near the ceiling. For the next two hours I answer questions and give my best recollection of the events leading up to Sal's murder and what happened immediately thereafter. I look at mug shots of criminals and speak with a sketch artist regarding the machine man. Near the end of the questioning, they show me a copy of Fiona's license and ask if this is the woman who fired the gun. She is smiling in the State of New York photo. The memories of my time spent with her flirt with my mind.

I see her playfully toss M&M's into the air.

I smell the hibiscus in her hair.

I feel the heat of her naked body as we meld together.

I hear her moans of ecstasy from the perfect rhythm we shared.

I want to say, "No, that's not the Fiona I know." But it is, so I reluctantly confirm the picture on the license is indeed the woman who killed Sal Santini.

As I am being escorted from the room, Toast is headed down the corridor to another room. When he recognizes me, he wails, "*Mon ami,* you're alive!" His eyes are red from crying. We embrace. "I'm so happy to see you. I thought she would kill you, too," he says.

I think, *so you ran away?* But I hold my tongue. I pat him on the back and suggest we get together before he leaves the island.

It's one of those things people say but don't really mean. In truth, I never want to see him again.

I join Phyllis and Megan in the front lobby. The excitement of the night is wearing thin as we each suppress yawns. Megan is stretched out on the bench. Phyllis is nodding off, but jolts awake at the slightest sound. I lean my head against the wall and count the pinholes in the ceiling tiles.

The clock on the wall is closing in on 6 A.M. A shift change is under way. The new officers arrive and gawk at us as if we are three disheveled winos found in a culvert by the side of the road. Well, two of us, anyway. They all seem to know Phyllis and say good morning to her.

An exhausted looking Sheriff Williamson finally makes an appearance in the lobby. He thanks us for our cooperation and informs us we are free to go. As we stand to leave, he pulls Phyllis aside and speaks with her in a hushed tone. Even though I am physically spent, my imagination is fully alert and doing chin-ups. I speculate on what the sheriff is saying in private to Phyllis. *Is he telling her to keep an eye on me? Did his investigation uncover my relationship with Fiona? Is he bringing in the CIA?* I want to go over and join their little huddle, but then the sheriff hugs Phyllis and they part ways.

We leave the police station and head to Phyllis's car. The morning light burns my eyes as I stretch and fantasize about a week's worth of sleep. But then I'm hit by a monkey wrench when I hear Megan whine, "I'm hungry." She is still here. I need to formulate a plan to extricate myself from her clutches, but I know it will be difficult with her right under my nose. I doubt I can count on Phyllis to help; she seems to be enjoying my predicament. But maybe after the sobering events of the past day, she might be easier to enlist.

We climb into the car, Megan in the back and me in the front. Phyllis sits behind the wheel seemingly in a trance. When she doesn't engage the ignition right away, I ask if she is all right.

"Guess what the sheriff just told me."

And there it is. I am screwed. *What did he have on me?* I try to mask my sudden anxiety by making light of the answer. "Is he gonna fine me for putting sand in the bags?"

"No. He informed me that Amber's stepfather is missing."

∞

I'M NOT sure how much more I can assimilate. To further complicate things, I'm the only person who can tie all this together, with the exception of the missing stepfather and I'm sure with my propensity for attracting trouble the answer to that conundrum awaits me at my house.

I don't have a mode of transportation back to Gulf Boulevard, so I suggest to Phyllis that she take me back to the island in exchange for breakfast. She thinks that is a good idea.

Megan lifts her hand in the back seat and says. "I'm in."

Maybe in a small skiff over rough intracoastal waters Megan will find herself . . . *out.*

It is my first all-nighter since college. I am drained as I try to summon the strength to tie the skiff lines to the cleats. I can't stop yawning, my eyelids are heavy, and I'm still clouded with a level of anxiety about what will happen next. And then there is Megan. She sits on the boat, checking her nails, unwilling to get her hands dirty. I need to get her out of here, but I'm too exhausted to formulate a plan.

I am relieved to find my house as I left it. The police haven't been back. Fiona isn't hiding out in my bedroom, and Amber's stepfather isn't slumped over on my deck. As soon as Montana sees me he squawks, *"Chi Chi, get the yeyo."* I feed the bird as Phyllis flops onto the sofa and starts making calls on her cellphone. Megan is taking the opportunity to familiarize herself with my house for the first time. She is walking in and out of rooms, lifting things, moving things, and looking too much like a prospective tenant. As I enter the kitchen she calls out, "Jason, I'm not too

~ 291 ~

keen on this gym room. I think we can better utilize this space."
Hello, migraine.

While preparing breakfast, I look out at the beach and find it naked and unkempt. My chairs are gone, the rake is gone, and the sand has taken a terrible pounding. A thin line of seaweed has already marked the highest tide. I need to get back to the mainland, after some sleep, and replace the rake and chairs taken by the police as evidence. I want to re-create Hermitville as it was, and maybe entice Harry to join Montana and me once again. But I wonder what it will feel like sitting in the spot where Fiona killed Sal. *Will I forever worry about someone sneaking up behind me?*

"The island has turned into a dangerous place to live and I sense more violence is imminent," I say for Megan's consumption. Phyllis smiles at my efforts to expel Megan from paradise, but Megan seems unconscious to my veiled threats. My facial expressions plead with Phyllis for help.

I work on Megan's expulsion as I serve bacon and eggs with hash browns for Phyllis and me, and a bowl of Holy Crap cereal with celery root to Megan. She loves it. Nothing is going my way. We spend breakfast talking about Sal and Fiona and how we still can't believe what took place.

"Have you thought about buying property down here, Megan? I have a lot of repossessed listings at very attractive prices," Phyllis says.

I toss Phyllis the stink eye.

Megan drops her spoon in the cereal and looks at Phyllis. "You mean like with a priest and all?"

And then it hits me. Megan is frightened by anything demonic. She can't be in the same zip code at the mention of Satan. Call it professional courtesy. In the last few months of my dreadful marriage, whenever I needed to put an end to her monotonous arguments, I would play *The Exorcist* on the DVD, which would result in Megan running from the house screaming.

I look at Phyllis and beg her with my eyes to follow my lead.

"Yes, Megan," I say. "A lot of properties down here are repossessed and have had unsuccessful exorcisms to boot. They just can't seem to eradicate the forces of evil. Why do you think the market in Florida is so depressed?" I ask.

Megan is unruffled. I can tell she has already found her comfort zone in my house.

"And now with the murder and all," I add, "it's a harbinger of manifestations to come."

"Doesn't matter, Poopsie, our beautiful house isn't repossessed."

"Oh yes it is," Phyllis says.

I bow my head. *Thank you. Thank you.*

"I sold this home to Jason and it was certainly a repossessed property at the time."

Megan appears lost in thought. She stands up and begins to look around the house. She is twitching and scratching and turning in circles. Her eyes are wide and her appearance turns pale. She is frightened and I have no doubt she has started to see objects moving. She stumbles back against the wall.

Phyllis glares angrily at me, but I'm looking around for someone to high-five.

"It's all right, honey. It's not what you think," Phyllis says in an attempt to calm her, but it's too late. The easy button has been pushed. The bell has been rung. Megan won't be able to spend another minute in my repossessed house.

"It's *re*possessed, not possessed," Phyllis says, but Megan is shaking her head in disagreement. I have no doubt in her mind she has already locked horns with Lucifer.

"I can't stay here, Jason. Something isn't right. I need to go home," Megan stutters.

"No, Megs, don't say that. I want you to stay," I plead, half-heartedly. "It's only bad here at night."

Megan bolts from the kitchen, grabs her luggage, and races out the front door.

From across the room: *"Say goodnight to the bad guy."*

"You're a horse's ass," Phyllis says to me.

"No, I'm a cuckold."

In the distance I can hear Megan screaming for someone to take her to the mainland.

"I suppose it's incumbent upon me to take her back to her car. You probably have no room with all that sand on your boat."

I nod.

"I thought so. Thanks for breakfast, you evil snowbird. I'll be in touch."

Phyllis hugs me and then follows in Megan's path. I watch from the deck as the skiff putters away from the dock. Megan never dares look back.

Aside from all that has taken place, I'm feeling pretty good. So good that I want to cover my face in blue paint and once again declare, *"Freedom!"*

Chapter Thirty

Island Holiday

"He has all the virtues I dislike and none of the vices
I admire."

—Winston Churchill

It is the Wednesday before Thanksgiving and I am on my way
to the boat condo to pick up my parents along with their lesser
halves. A four-day sleepover is scheduled, but I hope it turns into
a one-day inconvenience like some other family reunions do. I
don't mind having my parents visit, but putting them in separate
bedrooms with their *guests* will certainly keep me up all night,
especially if I hear noises. *Gasp!*

It's been just over two months since the incident on my
beach, and a lot of information has trickled out, all of which
has reached my ears by way of Phyllis's need to gossip. I learned
the guy I knew as Sal Santini, the music mogul, was in fact Salvatore Scalise, an alleged hit man known for his brutality. When
Phyllis relayed the information, I immediately reflected on all
the times he could have killed me for sport: from me not liking
his fake lobster tails, to the time I flipped him off at the bait
shop. I shivered at how close I came to being another one of his
victims.

The sheriff also shared with Phyllis facts obtained from the
FBI and Interpol regarding Fiona Tallahassee, aka Serafina Gior-
dano, aka *Il Serpente*. The woman I fell head over heels for, and
spent time under the sheets with, was a notorious international
assassin. Maybe Megan was right to feel an evil spirit in my house.
Nevertheless, my obsession with Fiona continues, albeit somewhat

diminished since learning of her occupation, but the flicker of a flame remains.

I also learned Toast left early for New York, intending never to return to this idyllic island. He told Phyllis he would not be renewing for the following year. *Whoopie!*

About a week after the "Sand Key Slaying," as the local newspaper headlines reported it, I opened the front door and found my steps lined with pots of flowers. There was a note in the first one telling me how much Amber enjoyed my company along with a request to kindly care for her plants until she returned. No date was given. I wish Amber hadn't been so clandestine with the flowers, because I wanted to ask her about her intentions that night on the beach when she was headed my way with a gun. I never got around to pursuing the question because the situation remained fluid with her stepbrothers and stepfather, so I felt it was best for me to keep my mouth shut. Phyllis was informed that Amber returned up north with her mother, leaving her beach house vacant. She hadn't put it up for rent, nor had she left instructions with Phyllis to have a caretaker tend to it. Phyllis had a spare key, so we decided to hire the island property management crew to tend to her home periodically, on my dime. It was the least I could do. The case of Amber's missing stepfather remains unsolved.

Memphis the Lighthouse claimed Sal's remains. The body was cremated and now resides in an urn on a shelf at the bait shop. Someday, when Memphis isn't eyeing me, I plan to spill Sal into a box and spread his remains over the gulf so the fish have some revenge for his bombing raids.

Several weeks after Megan escaped from the clutches of the satanic kingdom known as Gulf Boulevard, she sent a text message to say she was devoting her life to saving me, along with my checkbook I suspect, from the dark side. Megan wrote that she enlisted the advice of her local church, and had been in contact with the Vatican in an effort to secure the services of a priest with *exercise* experience. I texted her back suggesting she may want to search out some health clubs. She replied with two questions marks.

In her most recent text, she enlightened me on her progress and assured me as soon as the right priest was found, she would bring him down to Florida to conduct an *exercise* in my house. I texted her back inquiring if stomach crunches would be involved. She replied again with two question marks.

I know Megan is as serious as a laser-guided missile. I respect her tenacity and have no doubt she will try to convince a priest to perform an exorcism on my beach house. I'm sure in her mind it's like finding a safecracker who can open the vault to my assets. Whether she succeeds is anyone's guess, but I realized I needed some insurance, so I went out and purchased the new Blu-ray version of *The Exorcist*, just in case.

I pull into the boat condo to the waving arms of my mother and father. Tranquility is jumping up and down like a school girl, but Bradley is stoic; his hands are in his pockets and a pipe is in his mouth. There is nothing I admire about this guy; I dislike everything about him. I realize I can't do four days of this . . . I just can't.

I get everyone and their luggage onboard and head back to the waterway. Speed is my game, so I open up the throttle and advise only my parents to hold on. The *Ticket to Ride* jumps out of the water and rides the crest of each wave. I push her so hard my cheeks start to ripple. The hurricane-force winds combine with the roar of the engines to mute any conversation, so I am left to hope while at the helm there is panic behind me at the sudden loss of two passengers, nonfamily, who went airborne and overboard.

As I approach the mouth to Hermitville lagoon, I throttle down and glance back to find all my passengers intact. *Bummer.* They are all smiling and enjoying the vista. Tranny is trying to splash my dad with water, and my mother is in Brad's embrace leaning back against his chest. I feel the flicker within me. It makes me think of Fiona. For some time now I've questioned whether I can be a hermit in utopia without a hermitess to share it with.

I dock the boat, tie off the lines, and welcome everyone to Sand Key. My guests are turning in circles, utterly amazed as they walk along the sand path to Gulf Boulevard. When the house comes into view, I hear my mother exclaim, "This is unbelievable!"

We scale the staircase and once the view of the gulf appears, there is a collective wide-eyed exhilaration. Tranny grabs my dad by the arm and pulls him along the deck until they are on the walkover and running toward the beach. My mother remains on the deck next to Bradley, soaking in the panoramic view. For a quick second I wonder if Tranny is making my father younger, while Bradley is making my mother older—but it is just an observation.

After my guests frolic outside in paradise, it is time for a tour of the house. Of course the first topic of conversation is the African Grey parrot. The strange faces approaching his cage send Montana backpedaling as he opens up with a round of gunfire.

"Does he talk?" my mother asks.

"What's that noise he's making?" Bradley wants to know.

"Is his name Polly?" Tranny inquires.

"I've hated birds ever since a seagull stole my French fries at Revere Beach," my father blurts.

"He does talk when he's in the mood. Right now he's shooting at us," I say.

"Shooting as in bullets?" asks Bradley.

No, as in stars. "Yes, it's his defense mechanism," I reply.

"Well, that's lame and violent. I know a colleague who owns a parrot with an impressive vocabulary. The bird can actually recite lines of poetry from Emerson and Frost," Bradley brags.

"My bird is limited to the works of Pacino," I say.

"I'm not familiar with him," Bradley says.

"You will be by the end of the weekend."

I give the tour of the house and my parents are genuinely impressed. We gather on the deck outside my bedroom and marvel at the view. The beach is deserted which is to say, I'm not on it. Pelicans waver in the gusts, and sandpipers elude the incoming waves. My mother is taking pictures, and I'm sure an oil painting is not far behind.

"Why is your sand smooth as compared to the rest of the beach?" my father wonders aloud.

"I rake it, Dad."

"Really? Why do you feel the need to disturb the environment as it was meant to be?" Bradley inquires.

"I rake the beach, Brad, so the baby sea turtles have a smooth passage to the water. I find more survive because of my efforts." I didn't have facts and figures to back up my claim, nor had I even seen a baby turtle yet, but the bullshit is impressive.

"That is so real of you, Jason," Tranny says. She kisses me on the cheek. Okay, she can stay.

I gather the luggage and place my parents' bags in one spare room and the vagabonds' bags in the other.

"I put your bags in the rooms. Dad, you and Mom are in this room, Brad and Tranny can use that room," I say. My mother punches my arm.

After a stunning late autumn sunset and some reminiscing over drinks, day one is almost in the books as my guests retire early. As soon as they are tucked away, I search my war room for a marker and draw the number one on a piece of paper, not unlike a prisoner carving the number of days completed on the wall of his cell. I hang it on the refrigerator with a dolphin magnet as a reminder. To avoid the awkwardness of hearing noises I'm not unaccustomed to, I spend the night downstairs on the sofa under the spitting shells of my gangster bird.

Day two. I get up early on Thanksgiving morning to put the bird in the oven. Not the parrot, a turkey. With a little preplanning courtesy of Chef Phyllis Hammerstein, I manage to serve a full course meal by midday. At the dinner table, I entertain everyone with my experiences since moving in, beginning with my escape from Megan in Massachusetts to the escape from Florida by Fiona.

"Jason, I'm worried for you. Is it really safe here?" my mother asks.

I am about to calm her concerns when Montana calls out for his Thanksgiving fare.

"Chi Chi, get the yeyo."

My guests are stunned. All heads turn toward the cage.

"He talks," my father says, surprised.

"Yes, but it sounds Spanish. Does he have a green card, Jason?" Brad says, chuckling.

"He wants food. Excuse me while . . ."

Tranny jumps from the table and races over to Montana.

"Polly want a cwacker?" she asks in a baby voice. "Polly parrot wants a cwacker, don't he?"

I look at my father who is smiling. Tranquility is around the same age as Fiona, but light years behind in every other way. It has to be the sex.

I notice Montana is taking a liking to her. He gets close to the cage and tilts his head. This means he is getting ready to—

"Say hello to my little friend."

I'm relieved it's not an f-bomb. Laughter breaks out around the table. Tranny turns toward us with wide eyes and a big grin. She tells us, "I love Simon Says." She clears her throat and repeats, "Hello to my little friend."

I shake my head. Montana seems surprised by the mimic and takes a step back. My mother leans over to me and whispers, "Now you have two parrots."

I feed the gangster bird his lunch with help from Tranny. She is begging my father to buy a bird, but he grunts his displeasure at the thought as he lowers himself in front of the television to watch football. I join my mother in clearing the table as Brad joins Tranny by the cage.

"Don't they make a nice couple?" I say to my mother.

She looks up and rolls her eyes. "Look Jason, I'm very proud of you and what you've done for everyone, but you also have me concerned. That story over dinner . . . listen, can we talk in private upstairs?"

I nod, eager to hear the private part might involve helping my mother get rid of Brad. We load the dishwater and head toward the stairs. Tranny is sitting in a chair with my father, but there is no sign of any nostril exploration. Luckily, Brad is still on his feet using his finger to poke the cage instead of poking his toes. Montana looks agitated, but curious. I'm hoping my experiment with the Three Stooges will keep him from—

"You have a look in your eye like you haven't been fucked in a year."

I cringe. It is loud and clear enough that everyone turns toward Bradley. He throws his hands in the air and says, "What . . . I didn't do anything!"

My father starts laughing and Tranny is trying to understand why. My mother pauses on the steps. "Why did you teach your bird to talk like that, anyway?" she scolds me.

We sit on the upper deck, which is becoming my mother's favorite place. She starts lecturing, and once she does, it is difficult to get a word in edgewise.

"The violence and gangsters you told us about make me worry. A murder, right on your beach! I'm afraid for you here, Jason. What about repercussions, or revenge? I'd feel a lot better if you bought a home on the cape near Bradley and me. You'd also be closer to Megan, and by the way, I don't understand what's going on between you two. I spoke with her a few weeks ago and she sounded scared, as if the devil was knocking at her door. Why can't you two just work things out?"

I never told my mother that Megan cheated on me. I assume she always felt I was the cause of the breakup, but she never said anything to that effect—probably because she fears I'll raise her one dollar a year rent.

After hearing her out, I try to dispel the apprehension she harbors by claiming the events that took place were completely out of the ordinary. "Life on Sand Key is safe, and I doubt I will ever see a stranger walk on my beach again," I say.

"Then why do you have a mirror sticking out of the sand? Are you captivated with yourself or what? Who plants a mirror on the beach?" she asks with a furrowed brow.

I laugh. "I have it there so I can notice if my neighbors pay a visit bearing gifts, like say . . . lobster tails. Why else?" *It also works on detecting gun-wielding assassins.*

She doesn't appear totally convinced, and while I'm sure she would find comfort in me living closer to her, it ain't happening. And then one of the reasons for it not happening walks onto the deck to disturb my private moment.

"I must say, Jason, that's a strange parrot you have there. Certainly not a bird you can showcase in public," he chuckles.

"That's why I'm hiding out on an island," I reply.

He leans against the deck railing. "Hiding on an island," he repeats, while rubbing his chin. "That was quite the story you shared over dinner. My initial reaction was one of embellishment given the deserted nature of this area. I mean really, who commits a murder on a forsaken barrier island?"

I do, in a minute.

"We were just talking about that, Bradley. I'm trying to convince Jason to move to the cape where it is safer," my mother chimes in. "The most excitement we ever get is what happened to you at the university. Tell Jason about that."

Bradley shifts on his feet. "Ah, not as spectacular as your sordid tale, but I did entertain a visit from the state department regarding a suspicious package mailed to North Korea in *my* name, they claimed. The officials said it originated right here in Florida."

"No shit," I say, acting interested.

"I got the sense after they realized I held a prominent position at Harvard, they decided I wasn't the culprit in this matter. They only questioned me for a few minutes and I haven't heard from them since."

"Did they tell you what kind of shit was in the package?" I ask.

"No, they never shared with me the contents. I just hope it wasn't something insulting to the good people of North Korea. In the end, I suspect it was a student prank." Bradley turns toward the gulf. "So what is it about this place that captivates you, Jason?"

"He's like me," my mother says, answering the question. "He's always been drawn to nature." She stands up and joins Bradley at the railing.

"Yes, Gloria, but with all his found money, I'd consider traveling instead of taking root in a place like this, unless of course he has a Robinson Crusoe fantasy that needs to be played out." He looks at me with an elitist smirk.

"Where would you suggest I travel, Brad?"

"Well, you certainly have time to spare. Have you ever considered studying abroad?"

"Yes, I have, but I can't get a woman to sit still long enough."

"See, Gloria . . . it remains a challenge to engage in normal conversation with your son."

"Oh! My! Word!" my mother cries out, aghast. She exits the deck and calls down to my father. "Sam, your flower child is behaving lewdly on the beach."

I jump up from my chair and join Bradley, who is already leaning over the railing for a closer look. Tranny is cavorting around on my manicured sand. I usually don't stray from watching a woman's naked body in motion, but the realization that two ceremonial words would turn this woman into my stepmother is like the needle of a record scratching to a halt. Brad remains riveted. It makes me want to flip the professor over the railing, scream out suicide, and call it a day. But I refrain, knowing it would sadden my mother, not to mention the damage my lower deck would sustain.

When I hear my father calling out for Tranny, I am forced to take another peek. It is comical watching him chase her around the beach chairs with a towel. He finally catches her and they fall to the sand at about the same place that gravity claimed Sal. I'm thinking there must be some kind of magnetic force buried deep below the surface that brings people to a sudden halt on that spot.

After another sunset, day two comes to a close with a viral outbreak of turkey coma. I add another mark to the paper on the refrigerator.

DAY THREE is chilly for a Floridian, but my New England guests think it is balmy. I guess my blood is already thinning. The gulf is rough, so my plan to charter a fishing boat from the island of Boca Grande is scrubbed. Instead, we visit the quaint shops, which excite my mother and Tranny, and bore the life out of Bradley and my father. I remain neutral because day three is nearing an end and that means day four and their departure is within sight. I am almost giddy at the thought.

We have dinner at a marina on the waterway and later Tranny insists on a beach-blanket-bingo by the beach chairs, complete with a fire and marshmallows. My father and I hurry to collect driftwood, dried seaweed, and downed fronds. Bradley watches as he apparently fears breaking a nail. I dig a hole and to my surprise, I don't find any guns. I place the scrub inside and create fire, a bonfire to be exact. We sit circling the pit on stretched-out beach towels wearing sweaters and long pants. As the night grows long, the couples cuddle and then a suck-face competition is under way. I feel like a fifth wheel stoking the fire and watching these four make out like teenagers. I'm the youngest one in attendance, yet I am alone and getting nauseous. I find myself looking southward into the dark abyss hoping for an image, preferably female, to emerge.

The crackling fire masks the noise people make while kissing.

I try to project Fiona jogging in my direction, or Amber advancing toward me with a marigold hanging out of the barrel of a gun, or the young chick with the gorgeous smile from Two Palms Marina. Hell, I'd even take the uneven Double Ds at this point.

Later, when the house is still, I mark the third day on the paper. It gets me through the night.

∽∞∽

DAY FOUR has arrived and it is *hasta la vista day, baby*. I am up early with a little giddyup in my step, as I make as much of a ruckus as possible to get my guests to rise and shine. We have a quick breakfast and when I see their luggage in the foyer, I am overcome with euphoria. They all enjoy a final look at the early morning gulf, and each bids a farewell to Montana. The weekend wasn't filled with f-bombs like I feared, but the Three Stooges experiment hadn't taken effect either. So when I ask my parents to stand next to each other in front of the cage, I hope Montana gets the clue, but there is no reaction. Bradley then passes the cage and Montana flips him the wing. *Good boy.* Tranny is the last to say good-bye and she gushes all over the bird. I feel a parrot is in my father's near future. Tranny blows Montana some kisses and then turns toward the foyer. Montana scrambles along the perch to the edge of the cage. He bobs his head.

"Another Quaalude and she'll be mine again."

Everyone laughs and they start to gravitate back to the cage for more entertainment, but I open the front door and remind them they have a flight to catch. Enough is enough with people living with me. I need to be a hermit again. As I close the door to leave, I hear Montana squawk, *"Calling Doctor Howard, Doctor Fine, Doctor Howard!"* in perfect Three Stooges form.

⌘

At the boat condo, I hug my parents good-bye. My mother suggests again that I consider the cape, and I nod out of respect. Bradley offers his hand, but I counter with a bump fist. I have no idea where his hands have been, and that triggers a mental note to have the island cleaning company do a double fumigate on my guest rooms.

Tranny embraces me a little too tightly and I have to fight the image of her naked on the beach.

"Promise me you'll find safeness under the sun and keep Montana's feathers aflutter," she says.

Huh?

Her eyes are glassy and red as if she has been stoned since she arrived, but I haven't seen any evidence of cannabis so I assume this is Tranny's biological makeup and it clarifies for me her unwillingness to shift out of first gear.

I ask them all to come back soon; the things people say that they don't really mean. My parents nod eagerly at the invitation. Brad shrugs his shoulders and Tranny asks, "Why should we come back if we're already here?" This causes my mother to roll her eyes. They climb into their rental car, wave for a final time, and drive away.

I stand on the cement dock and watch the car exit the parking lot. The covered docks are quiet. The air is warm for an autumn day. These are the best of times because the humidity and the bugs are on vacation. A boat appears at the entrance to the dock area.

"Jason, how are you?" the captain calls out.

I step aboard the *Ticket* and greet my boat-condo neighbor as he eases closer. The man is old and scruffy; his skin tanned and wrinkled. He is a retired autoworker, living the dream of sun worshipping, fishing, and sleeping. After he maneuvers into his berth, he holds up a string of fish.

"Had a good morning out there, can you take some?"

I've acquired a palate for grouper. I think nature made this fish so ugly she felt bad afterward and gave it flavor. I locate a few on his line and say, "Thanks! I'll take one of those groupers if they haven't been spoken for."

He wrestles one off the line and tosses it over. I thank him and start up the boat to head back home.

I tie up at the lagoon and decide to clean the fish on board. I haven't done this since my fishing expedition with Sal, so I have to stop and think where I stowed the knives. I pull out a wood block and place the fish on top. Then I search a few small compartments until I find the cleaning knives along with some keys I don't recognize right away. But then it hits me . . . *Sal.*

Chapter Thirty-One

Island Discovery

"I don't suffer from my insanity—I enjoy every minute of it."

—Sherrilyn Kenyon

I'm sitting on the gunwale with the keys in my hand, trying to recall my conversation with Sal about trust, a Dean Martin CD, and some secret codes to a combination lock for a storage locker somewhere on the mainland. It's all a blur to me now because once Sal died, I tried to jettison everything I knew about him. I wanted no part of his dealings: past, present, or future. But now that the dust has settled around him and I find myself holding the keys, my curiosity gains momentum. *What was he hiding in a storage unit?* I struggle between being a hermit and being nosey. I want to know what unfinished business Sal may have left behind.

The simple fix to my dilemma is to throw the keys in the lagoon and forget I ever found them. No harm with that unless I subscribe to the fear of ethereal payback in which Sal will seek retribution upon me for breaking his trust. No doubt, I am treading on a Megan moment. I come up with a solution. I will fry some grouper fillets for supper, sit with Harry and Montana by the shoreline, and put off until tomorrow what trouble I could get myself into today.

∞

THE NEXT day I cruise over to Two Palms Marina to pay my good buddy Memphis the Lighthouse a visit. As the investigation unfolded into the death of Sal Santini/Scalise, Phyllis told me the police were stumped with the whereabouts of Sal's boat and Cadillac Escalade. They were hoping to find clues about the man, his life, and why he was the victim of an assassination, but the boat and SUV seemed to have vanished into thin air. That was good for me, because if I can't find the Dean Martin CD, then I am exonerated from fulfilling my responsibilities as trustee to Sal's secrets.

When the fingerprints came back and Sal's true identity was revealed, the search for his assets subsided. Months later, island folklore had it that Sal sank the boat one night, along with the Escalade, which would make for some ecstatic manatees. I don't buy it though, because I have trouble believing Sal would sink his vehicle after giving me explicit instructions on what to do should he meet his demise. My theory is Memphis knows more than his chest-headlight is illuminating. It is common knowledge these two knew each other, but I had seen them exchange surreptitious winks and nods that indicated to me they were more than just acquaintances. *Did Sal entrust Memphis like he did me?* I originally suspected they were in cahoots to make my life on the island miserable, but now that I am the last man standing on Gulf Boulevard, I think Memphis may hold some secrets that need to be shared.

I dock the *Ticket* and step onto the floating dock. Business is slowing to a crawl around these parts. The help is back at school, and the Two Palms Snack Shack is only open on weekends. I linger near the bait tubs waiting for Memphis to sneak up on me.

"What yous want, Na-jar-bin-laden?"

I turn quickly. *How the hell does he do that?*

"Hey, Memphis, something has come to light and it ain't your lamp."

He wipes his hands on a rag and stuffs it in a back pocket. "Seems peoples 'round these parts are turnin' up dead since yous showed yous face. How comes dat is, snowbird?"

"Technically speaking, I'm not a snowbird. I live here year-round."

Memphis riles up some phlegm and expels it into the canal.

"I think we need to talk, just you and me." I jingle Sal's car keys in front of him. "You *guts* any idea where I might find Sal's big SUV?"

Memphis turns his head in all directions looking to see if anyone is within earshot. The marina is deserted. "Who's doin' da askin'?" he asks.

Now I look in all directions. "I think I am."

"Yous sures, Na-ja-bin-laden?"

As if someone just spiked the volume control knob, the dueling banjos start playing loudly in my head. "Yeah, I is sures I am me," I say.

He stares suspiciously at me for too long a moment, and then seems to succumb. "Sal says while he was in the livin' dat you'd be by for him, dats the only reason we is talkin'."

"Ain't dat so," I reply.

"Sure dang. Now y'all follow me." He hitches up his overalls and starts walking toward the structure where boats are drydocked during the winter months. He climbs onto a forklift and drives it deep inside the building. I hurry to keep pace. When Memphis reaches the end, he turns the truck and starts raising the forks. I look up and see something large covered in canvas. The forks slip underneath a metal pallet, and then it slowly lowers the mystery down to the floor. Memphis shuts down the lift and jumps off.

"Yous guts five minutes," he says, holding up ten fingers, then turns and walks away.

I lift the canvas on one side and find Sal's Escalade. I insert the key into the door and crawl inside. The battery is either dead or disconnected, so I use what little light there is inside the building to search through Sal's collection of music until I find Dean Martin's *Greatest Hits*. I open the case and pull out the bio sleeve. On page one is a picture of Martin. On page two the only number I find is the year 1964. Under the nineteen is a line drawn in ink. I assume nineteen is my first number. I flip the pages until I see another dash on page six. It is under the year 1995. One of the nines is underlined. I keep turning pages until I find a playlist of songs. *"Ain't that a kick in the head"* is number ten on the list, and that number is circled. I search the remaining pages and find nothing. The numbers are nineteen, nine, and ten.

I have no idea what to do next. I recall Sal mentioning a storage unit and some combination, but that is it. A rap on the window startles me.

Memphis points to a watch that doesn't exist on his wrist and says, "Yous five minutes is up." I exit the SUV as Memphis climbs onto the forklift. In a minute Sal's Escalade is covered and hoisted back up to a dark corner of the cavernous building and disappears among the various boats of different shapes and sizes.

Memphis wheels the forklift around until he is parallel to me. "I dones my favor for Sal. Now yous best forget what yous seen. It don't matter yous friends with Ms. Phyllis, guts it?"

I ignore his veiled threat. "Is there a storage unit company on the mainland?" I ask.

"Yous means dem things wid all dem gay-rages glued together real tight?"

"In simpler terms, yes, with the garages all glued together."

"I'm thinkin' Stor-Mor on 776 headin' to Punta Gorda." He gives me the two eyes, two fingers watching me thing, and then speeds off. I flip him the finger, hoping he can see it in his rear-view mirror.

The name of the storage company rings a bell, so I hurry out of Two Palms Marina and set course up the Intracoastal Water-way for my boat condo. Once there, I transfer to the F-150 and head south to Route 776. About thirty minutes later, I arrive at a modern looking self-storage facility composed of several one-story buildings with stone siding and bright red storage-unit doors. It is a gated facility with video cameras and a security office. I notice the signs requesting identification before entering. There is no way I am getting past this fortress, and I can't understand why Sal would send me on this mission if I can't even get in. I park the truck and head over to the office to make a fool out of myself.

As I approach the counter, a young, attractive woman stands talking on the phone. Behind her are stacks of flat boxes in different sizes. On a wall display hang sealing tape and an assortment of key and combination locks. The woman notices me and ends her call.

"Can I help you?" she asks with a soft voice. Her nametag reads: Sue McGrath – Manager.

"Hi, I'm here for the Salvatore Santini unit." I'm not even sure if that is the name he used.

As she taps something into her computer, I notice she isn't wearing a ring. I think she is cute, so I debate whether to ask her out to dinner, followed by a chilly island sunset, a handful of chick-magnet M&M's, and some insults from my gangster bird. What woman can refuse all that?

"Yes, here it is. Salvatore Santini, building B, unit 17," she says. "You're paid up through the end of 2011. May I see some identification, Mr. Santini?"

"Ah . . . here's the thing. I'm not Mr. Santini. He's traveling south at the moment, so he asked if I could look in on his storage unit."

"I'm really sorry, sir, but I can't let you in without a proper I.D."

Fine, I didn't want to be here anyway. "No, that's all right, I understand. Thanks for checking. I'm surprised Mr. Santini didn't foresee this problem."

She nods with an expression of concern. I shuffle my feet while being stuck in the in-between moment. I am financially secure, but woefully insecure when it comes to the opposite sex. *What are the odds she is a mechanic?* At the risk of rejection, I introduce myself.

"My name is Jason," I say, as I extend my hand over the counter. "I'm wondering if you would be interested in joining me for dinner later."

Sue McGrath displays a broad smile until it appears a thought hijacks her attention. She looks at the computer screen while I slowly withdraw my unwanted hand.

"Did you say Jason as in Jason Najarian?"

I raise my eyebrows, surprised. "Yes, most people stumble over my name. How did you know that?"

"Mr. Santini listed you as an approved visitor. If you show me identification, I can let you in."

I pull out my wallet and display my license.

"Perfect. Again, it's building B, unit 17. If you drive up to the entrance, I'll open the gates so you can enter. Building B will be on your left."

"Can you do me a favor?"

She nods.

"Please remove my name from the list. I'm leaving the country."

"No problem, Mr. Najarian. You are removed."

Apparently she has forgotten about my dinner invitation. I thank her and exit the office confident she will flag me down on my way out to give me her phone number.

I drive up to the entrance and the gates automatically part like the Red Sea. I ease into the complex and turn down a corridor separating buildings B and C until I arrive at unit 17. I park the truck and approach the outdoor storage unit. Sure enough it has a combination lock. I pull the numbers from my pocket. Left to right or right to left? I have no clue, so I start the dial at zero and turn right until I hit nineteen. Next, I turn it left until I reach number nine, and then I turn it right all the way around until it stops on number ten. I give the lock a tug and surprisingly it falls open.

I scan the area for inquiring eyes. My growing fear is as soon as I lift the door, Homeland Security, the FBI, the CIA, and the IRS will appear on the rooftops pointing machine guns at me and wanting to know my connection to the secrets Sal, the hit man, has hidden inside.

What is behind door number one? Will I find bomb-making material for his fishing excursions? How about humidors filled with illegal Cuban or Abucan cigars? Maybe I'll find cases of lobster tail pastries gone bad. My best guess is Sal has stored his cache of weapons. But what would he expect me to do with them?

I suddenly wish there were people around so I could corral them in front of Sal's unit and auction it off to the highest bidder. At the very least, the crowd would deflect the bullets destined to rain down on me as soon as I open the door.

I reach down and lift the bright red aluminum door. No alarms. No trip wires. No explosions. Light filled with dust particles brightens the darkened room. As I stand outside looking in, I see an old wooden table with a wood-frame chair on the far side. On the table I notice three large envelopes at one end and some scruffy clothes with sneakers on the other. Behind the chair is a dark tarpaulin attached by grommets to a ceiling rod that stretches across the width of the unit like a shower curtain. I step from the fresh air and enter the musky storage space of a forgotten dead man.

Next to the large envelopes I find a smaller envelope covered in fine dust. My name is printed on it. I open the seal and remove a letter and an odd looking small key. I grip the key and unfold the note. It is handwritten and reads:

> "Hey Trust Fund,
> You here reading this means I'm dead. Or, maybe your here reading this and I'm still alive, which means your fucking dead, capisce? But I don't think your that dumb, so I'm gonna go with me being dead. I need to know who did me in. Tell me now. Say it out loud."

"Fiona."

> "I'm guessing the boys from Philly, but you wouldn't know that. Anyway, I need a favor. It's payback time. The three envelopes on the table need to be mailed. If they want a fucking war, I'll give them a fucking war from the grave."

"Actually it would be from the urn."

> "I put postage on them, but if it ain't enough, cover it and I'll pay you back. Hey, it was fun while it lasted,

huh? You enjoy the sunsets, your M&M's, and Running
Bush—the future Mrs. Trust Fund. Make sure you check
in with Memphis. See ya on the other side.
Sal"

It is eerie reading the words of a dead man. Sal didn't mention
the key in his note, so I have no idea of its purpose. I fold the
letter and shove it, along with the key, into my pocket. I glance at
the three larger envelopes. The first is addressed to *The Providence
Journal,* the second to Raymond Gulioti, and the last one to Arturo
Moretti. Based on the perceived tone of Sal's message, I doubt
the contents of the envelopes represent a mea culpa on his part.
Rather, Sal appears intent on revenge. That means if I mail them,
I could be scratching the scab off the détente currently existing
between the Mafia families, as reported in the newspaper. It also
means if a new round of retaliatory violence breaks out, someone
will inevitably die. I'm not sure I can carry that burden.

I look at the clothes on the table. Sand has crusted on the
soles of the sneakers. The pants offer a whiff of what appears to be
urine. I move closer to the shirt and see a dark stain encircling a
hole in the fabric where it once covered a heartbeat. Sal was shot
in the head, so I'm left to speculate on the unfortunate owner of
these clothes. I lift the envelopes from the table with the intent
to leave, but I'm drawn like a magnet to what lies in the dark
recesses of the unit.

A slight breeze drifts in creating a ripple along the base of the
tarpaulin.

What is behind the curtain? I am sure there are no dead bodies
in here, as Sal once joked, because there is no stench of death
in the air. Recalling what I had seen on the boat, I suspect his
collection of armaments lies beyond the partition. I'm curious to
see the weapons one last time. But first, I step outside for some
fresh air and scan the area to make sure I'm alone. Satisfied, I
drift back in.

I feel like I am violating Sal's crypt as I maneuver around the
table and approach the center of the thick tarp. It is heavy and

hangs rigid. Doubts are amassing in my mind like a sudden flash mob. It has to be his guns, right? Right?

Am I insane or what? I reach out to pull the tarp aside.

A dusty gust of wind startles me. I quickly pull my hand back from the partition. *Is Sal sending me a signal from the netherworld? Was this sudden draft an exhale from his cigar as a warning to take the envelopes and leave without probing further?* My curiosity of what lies beyond the tarpaulin weakens, like my knees. Maybe I don't really want to see what I suspect is his elaborate gun collection after all. Maybe I should retreat back to my sand dune of an island and delete all memories of Sal—from the time I pulled his boat off the sandbar, to the moment Fiona put a bullet in his head.

But I can't, and this is why I will never be a hermit in good standing.

I reach for the tarp and ease it slowly to one side. Daylight seeps through erasing segments of darkness that had lingered intact behind the partition. Something large is immediately illuminated, eerily so, and once my eyes adjust to the dim light, it appears to be a person. I can see the extended arms of the figure as it reaches out to grab me.

A rush of adrenaline blasts through my body.

Within a nanosecond, most of me has already exited the storage facility and is boarding a plane to anywhere, but for some reason my feet remain in place unwilling to budge.

My eyes are wide open.

My heart is pounding.

CHAPTER THIRTY-TWO

Island Sunset

"The future ain't what it used to be."
—YOGI BERRA

As light takes hold, like a sunrise over the shrouded depths of the storage unit, I can see additional figures begin to take shape. They seem to be marching toward me. Light floods in. There are mannequins everywhere. Some have bloodied faces, some have protruding knives. One has a rope around its neck. Another has a small axe stuck between its eyes. I'm amazed at the carnage.

I count twenty-three mannequins, each tagged with a date, and on a table there are enough guns to invade a Third World country. What the hell was Sal into? Close to me are two figures dressed in black with bullet holes and bloodstains. I look at the day, month, and year, and then stumble back. I reflect back on my conversations with Sal. There is only one conclusion to explain this place. These are Sal's trophies.

I turn in circles, not knowing what to do. If I report this to the police, I will implicate myself. My accounting mind seeks balance. The storage unit is prepaid through the end of next year. That's a lot of distance between now and then. When Stor-Mor doesn't receive any payments come early 2012, the locker will go to auction. Whoever wins the bid will need to check with the police to see if the weapons have any history. I believe by the evidence before me, Sal's weapons have history. Afterward, the *CSI: Miami* types will have a field day connecting the clothes on these mannequins to Sal's victims.

As I look around, I realize this was Sal's life. He made all this happen and then paid the price. It sends shivers down my spine when I recall sitting with him on the beach, being out on his boat, and pissing him off on numerous occasions. There could've been a mannequin in here wearing my clothes.

I sweep the entire locker for any evidence of my association with Sal. Confident there is nothing to implicate me, I make my way out, roll down the door, and lock Sal's secrets inside. I climb back into the truck and expedite my exit from the storage facility.

As I drive back to my boat, I have one last responsibility to fulfill. Although I vacillated, I decide to make good on Sal's request to mail his envelopes. When I arrive at Phyllis's office to pick up my mail, I hand her what Sal entrusted to me. With his letters in the mail, my obligation to Sal is over. I can resign as his pawn and leave behind all memories of his sordid existence. I just hope he agrees with me. But I sense I will never thoroughly be free of him. Sort of like my ex-wife.

It is late afternoon when I arrive at the dock. I tie off the boat and take a deep breath. I can smell the island flora and feel the embrace of serenity. I can even hear the crashing surf—or is it Montana screeching for food? I can't tell.

After grilling some fish for dinner, I make it down to the shoreline in time to take in another stunning sunset. Montana munches on a banana in his cage to my right and Harry the Heron is a few steps beyond probably wondering what parrot and banana would taste like combined. I filter through the mail in my lap until I come upon a postcard. It reads, "Greetings from Argentina," and the picture captures the night life in Buenos Aires. I don't know anyone in Argentina, and I don't know anyone traveling there. For a moment, I'm overwhelmed with exhilaration. Maybe Megan took a wrong turn and ended up in Argentina without the means to get back. I excitedly turn the card over seeking confirmation. Instead, the only written word is, "Freedom!"

I'm hypnotized. I stare at the word for several seconds. Could it be? I gaze out across the sunset. Boats drift in the gulf. A gentle breeze drifts ashore. There is an element of closure in my life, but now the postcard calls out to me.

Freedom!

I want to get on with my hermit existence. I want to be left alone. That was the future I anticipated when I first arrived at Gulf Boulevard.

But the future ain't what it used to be.

Dobbs Ferry Public Library
55 Main St.
Dobbs Ferry, NY 10522